Penguin Books
I'll Never Be Young Again

P9-CRQ-192

Daphne du Maurier is the second daughter of the famous
actor and theatre manager-producer, the late Sir Gerald
du Maurier, and grand-daughter of George du Maurier, the
much-loved *Punch* artist and author of *Trilby* and *Peter
Ibbetson*. After being educated at home with her sisters
and then in Paris, she began writing short stories and
articles in 1928, and in 1931 her first novel, *The Loving
Spirit*, was published. Two others followed. Her reputation
was established with her frank biography of her father,
Gerald: A Portrait, and her Cornish novel, *Jamaica Inn*.
When *Rebecca* came out in 1938 she suddenly found herself,
to her great surprise, one of the most popular authors of
the day. The book went into thirty-nine English
impressions in the next twenty years and has been
translated into more than twenty languages. Sir Laurence
Olivier starred in the film under Hitchcock's direction.

Since then, besides several best-selling novels, which are
available in Penguins, she has written plays, short stories,
and a biography of Branwell Brontë. *The Du Mauriers*, her
account of her relations in the last century, was published as
a Penguin in 1949. Her latest novels are *The Flight
of the Falcon* and *The House on the Strand*.

Her three most popular novels were all inspired by her
Cornish home, Menabilly, where she and her family
lived for twenty years. Daphne du Maurier was married
to the late Lieut.-General Sir Frederick Browning, wartime
commander of Airborne Forces. She has two married
daughters and a son.

Daphne du Maurier

I'll Never Be Young Again

Penguin Books

Penguin Books Ltd, Harmondsworth,
Middlesex, England
Penguin Books Australia Ltd, Ringwood,
Victoria, Australia

First published by William Heinemann Ltd 1932
Published in Penguin Books 1966
Reprinted 1969, 1971
Copyright © Daphne du Maurier, 1932

Made and printed in Great Britain by
Hazell Watson & Viney Ltd, Aylesbury, Bucks
Set in Monotype Times

'If it must be so, let's not weep nor complain
If I have failed, or you, or life turned sullen.
We have had these things, they do not come again,
But the flag still flies and the city has not fallen.'
HUMBERT WOLFE

Part One: JAKE

1

When the sun had gone, I saw that the water was streaked with great patches of crimson and gold. They formed a ripple under the bridge that was part of the wake belonging to the barge. She was perhaps two cables' length from me now, low in the water, deeply loaded with timber, the brown sail flapping uselessly against the mast. There was scarcely a suggestion of a breeze, and it was the ebb-tide that carried her down-stream. I could see one man aboard her, his arm flung carelessly over the tiller, his legs crossed, and a cap on the back of his head.

His pipe must have gone out, for I saw him bend swiftly and fumble in his pocket, steadying the tiller with his knee, then he cupped the pipe in his hands, and threw away the match. I imagined myself in his place, glancing half-curiously in the wake of the barge, where the little match drifted with the tide.

The air to this man would be strong with the harsh smell of tobacco, and the peculiar sweet flavour of well-seasoned timber that clings to a barge. His hands and his clothes would be of it too, the sticky mixture of tar and cutch, and a burnt rope's end dangling near an empty barrel.

While beyond all these things, so intimate a part of his life, there would come floating up to him, from nowhere in particular, the old unchanging smell of the river, borne from the mud flats beneath the wharves and the dingy warehouses; a smell of refuse left on these beaches to be carried away by the tide, a hint on those mysterious houses where no faces are ever seen and whose dark windows look out upon the Lower Pool, a whiff of oil upon the surface of the water cast by some passing tug-boat.

And strange and unbelievable, mingled with the smoke of London rising into the hazy orange sky of the spent day, a suggestion of some world farther than the tired City and the river, a world where there would be no stretch of buildings flattened in a half-light with the spire of St. Paul's companion to a ware-house chimney, but a grey sea not encompassed by the smallest ridge of land, cold and white-crested, under a grey sky.

Now the barge was no more than a black smudge amongst the traffic in the Pool, a tug-boat was frothing in her wake, smoke screaming from her stout funnel, her propeller churning the water as she went astern.

The iron of the bridge felt hot under my hand. The sun had been upon it all the day.

Gripping hard with my hands I lifted myself on to the bar and gazed down steadily on the water passing under the bridge.

The flaming colours had gone with the sun, the little ripples still formed and bubbled, but they were brown now, dull, and shadowed by the archways of the bridge.

The sight of the barge had taken me away from myself, and because she had left me I fell back again into my first despon-dency, seeing nothing but my own black mood of bitterness, caring for nothing but that the night should come quickly and allow me to slip away unseen. I waited then, for time was some-thing with which I had no more concern, except for the furthering of my purpose, and as I leant against the stanchion of the bridge I closed my eyes so that I need not look upon the faces of the men and women who passed me by.

In this way I could cling to some sort of security, and my plans would not be hindered by a momentary weakness thrusting itself into my view, a weakness coming to me from the strength and solidity of people.

My ears would not be deafened, though, and in spite of myself I listened to the safe and steady rumble of traffic over the bridge, the hard, grating wheels of lorries, the painful grind of a tram homeward-bound, the jolt of a bus, the smooth wheels of cars, and the silly rattle of a stray taxi. I pretended that these things were meaningless in themselves, and could not drag me away from the river to be part of them, but even as I argued thus I heard the voices of women as they trudged along the pavement, brushing against me as they went, the shoulder of one just touching the back of my coat. And these women, whom I had

8

never seen, seemed by this simple action to enter my life, becoming definite personalities of reality.

Coward-like, I would have turned to them and stretched out my hands, saying as I did so: 'Perhaps you would stand here a little longer so that I may listen to your voices; nothing more than this.' Maybe they would have understood. Stupidly, with the dumb knowledge that such a moment was impossible, I longed for them to linger a while, and consider the matter, and then accepting me as one of themselves suggest that I return with them. Gravely, kindly, they would watch my face, and with a quick, shy gesture, as though ashamed of their charity, they would say to me: 'You can come back with us, you know, it isn't much of a place. . . .'

I would walk then with them, somewhat apart, conscious of their superiority, and we would arrive at some drab tenement building, where iron-railed balconies stretched from window to window. There would be a canary swinging in a high cage, and a faded odd-patterned screen. These women would busy themselves, familiar with their surroundings, and the drip of a tap or the moving of cups and saucers would seem blessed tokens of friendship to me, humble in a quiet corner, blinking my eyes because of the sudden flare of a gas-jet. I would enter the moods of these people, share their troubles, love their friends, act in some way as a faithful servant if only they should not cast me away from them, leaving me to wander back to the bridge once more.

I opened my eyes, and the women had passed from me along the pavement; I could scarcely distinguish their backs amongst the crowd pushing each other where the tram stopped.

They were away and out of my remnant of existence, like the low hull of the barge and the man with his arm flung over the tiller.

I took a folded newspaper from my pocket, smoothing the creases carefully and read with interest some advertisement for furs.

The print mocked me, knowing that the words they spelt could have no meaning to me, for soon I would be a bent, contorted thing of ugliness, sucked and drawn by the swirling eddies of the Pool, and the paper and its advertisement floating placidly to some unknown destination upon the surface of the water.

It seemed strange that things could still be done to me after I was dead, that my body would perhaps be found and handled by people I should never know, that really a little life would go on about me which I should never feel.

The tiresome business of burial, and decay. These sordid actualities of death would be spared me at least.

For me, the present agony of departure, the silent terror of leaving a place known to me if hated, the well-nigh impossible task of conquering the fear that possessed me. Not the fear of that hasty look round, the sudden plunge headlong and the giddy shock of hard, cold water, the river itself entering my lungs, rising in my throat, tossing me upon my back with my arms outflung – I could hear the sob strangled in my chest and the blood leave me – but fear of the certain knowledge that there was no returning, no possible means of escape, and no other thing beyond.

It would not matter to the world that I was gone, odd doubtful thought, entering my mind at such a moment. I felt the flesh that was mine and the body that belonged to me; queer to think it was in my power to destroy them so swiftly.

During these last moments I stood apart then from the world I had not left. No longer of it, and yet not broken away.

That man on the top of a bus, brushing his hair away from his face, a cigarette hanging from his mouth, he belonged – he would know many days and many nights. That lorry-driver, his face white with cement from a load of bricks, shouting to his companion; and a hurrying girl, parcels in her hands, glancing to right and left. One after another they flashed before me, imprinting themselves for ever on my mind, living, breathing figures I had no right to touch. I envied them their food, their sleep, their snatches of conversation, the smell even of their clothes, dusty after a long day. I thought of places I should never see, and women I should never love. A white sea breaking upon a beach, the slow rustle of a shivering tree, the hot scent of grass. A crowded café, and the laughter of some man, a car passing over cobbled stones.

A dark close room and a girl still against the shadowed pillow, her hands across my back.

I remembered as a child standing in a field where a stream crossed my path, and a yellow iris grew next a background of green rushes. The stream sang as it tumbled over the flat stones. And as a child I thought how strange it was that such things should continue after I had left them, as though when turning a corner with the stream hidden from view, a mist must fall about them, shrouding them carefully, until I should pass again.

It was like this now, with the traffic and the moving people. Impossible that they should live while I was no more a part of existence.

Once more I looked down upon the swirling water beneath the bridge. I threw away my paper and watched it twirl slowly, caught in a sudden eddy, and then, limp and tragic, float from me, borne by the current. A crinkled edge stared up at me, as yet unsodden, like a faint protest.

I resolved that I would not wait any more. The dust and the noise of humanity, the nearness of men and women, were urging some claim upon me that was robbing me of my strength and will.

They were united in a conspiracy to keep me from the peace I had promised myself.

It was not thus I had imagined it would be.

I wanted it to be made easier for me. In my preparations for this moment I had been overcome by a great weariness, my eyes had seen nothing but the wide placid sheet of water ready to receive me, my ears had heard nothing but the soft, steady ripple of the wash against the archway of the bridge.

There was no throb of traffic then, no hum of city, no smell of dust, and body, and life, no shouts of men, nor the clear whistle of a boy with his hands in his pockets.

I wanted to be tired, I wanted to be old, I wanted to lose myself and not be reminded of things I had never done.

I looked up at the sky and saw a great dark-edged cloud hover over the distant spire of St Paul's. Where the west had been golden was a shadowed blanket, a grim reflection of the murky buildings by the water's edge. Soon the million lights that

11

belonged to London would cast a halo of light into the sky, and one faint star would flicker against the purple.

There seemed no reason for staying any longer. I would not even be dramatic and make a gesture of farewell. There should be no sentimentality where I was concerned. It was not worth the trouble of tears, not my life, anyway. I would make a ripple upon the water for a moment, not much more than a stone thrown by a child from a bank. Nothing mattered very much. I wondered why my heart felt so heavy and afraid, why the sweat clung to my hands and could not be wiped away.

I swung my legs over, holding on to the bridge with desperate fingers. An odd snatch of breeze blew across my hair. I supposed that this was the very last thing of the world to come to me.

I breathed deeply, and I felt as though the waiting water rose up in front of me and would not let me go.

This was my final impression of horror, when fear and fascination took hold upon me, and I knew that I should have no other moment but this before the river itself closed in upon me. My fingers slackened, and I lowered myself for the fall.

It was then that someone laid his hands upon my shoulder, and turning to clutch him instinctively as a means of safety, I saw Jake for the first time, his head thrown back, a smile on his lips.

2

'You don't want to do that,' he said; 'it doesn't do any good really, you know. Because nobody has ever proved that there isn't something beyond. The chances are you might find yourself up against something terrific, something too big for you, and you wouldn't know how to get out of it. Besides – wait until you're sixty-five if you must finish that way.'

I was ready to break down like a boy and cry. I kept my hand on his arm as though it afforded me some measure of protection. Yet somewhere inside me there was a feeling of revolt, a stupid sense of frustration. This fellow had not any right to stop me from making a fool of myself. And, anyway, I did not care a damn for his opinion. Mechanically I heard myself speaking in a small tired voice I scarcely recognised as my own.

'You don't understand,' I kept saying, 'you don't understand – I'm not going to explain to you or to anybody. This is my affair, you don't understand.'

He swung himself up on the bridge beside me. He pulled a packet of cigarettes from his pocket.

I took one, and this very action of turning it in my fingers and lighting it, in the familiar drawing-in of my breath, gave me such a sense of life new-found with the blessed relief that I had so far escaped the horror of death, that I smiled and was no longer fearful or ashamed to meet his eyes.

He smiled too, and then stayed silent for some minutes, allowing me time to recover my mental balance, while his shoulder just touched my shoulder, and his knee just touched my knee, so that I was aware of the immense security of his presence.

He must have been following some train of thought in his mind, for when he spoke again it was like the continuation of things unsaid.

'There's always been a whole lot talked about responsibilities,' he went on, 'and citizenship, and duty, which is a funny word. None of these matters to you or to me, I guess. Maybe we're built on a lower level. We're not belonging to the crowd of real people. They exist apart, in their true, even way of living. But there's something in me and in you that can't be cheated for all that, it's like a spark of light that burns in spite of ourselves, we can't throw it away, we can't destroy the only chance we've got to live for our own purpose. We wouldn't have been born otherwise.'

He broke off abruptly and looked at me sideways, not to watch the effect of his words, but to see how I was taking my new lease of life.

'What were you thinking about?' he asked. I saw that he meant by this what was I thinking before I tried to throw myself down from the bridge.

'I don't know,' I said; 'pictures came into my mind that I couldn't stop. The smell of grass in early summer, a gull dipping its wing into the sea, a ploughman on a hill resting, his hand on his horse's back, and the touch of earth. No, now I come to remember, these faded before things I had never known. Impossible dusty cities and men swearing and fighting; then I getting terribly drunk, getting terribly tired sleeping with women who laughed against my shoulder, not caring about me at all. Then eating and riding, and a long rest and a dream.'

Somehow we found ourselves smiling at the pictures my imagination had so swiftly conjured.

'That's the sort of mood you've got to cling to,' he said, 'don't get away from it. I want you to feel like that.'

Once more I was a boy again, shy, sullen, resentful of the attitude he had adopted. I didn't know him. It wasn't his business.

I leant forward on the bridge, biting my nails.

'I don't see,' I said, 'what all this has got to do with you. You might as well have left me to clear out. I'm no use, I don't want to live.'

He did not bother about me, he made no attempt to ask questions, and I felt like some silly girl snubbed by a man older than herself, failing to win her impression, and sitting back confused and immature.

'Oh! hell,' I said, and to my shame and misery I heard my voice break off in the middle, and I felt the tears come in my eyes.

I was not even a boy, but a little sniffing child wiping his nose against the shoulder of his companion.

'I've been such a fool,' I said, 'such a bloody fool.'

Then he laid his hand on my arm, and I knew he was not looking at my face, but that he meant to show he was with me and that my boy's tears could not spoil anything.

'We'll pull along together,' he said, and that was all.

I knew then that I did not have to worry about things again, that I could lean upon him, weak though it might seem, and that he would not leave me to the horror of being alone. I began to notice his face, his curious grey eyes and the scar that ran the length of his left cheek. His hair was black, and he wore no hat. His clothes were shabby too, as though he did not care. I did not mind who he was or where he came from, all I knew was that there was something of splendour about him that had lifted me away from myself, making the coward in me sorry and lamentable beside his grandeur. He must have been some six or seven years older than me, but I felt there was no necessity to ask these sort of questions.

14

We accepted each other and that was all.

'My name's Jake,' he said, throwing away his cigarette, 'what do you call yourself?'

I hesitated like a poor fool, and then stumbled over my words, realising that my father's name could not matter to such as he, fame would be one of those things that would leave him untouched, save for a smile and a shrug of his shoulder.

'Oh! call me Dick,' I said, 'that's good enough for me,' but even as I muttered this stupidly I hated to feel he had been aware of my hesitation. It was as though some remnant of family pride still clung about me, reminding me that the shackles of relationship could never be shaken off.

At that moment I loathed the memory of my home more than ever; I could not bear that instinctively it should step between me and my freedom.

He asked me suddenly how old I was, and I told him I was twenty-one.

'You mustn't throw it away,' he said.

'No,' I said.

I don't think I really knew what he meant.

'Life,' he said, 'isn't just whining about things. There's something tremendous in it. We don't want to go messing up our chances. There's so much to know, so much to do. No reason for us to crumple.'

I wondered why he included himself in my inferiority, and I thought that this was his way of showing sympathy. He was pulling himself down to my level. I didn't want him to do that, it was a humiliation to both of us, but especially to him. I knew that however desperate his life might have been, however lonely and bitter and distressed, he would not have done what I had tried to do.

He would have been sufficient to himself and never lonely.

'Oh! you,' I said, 'you're different –'

I felt hot and ashamed, but he did not notice this, unless he kept his thoughts to himself.

The darkness had come while we had been talking, and there were no wide streaks left in the sky and no dark patches.

There was a star above the black smudge of St Paul's.

I was grateful to the darkness and grateful to the vast sound of London in the distance. I loved the warm air and the spent dust, the lights of the world that still accepted me, the listless scent of a summer evening, the movement of people, and the blessed certitude of the small star. And above all the voice and nearness of my companion.

The river beneath the bridge was remote now and beyond me, the very water running so swift and silently held no suggestion of horror. It had even lost its power of fascination. I was superior on my firm bridge and it could not reach me. I would not be afraid of it again.

Perhaps in a way I was dazzled at the thrill of escape, I was oddly excited at the possibility of adventure, I wanted to show off. I swung my legs carelessly over the parapet, whistling to myself, knowing I should not fall.

Jake laughed, and steadied my arm as though I were a child.

'You're safe now, aren't you?' he said.

I felt small and ridiculous, and was not sure how much of a fool he thought me. I wished I was different, I wished I were stronger than he.

It would be good to win his approval over anything.

'What are we going to do?' I asked, and I wondered whether he realized how I hung upon his words. He did not answer me directly, his face was in shadow and I could not learn the expression in his eyes. Once more he continued in a channel of his own thoughts.

'Being young,' he said, 'is something you won't understand until its gone from you, and then it will come in a flash, leaving you a little wiser than before. You won't be lonely, you won't be unhappy, possibly there will be a great peace and security. You'll go on, you see, as others have gone on, just that and no more. You'll love and live, and the rest of it. But because of stupidity, or carelessness, or a belief in the lasting glamour of things, you'll throw away what you wanted to throw away tonight. I guess you won't notice any difference. You won't know what you're losing, and you won't care.'

He laughed softly, and laying his hand on my shoulder I knew that he understood me better than I did myself. And there was a shadow across his eyes which made me feel as if he were sorry about something.

'You'll be all right,' he said, 'you'll be fine, and stronger than before. But if you listen you'll hear the echo of a lost thing away in the air, like a bird with a song you can't name, high up above you where you can't reach.

' "I'll never be young again," it says, "I'll never be young again." '

Still he had not answered my question. And I did not want to be treated as a child. Nor did I understand. I spoke roughly, not choosing my words.

'Oh! damn your sermons, let's clear out of this place, it doesn't matter where.'

Away down the Pool I heard the siren of a ship, and the echoing siren of a tug.

Lights winked in the darkness, and the still rotten smell of the river floated up to me, bringing a memory of the barge that had gone with the tide and the setting of the sun.

Jake lifted his head, and he seemed to be listening to the siren and the hundred-odd sounds of the Pool. It may be there was a distant whistle and the scraping of feet on a deck, the rattle of a chain, the hoarse shout of a pilot. None of this could we see, only the flashes of light and the dim outline of moving things upon the water. I fell to wondering about the sea that lay beyond this river, and how the sight of it would meet our eyes at dawn like a strange shock of beauty after the mud reaches and the green plains. Somewhere there would be tall cliffs, white against the morning, and loose chalk and stone crumbling to a beach. I fancied there would be breakers upon the shore, a thin line of foam and a soft wind coming from the land. Little houses would stand on these cliffs, snugly asleep, the windows closed to the air. They would not matter to us as we passed, for we would have done with them. We would be away, and long after men would come from those houses and make for the fields, staring at the warm sky, calling to a dog over their shoulder, while the women bent low over their tubs, wringing their hands in the blue soapy water, harkening to the kitchen clock and aware of the good dinner smell. Staring towards the sea, shielding their eyes from the sun with their hand upraised, perhaps they would see a grey whisper of spent smoke upon the horizon to tell them we had passed. Or the square corner of a sail dipping below the line, the tip of a mast-head smudged against the sky.

Then I sighed, for these things had become real to me in a moment, and here we were only upon the bridge, and we must turn to the streets, and the noise of the traffic, and think of the necessity of eating, stand shoulder to shoulder with people on pleasure bent, mounting like beetles from the hot Underground, our eyes blinking at the glaring lights of a crowded cinema, and so to a drab lodging-house with the narrow beds and the grey cotton sheets.

So once more I turned to Jake and repeated: 'What shall we do?' scarce caring for his reply, aware that despondency would come to me in any case. And his answer was one that showed me he had an intuition of my every mood, that he joined in with them as though he were part of myself, that even my thoughts were not hidden from him, that we were bound henceforth as comrades and I loved him and he understood.

'We'll get away in a ship together, you and I,' he said.

3

After I had eaten I felt strong, with no shade of weariness clinging to me. We sat at a little table in a dark corner, and the shabby waiter had flicked the last crumb off the greasy cloth. We had told him to go away and not to worry us. The air about us was thick with the smoke from our cigarettes. This and the swinging light from the opposite wall worried my eyes, but Jake's face was in shadow and he sat motionless, though I knew he was watching me. The ash fell from my cigarette on to the plate beneath me, and I kept picking at the crumbs on the cloth, and drawing imaginary figures. Jake had suggested a brandy and soda to pull me together, and perhaps this and the food had gone to my head, for I moved about in my chair excitedly, and my face was burning, and I wanted to go on talking and talking, and explaining to Jake the reason for things. With the outpouring of my words I seemed to get right clear of the atmosphere of the place, and to find myself once more standing on the lawns below the windows at home. Smooth even lawns stretching away to the sunk garden and the lily pond.

I could hear the distant whirr of the mowing machine, and one of the gardeners snipping at the laurel bushes leading to the drive. A dog barked away by the stables. And I would look into the cool long room that was the drawing-room, with its shiny chintz covers, the air filled with the scent of flowers so fresh compared to the solidity and stale mustiness of furniture never moved, while my mother's voice, cold and impersonal, continued in a strange monotony to my father their endless discussion of things that did not matter to me.

Then he would push back his chair and wander towards the door, returning to the library, where he would continue his work, and on his way pausing, his hand on the handle of the door: 'Have you spoken to Richard?'

My mother answered something I could not hear, but I could see him shrug his shoulders as though to dismiss such a trivial thing as me from his mind, and then he would add contemptuously with a half-laugh: 'He'll never make anything of himself.'

She probably nodded her head as she always did, in complete agreement to any of his words, and when he was gone she would forget me as he had done and give herself up to that self-effacing work which was her life's pleasure, the copying of his spidery manuscripts in her own neat handwriting.

And I, standing without on the smooth lawn, would glance towards the large bay window of the library, and would see the figure of this man that was my father standing an instant, his hands clasped behind his back, gazing at the son of whom he had so piteous an opinion; then turning to the heavy desk, the curtain blowing and fanning the litter of his papers, he would seat himself, his head lower than his hunched shoulders, and in the room there would be no sound but the steady scratching of his pen and the tassel of the blind tap-tapping against the window-pane.

Every word he wrote would be strong with that sweet purity and simplicity that was his gift alone, placing him higher than any living poet, secure on his pedestal apart from the world, like a great silent god above the little dwarfs of men tossed hither and thither in the stream of life. From the crystal clearness of his brain the images became words, and the words became magic, and the whole was transcendent of beauty, one thread touching another, alike in their perfection and their certitude of immortality.

Thus it seemed to me he was not a living figure of flesh and blood, but a monument to the national pride of his country, his England, and now and then he would bow gravely from his pedestal and scatter to the people a small quantity of his thought, which they would grub for on their poor rough ground, then clasp to their hungry hearts as treasure.

My father was a legend, and he had created his legend, his life, his atmosphere, he continued as something changeless and immortal like some saga whispered from generation to generation. His home was no more than a reflection of himself where his wife and his servants moved like dumb things, stray patterns on a screen of his own weaving, and he a giant in the huge musty library, his sombre eyes set deep in his carven face, untouched by the world, as the frozen snow of a far mountain, splendid on his pinnacle, alone with his thoughts.

Like a medieval king he accepted the homage due to him, and I could remember the line of people waiting in the stone hall until he should come to them, my mother moving amongst them as graciously as the queen she felt herself to be.

The little crowd of worshippers would fade away when the audience was finished, and, dazzled and awestruck, find themselves out on the great paved terrace with the magnificent image of their god printed for ever on their minds.

This was as it should be; this was what they had imagined, the poet secure in a background of tradition, while England and themselves bowed low in recognition of his supremacy.

And so away down the long chestnut drive and through the park where the deer grazed, and the deep woods beyond, and out past the lodge and the high iron gates on to the main road that led to Lessington.

They would sigh, shaking their heads at the loveliness of what they had seen, the peace of the house, the marvel of my father's presence, but even as they envied him, deep in their hearts they would smile at the memory of the homes awaiting them, and their own little joys and their own little worries.

These were some of the things I told Jake that night in the corner of the dirty smoke-filled eating-house. Nor did he interrupt me to put some question, for I spoke as though talking to myself and he a silent witness.

Even as the words came from my mouth my eyes fell upon the torn half of a newspaper left on another table, and this was the same edition I had read myself that evening on the bridge. And here was a column of a speech, and here was my father's face staring up at me from the print to torture me once more. I struck at it with my fist and threw it over to Jake in his shadowed corner.

'There,' I said to him, 'there is my father,' with triumph and defiance in my voice as though I expected his surprise and disapproval, and I didn't care at all, not I.

He looked at the photograph and the name beneath, then handed it back to me without a word. Then I continued speaking my thoughts aloud. Once again I was back at home, and wandering lost along the narrow dusty corridors of the silent house, passing the doors of the bedrooms never used, peering into the great empty wing that was shut away from the part in which we lived.

The furniture, draped in white sheets, stared strangely through the gloom. If I opened a window the hinges creaked, the pane shook, and the stream of day filtering through into the room seemed like a sacrilege and the intrusion of shame. A blind moth fluttered its way to the light. Then I shut the window again and drew close the shutters and crept from this atmosphere of decay and silent antagonism, and away down the murky passages and down the stone stairway of the servants' quarters, out into the bright sunlight of the gardens even as the moth with its fluttering wings had done. Yet the moth was free and I was still in prison.

And I wanted to shout and I wanted to sing, and I wanted to throw a ball into the air.

For I wished to be a boy with other boys, wandering in early morning in wet fields, astir with the lark, the dew soaking my shoes and the mud from the valley stream clinging to my clothes.

I wanted to rob a nest, careless of the disconsolate bird; I wanted to dive into the stagnant lake from the low branches of a crouching willow. I wanted to feel a cricket bat in my hands, bending the spring handle, and hear the sharp crack of the leather against the wood.

I wanted to use my fists against the faces of boys, to fight with them, laughing, sprawling on the ground, and then run with them, catching at my breath, flinging a stone to the top of a tree.

I wanted to smell the hot, damp flesh of horses, they snuggling their warm noses in my hand, and then up, and a kick, and a jerk at the rein and off towards the low meadows and the rough hussocks of turf.

I wanted to have a father who cared for the glory of these things, who gave me a gun, who rode with me calling to his dogs, who laughed loudly and long, whose breath smelt of whisky and tobacco, and then after dinner would lean back in his chair and smile at me across the candles on the dining-room table, and bid me tell him what was passing in my mind.

I would have a mother whose beauty made me ashamed of my own clumsiness, whose voice was low, whose smile was a caress; who knew my thoughts without my telling her; who loved me to lie silent in her room when I wished to be alone thinking of nothing, whose scent would always be the same behind her ears and in the hollow of her hands, and who would come to me at night and let me be a child.

And none of this belonged to me, but existed only in my imagination, for I had a poet for a father, and my mother was his slave, while I sat stiffly in the schoolroom with my tutor, his weak eyes blinking behind his spectacles, his scholarly voice accentuating with punctilious correction the steady metre of Greek verse. So I learnt that I must follow meekly like a humble shadow in the footsteps of my father, train my mind gradually and patiently to the polished beauty of words, fold my hands reverently on the covers of books, care for no smell save that of ancient manuscript, the faded ink, the yellow parchment.

22

To be able to write then was the only object in my life; without this achievement there was no purpose in my being born at all. My tutor was like the thin echo of my father's voice, repeating his phrases as a disciple murmurs the teachings of his master. And I grew to loathe my father, loathe his genius that made such a mockery of his son; and my spirit rebelled against all the things he stood for, it struggled to resist his power, it fought to escape from the net that bound me imprisoned in his atmosphere. I hated him, alone in his library, distant and intangible, his cold brain wandering amongst heights which I could never attain, worshipped by the world and remaining aloof, untouched and un-harmed by his own fame. How could I interest him, with my boy's body and my restlessness, and what were my dreams to him? We sat round the table in the dining-room, my mother shadowy and ineffectual, keeping up a little patter of words to the tutor, who turned his own face towards her with pretended interest; and my father silent in his oak chair chewing his food slowly, his eyes fixed on the table-cloth like a dumb idiot.

Sometimes my mother would glance in my direction, and I would guess at the puzzled thought behind her brow.

'Richard,' she said, 'looks pale today. I think he might take his bicycle into Lessington.'

And my tutor would fall in with her agreement, and im-mediately they would make a business of this going into Lessing-ton, the time of starting and the time of returning, and what I should do there and what I should see. So much so that instinc-tively I resented their idea, and scowling over my meat I would mutter that I did not care to go.

Then my mother appealed to my father at his end of the table, with a glance of reproach in my direction for being the cause of disturbance to his great thoughts, and putting on the special voice she used for him would say: 'My dear, we think Richard should bicycle into Lessington.'

My father would turn his eyes upon me, as a scientist looks at an unimportant insect whose name he does not even bother to remember, and then pausing to consider the matter, for his manners were excellent, he nodded his head gravely as though he had turned the subject over in his mind.

'Yes,' he said, 'Richard must certainly bicycle into Lessington.'

Thus the subject was closed for ever, and early in the afternoon I would be dragging my machine from the empty stable, and pedalling along the silent drive out on to the hard high road bounded on either side by the ugly telegraph-poles.

In the evening my father would still be working in the library, and we would sit in the drawing-room, the tutor with his spectacles balanced on his nose reading aloud to my mother, who lay back in her chair, her eyes shut, sleeping, her work on her knee.

And I would run upstairs to the empty schoolroom, my mind afire with a poem I should write, but once I took the pencil in my hand the ideas floated away from me, mocking me, and the words would not come. I would scribble something in a last desperate effort to be unbeaten, but the lines stared up at me pathetic in their immaturity, and in a wave of misery I tore the paper, aware of my failure. There was silence in the house and the garden was hushed. There was no movement even in the branches of the trees.

'You talked to me of being young,' I said to Jake, 'you talked this evening on the bridge of losing something I would never understand. Don't you see what all that has meant to me? I was a boy without the life of a boy. Being young means bondage to me, it means a gaping sepulchre of a house smelling of dust and decay, it means people I have never loved living apart from me in a world of their own where there's no time, it means the stifling personality of my father crushing the spirit of his son, it means the agony of restlessness, the torture of longings which nobody would explain, and always with me the certainty I was a failure, unable to write, unable to live – don't you see, don't you see?'

I did not really care whether Jake followed my words or not, I was speaking to persuade myself.

I went on to tell him of this business of growing up in my father's shadow, of no longer being a boy and my tutor leaving, my supposed education being finished, while my mother still looked upon me as a child of ten and my father never looked on me at all, unless it was to ask me courteously if I had finished the play I had begun.

For I had started a drama in blank verse, one scene of which had been written and re-written, and because of this I shut myself up in a room all day pretending to be working, while most of the time I bit the end of my penholder and gazed out of the window over the trees in the park to the hills beyond.

I hated blank verse, and I hated the Greek form which was nothing but a wretched, slavish imitation of my father's metre, and forgetting the pompous mouthings of my hero I dreamt idly as the long hours passed.

I would be a man with other men, I would lose myself in a conversation of trivial things where poetry was scorned; I would go where there were no trees and no placid grazing deer but the hot dust of a city and the scream of moving things, where life was a jest and a laugh, where life was an oath and a tear, where people hated and people loved, and beauty meant no empty word in the cool impersonality of a poem but the body of a woman. And so on, and so on, I dreamt with the pen still clutched between my fingers and the poor hidden life in me yearning to be free.

As I explained these things to Jake it seemed as though the old hatred of my home rose strong in me as ever, and I was still passionately bound to it for all my breaking away, for all my thankful realisation of the hot drab restaurant and my hands on the greasy cloth and Jake's face secure in the dark corner before me. My father still wrote unmoved in the library, and whatever I did could not change him, for he would always know me as unworthy, a wretched abortion of himself, and therefore something to be cast aside from his thoughts lest I should disturb their crystal clarity.

So all I had been saying was no more than an attempt to show this man my father and the atmosphere grown up about him, and once more Jake must bring his mind back to the picture I had drawn for him, of the open windows of the drawing-room and I standing on the lawn with the echo of my father's voice ringing in my ears: 'He'll never make anything of himself.'

Even the first sentence: 'Have you spoken to Richard?' proved in a few words his contempt for his son, so much that it was not worth the trouble of taking him to task, but such a matter was best left to the handling of my mother. For why should he worry, and why should he care?

Then in a blind frenzy of rage I must run upstairs to the poor forsaken schoolroom and rummage in a dusty drawer, and from beneath the scarce-started manuscript of my Greek play, which rapidly I tore across, flinging it in pieces about the floor, I drew page after page of my own poetry hidden in a thin black exercise-book, poetry that I had not dared read over even to myself, for here were lines of hatred and revolt, bitterness and despair; here were my dreams of women, lust-ridden and obscene, images conjured by the loathing of my father's simplicity and purity. Pitiful and stark, they expressed no more than a defiance of his beauty. And seizing these I went down to the library, and flung open the door, looking upon him where he sat before his desk, his heavy brown face resting in his hands, and I went to him and threw my poems in front of him, stammering over my words as I spoke. 'Read them, read them, I wrote them because of you,' and then called out of the window to my mother bending over her flowers: 'You come too, and listen to my poems.' Then the horror grew upon me as she came through the long windows, a dawn of a smile on her face, and leant over my father's shoulder, who, slowly drawing his spectacles from his case, fumbled with my litter of paper.

So he began to read aloud in his resonant voice, unaware at first of the sense, the pornographic outpourings of his son. This scene I had staged seemed to me so untrue that I was afraid, and even as I shuddered a wave of disgust came upon me for the diabolical cruelty of my action, and in something more than shame and despair I saw the papers fall from my father's hand and his great eyes turn upon me, while my mother, understanding less than he, would have put some question, for I noticed her puzzled frown and the beginning of a sentence: 'Why, Richard –' she said. 'Why, Richard . . .?' But my father never moved, he only kept his eyes upon my face. So then there was no more than my curse, and my stumble from the room, and running away down the drive with the memory of his eyes, and past the deer in the park, and the crying rooks hovering above the woods, and out of the iron gates for the last time, never once looking back over my shoulder. After this, three days and three nights which passed as a dream swiftly forgotten, leaving nothing but a sensation of despair, and then the sight of London friendless, and cold, and feeling hungry and feeling tired and thinking about things, and still thinking, and so standing on the bridge above the river.

Now I was tired and I leant on the table with my head pillowed on my arms, and waited for Jake to speak to me.

'You're blaming me, of course,' I said; 'I don't care.'

I took his silence for a confirmation of my words.

'Even now you don't understand what I've been through,' I told him; 'you can't know what those years have meant to me. Lost and wasted. A misery and a denial of everything that was living. Then you talk of the glory of being young.'

Jake's voice sounded gentle coming from out of the shadows.

'I believe you've felt all you've told me,' he said; 'I can understand everything and a little more. But against all this you had things you could have loved.'

'Had things? What do you mean?' I asked.

'There was a garden,' he said, 'and woods and rooks, and the smell of flowers, and the voices of people.'

I thought he must be mad. I stared at him in amazement.

'A garden? What was that to me? I tell you I was buried; you can't have any conception of suffering when you say that.'

He was silent again.

'It's all very well for you to talk,' I said; 'all the years I've wasted you must have spent loving and living, and not caring a damn. You're crazy to talk about woods, and flowers in a garden – you haven't understood, then, after all? Where have you been these last five years, anyway?'

I was superior to him in my knowledge of suffering. He did not know what it was to be sensitive.

Jake waited a moment, and when he spoke it was as though he were sorry for me, and the fool I had made of myself, but for himself he did not care.

'I've been in prison,' he said.

When Jake told me this I got up blindly from the table and went out, through the swing doors into the street, and began to walk like a drunkard along the pavement brushing against people I did not see, never caring how I went or where I should end. I did not realize that he had followed me, but looking over my shoulder I found that he was walking by my side, and turning my head so he should not see my face, I told him roughly to go, and leave me by myself.

'Don't be a fool,' said Jake, and he caught at my wrist before I could strike him. 'Don't be a fool,' he said.

I wanted to knock him down, for every word of his was like a sting and a reproach to me, who in my ignorance had accused him of a lack of sympathy and an ignorance of sorrow. He had listened without speaking to my interminable rambling story of repression and introspection, with no hint or comparison of what his own life must have been, and he had let me run on, the silly boyish words pouring from my mouth, I who for all my discontent had lived in comfort and security. And in his understanding of my feelings all he had suggested for the difference between us was my possession of woods and rooks, the smell of flowers and the voices of people.

It seemed to me that I could see him in his cell watching for a glint of light through the grated window, and there would be a smile on his face for the blessed comfort this light would bring to him, whilst I, my hands and my lips buried in the scarlet and golden petals fallen from the azalea and the rhododendron bushes on the lawn at home, the sun on my back, and in my ears the song of a thrush on the sweeping branches of the chestnut tree, would groan and struggle against the impossibility of escape.

'You'd better go away,' I said to Jake; 'you can't hang around with me after what I've said. I'm not worth a curse; I'll clear out, I'll go with people who don't matter.'

'Don't be a fool,' he said again. We were standing now by a lamp-post at the corner of a street. 'You don't have to mind what you say to me,' he went on, 'and you don't need to worry over my years in prison. That's all gone, and locked away in myself, minding, I mean. You can talk about it whenever you like if it helps you.'

'I feel a swine,' I said, 'the way I've been throwing about my own story like some fake martyr and you going through hell. . . .'

'Oh! that's all right,' he said, and he laughed to show me I need not be shy of him over this.

'What did you do?' I asked stupidly, and then felt myself go scarlet, for what business was it of mine, anyway?

'I killed a man,' said Jake.

I did not know what to say, I wanted to show him that it did not matter to me what he had done, that he would be justified in anything.

'Oh! well,' I said lamely, 'I dare say . . .' but I did not know how to go on with my sentence.

'I expect the other chap deserved all he got. . . .' I ended, feeling a fool.

'No,' said Jake, 'whatever anybody does it can't give you the excuse to take their lives. I reasoned that out in prison. You get a whole lot of time for thinking there.'

His words were simple enough, but it hurt me to think of him alone with his thoughts, fighting out the reason for life and death.

'I don't know,' I said, wishing to argue on his side, 'if your chap had done something you couldn't forgive?'

'Oh! forgiveness,' smiled Jake, 'that's nothing. You soon get over that. I was your age when this thing came along, and I guess I thought very much like you then. I wanted to hurt, and only succeeded in hurting myself. The man I killed wasn't any the wiser. In prison I soon forgot about him, and what he'd done; all I remembered were the years he might have had, and mine too, gone because I hadn't stopped to think.'

'What happened quite?' I said.

He did not answer me directly.

'When you're young,' he said, 'you make the mistake of plunging too deeply into things. That's what I did, anyway. I reckoned myself capable of judging men by standards I'd built up for myself. I resented illusions crashing about the place.'

'Yes,' I said.

'I didn't see that my concern was with myself, and that however much I fought I couldn't change things, and the way people went. I believed a great deal in that fellow, and I killed him because he had spoilt the life of some woman I had never even met.'

As he spoke I could see the Jake of seven years back, and the hatred in his eyes not for the man whom he had destroyed, but for the loss of an ideal. He would crucify himself for no reason. Beneath all this I saw his superiority to myself, for I would have no principles and no standards; I would accept such a thing as natural, making excuses for the conduct of a friend, laughing perhaps, wondering idly as to the attraction of the woman, and wanting to know her.

'Oh! well, if he was like that . . .' I began, but I was aware my voice did not ring true with sincerity. 'Anyway, what had he done?'

Now I was curious, and at the same time I despised my curiosity. Jake looked at me and the expression in his eyes made me uncomfortable, as though I were a little schoolboy grubbing over a coarse passage in the Bible.

'Just been selfish,' he said, 'and thinking about his body.'

He did not say any more than this.

'She died of consumption out in Switzerland. She went to pieces after he left her. He was the first, you see, and he hadn't bothered to think.'

I nodded, biting my nails; I wanted to get away from the subject of the woman. I felt I wasn't qualified to judge.

'How did you kill him?' I asked.

'Fighting in the ring,' he said, 'just a cheap prize-fight, one of those affairs in a tent at a circus where you pay half a crown to watch. I broke his neck. Nobody but myself knew how much it was on purpose. At the trial the jury brought in a verdict of manslaughter. I knew I was guilty and I didn't tell. That's being a coward. Now you know why I'm here. I've served my little sentence.'

He laughed, and I thought how bitter I would be, how resentful of the world, how bent and broken by the punishment brought on myself. And he was laughing, standing under the lamp-post, lighting another cigarette.

'Maybe I've been boring you,' he said; 'let's forget about all that. I've told you this just to show you that you don't have to chuck yourself over a bridge.'

I wished he did not have this power of making me feel aware of my shame, leaving me stripped before my own eyes without the shadow of an excuse.

Perhaps for the first time that night I realized what he had saved me from, and but for him I would now be drifting swollen and horrible at the mercy of the river tides.

He must have seen what was passing in my mind.

'I'm glad I came along,' he said. Now I knew that because of him there was some meaning left to my existence, and that wheresoever I should go in the future, and whatever the days might have in store for me, I should not be alone.

My knowledge of what he had done, and those years of suffering in prison, had in the little space of time he had taken to tell me so succeeded in making me forget myself that now the thought of my father and the home I had left were become shadowy, ineffectual memories in my mind, and I believed myself free of their clinging atmosphere at last.

For Jake was more real to me in the few hours I had known him than the shrouded intangibility of my father, and Jake's personality had carried me away from my dusty dreams to the reality of hardship and suffering.

To me this was the meaning of being alive, this very sensation of the pavement beneath our feet, and the lamp shining upon a square, the smell of the warm air, the careless knowledge that it mattered little where we went, with no one to care but our two selves.

Jake and I wandered wherever the streets should lead us, and it was good to know that there was not the necessity of talking, but a word thrown now and again, and a whistle of a song, and a glance at the sky and a smile.

I could know his thoughts if I wanted, and it was the same for him.

I knew then that this night was a thing which could never be forgotten, nor the hard ring of our feet as we walked, nor the scattered groups of people in the slum streets, nor the wind rising from odd corners to blow upon our hair, nor the thrill of adventure, nor the mud-tang of the river smell from the docks and the lights of ships at anchor.

And never forgotten the sight that met our eyes before morning when we looked over a great bank of coal and black dust and saw the grey outline of a sleeping barque, her yards scarce discernible through the mist, the shrouds as shadowy as a cobweb, and the white letters on her stern: '*Hedwig* – Oslo.'

Jake and I stared at her without a word, and then turning smiled at one another, for the same thought belonged to us both, and we knew we were looking upon the ship that would carry us away.

Then we lay down on a piece of sacking on the wharf, and pillowed our faces in our hands, and slept.

5

As she went down the river the ship seemed like a phantom on the surface of black water, and the lights of London burned and flared in the darkness, sending a tongue of yellow flame to the sky. These lights and the dim buildings, this sound and clamour of London belonged to the world which we were leaving, and we passed them by, careless, unheeding, our eyes turned to new vistas ahead and to new sounds. There were the lights of other ships, there was the wash from a swift tug-boat, and faintly – coming from beyond, borne on the air – the siren of a homebound cargo vessel. London was gone, and vanished soon the flat marshes of Essex, and nothing awaited us but the great turn and span of the river, and a cold fresh wind; new lights winking from a headland, a spatter of rain, and the smell of the sea.

I leant against the bulwark of the ship and the first spray licked my face, and I felt the deck rise and fall beneath my feet as the barque met the sea. The coast of England slipped away from us, strange and unfamiliar in the grey light of morning, while ahead lay a hard unbroken line of sea, and another day and another sky.

It came to me that this was the beginning of adventure, and the starting of a dream, and as I felt the sea on my lips and heard the voices of men around me, I knew that I was no longer a boy who yearned to break the shackles of home and be free, but I was sailing before the mast of a Norwegian barque, and I was a man with other men.

So I should know what it would be to sail in a ship, to be weary and worn, to be hungry and happy.

I should learn the feel of ropes, the pressure of wind in canvas, I should know sickness and torture, but beyond these things there would be a fierce wild pleasure that I could not explain, a tumult of my body and a madness of my brain, laughter, and shouting in the air.

At first there was confusion and distress, and a lost sensation of my own helplessness, and then I conquered the misery of sickness, clinging to Jake like a weeping child, and I came out of the fo'c'sle upon the deck with my belly empty and my tongue afire, and there was the barque straining to be free as I had striven, a high sea running and a high wind blowing.

There were days and there were nights when living was tremendous, and living was hell, and I worked, and I slept, and I worked again. And there was no time for thinking, no time for dreams, but only this bare fighting for existence, the hunger of an animal, a sudden calm and a sleep. I had rough hands and a growth of beard like any man, I cursed and I laughed, I fought and I was happy. Soon there would be another country, and faces I had never seen. Nothing mattered but the harsh beauty of this life, this pleasure and the pain, nothing mattered because Jake was beside me, and I was not alone.

The high masts strained under the press of the heavy canvas, looking down and from the fore-t'gallant yard the deck sheered away, long and narrow, small space for movement because of the stacked timber. We worked our way along the yard, treading the slippery foot rope, clinging with one hand to the swinging ratlin above. There seemed every prospect of a fresh breeze, and this was an advantage not to be neglected, for we were already forty-

eight hours behind our stated time, and now with every sail set
we must make up for what we had lost after leaving Finland,
when the westerly gale had set us off our course, and we had been
obliged to beat against it, snugged down to lower tops'ls, with
the fo'c'sle head covered every few minutes with a grey sea.
Now the wind came true from the north, and the watch crowded
aloft, Jake and I flinging the gaskets from the fore-t'gallant while
the great sail bellowed loose and the halyards shook, and the
wind whistled in the rigging like a joyous devil.

Jake shook his head and laughed at me, his hair falling over
his eyes, and I ducked to avoid a swinging blow from the shaking
sail before it was sheeted home. And now I balanced myself on
the foot rope, one hand on the back stay, and giddily I looked
below me and saw the green water rushing past our bows, and
heard the pressure of wind in the canvas and saw the figure of
the cook peering up at us from his galley abaft the mast, a small
dot of a figure beside the white deck-house. Then for all my torn
hands and my dizzy head, and my rough clothes still sodden from
the soaking they had received in the gale, I smiled back at Jake,
for this was something that meant the thrill of living, and the
joy of being young. Somewhere there was a bitter shame-faced
boy, running down the avenue of his home to the lodge gates
and the high road leading to Lessington, but here was a man
who was learning to work with his hands, to fight for his life, to
conquer the wild forces of wind and sea, to curse and laugh with
his companions in a strange language, to fill his aching stomach
with filth and be grateful, to cast himself in his cot, dog-weary,
with his wet clothes clinging to him and his head at the wrong
angle, and to smile and be happy, caring not at all.

Never for one moment, even with the agony of the work and
the terrible fatigue, did I regret what I had done, for this was a
freedom in itself and Jake was beside me.

His cot swung above mine in the dingy fo'c'sle, and there was
always an assuring comfort in his presence, even from that first
night at sea when we had staggered down from the deck to the
watch below, I bewildered and helpless with the unaccustomed
orders, and groping my way in the dim light to my cot I heard
him climb to the one above me, and felt his hand touch my

shoulder for a minute, and his voice, half anxious: 'All right, Dick?' in my ear.

So we were together from the start, both being cast in the same watch, and we ate side by side, carrying our tin of food from the galley to the fo'c'sle, and we tramped the deck by night talking of things or not talking, and picking up a smattering of Norwegian or Danish from our companions.

I learnt to take my trick at the wheel with the others, and it seemed to me that this must be the grandest moment of my life – one fine clear night it was in the middle of the Baltic Sea on our way to Finland from London, with a fair wind on the quarter, and a black sea around me, and the tall masts before me pointing to the stars.

I heard the sigh of wind in the canvas and I felt the strain of the wheel, and I looked down upon my course marked on the compass in the light of the binnacle, and there was no sight or sound of any moving thing upon the sea save us and the ship, and I felt that this moment was good and could never be destroyed.

And when Jake came to relieve me he waited a while, seeing my arms flung carelessly through the spokes as though I had been born for this, I showing off a little to both him and myself, and as he watched me I could not hide the smile on my face which would not leave me for the beauty of this moment. He did not bother to laugh at me, but he said: 'You're happy, aren't you?' and he knew.

Days and nights had gone past now though, and we were bound from Helsingfors to Copenhagen to discharge our cargo of timber, and from thence we were uncertain, but there were rumours of our proceeding round the coast to Oslo in ballast, and there to wait our turn for a freight.

It mattered little to Jake and myself, for we had no plans, only to take what chances should come our way, and when we became tired of a thing to go off on our own once more, and work or stay idle, whichever should come to our minds. The wind held fair from the north as I have said, and we made a quick passage to Copenhagen, but there was a dirty colour in the sky and we saw a long line of sailing yachts, running to their moorings before the weather broke, following close upon one another's heels, a lovely sight in the half-light before the sun went down.

Then the sky filled with grey, and I saw the city of Copenhagen through a mist of rain that fell gently on the red roofs and the towers, making it seem like England and home.

I was as thrilled as a schoolboy on holiday, and Jake and I went ashore that night with the rest of the crowd from the ship, and we made straight for the Tivoli, the fun fair of the people of Copenhagen, where we scattered kronen without bothering about the cost of anything, riding the switchbacks and throwing darts, seeing ourselves in distorted mirrors, driving ridiculous little cars controlled by electricity, peering at the girls on the dancing-floor where some of the boys were bold enough to venture, but I felt shy about this and hung back with Jake, pretending I did not care to dance. All the time the rain fell, and we splashed about in puddles with the lights of the Tivoli reflected in them green and gold, and a band played a dance tune that was good to hear.

Then Jake and I moved off to explore the streets, and I left the Tivoli with the sound of that tune in my head and a memory of a girl with a great cloud of flaxen hair looking over somebody's shoulder to where we had stood some minutes before, jammed in the crowd, and I wondered if I had really been shy to mingle with the other boys on the dancing-floor or if it was a desire to be on the same level as Jake, who cared only to find the cobbled stones of a market square and a canal by a twisted bridge. So we walked about the streets in the rain until I was tired, and I felt flat after the excitement of landing earlier in the evening, but Jake looked as if he could keep this up all night, taking a passionate interest in the shape of buildings and the corner of some old house, so that my mood was out of tune with his for perhaps the first time since we had been together, though I managed to hide it from him.

I could not forget that it was my first night in Copenhagen and I was a sailor ashore, and that every minute should be filled with the possibility of adventure, while here we were plodding the wet streets that might, in the light we saw them, have belonged to an English country town, and I was not sure if it was a girl I wanted or a drink or neither, but all I knew was that I wanted it to be different from this.

We got back to the landing-stage just as the rain had stopped and it was getting light.

The boys were in the boat wondering if they should bother to wait for us. They were most of them happily drunk, and a young Norwegian who spoke English told me with a sleepy grin he had picked the best girl in Denmark and had gone home with her. They all laughed at him and said he had been too drunk to do anything, and then they chaffed one another in their own language, and I watched them, rather foolish and apart, not being able to understand what they said. I wished I was drunk too and exhausted in the same way, having known something about Danish girls, and lighting a cigarette I glanced over to where Jake was crouching in the bows, his knees drawn up to his chin, his eyes narrowing as he looked away from all of us to where the dawn was breaking clear and cold over the water. I knew his thoughts were of Copenhagen shrouded still in a grey light, the green patch of colour in the sky and the beauty of a spire, and he had not listened to our chatter and our laughter.

I supposed we must have sounded like a flock of cackling geese, and I did not laugh much after that, but somehow I envied Jake's mood and I envied the boys too, and I felt very dull, for whichever way I looked at it my evening had been a failure.

I don't think it was fine all the time we were in Copenhagen. We were kept busy most of the time discharging our cargo, and when we were free of the timber we had to set about shifting our own ballast to get the right trim. There were not many hours for going ashore with all this work on our hands. I was not sorry when we weighed anchor once more, and made for the open sea with Copenhagen astern of us in a curtain of rain.

We were making all the sail we could, for the breeze was light, and high up in the rigging Jake leaned across the yardarm, and shouted to me, pointing to a ridge of land away on the quarter. 'That's Helsinor,' he said, and I could not help smiling at his excitement, and then fell to wondering at this man who had been a sailor, and a prize-fighter, and had killed his friend because of an ideal, and had spent seven years in prison, and who liked me, and who knew about Hamlet.

But there was not time to puzzle out these things, for the mate shouted up to us from the poop, his hands to his mouth, and I had picked up enough Norwegian by now to know that he was cursing us to work smartly, and put some muscle into the job, and I tore at the beating canvas and the ropes stiffened with the disuse in the harbour and the rain, the blood running from under my broken nails.

As we had imagined, the *Hedwig* was bound for her home port of Oslo, and many of the boys were talking of leaving the ship when she docked, and going ashore for a spell, for it was likely she would have to go into dry dock and be overhauled before she secured a freight, and this might take several weeks, so, anyway, the crew would be paid off. The boys could sign on with another ship when their money was spent if the *Hedwig* was not ready by then. So much we gathered from the smattering of Danish and Norwegian in the fo'c'sle, and Jake and I talked the matter over in our watch below, he smoking cigarette after cigarette stretched out in his cot, his feet on the bulkhead, while I lay below him, my head pillowed in my arms, watching the swinging light and the haze of smoke and the sleeping faces of the watch.

'We'll lay off the sea for a while,' said Jake; 'I'll buy a map when we get to Oslo and we'll strike inland, north of course, to the mountains.'

'Yes,' I said.

'I don't care how we get there, do you? We'll walk and ride and get lifts in a truck. We don't have to worry about anything, do we?' he said.

'No.'

'I've got some money,' he said; 'we shan't want much, as a matter of fact. That's an advantage of prison, Dick, you're clear of bills, and your balance mounts steadily.'

'Oh! hell!' I said, 'I can't hang on to you like this, Jake.'

'Don't be a fool. Who brought you on this trip, anyway?'

'No – listen here. . . .'

'I'm sick of your voice; go to sleep, can't you?' he said.

'It's all damn funny for you,' I muttered, 'but what do I look like, mucking around on your savings?'

'Who's going to look at you?'

'Oh! I don't know, but what am I going to feel like?'

'You haven't got any feelings, Dick.'

'Sure, I have.'

'Forget 'em, then, they're not worth a cent.'

'No, but look here. . . .'

'Go to sleep, little boy, you're no nerve tonic to a tired sailor.'

I laughed, cursing him at the same time. I saw that it was no use protesting, and, anyway, it did not matter very much.

I fell asleep, smiling at the thought of my father, who scarcely existed any more for me, sitting at his desk in the old library gazing out of the windows on to the smooth lawn, and I, stretched in a cot of a fo'c'sle with an unknown country before me to explore, and a rough track through the mountains, and forests, and a frozen lake, and no night and jumbled up with this the imagined approach to Oslo, another strange city, the lights and laughing, and a song and maybe a girl somewhere. . . .

Every moment was new to me on the passage to Oslo, and there were a thousand and one things to make me wonder, or smile, or curse, and the work was hard, nor did we ever get much sleep. I dare say I should have grumbled if it hadn't been for Jake, who seemed eternally to understand the light and shade of my moments, the heights and the depths, and he had the power of knowing when to throw a word at me and when to leave me alone.

The hardships and the monotony were forgotten when I remembered that each minute we were getting farther north, and the summer evenings stretched themselves indefinitely with scarcely a breaking up of day into night. The ship would slip over the surface of the water with every rag set to catch a breath of the inconsistent wind, and suddenly the sun would be gone without my having known, and no cover of darkness would fall upon the sea, only a hard white light that seemed to be born of distant mountains and cold glaciers, a light that belonged to a rushing stream set in a forest of great hills and the silence of lakes, frozen in midsummer. We were in the midst of the sea with no land near to us, but there was something in the stark purity of the air that told us these things existed 'way ahead to the north of us, and I was aware of a dumb sorrow in me that I could not explain for the beauty of what lay around me and I had not seen.

Then I was glad of the presence of Jake near to me at all times, for a horror would come upon me because of the vast solitude of space and the solitary splendour of the regions where we were drifting; even the white stars seemed cold and terribly remote, and we, poor human beings on our little ship, were wretched and pathetic in our attempts to equal their wisdom, nor had we any right to venture upon the imperturbability of these waters.

Something inside me wept I knew not why, and my heart hungered for unattainable things that had no name, so that I would gaze upon the still sea bathed in its white light with a shudder and a strange despair, till Jake stood beside me on the deck, and the touch of his shoulder and the smell of his cigarette brought me to some sense of reality, I clutching at the sound of his voice so natural and unafraid, as a crumb of comfort and a sign of security.

Then perhaps there would be a shift of wind, and a call from the mate on the poop to go aloft or lay a hand on the braces, so there would have to be a forgetting of one's thoughts, shy and unexplained, and a casting of mind and body into this business of wind and sail.

It would seem to me that the smell of ships and the sea was in my blood now, and I had never known any life but this.

We docked in Oslo early one morning before the sound and movement of the day. A large tramp steamer had come to her moorings before us, and the belching smoke from her funnel made a curtain in the sky, so that all I could perceive of Oslo in the faint light were the forms of many ships, the ugly cranes of the docks, and stretching away from this the old town on a hill, and on the left the buildings of the modern capital, with a sparkle of blue water and blue hills beyond.

Jake and I were paid off with the rest of the crew at Oslo, and we looked back with regret to the steel outline of the barque that had been our home. For all the discomfort we had endured there had been moments of glory and exultation and the thrill of this first adventure could not surely be surpassed.

I resented the idea that when the *Hedwig* sailed again there would be some strange Norwegian snoring in my cot in the dingy fo'c'sle, for places where we have lived intensely become part of ourselves, I always think. However much now Jake and I might resolve to return when the barque was out of dry dock, I felt there would be other things claiming us by then and the *Hedwig* would belong to the past as surely as the bridge over London river belonged to the past, with the sailor as vanished as the boy who trembled at death.

Even now, with the spars of the ship hidden from view by a tall crane, I turned forgetting her a little, and looked towards Oslo and the blue hills beyond. We said good-bye to the boys, some of them had their homes far away, one or two were going to look for another ship. It seemed odd parting from them, after having worked side by side and eaten and slept with them. My friend the Norwegian made some joke and waved his cap and smiled, but I knew I would not see him again.

Jake and I wandered about looking for shops in Oslo. There were avenues of trees and trams, and the colour of the buildings was yellow. I got some dungaree trousers and a pair of canvas shoes, and a blue cap with a peak, but Jake only bought a toothbrush and a map.

We found a cheap restaurant where they knew about beer, and we spread the map out on the table in front of us. I could not make head nor tail of it, I wanted to get away up north to the patches of blue that looked like water. 'They're the fjords,' said Jake; 'we'll strike them on our way. Look here, these are the mountains, and that's Turin right in the heart of them before you get to the fjords. We'll have to work this way, and follow the roads.' His thumbnail was pointing to something called Fagerness, away in the wilds, and miles from Oslo.

His voice was excited, and his hair fell over his eyes. He looked younger than I had ever seen him.

Somebody laughed at another table, and the smell of food was good. Soon it would be evening, and the lights, and more people crowding together, and outside the still air and the white sky, although it was night. I thought how splendid it all was, and how I might have been dead.

'I want to get drunk,' I said to Jake. He laughed, he did not care.

We went out after a while and we found somewhere to sleep that night; it seemed cheap enough, and a paradise of luxury to us after the cramped fo'c'sle of the barque *Hedwig*.

I was not tired enough and I did not want to go to bed yet awhile.

'Come on,' I said to Jake, and we looked about us for a theatre, but there did not seem anything much on, though he suggested trying the opera; they were giving *Tosca*, and I told him to go to hell, so once more we found ourselves in one of those café-restaurant places ordering drinks. I did not think much of the night life of Scandinavia. Even the Tivoli at Copenhagen was better than this.

'We ought to have tried Stockholm,' I said to Jake, but he was dragging out his damned map again and did not listen to me, so I kept calling the waiter fellow to bring us more drinks, and then looking around me, but there weren't any girls worth worrying over, and they all had their own parties, anyway.

'We can get a train to take us to Fagerness,' said Jake; 'I reckon it to be about ten hours' journey from Oslo. Then we'll see if we can get horses and strike away for the mountains – you can ride, can't you, Dick?'

'Sure I can ride,' I said, but his words seemed nonsense to me, and the air was very thick, and his voice was coming from a long way away.

I did not know how to stop myself from smiling.

'We ought to get out to the glaciers somehow,' said Jake, 'but that's right north in another group of fjords. See here's Sandene, and there's the Briksdol glacier we ought to see.'

'Oh! shut up,' I thought, 'who cares?' and I tried to keep my eyes focused on something on the table, but they kept wandering away to the corner of the room where there were a couple of men, and an ugly girl who had something queer on her hat, not that it mattered to me, but the light caught it and it was aggravating not to know, and some damn fool orchestra started which muddled itself up with the sound of Jake's voice and the movement of a passing waiter.

I began to wish I hadn't drunk so much, but it was too late

now, and perhaps none of this was going on really at all, but I was asleep, and it was happening in my imagination. It would have been a relief to sweep the things off the table and stretch out my arms, and then lay my face in my hands and not bother any more. There was no fun in getting drunk this way; I ought to be talking a lot or being amusing, or singing from sheer joy and the strength of life. I knew that Jake would be able to drink anything and even then not show the slightest sign, but walk twenty miles or climb a mountain, or maybe go out laughing and kill a fellow.

I steadied my hands on the table and looked across at him, but his face did not seem to hang at the right angle, and I wondered if it was he who smiled so stupidly or myself reflected in the glass opposite.

'You sit quiet awhile,' he said, 'or d'you want me to take you home?'

There was not any need to laugh at me like that, I thought.

'Here, I'm not drunk,' I said.

'That's fine,' he said.

'You think because I've lived all my bloody life buried in England I don't know anything,' I went on. I supposed it was my voice talking loudly, but was not sure. It did not seem to matter whose it was.

'Never mind about all that,' said Jake.

The silly idiot was treating me like a child.

'I bloody well do mind,' I said. 'What sort of fun d'you think I'm getting out of this? You sit there, grinning at me, with your big face. I know a hell of a lot, I do. Listen here, my father's a damned old scoundrel, isn't he? I've told you about him, haven't I? He's just a damned old scoundrel who thinks because he can write a whole lot of rotten poetry, he can tell me what to do.'

'Shut up, Dick,' said Jake. 'If you don't sit quiet I'll take you out of here.'

'I'll go when I bloody well choose, and not before. You can't tell me what to do any more than my father. And he does write damned rotten poetry. I could write better than him if I wanted to. Do you say I can't write, Jake?'

'I don't mind, Dick, tell me about it another time.'

'I showed my father what I'd written. I chucked it down on the desk in front of him. "Read that," I said, and he took hold of it in his hands. He didn't know what was coming, and he read it out loud, Jake. I tell you I can bloody well write if I want to. I don't care what my father thinks; my poem was all about wanting to sleep with a woman and the feeling you get.'

'Yes, Dick, I know.'

'My father didn't understand a word, he's about seventy; what should he care, Jake, he's a damned old scoundrel, isn't he? Listen, I wrote another poem, too.'

'Shut up.'

'I won't shut up, why should I? I want to talk about women and things, you don't ever want to. You're just damned sexless, that's what you are. Here, you think I'm drunk, don't you, you think I'm drunk?'

'So you are, Dick.'

'No, I'm not. Listen, I want to go to all sorts of places and do things; I want to be famous one day, Jake. I'll know a hell of a lot then. Listen, I want to go to Mexico or somewhere, and drive cattle, and make a whole packet of money and then come back to Europe and bust it all in Paris on women. Here, you think I'm mad, don't you?'

'No, Dick, only young.'

'That's a damned offensive remark, anyway. I'm not young. Listen, I'm going to write a book one day.'

'Of course you are.'

'Here, this isn't much of a place; what sort of a town do they think Oslo is; it's a bloody dull town, isn't it, Jake? No girls, nothing; come on, let's start a fight; let's get knocking people about; I'm going to hit the red thing off that girl's hat, here – I wish the boys were in this crowd; come on, let's start something.'

I remember getting up, but there did not seem to be any floor and the door was zigzagging away in the corner. I could not get the feel of my feet at all.

'Here, let go my arm,' I said to Jake.

'Steady, Dick,' he said.

I was not sure whether I wanted to cry or to burst out laughing.

'Come on, fight,' I shouted; 'let's start a bloody good row.'

A whole crowd of people got up and began knocking in to me.

'Walk straight, you damn fool,' said Jake.

The door crashed into my face, hurting like hell.

Everyone was being unfair, it wasn't my fault. I sat down on the pavement outside holding on to the kerb. When I shut my eyes it felt as though somebody were swinging me upside down by my heels.

'Here, I'm going to be sick,' I said. And it seemed to me that life was not such a grand thing after all.

6

We got a train and went to Fagerness in the mountains. It was only the start of them there, but right away in the distance they stretched to the sky, covered in forest, with white falls born from the snow on the summits, crashing down into the valleys below.

At Fagerness there were wooded hills, and farms for breeding silver foxes, and a shallow silent lake surrounded by narrow beaches where nobody ever went.

Jake stayed in the village, talking to some fellow about getting hold of horses, and I found a track through a wood, full of fern and broken stone, and climbed high up somewhere surrounded by the close trees, never coming out into the light. It began to rain, and there seemed something of terror in the silence of this place, with no other sound but the steady falling of rain in the trees, and the drip-dripping of it on the leaves, till I started to run, some instinct taking me downward all the time, and I wondered what should happen if I caught my foot in a root of a tree or in the loose earth, and fell to the ground with a twisted ankle, helpless and alone. I knew how I should lie there with the rain upon my face, and listen to the patter of it on the rustling leaves above me, and no darkness would come to shroud the trees and bring a relaxation of my wakened senses, for in this land night was no more than a continuation of the fading day, and the forest would seem to stand more coldly aloof at midnight than before, strange, with an unnatural clarity scornful of shadows. So I ran away from the silence, and breaking from the belt of trees I came once more with relief sweeping upon me and a glance back over my shoulder, to the village of Fagerness with Jake standing in the middle of the road looking to right and left, wondering where I had been.

'Where have you come from?' he said.

'Out in those woods,' I told him. 'It's terrible the feeling you get there, that you're not wanted. I hate being alone, Jake.'

'What d'you go for?'

'Oh! just to see. I'd try anything once.'

'I've got horses, Dick.'

'Listen – I'll make a fool of myself riding.'

'That doesn't matter.'

'How did you pay for 'em?'

'Got 'em cheap. The fellow had a squint, he didn't know much.'

'Where are we going?'

'Over the mountains to the fjords.'

'We shan't ever get there.'

'Sure we will.'

'I'll get the horrors, Jake, in these hills. They're too big for me.'

'You won't be alone.'

'There's something queer about this country – I don't know. The silence, and never getting dark, and all those trees above you that you can't touch.'

'I like it,' he said.

'You're different to me, Jake. If I wasn't here you'd ride off by yourself with a smile on your face, and get lost on a mountain, and you wouldn't care.'

'I don't know.'

'What'll we do about food?'

'Get it as we go.'

'There aren't any towns.'

'There'll be villages scattered, and huts, Dick.'

'We'll have to sleep somewhere.'

'We'll be all right.'

'It'll seem funny, won't it, right away in the hills and no sound or anything?'

'You won't be scared.'

'I'm a damn fool, aren't I, Jake?'

'No.'

'There's part of me wants this more than anything in the world, and another part feels like running away, and being in a street somewhere full of traffic, tired on a hot pavement, waiting in a queue of sweating people to catch a bus. . . .'

'Never mind about that.'

'I wish I was different.'

'You're all right.'

'I wish I knew how to keep up with grand things and not just stick to the rotten.'

'You're like a sheet of blank paper, Dick, waiting for impressions.'

'Being with you is fine.'

'That's good.'

'I wish I could write like my father.'

'You could if you wanted.'

'No, I couldn't, Jake. I'm only an ordinary fellow without any guts.'

'You don't train yourself. You don't know about discipline. There's a whole lot of you that you're too lazy to bring out.'

'That's it, laziness,' I said.

'You ought to take a pull on yourself.'

'Maybe I will, later, but there's plenty of time. I want to get fun out of things now.'

'You'll go on and forget, till it's too late.'

'I don't know, I don't see it matters. I can only be young once.'

'Everybody says that. You'll find it's over without anything to show for it.'

'There'll be moments like this to show for it, Jake, and being on the ship, and taking my trick at the wheel, and hanging round Oslo, and knowing you.'

'That won't be enough.'

'I'll have lived a whole lot.'

'Only in little things, Dick.'

'This is big enough, anyway.'

'There won't always be this.'

'You won't chuck me, Jake?'

'No.'

'I'd be a mess without you hanging around.'

'You ought to stand by yourself.'

'I can't cope.'

'We'll make an early start tomorrow, Dick, and strike off on that road to the left. We'll get right away over on those hills.'

'That'll be grand.'

'There's a white stream somewhere we can follow.'

'Yes.'

'How do you feel now, Dick?'

'I feel fine.'

We did not talk any more after this. We went inside the little hotel to our rooms, and I was asleep very soon.

I felt as if I had been born again when I got out into the mountains. There was something tremendous in the way they took a hold on me, making me feel sick at myself for anything I had done. I did not know where I was, the first few days of that journey. I looked about me dazed and half-conscious, leaving my horse to pick his own way after Jake, who was always a little ahead; and Jake would turn round on his saddle ever and again with a smile on his lips and a call to me 'You all right?' nor would I answer save for a nod of my head.

At first the mountains did not seem to get any nearer; we could see them away beyond the rolling hills stretching their rugged shoulders, line upon line, one peak for ever higher than the other, snow-capped under a white sky.

It was frightening, this great distance. I felt the summits were unattainable, nobody had ever leant his cheek against the rough surface of the rock, and listened to the boiling cataract of foam that fell like the crashing of thunder down on to the forested slopes.

There would be no hands to touch, no voices to break upon the silence of these places, and the snow would be untrodden.

Where we rode in the valleys there were forests rising away from us on either side, fir trees I suppose they were, and growing massed together there was every possible coloured green amongst them, vivid startled patches toning with the soft and the pale, while below and above were the silver greens, and the sombre, darkly clustered like a carpet of shadows. They stretched from us tier upon tier, immeasurable and bewildering, losing themselves finally in the crags of mountains.

Way up above, lost in the heights, where there was no pathway, and no movement of a living thing, the untrodden snow became frozen and crystallized, and when a breath of warmer air blew upon this the falls were born in a thundering cascade of water, striking a high ledge of rock and running into the valleys, singing over the stones, twisting and turning as they fell, a white stream of rushing melted snow.

Wherever we went these streams were with us, a torrent of sound like a song in our ears. The mountain snows were white, the streams were white, and the sky, and white was the light that bathed us when evening came, making the forest pale ghosts with shadowed fingers, and us strange things of clarity till the dawn.

The sun beat down on us all the day, and we rode carelessly, our shoulders bent and our knees slack, scarce touching a rein, the horses drooping too, twitching their ears at the sun.

At midday or sooner we baited them awhile, and as they nosed amongst the short grass or the stones, we lay with our faces in our hands, sleeping sometimes, the heat upon our backs, and then turned and stretched ourselves, looking away to the forests and the mountains beyond, and smiled, saying a word or two, and reached for a cigarette.

Often we slept thus during the heat of the day, and rode on again at evening, for there was no darkness to bewilder us and the way was clear.

Jake had his map before him on the saddle, but it mattered little how we should go or where we should end.

As the road crept onward, climbing higher, and the green valleys sloped away from us, the mountains began to close in upon us and the sound now of the cascades falling upon the rocks was an everlasting crescendo of sound, while the sky seemed nearer to us, like a white hand on the face of the mountains, and we shivered in spite of the sun, because of the stark purity of the air.

Now I was here I was no longer fearful of the majesty of beauty or the solitude, my mood of dumb wonder and silent terror at their approach had given way to something sublime and almost terrific. I felt as though I had risen above myself, leaving the old self in the valleys below, and with this shaking off of mediocrity had been re-born with a new strength and a new understanding. Jake would not be so far away from me now; we might ride together as companions. He would always be ahead, of course, and I retaining my measure of humility, would follow his lead. Up in the mountains Jake seemed even grander than before. It was as if this was his own element, the snow, the air, and the white skies.

He belonged here, having a supreme instinctive knowledge of these things, whilst I was only learning, and keeping in the track of his footprints, my eyes watching for a reflection of what he should see.

The thrill of the daily life aboard the barque *Hedwig*, the vigorous toil, the fight against wind and sea, the weary hardships, all these seemed far from me now, for we had embarked upon a longer journey where the mind travelled beyond the body riding on its horse, and there was no monotony of work to break upon a train of thought.

It was like existing indefinitely in a land of dreams, clearer than reality where the spirit wandered of its own free will, untrammelled by desire and discontent. Jake and I had entered into a strange intimacy, when silence meant more to us than words. We knew that we were happy without going into an explanation of what we felt. We rode side by side like two pilgrims to no shrine. We had no prayers, but every moment was something to be worshipped, and our gods were the things we looked upon, the mountains, and the cold air.

Somewhere there was a little withered boy with a dusty mind who, stifling in the atmosphere of his father, wrote shabby pornographic poems crouched in a lonely room full of shadows, but he was not here in the silent hills amongst the singing falls and the untrodden snow.

Maybe, Jake too looked down from his heights on the face of a prisoner, barred from the light of the sun, who sat tortured by the thought of a life lain waste that might have been as splendid as the one that followed on.

I did not want ever to go down into the world again. I wished I were a writer, I wished I knew how to write down on paper the beauty of things. My father, having seen nothing of all this, would sit alone in the library before his open desk, and from his pen little thoughts would run forming themselves into words, becoming in one stroke, in one flash, living images of strange loveliness grouped like a string of pictures without names.

Whilst I, groping in the darkness, could only wonder and worship, with the mountains rising up before me, their shoulders stretched above a bank of cloud, their frozen faces lifted in dumb expectation to a white intangible sky.

And below the green forests clustered, the spreading branches turning away from the hard rock surface like reluctant fingers.

I would describe the silence of a frozen lake, and the sudden sound of a foaming cataract of water splashing its way down into a forest stream. I would make some melody of music, linking the echoes of falls in a valley with the song of the stream, and mingling with this a gold pattern of lost sunlight on a trembling leaf.

I would paint the still air, and the other mountains that I could not reach, and the white light at midnight, and the shiver before dawn.

I would draw with a shadowed pencil the figures of two men, their horses motionless, standing on the sloping ground of a rough track watching the sun go down behind a blue mountain, and when it was gone there were patches of pink and silver like fingerprints in the untouched snow.

And the first man had a face that might have been carven out of stone, with the scar that ran down his left cheek as a crevice in a rock. He belonged here, to the colours of the setting sun, to the ridge of the mountains never climbed, and to the frozen air.

I wished I had some gift of explanation, but in my mind there is this picture burnt with strokes of fire, treasured and unforgettable, of Jake astride his horse, the reins hanging loose on the

51

horse's neck, while he sat with his arms folded and his head turned to that suggestion of pale light upon a mountain where the sun had been. And below us the soft snow crinkled and melted, and the white rushing streams fell into the valleys.

We had climbed the highest point of our journey, and we stayed here transfigured, saying never a word, Jake happier than he had ever been and out of my reach for ever.

If we could have stayed there perhaps a breath of ice could have been blown upon us, and we would have stood crystallized into eternity, the smiles frozen on our lips, the moment never changing and the beauty of a thought remaining with us everlasting.

It would have been good to die in such a way, with Jake by my side, and no fear in my heart. It seemed strange that life must go on without our need for it. I wanted to cry out to Jake to stay, to linger here only a little longer, away from the world, so that we could carry a greater memory of it which would not forsake us, but he waved his hand to me as a signal and I knew it was the end. We turned then and went down the stony track into the forests below.

That night we camped in a clearing of trees, and we lit a fire that crackled and glowed, rising high into the air with a red tongue of flame. We leant forward, our knees drawn up to our chins, the firelight on our faces, and smoked and listened to silence.

'I don't want this to end,' I said; 'I wish it would go on for ever.'

'Tomorrow,' said Jake, 'we get to Laardal and the first fjord. There'll be some sort of a village, I expect. Maybe there'll be one of those cruising steamers that'll take us on.'

'I don't want it,' I said, 'not to see people once more and hear them laugh and talk. Everything and everyone after this will seem a sham.'

'You'll change your mind when you leave the mountains behind, Dick. You'll feel same as you did in Oslo.'

'No, I shan't, I'll never feel like that again. These mountains have done something to me – I don't know. I hate everything I've been before. I want to go on feeling like I do now.'

'Yes?'

'We ought to build a hut, Jake, and live up here.'

'You wouldn't care about it for long.'

'I would. I'd like it better than anything in the world. There'd be a reason for being alive. What are you smiling at?'

'I'm not smiling.'

'Yes, you are. You've got me all wrong, Jake; you think I'm just a damn fool hanging round in towns trying to get drunk.'

'No.'

'Do you know what this has meant to me, seeing what we've seen, and riding, and listening, and not bothering about anything?'

'I think so.'

'I never could explain much, Jake.'

'You don't have to.'

'You've liked it too, haven't you, Jake?'

'Yes, I've liked it.'

'I'd never have thought of it on my own. Remember you spreading out the map in that café at Oslo? I wasn't much good that night. That's ages ago, isn't it?'

'Not so long.'

'It's centuries to me. I feel a whole lot of difference in myself. What do you feel?'

'Oh! I guess I'm just the same.'

'You'd say that anyway. You know, Jake, being up here has made me hate the thoughts I used to have. There's something so small in looking back on that life at home, whining about nothing, grubbing over my own bad poetry. I hate to remember it.'

'Don't remember it.'

'Well, it's difficult to quite get away. It's fine, the time one gets for thinking on this trip though, like giving one's mind a wash. Do you feel that too?'

'I think I've probably been giving my mind a rest, Dick. I used up all my thoughts in prison.'

'Now you're laughing at me,' I said.

'No, I mean that.'

'Did prison alter you, Jake, at all?'

'Yes.'

'What – you got a different angle on things?'

'I saw clearer there.'

'I can't understand that. I'd have gone mad. I'd have wanted to bash somebody's head in.'

'That had been done already.'

'Oh! hell, Jake – you know what I mean. I'm sorry.'

'It doesn't matter.'

He smiled at me across the fire and I knew I had not hurt him. I wanted him to go on talking. 'Tell me about that chap,' I said.

'There isn't much,' said Jake, 'that I can make into a story for you. He was all right, just like a million other fellows, that's all. I made the mistake of believing he was different.'

'How d'you mean?'

'We were on a ranch together for a while – there's another thing I've done, Dick, besides sailing and boxing and being in prison!'

'Was it fun?'

'Sure, it was grand. We used to like it.'

He laughed, and I felt I should never really understand how he could have killed this man who had been his friend.

'We used to talk ourselves sick in those days,' said Jake; 'we had ideas on everything. He was an enthusiast all right. We thought of going to a leper colony at one time.'

'Hell.'

'I know – youthful, wasn't it? That's the sort of chap he was. I loved watching him with the cattle; he knew instinctively how to handle one of them when it got sick. He knew what to do. He was fond of horses too. He'd have liked this trip.'

There was something terrible in the way Jake talked about the man he had murdered. It seemed impossible and unreal. He did not appear to mind. It was as though the years of suffering in prison had done away with feeling.

'I don't know how you could have done it,' I said.

'Done what? Oh! killed him, you mean. No – I ought to have hanged for it, of course.'

'Jake – don't.'

'You think this is all very cold-blooded, don't you? You see, it happened so long ago.'

'Seven years?' I said.

'It doesn't sound much to you, but then you see, you've never been in prison.'

'Jake . . .'

'You have time to worry everything out then.'

'Go on telling me,' I said.

'We went to England after a while,' he said. 'I took up boxing, I hung around with a moving fair. I enjoyed all that. I didn't see much of him, though; he was in London. I felt he'd be doing something great, wherever he was. We'd never quite given up the thought of the leper scheme, and I was ready to break away whenever he was. I wrote to him after a while, asking him how things were. Got a funny letter back. Said now he was in London life and people had made him feel different. He laughed at the leper business, said I must have been crazy to think he'd meant it seriously. He was going about a lot. Somebody must have lent him the money; he was always broke.'

Jake smiled as he said this. He leant back, his head against his hands. I saw the firelight reflected on his face.

'What did you feel about it?' I said.

'Oh! I didn't think much. In a way I imagined the whole letter was a joke. Then I heard about the girl.'

'Who told you?'

'A fellow I'd known in America came to see me fight one day. He was amused at this circus life I was leading. We got talking about things, vaguely, you know. He was quite a nice chap, but spoilt himself by drinking and running after women who didn't want him. He suddenly showed me a letter from some girl – written out in Switzerland. Terrible letter it was. She'd got consumption, and everything was hopeless. And this little fellow, who wasn't anything much himself, mark you, got white in the face and said to me – I remember the exact words – "I knew that girl when she was hardly more than a kid – and now she's dying, all because of some swine like you or me." He told me she'd led a

55

hell of a life for about two years. He seemed to have all the details. It was an unattractive story.'

I wanted to know everything though.

'Go on,' I said to Jake.

'I listened – much as you're listening now, Dick, but it wasn't from curiosity, it was something more. I hated the thought of this world that must be lived in – the sordid pitiful lives of men and women, who can't get beyond their own bodies. I could see this girl, living as she did without the excuse of poverty – she wasn't any prostitute having to keep herself, but spoiling her beauty, her health, and her own precious individuality, which is greater than anything in life, Dick, because some man had taught her to be self-indulgent. There wasn't anything more in it than that.'

'But look here, Jake, damn it – life, I mean . . .'

'Oh! I know. The same thing happens every day and night. But there didn't seem to me to be any need for a girl to die out in Switzerland because of it. Animals are wiser. Making love is a physical necessity to them, and they have young.'

'Yes – but, Jake . . .'

'That's the way I looked at it, Dick, sitting over a drink with this fellow. He said: "I'd like to wring the necks of all the men who've had her," and I couldn't help smiling to myself, for, thought I, there speaks the one man who hasn't. At the same time I didn't agree with him. It went further back than that. "They don't matter at all," I said, "the man to kill is the first – the rest don't count."

' "You know who he was?" he said. How should I? I shook my head. "Why," he said, "your pal out on that ranch, I forgot his name. Saw him the other day in town. That's the whole point of my telling you this story – I thought you knew who I was talking about?"

' "No," I said.

' "Oh! well, I suppose I've been rather indiscreet.' He looked very taken aback. I thought he was a fool, blabbing over two whisky and sodas.

' "Are you speaking the truth?" I asked.

' "Why – I can give you details," he said. I did not want them though. I got up and walked away. He thought I was crazy. My ideas had all gone smash in a second.

'Because I was young and it wasn't my business, I wrote to him. He came down the next day. I remember standing up, very proud and serious, and telling him the story I had heard. And I remember him throwing back his head and roaring with laughter.

' "Good Lord, Jake," he said, "if you expect me to feel responsible for every woman I've slept with . . ."

'I hated him then. I hated the way he didn't even bother to finish his sentence, and I hated his laugh. But most of all I hated him for having destroyed my idea of him. That's being young, Dick, and that's why I killed him.'

I nodded, for this much I understood, and it seemed to me that I was living far more in this story than was Jake, the teller of it, for he leant back with his head against his hands and the firelight on his face, the sound of his voice calm and detached, as though he were reading some impersonal tale from a book; while I leant forward, my chin in my hands, and I didn't see the fire or the trees of the forest around me, but only the figure of the old Jake standing with his hands clenched in the hot circus tent, with all his illusions crashing about his ears, and before him the laughing face of his friend, who, in a terrible subconscious fashion I could only identify as myself. I had never known this man whom Jake had killed, and yet I knew it was myself and that it was my story.

'When he had finished laughing,' said Jake, 'he came over to me and laid his hand on my shoulder. "You take life too seriously, Jake," he said. "You're like the leader of a lost cause. Smile, boy, smile. I want to see you fight." Then I went into the ring, and he watched me, applauding, looking so like his old self of the ranch that it seemed hard to believe the truth of everything that had happened.

'I looked down from my corner on the faces of the men gathered at the ring-side, and there he was, smiling at me, winking because of the fun of it all.

' "I'll pay my two bobs' worth and have a knock at you myself, Jake," he said.

' "Come on," I said. People were laughing all around; they knew we were friends, and it would be a rag.

' "Smash up your pal," somebody shouted, and outside the tent I could hear the thumping of the drum and the yell of the chap who worked the crowd to come inside.

' "Walk up – walk up – and see the greatest fight of your life. Champion Jake against an unknown Amatoor."

'I waited for him in my corner. We were about the same size. Often we had knocked each other about out on the ranch. He didn't look good stripped; I noticed he'd put on flesh, and he'd gone flabby. He wouldn't be quick on his feet, I thought.

' "This is going to be a hell of a rag," he called to me; "I'll lay you out on the floor inside ten minutes."

'The crowd gaped at us, grinning. The shabby little referee lifted his hand excitedly, and held out his watch, calling time. I worked round to the centre of the ring, while my opponent shuffled on his feet towards me.

'The first blow came from him, he feinted with his left and then swung under my guard and landed on my ribs with his right. I shook him off, and then followed him up closely with a short right and left on the mark. He tried a left hook to my jaw, but I dodged, and got in a stab from my right above his heart. This shook him a little, and he came at me with a rush. He was smiling, as he had often smiled when we had sparred together on the ranch, and I heard him say – "Come on – Jake." I knew then that I should kill him. Something inside me was bleeding because of him, and I was young, and I'd never been hurt before. I thought more of my own lost faith than of the girl, dying out in Switzerland. Then I remembered the leper colony, and the way he had talked on the ranch with his face uplifted like a priest who dies for his belief. I remembered his hands, and a sick animal in pain, watching him with wounded eyes, trusting him. I felt as though I possessed all the strength of the world at that moment. He rushed at me then, shaken by the blow above his heart as I have said, and his guard was careless, for he was swinging to attack. I saw his smile and the point of his jaw, and then I smiled too, and I struck him – just below his jaw – I saw his head fall back horribly, and his hands spreading – clutching at the air, and then he crashed down on to the floor to lie limp and helpless, with his neck broken, and the veins standing out strangely in his throat.

'He died there at my feet.

'Then I remember somebody shouting and people climbing up through the ropes on to the ring, and the thin hysterical voice of someone screaming in my ear, pulling at my shoulder with their hands . . .'

Jake broke off, and I saw his eyes staring at me over the light of the fire, and they were black and burning against the pallor of his face.

'Why – what's wrong, Dick?' he said.

When he spoke to me the picture of the ringside vanished, and the hot air was gone, and his eyes were no longer the eyes of the murderer bearing down upon me, his friend, but the grave gentle eyes of the Jake I knew, and there was not any hatred after all, and there was no death from which I could not escape, but only the firelight and the pale branches of the trees, and he and I talking together of something that had happened long ago.

'Nothing,' I said. 'It's all right – it doesn't matter any more.'

'Why,' he said, 'you look like a pale ghost, scared in the dim light. You're white and drawn, and your eyes are black like two hollows in your face.'

I shivered for no reason.

'You're drawing a picture of yourself,' I said. He shook his head at me. 'You don't have to be scared,' he said.

'I'm not scared,' I told him, 'I'm only glad that all this here is real, and that your story is over and done with. It can't happen again.'

'No, never again.'

'Being in prison hasn't made you hard, Jake. I can imagine what you were before, but you're bigger now in every way.'

'No – I only see straight.'

'I shan't ever be able to do that.'

'Yes, you will.'

'I don't see how.'

'After you've suffered a while.'

'I did, as a boy, in my own way.'

'That's different.'

'It would take me wrong, Jake. I'd crumple up over anything.'

'No, you wouldn't. At first, perhaps, not afterwards.'

'It would be all right if you were around.'

'You can't depend on that.'

'You said I could always depend on you,' I said.

'I meant, you mustn't give way to the idea of your own weakness,' he answered.

'I'm a rotter, aren't I?'

'I've told you – you're young.'

'Jake, I don't want ever to be old. I want always to get up in the morning and feel there's something grand lying just ahead of me, round the corner, over a hill. I want always to feel that if I stand still, only for a minute, I'm missing something a few yards away. I don't want ever to find myself thinking: "What's the use of going across that street?" That's the end of everything, Jake, when looking for things doesn't count any more. When you sit back happily in a chair, content with what you've got – that's being old.'

'There's no need to get that way. It's your own thoughts that keep you young, Dick. And age hasn't anything to do with it. It's a question of your state of mind.'

'I don't care about all that. Oh! Jake – if I could live tremendously, and then die.'

'What do you call "tremendously"?'

'I don't know – but there are a whole lot of things I want to know and to feel. They won't ever happen though. Fate'll be against me.'

'Don't talk like a fool. There isn't such a thing as Fate. Everything depends on yourself,' he said.

'Everything?'

'Yes.'

'I wish I could think like you, Jake.'

'It's easy enough.'

'You're strong, you'd win whatever came up against you. You've been in hell – in prison – and you weren't beaten. You'd never have thought of chucking yourself over a bridge even if there'd been the chance – would you?'

'No, I don't think so.'

'There's a difference in us,' I said.

'That'll never happen to you again,' he said.

'How can you tell?'

'Because that's just one little piece of weakness that's slipped away. You value your life now.'

'Why do I?'

'You told me you wanted to make something of it.'

'Yes.'

'Go on wanting, then.'

'Dreams won't get me far.'

'I'm not telling you to dream.'

'You won't leave me, Jake?'

'No.'

'Now we're getting damned serious, aren't we?'

'I wonder.'

'Don't laugh – you always laugh in the middle of something that means a lot to me.'

'Does it mean such a lot?'

'Hell – it does. You think I'm a child, Jake.'

'Yes.'

'And a fool.'

'No.'

'Why do you bother with me?'

'Because you're what you are.'

'I don't see.'

'No.'

He laughed again. I wanted to go on being serious, but it was hopeless if he was laughing at everything I said.

'I'm going to turn in,' I said. My sulking only amused him.

'Put that horse blanket over you or you'll be cold later on,' he said. The fire was dying and I kicked some of the ashes with my feet. High above us I could see the mountains where we had been, and the rough stone track leading away through the trees. I could imagine the cold air and the silence of the snow. Around us the trees rustled, shivering before morning, and in the distance, unseen, ran the mountain stream down into the valley.

The white light of the sky belonged to the snow, I thought, and the pale stars, and the sound of the rushing stream. This was our last night, and we would never come here again. Tomorrow we would be in the world once more.

I did not want ever to forget all that had happened.

I lay with my face in my hands, and turning sideways I could see Jake sitting motionless with his back to the tree, staring at the same mountains.

'What do you think about, when you look like that?' I said.

'Different things,' he said.

'What sort of things?'

'You sometimes.'

'What about me?'

'Wondering how you'll get on.'

'I'll be all right.'

'I think so.'

'It doesn't matter much, anyway.'

'It does to me,' he said.

'Why should you worry?'

'I don't know.'

'This has been fun, hasn't it, Jake?'

'Yes.'

'We won't change anything, getting away from here?'

'No.'

'I'll never like anything as I've liked this.'

'I wonder.'

'I just couldn't. I feel as happy as hell.'

'Do you?'

'Sure. It's the greatest thing that's ever happened to me.'

'I'm glad.'

'You're a queer chap, Jake.'

'Think so?'

'Yes. I don't want to be with anyone else.'

'That's fine.'

'You never say anything much, do you?'

'No.'

'Good night, Jake.'

'Good night,' he said.

Next day we had our first sight of the fjords. The road came away from the mountains down into the valley, and there before us we saw the stretch of blue water like a channel, with the high

62

mountains on either side standing as a chain of sentinels, their snow heads turned to the white sky.

It seemed strange to come across people once more. Even the grass huts on the hillsides looked civilized after the lonely mountains. Laardel was the name of the village. The men and women stared after us on our horses as though we were madmen.

There was not anywhere much in Laardel where we could stay. Some fellow came up to Jake and started to talk, pointing to his own house, where I gathered we might have a room for the night. I did not bother to listen. I left Jake to make any arrangements. I got down from my horse, and went to the edge of the blue water.

Up in the silent hills I had not imagined a fjord could be as beautiful as this. The air was hot, and the sun was shining. The water was the same colour as the sky.

The fjord seemed hemmed in by the mountains, from where I stood I could see no outlet, but I supposed that away ahead there would be a narrow channel. The fjord was as still as a lake without the suggestion of a ripple; I felt the touch of it would be colder than the white streams and the ice from the glaciers, and the depth of it unfathomable, greater than any ocean.

I could see the mountains reflected in the water.

There would be no shadows even when the sun was gone, and no sound. The light on the water would be the same, night and day. I could imagine there would be no birds here to sing. They would be afraid of the sound of their own voices.

It was beautiful, but it was too big for me and too remote. I knew I could never get close to it. I went back to Jake and the horses.

'I wish we hadn't come,' I said.

He laughed at me, looking down on me from his horse.

'Why, where do you want to be?' he said.

'I don't know – somewhere on a stretch of land where I can breathe. Or I'd like to be on the *Hedwig* with a gale of wind blowing, and some chap shouting from the deck. There's no air here, and no sound. It's all shut in.'

'We'll get away to-morrow,' said Jake. 'This fellow tells me the steamer touches here. She goes on to another belt of fjords. She'll take us to Balholm. Maybe you'll like them better!'

'I don't know,' I said; 'I wish we hadn't come.'

I asked Jake what we should do with the horses.

'We don't need them any more,' he said; 'we can leave them here. One of these fellows will buy them.'

'I don't like getting rid of them, Jake.'

'No, nor do I, but we can't take them on the water. We knew we had to leave them somewhere.'

'I don't know why we have to go on like this.'

'I thought you wanted to,' he said.

'Yes – I do really. Only every time you leave something – it's like leaving a bit of yourself.'

'I know.'

'It'll be a rest sleeping in a bed again, anyway.'

'Yes.'

'Funny – last night we were alone up in the mountains and now we're here, and people around.'

'You don't hate it, Dick?'

'No – but every minute, every second time is slipping away from us – and things don't last – and we don't know what's going to happen.'

'You like that generally, Dick.'

'Yes. Oh! hell, Jake, I never know how I'm going to feel over anything.'

'Come and get some food, boy,' he said. We went along the road to the house. I felt better after I had something inside me. I suppose this was the first real square meal we had had for days.

'This is grand,' I said to Jake. I got up and stretched myself and we stood outside the little house, and looked down the road to the still water. The sun would soon be gone behind the high rim of a mountain. The sky was orange, and long orange fingers crept across the snow.

Then a black crag hid the sun from sight, but still the light did not change. Everything stood out clearer than before. A man was rowing a boat over the water. He looked as though he were painted against the background. A child ran down from a hill and called to him. He called back, waving his hand. Then a woman came from a house with a blue handkerchief on her head, and she took the child up in her arms. Soon there did not seem to be anyone standing around. The sun was gone, and the sky was olive green. The mountains were reflected like black shadows in the water. There was no other sound but the white falls streaming down the rocks and crashing thousands of feet below. It never got any darker than this.

I smiled across at Jake.

The fjords were pretty good after all.

7

When we woke we saw the steamer had dropped anchor opposite Laardel jetty. She must have come in while we were sleeping. She was painted white, and looked rather fine against the blue water. She flew Norwegian colours.

Her decks were crowded with people. There were two little steam launches fussing round to take the passengers ashore.

'We'll never find room on that packet,' I said.

'Sure we will,' he answered; 'it's early in the year, she's not as full as you think.'

'I don't care about mixing with all that crowd,' I said.

'You don't have to talk to them,' said Jake.

I felt hot and self-conscious about meeting a whole bunch of men and women. Our clothes were all wrong, we looked like advertisements for a Western picture. Everybody would laugh at us. They were just a smart gang of tourists on that boat. We probably should not be allowed to go aboard.

'I say, we're going to look a couple of fools, Jake, honestly we are.'

'Who cares?' he said.

'I hate being stared at,' I told him.

'No one's going to stare at you.'

'Well, anyway, I don't like it.'

'We'll be all right.'

He paid for our night's lodging while I shambled about, my hands in my pockets, wondering why I did not mind being dependent on him for everything. We walked down the road to the jetty.

Some of the people from the steamer were just landing in one of the launches. I heard them talking excitedly over the chug-chug of the engine, and somebody was pretending to sing in a high falsetto voice, and a woman laughed, a silly high cackle of laughter.

I scowled, with my eyes on the ground. I would not even look at them, I hated them all. I wanted to be back in the mountains and never to hear the voices of people, nor to mingle in their idiotic lives.

Some man, a guide I suppose, marshalled them out of the launch on to the landing-stage, and then waited for them to gather round him in a little group. He held up his hand for silence. He called out, speaking first in Norwegian and then in English. 'We are here for one hour,' he said, 'we see many things. Those who wish to walk may take the road to the left. The rest, who wish to be explained the sights, please follow me.'

He set off, poor fool, at a rapid stride, his anxious face sweating beneath large horn-rimmed spectacles, and the crowd went after him, tripping over their feet, running like silly geese to buy picture postcards from a stall.

Jake was bending down to the launch, talking to one of the sailors. Then he straightened himself and winked at me.

'Come on,' he said, 'this chap will run us over in the launch. He thinks we'll get a cabin all right.'

In a few minutes we were chugging over the water to the steamer. She looked large as we drew alongside, passing under her stern.

Christiana was her name.

We went up the ladder, and on to the main deck.

Everything was white and scraped. The brass was polished. It was very different from the barque *Hedwig*. I did not want to be there at all. Jake disappeared in search of the purser. I waited by the gangway until he should return. I could hear feet scraping on the lounge deck overhead and somebody started a gramophone.

A girl hummed in time to the music, and I supposed it was her foot tapping on the deck.

Half-unconsciously I whistled the tune under my breath, wondering what sort of a face she had.

This tourist steamer was spoiling all the beauty and grandeur of the fjord. Still, it couldn't be helped.

'You haven't been long,' I said to Jake when he came back.

'It's all right,' he said, 'we can go as far as Balholm. We can keep to ourselves,' he went on; 'we needn't worry with this crowd.'

He made a face at the sound of the gramophone overhead.

'That's not so good, Dick.'

I shrugged my shoulders; I did not mind it so much as I thought I would.

We stood for an instant, looking up at the mountains where we had come from the day before. They seemed very far away to me. The record was changed on the gramophone, and I went on whistling the new tune.

'Those machines ought to be condemned,' said Jake, still looking at the mountains.

'Oh! I don't know,' I said.

I went up to have a look at the view from the top deck.

The *Christiana* left Laardel about midday for Gudvangen. Jake and I looked about for some quiet corner on the boat where we could get away from the crowd. The weather was marvellous, and it was impossible to sit down in our rather poky cabin with its two narrow berths, one above the other, so we had to become tourists like the rest of them, with a couple of deck-chairs under a large tarpaulin, while people near us exclaimed at the beauty of the view and ran about the deck clicking their wretched little kodaks. They were a mixed crowd. A few Scandinavians, one or two English, with the majority German and American. They looked all wrong against the background of mountains. I felt they did not have any right to be there at all, neither they nor the steamer with its spotless deck and its polished brass, and the chugging swish of the propeller through the deep water. Jake and I ought to have been in a boat by ourselves. I wondered if one could sail through these fjords. It would be glorious, but the water looked dark and treacherous and there was never any wind.

Jake had found an American paper. He was reading up baseball news. Funny, the way he fitted in to any sort of atmosphere. The crowd did not seem to worry him.

I could not settle to read or to sleep. I felt restless for no reason. I did not know what I wanted to do. There was a party of Americans lying on rugs opposite, placed against the skylight of the saloon below. They were the people who had the gramophone. It was rather amusing to watch them. They were a party of five, three men and two girls. I leant back in my chair and wondered on the relationship between them all. Who was married to whom, and so on. They none of them behaved as though they were married. One fellow looked dull. He wore spectacles and was reading a book. I thought he must be the brother of the girl with dark hair, because when she asked him to go and get her a rug he said he couldn't be bothered, and then one of the other fellows leapt up and found one for her instead. He seemed pleased to be able to do it, but she didn't smile at him much. The other boy kept playing the fool with a camera, and taking photographs of them in ridiculous positions. He was the comic of the party. Everyone laughed whenever he opened his mouth. The other girl was asleep, or pretending to be. She had red hair. She wore a white dress without any sleeves. She buried her face in the crook of her arm and smiled for no reason in her sleep.

She was pretty good. I looked at her most of the time. I wondered which of the men she worried over – surely not the chap in the spectacles. Some fellows knew how to get away with anything. She probably treated them all alike, though. She sat up after a while and combed her hair. It didn't need anything doing to it. Then she reached over with a lazy hand and started the gramophone. It was the same tune I had whistled in the morning. She shrugged her shoulders in time to the music, and the comic boy lit a cigarette for her and put it in her mouth. She hummed in a low key. Jake moaned faintly when the gramophone started and he got up from his chair.

'I'm going to see if they'll let me up on the bridge,' he said;

'I'd like to have a chat with one of those fellows. The second officer seemed all right. It'll be quiet there, and the mountains will be grand.'

'Yes,' I said.

'Are you coming, Dick?'

I yawned and stretched myself.

'No – I think I'll stay here,' I said.

'Right.' He disappeared along the deck. His getting up had attracted the attention of the American party. They all looked at him, and then back at me. I felt a fool sitting there by myself. I picked up Jake's paper and pretended to read it, but it was upside down. Somebody laughed. I was sure it was the girl with red hair. I kept my face glued to the newspaper, so that they should not see the colour of my face. After a while I lowered it, and found they were not looking at me at all. I fumbled for a cigarette to give me something to do. Then I found I hadn't got a match. I felt more of a fool than ever. The comic boy looked across and saw me with the unlit cigarette in my mouth.

'Here,' he said, 'd'you want a match?'

They all looked at me. This was terrible. They probably thought I had done it on purpose, so as to be able to talk to them.

'Thanks awfully,' I said, and got up, tripping over the chair.

'Did you come on board at Laardel?' said the red-haired girl.

'Yes,' I said, 'we'd ridden from Fagerness through the mountains.'

'Oh! boy!' The man in spectacles looked up from his book.

'That's a devil of a way on horseback, surely?'

'Yes, it is quite,' I said. 'It was worth it, though.'

'I suppose you came through the most fascinating country,' said the other girl, and the red one smiled and put on another record.

'Wasn't it just too romantic for words right up in those big hills?' she asked me.

It was a damn silly remark, but she was pretty enough to get away with it. I smiled too.

'I don't know about that,' I said.

'Oh, I'd love to have done it,' she went on; 'I'm just crazy over mountains and things.'

The chap with glasses began to ask boring questions about our average mileage a day, and how we had managed about food and sleep. I answered him anyhow, because I was trying to listen to what the red girl was saying to the boy with the camera.

'. . . you'll get me mad, Bill, clicking that li'l thing at me,' she said.

Then there was a pause for a few minutes, and I looked down at the red girl, who was swaying in time to the music.

'That's a good record,' I said.

'It sounds swell on a real band,' she said; 'it sends me cold all over and crazy to dance. Do you dance?'

'No – I'm not much good at anything like that,' I said.

'What about your friend?'

'No – I don't think he does either.'

'How far are you going?' asked the man in spectacles.

'I think we only go as far as Balholm,' I said.

'They say that Vadheim beyond is a great spot,' said Bill.

'Yes – you ought to come on to Vadheim,' said the girl with the red hair.

'What sort of a trip have you had so far?' I asked the dark girl. It did not look too good to be only bothering about the red one.

'Why, it's been divine,' she said, 'we can't get over these fjords. They're better than anything I've seen back at home. This is my first visit to Europe and we've done England and France and Germany all in two months. What do you think of that?'

'Marvellous,' I lied.

'Isn't it just marvellous? Of course Carrie has been over before.'

So she was called Carrie, my red girl. Bad name. I turned to her again.

'How do you enjoy it?' I asked her.

'Oh! I like Europe a lot,' she said, and she smiled in a careless way as though to suggest she had done a lot in Europe as well as liked it. She was grand. Pity her name was Carrie. I liked these people, they were fun. So easy to talk to. They did not make one feel a fool at all.

'Mixed crowd on this boat,' I said, and then remembered my own appearance, which didn't look up to much.

'They're just terrible,' said Carrie, 'I don't believe there's anyone here of any social standing at all.'

What a remark! I was glad Jake was not there. Never mind. A girl with a face like that could get away with murder.

'Besides, they're so bored and tame,' she went on; 'there's no one under fifty, I declare. I'd like to rouse them and put some pep into them. We might have some sort of a party then.'

'I wonder what Gudvangen will be like,' I said.

'They say it's no size at all,' said the dark girl's boy, 'there won't be any real fun till we get to Balholm. We'll start an excursion from there.'

'I tell you what would be really cute,' said Carrie, 'if we didn't have to join the rest of the crowd from the boat, but just went off in the wilds to explore. You and your friend ought to join us to swell our party.'

'That's an idea,' I said. I did not know what Jake would think of this. It sounded all right to me.

'I want to get somewhere and bathe,' said the dark girl.

'Gee – I wanner bathe too,' said the boy who bothered over her rug.

'If you two fellows join us we might get hold of some sort of conveyance,' said the spectacled man. He seemed to be the boss of the party. I guessed he was inviting us because there would be more money, and with added funds we'd be able to hire a car.

'It would be rather a rag,' I said.

'Wouldn't it be swell?' said Carrie.

The dressing-gong for dinner sounded then. I supposed they would all go below. Jake and I had not any kit with us.

'Won't you dine with us?' asked the dark girl.

'Oh! thanks very much, but we don't change,' I said, 'we'll be feeding in the other saloon. Maybe we'll see you afterwards on deck.'

'That's O.K. then,' she said.

She and the spectacled chap, her brother I supposed, were running the show.

They all got up and looked for their various coats and things. I pretended to help them with the gramophone and a rug, but I was not much use. The dark girl let her boy carry everything.

It was probably one of the thrills of his day. I did not know whether to go or to stay. It looked funny to go just because they were.

Carrie hung back a second after the others. She was powdering her nose. Bill, the chap with the camera, looked after her over his shoulder.

'Come on, baby,' he called.

She picked up her coat from the ground and threw it over her arm. She smiled, and it was fun to think nobody but me saw the smile.

'See you later,' she said.

She followed the rest of them below. I went off to find Jake. I met him coming down from the bridge.

'Wasn't it fine?' he said. 'Did you see well from where you were?'

'What?' I said.

'Why, the colour of the sky beyond that mountain just ahead.'

'Oh! sure,' I said. 'Listen, I've been talking to the party with the gramophone. They're terribly nice. They suggest that when we go ashore at Balholm we sort of hire a car all together and see everything. We can keep away from the rest of the tourist gang.'

'Oh!' he said.

'It wouldn't bore you, would it, Jake? What I mean is it's rather fun being with people, d'you know, just for a change? And they really are easy and amusing. Not stiff at all. There's a chap – the one with glasses who was reading – he seemed keen to know all about how we'd ridden down from Fagerness through the mountains. I think you'd like him. I believe the dark girl is his sister.'

'I didn't notice any of them,' said Jake.

'They said something about us dining with them, but I said we hadn't any clothes. We might see them up on deck later and talk it all over.'

'Yes,' said Jake.

'I mean, we don't have to if you're not keen.'

'No.'

'It would make a sort of a change though, don't you think? It's rather good for one to mix with people now and again. I don't want to drag you in for something that's going to bore you, though.'

'Oh! it'll be all right,' said Jake.

We had some food and afterwards we went on deck. The boat was just going to anchor, and Gudvangen was before us. The fjord here was very narrow, with the high forbidding mountains rising on either side. The water was black, and of an impossible depth. The white falls crashed down from the ledges of rock. The little village lay ahead. Everything seemed an enormous distance. It was too much.

I left Jake talking to the fellow with spectacles, and Carrie and I went into the bows of the ship and watched the men working at the anchor. I was able to explain the various reasons for things.

She looked up at me with big eyes – 'Isn't that just too amazing,' she said.

I told her about Jake and I working our passage to Oslo in the barque. She could not get over this. She made me go into every detail of the life, and all the while she leant with her arms on the side of the bridge, her thin dress fluttering in the cool air.

'My, you've done a lot,' she said.

'Here – you'll get cold,' I said after a while, and we wandered away to find the others, though I did not want to look for them at all.

'I wish we could dance,' she said.

'I can't dance,' I said.

'I guess I could make you learn.'

'You wouldn't try me for long,' I told her.

'How should I know?'

We laughed, and then the boy called Bill and the other one caught sight of us.

'Here they are,' they shouted. Jake was standing there too. He did not seem to be talking to anyone.

'Why, where have you been, Carrie?' asked the dark girl, and then they both laughed, and everybody looked at us. I knew I was turning red in the face for no reason. Why did they all have to make such a thing of us having been up in the bows of the steamer? It was damn silly.

'He's been telling me all about his romantic past,' said Carrie. That was all right for her. The line got a laugh of course. It made me look a fool, though. I wondered what Jake would think.

'Hullo, old boy,' I said unnaturally, 'why didn't you come along with us?' I had a feeling that he thought that I was thinking he was out of things.

'Hullo,' he said.

I smiled foolishly, humming a tune under my breath. The fellow in glasses came up.

'Do you boys play bridge?' he said.

'I do,' said Jake.

'That's splendid now, can't we make up a four? You and myself, and my sister and Matty?' Matty was the bloke who hung round with the dark girl.

'I didn't know you played, Jake?' I said.

'Didn't you?' he said.

I wondered if it was my manner that was forced or his.

Somehow I felt as though I didn't know him so well as I did. I hoped the bridge would not bore him. It would spoil the fun of my evening if I thought he was hating it.

'You'll play, won't you, Jake?' I said anxiously.

'Sure,' he said, 'I'd love to.'

That left out Carrie and myself. Also the boy with the camera, Bill. I wondered if he would hang around all the time. He did. We went below on the other deck and he came too. We took the gramophone and the case of records. She tried to teach me to dance. I could see the other boy danced well. She looked good against him. I'd have got on all right if he hadn't been there. He was funny too, he kept making her laugh. She was enjoying herself with the pair of us. I supposed this was what girls considered having a good time. I did not think it was great fun. It could have been so much better.

'Don't you play bridge?' I asked the boy.

'Why, he can't play any of these indoor sports,' said Carrie.

'Can't I, baby?' he said.

They both laughed. I supposed they had some bloody feeble joke. They probably knew each other very well, anyway.

There was a bar in the smoking-room. We went along and had drinks. She laughed at each of us in turn over the rim of her glass.

'Go and see if the others have finished their bridge, Bill,' she said.

I wondered whether we had to stay there until he came back. He'd probably only be gone a minute.

'Are you going ashore in the morning?' I asked her.

'Maybe I will,' she said.

'What sort of time?'

'Oh! any time.'

'I wonder if there's much to see,' I said.

'You'd better come along and find out.'

'Will you all be going ashore together?'

'I can't tell,' she said.

The wretched boy came back after that. 'They've all gone to bed,' he said, 'I can't find any of them.'

'I guess I'll go to bed if Mary's gone,' said Carrie. So that was that. Nothing much of an evening after all. We walked along with her to her cabin. 'You boys don't have to turn in just because of me,' she said; 'I'm not breaking up your party, am I?' She knew perfectly well she was. As if we were going to hang about talking when she was not there.

We fooled about outside her door. The boy did his comic stuff and pretended to go into the next cabin. I thought I'd seize my chance and say something.

'Listen,' I said, 'will you come ashore early tomorrow? I'll get a boat – we needn't wait for the others, unless you want to.'

She kept one shoulder through the crack of the door.

'I might,' she said.

'Do – say yes – will you?'

She smiled, with her tongue in her cheek. She wasn't going to give anything away.

'You never can tell,' she said. Then she shut the door. I felt tomorrow would be all right.

'Good night,' I said to the boy.

I went along to our cabin, which was at the other end of the ship. Jake was already in his berth. He had chosen the top one.

He was reading. I whistled, chucking off my things anyhow. There wasn't much room.

'Had a good time?' he said.

'Oh! not so bad,' I said.

He did not say anything after that. I funked asking him how he had liked the crowd. If he had enjoyed it he would have said so without my having to mention them. I wondered what he would do in the morning. I wished he could get some amusement somewhere. Still, he was always all right by himself. It would not matter leaving him. I climbed into my berth and lay with my hands under my head. It would be fun going ashore with the girl in the morning. Perhaps when we got to Balholm later in the day we would take a boat and bathe. It would be fun whatever one did, I thought. I supposed she let the comic chap sleep with her. They'd scarcely all go away in a party together unless they did. The other girl would cope with the boy called Matty. The spectacled fellow did not seem to come into it much.

Carrie seemed easy enough to know. I wondered if she held everyone in the same way when she danced. It had been pretty good. Her hair was good too. Everything was good.

'Jake,' I said, 'are you asleep?'

'No.'

'Well, listen – why do we have to get off at Balholm? Can't we go on to Vadheim?'

'I'll find out,' he said, 'if you're keen. What makes you want to go there?'

'Oh! nothing,' I said, 'but I feel we ought to see all these places now we're here.'

I did not sleep much that night. I felt restless and excited, for no reason. I wanted to go for a ten-mile walk or pull a boat about in the fjord. There was something in the air of this place that was not helpful to sleep. Pure and still. The white light, too. It was demoralizing the way it never got dark. I wanted to be doing things all the time, and I felt hemmed in by those high black mountains unable to get away. The sound of the crashing falls got on my nerves. I got up very early and went on deck. Gudvangen looked a tiny place, dead or asleep, across the still water. Nobody moved from the houses. It seemed impossible to believe that there were living people within miles. The grey mountains towered overhead, it was as if they were leaning towards the anchored ship ready to close in upon her. I leant over the side of the steamer and looked down on the dark water. There was never a ripple, never the slightest disturbance of the surface. And all the while the falls tumbled from the rocks like the hiss of rain.

There would be no change ever in this atmosphere. It was sinister, overpowering; it was like a troubled dream conjured by the evil thoughts of a past day.

There was no suggestion of ultimate hope, and no possibility of escape. It was a terrible place.

I sat up on the deck with my chin in my hands, looking in front of me thinking of nothing, my heart heavy, longing for some nameless thing that I could not explain even to myself. I did not want to feel depressed like this. I wanted to laugh, and not to care about a thought, and to be with people who did not matter, and to have some fun taking that girl ashore. I did not want to be in a lost mood, wretched and distressed. I wished Gudvangen was different, and the mountains wider apart, and the sun shining in a clear sky, and the blue water warm and shallow.

I went below and found Jake was awake, and sitting up in his berth. 'I woke up and wondered where you'd gone,' he said. 'I was just coming up to find you. I had a feeling something was wrong.'

'Jake,' I said, 'I feel like hell.'

He looked at me without saying anything for a moment. Then he spoke.

'Tell you what, how about taking a boat from Gudvangen and climbing somewhere to get close to those falls. You can stretch your legs a bit. It would be fine getting away again.'

When Jake suggested this, I was glad for a minute, and then I knew I did not want to go. I had it fixed in my mind about that girl and I was not going to change everything.

'I can't,' I said, 'I arranged something last night with one of those girls.'

'Oh! I see,' said Jake.

'We don't get much time ashore, anyway,' I went on, 'the boat goes off to Balholm at midday. It wouldn't be worth climbing anywhere.'

'No.'

I wondered whether he thought I was making excuses.

'Why don't you come too?' I suggested.

'I think I'll be lazy this morning,' he said, 'I'm not really keen.'

'Just as you like,' I said.

I whistled to be natural, but it seemed as though we were hiding our inner thoughts from one another. There was nothing to hide either. I had only told him perfectly frankly that I had arranged to take the girl ashore. That was all. I don't know why we had to act a part in front of one another. Life was a queer business. The steward sounded a gong for breakfast.

'I'm going up to the saloon,' I said.

'Right,' he said.

Now that people were about and the day had got started, my depression seemed to have gone.

The Americans waved their hands to me. I went over to their table and said good morning. The dark girl Mary had a pink blouse. She looked wrong, somehow. Her boy Matty sat beside her. The spectacled brother was making a large meal. He was very boring, wanting to arrange plans.

'I'll tell you what,' he was saying, 'if we all get together by ten o'clock and go ashore in the same boat, we could get carriages and then see all there is to see, coming back in time to join the steamer at twelve.'

Nobody was particularly enthusiastic. I thought it a rotten idea. Carrie was not there. Bill was in high spirits making an ass of himself chucking cherry-stones about the room. One of the stewards came and complained. The party thought this the greatest joke. Presently Carrie came in. She had a sort of green thing on without any sleeves. She looked grand. I felt all right then.

'Hullo, everybody,' she said, 'what are we all going to do? No – I don't want any breakfast – I can't eat a thing ever.'

'We're going ashore,' said Mary, 'are you coming?'

'I can't make up my mind,' said Carrie.

I kept silent. I was not going to commit myself either way.

'There's no hurry,' said Bill. Of course, wherever she went he would go too, I had that as a definite impression. I found it a bore. I could not cope with that sort of situation.

'Well, I'll be getting along,' I said. I left them all to it. I went and buried myself in the smoking-room. I'd sit there all the morning and read a paper. I did not care a damn what happened, or who went with whom or where. I wished I had gone with Jake. It was too late to go and hunt him up now. He was probably talking to one of the officers on the bridge. About half-past ten Carrie suddenly appeared in the smoking-room. She had a hat on. She was swinging a bag in her hands. 'I think you're mean,' she said.

'Why – what's the matter?' I asked.

'You told me last night you were going to take me ashore. What d'you think I am, to leave me waiting half an hour up on that old gangway?'

'I thought you didn't care to go,' I said, 'you didn't seem keen at breakfast just now.'

She laughed under her hat.

'Where d'you keep your brains, little boy? I've sent the rest off hours ago. Don't you know anything about women?'

I stared at her for a minute and then I smiled. That was all right then. I knew where I was now. 'I've learnt a whole lot in two minutes,' I said. Then we went on deck to see if there was a boat going ashore. We got one to ourselves. We sat back in the stern. She sat on my handkerchief so she didn't have to dirty her dress.

'I'll fall if you don't hold on to me,' she said. I put my arm round her and she leant against my shoulder. It was all right. I heard myself laughing rather too loudly.

'There's your friend,' she said. I looked up and saw Jake watching us from the bridge. He waved his hand. I waved back, feeling a fool. Why did he have to be there?

'He's quiet, isn't he?' said Carrie, 'he's ever so different to you.'

'Yes,' I said.

I did not want to think about Jake. I wanted the morning to be fun. Somehow I wished he had not been up on the bridge to see us go.

The excursion party had left when we got ashore. They had all taken little pony carriages up to some mountain. There weren't any we could have.

'We don't need to go, anyway,' said Carrie, 'there isn't a thing to see way up there but a view.'

'I was afraid you'd be disappointed,' I said.

'I don't care. Say, what sort of a place is this? Anyone would be buried alive living here.'

'You don't like it?' I asked.

'It sends shivers down my little spine. There aren't any of those cute shops like you see in some of these villages. I was hoping I'd see something I'd like in a fancy way. A bag, or a scarf made up in those fascinating colours you find everywhere. You'd have got it me, wouldn't you?'

'Of course I would.'

I was glad there were not any shops in Gudvangen. What sort of a fool would I have looked, turning out my pockets to search for money that wasn't there. I'd have to borrow some off Jake when we got to Balholm. We strolled along by the water's edge and we found a path that ran beside the fjord at the foot of the mountain. One of the white falls crashed down ahead of us. That was where Jake and I would have climbed had we started off early in the morning. It would be too far for the girl, of course. I helped her up to a ledge of rock; she sat there with her legs dangling over the side, and took her hat off and I guessed she thought she was looking good. She was, too. I swung myself up on the ledge beside her.

'You'll get bored at this, won't you?' I asked.

'Oh! I hardly ever get bored,' she said, 'I get a kick out of almost everything. Don't you?'

'Rather.'

'I bet you got kind of lonesome up in those mountains with that quiet friend of yours, didn't you?' she asked.

'No – I liked it.'

'It must have seemed slow at times. I just love beautiful things,

80

but I do like a bit of excitement thrown in. Why, I'm crazy over excitement. Didn't you ever think of all the fun back in London, and movies, and dancing, and all your girl friends crying for you?'

'I don't live in London,' I said.

'You don't? Why, I think London's just fascinating. I've had the time of my life in London. I knew a boy there who looked like you. He used to take me motoring every night in his automobile.'

'Who shall blame him?' I said. 'I'd hire a char-à-banc if you drove with me.'

'You're kidding.'

'No, I'm not.'

'Say, can't you get rid of that bum friend of yours and you come along and join us for the trip. We'd have lots of fun.'

'I can't – we hang around together, Jake and I.'

'I can see he's not your sort, he's not got an ounce of pep.'

'He's fine,' I said.

'I don't know what you call fine. I think you're mean if you don't come with us. I'm having a terrible time on this party, I don't mind saying. Mary and Matty looking at each other with great eyes. . . .'

'You've got two other fellows.'

'I know them too well. What's the fun of anything when you know a boy too well?'

'Sounds all right to me,' I said.

'Aren't you a little ray of sunshine? I guess we like the same sort of fun, don't we?'

'I'm going to find out,' I told her.

'Optimistic, aren't you?'

'Yes.'

'You make me laugh a lot.'

'Do I?'

'Say – we'll have a party tonight at Balholm, what d'you think?'

'I think it's an idea,' I said.

'We'll find a char-à-banc and then you can put over some of your rough stuff.'

'That suits me all right.'

'Listen to me, big boy; are you one of these hundred-per-cent tiger men who rush at a girl and get her flustered?'

'I don't know –'

'Well, aren't you going to show me?' she said.

We looked up and saw the little line of pony carriages coming down the mountain path above Gudvangen. She reached for her bag and dabbed at her nose with an inch of powder.

'Of course those jokers *would* show up just as you were getting me excited,' she said. 'Isn't it just like life with a big L? Come on, baby, we don't want to be left behind in this place.'

It was all right for her. She didn't seem to feel anything. She'd powder her nose and stay cool whatever happened. It wasn't so good for me. I felt terrible.

'We don't have to go,' I said, 'we're all right here. The boat doesn't start for hours yet.'

'Yes? And do you promise to sit here and keep your hands to yourself?'

'Don't be a swine,' I said.

'That's it – just like a man, calling me names. Is it my fault the pony carriages came down the hill at that moment?'

'Come and sit down again,' I said.

'No – not in these great open spaces. Not with your friend looking at us with field-glasses from the top deck.'

'He's not looking, damn his eyes.'

'I guess he is. He doesn't like me, he thinks I'm leading you astray.'

'Did he tell you so?' I asked.

'No – but I can see it in his big grey eyes. Get up.'

We scrambled down the hill and joined the launch as it was putting off to the steamer. The others had gone on in the first launch. I was glad we did not have to meet them.

'You're going to feed with us,' said Carrie.

I took her word for it. I did not care what happened. I did not want to eat, anyway. I made no attempt to look for Jake when we came on board. I thought I caught sight of his back in the smoking-room, but I didn't bother to find out. After all, he could look after himself. If he didn't care about my party nobody forced him to join it. I felt somehow awkward with them in front of him. I looked a fool before all of them. When he was not there I got along famously with the whole crowd. If he joined us I'd be uneasy at once. He made them look silly because he was so different. I liked him being different, but I'd rather he was different alone with me. Fooling with them was not the same as fooling with him. I could do both equally well and be on my own ground, but if he saw me talking and laughing with them I should be self-conscious at once, as though I were forcing things and being unnatural.

They treated me like one of themselves, but Jake would always stand alone. He would never change. It was all very difficult. I did not want to have to think about it.

We all went in to lunch. I asked the steward if he had seen Jake. He said he had had his food early and had finished some time ago. That was all right then, and I did not have to keep looking to the door in case he should come in. Perhaps he'd be up on the bridge all the afternoon. Carrie and I were going to take rugs and the gramophone on the top deck. We had found a place behind one of the launches swung on the davits. I sat next to her at lunch. I put my hand under the table and felt for her. She did not mind. Nobody else saw. I did not care much if they did. She talked all the time, and said a heap of idiotic things about the beauty of the mountains and how she loved nature, and she'd like to settle in Europe and never go back to America again. This started an argument from the rest of the crowd, and they were all against her. I don't know why she had to say all this. Just for the sake of talking, I suppose. It did not impress me much. When anyone talked about beauty in that way I knew they were doing it for effect. Perhaps she wanted me to think she was intelligent. She had only to open her mouth to show me she was not. Why didn't she just rely on her looks? Nobody expected her to be clever. I did not, anyway. The dark girl Mary had more sense, but then she had to have something to make you forget she wasn't pretty.

After lunch we went up on deck and lay there all the afternoon. Bill joined us for a while and then he drifted away. He had his camera with him, but he did not seem to make Carrie laugh as much as he had the afternoon before.

The others were reading on another part of the deck under the awning. There were not a great many people near us. Still no sign of Jake. Carrie lay on her side pretending to sleep again. I lay and looked at her, and put on different gramophone records when she asked me.

I don't know what sort of scenery we passed through, it all looked alike. Narrow channels of water between high cliffs. These were the fjords.

'If you've seen one you've seen the lot,' said Carrie, and I agreed with her. Yet I had not felt like that when I was up in the mountains with Jake. There the smallest patch of colour on the smooth untrodden snow had been a thing of wonder, and the winding paths through the trees, and the white streams and the falls had made us rein in our horses with the words unspoken on our lips. I supposed I had been in a different mood. Carrie shook her hair and I blew cigarette smoke into the air.

She sang, and then she prodded me in the arm – 'You're letting the machine run down; what are you thinking about?' she said.

We got to Balholm about seven in the evening. It was a much larger place than Gudvangen. There was quite a big village here, and an hotel. It was not shut in, either. The fjord stretched away from it like a lake. The mountains looked blue in the distance. The sun shone on the water and the light was wonderful. I liked Balholm. Matty came over and found us.

'We're all going ashore,' he said, 'we can get dinner at the hotel and then explore afterwards. The boat doesn't leave again until after midnight. Then we get to Vadheim in the morning. Sounds like a good party, Carrie.'

'Come on, chaps,' she said.

'I'd better go and hunt up Jake,' I said.

'Yes – bring him along too.'

I found Jake below in our cabin. He smiled and seemed pleased to see me. His smile hurt me somehow; I rushed into conversation before I had time to think of reproaching myself for anything.

'Hullo!' I said. 'Where have you hidden yourself all day? Listen, we're going ashore. You must come too. There's an hotel at Balholm where we can get dinner. It looks a good place, doesn't it? What about it?'

'I'll come,' he said.

'Splendid.' I washed my hands in the basin for no reason except that it gave me something to do.

'I say,' I began, suddenly remembering the morning, 'give me some cash, will you? It's hell being without anything.'

'Sure – take this.' He gave me his pocket-book.

'No – I shan't want all that.' I took a note and some change. Then we went up on deck. The party was waiting in the crowd by the gangway. They smiled when they saw Jake.

'So glad you're coming along too,' said Mary.

I looked at Jake as though to say: 'There, you see, they do like you – they do want you to be one of us.' It was nice of Mary to say that. I wanted it to be a good party with everyone getting on fine with everyone else. When we got ashore some of them went to arrange about the dinner in the hotel. Jake went, too. Carrie hung back. She wanted to see if there were anything she liked in the little shops.

'Oh! look at that jersey,' she said. 'My! I'm crazy over that. Isn't it just too cunning for words? I wonder if it's dear.'

'We'll go in and ask,' I said. When we got inside she became enthusiastic over a cap to match. There was a silver bangle too. I bought the lot. Thank God I had enough money.

'Are you going to give me all these?' she asked, with big eyes, and putting on a baby voice.

'Anything else?' I said.

'Oh! I've plenty here. I think you're swell,' she said.

She leant on my arm and we went along to the hotel to find the others. They were all sitting at a table. The room was rather crowded. Carrie went on with her baby stuff.

'Look what I've got,' she said. She held up the jumper and the cap, she had the bangle on her wrist.

'Enter the original gold-digger and her baby boy,' said Bill.

The others laughed. Jake didn't say anything and I didn't look at him. I hoped everyone would keep talking and there wouldn't be any silences.

Bill was in high spirits, which was a relief. He kept the laughter going. Matty was in good form, too. Mary's brother was not so good. I think he was worrying about the bill. There was a lot to eat and drink, and I suppose he was afraid the waiter would think it was his party. I wasn't going to worry. Jake was grand over things like that. The pair of them could settle up together.

The waiter brought cocktails that tasted of lemon, and afterwards I found there was too much gin in them. We all had about three each and then white wine that was corked. Carrie asked for champagne, but nobody took any notice. Everyone's faces seemed to be in a haze. I imagined they all felt the same as I did. It was a great party now it had got going.

'Can't we see about getting hold of cars and driving somewhere?' said Bill.

'No,' said Mary, 'let's stay here and dance.'

'Have you forgotten your bathing stunt?' asked Matty.

'No – it's not warm enough to bathe.'

'Let's go in cars as Bill said.'

'I'm crazy to drive anywhere,' said Carrie; 'what about you?'

'Oh! I'll do anything,' I said.

Mary turned to her brother. 'You're the boss of this crowd,' she said, 'you go and see what you can find in the shape of an automobile.'

People at other tables were looking in our direction. We were making a devil of a row.

'My! Look at that woman in the peach-coloured gown,' screamed Carrie. 'Doesn't she look as if she came out of the Ark?'

We all laughed. I fell over the table, I laughed so much. It wasn't a bit funny either.

'Let's start a chorus, boys,' said Matty. 'Come on – one – two – three – "I want somebody to Lo-o-ve . . ."'

We joined in on different keys. It was the most appalling sound. We swayed from side to side in time to the music.

'Hullo – where's your pal gone?' said Bill. I looked about for Jake. He had disappeared.

'Oh! hell, don't worry about him,' I said, 'let's carry on with the chorus.'

A waiter came over and asked us to stop. We yelled with laughter and told him to go away.

Mary's brother waved to us from the door.

'Come on,' he shouted, 'there are carriages outside. I couldn't get any cars.'

We all got up noisily from the table. Carrie seized hold of my hand.

'We don't want to go with them,' she whispered, 'let them start without us. You wait for me here while I go in the cloak-room.'

I felt queer. I leant against a pillar in the dining-room. I'd be all right once I was out in the air. Drinking was no good with me. I heard the others shouting for us outside the hotel, and there was a sound of carriages moving off, and Mary laughing. I wondered who had paid the bill. There was no sign of Jake anywhere. I did not see why I should bother about him. He had probably gone with the others, anyway. Carrie came out of the cloak-room.

'Have they gone?' she said.

'Yes,' I said. 'Come on.'

There was one donkey-cart left, and a driver.

'Here, we don't want you,' I said to him. Carrie laughed, and we climbed into the cart.

'Where shall we go?' I said.

'Up there, where that little path leads into the woods,' she said.

We could not see which way the others had gone. I took the reins and touched the donkey with the whip. He set off at quite a rattling pace. Carrie leaned against me and her hair blew about in the air. She did not bother about her cap. The sun had gone now, and the white light bathed everything. There seemed to be a mist over the water though, and against the mountains.

We could see the yellow lights of our anchored steamer. She looked as if she were painted on the water. The path went on. I did not see where I was going. I did not see anything. I heard my heart thumping and I could scarcely hold the reins, because my hands trembled. I didn't know how I was feeling. Then the path turned into the woods. It was darker here. The donkey went more slowly now; he was climbing a steep part of the track. There was grass all around us. The trees grew very thick, it was almost difficult to see.

'Gee – I'm scared,' said Carrie.

I put my arm round her and she felt for my hand, but I was holding the reins. I stopped the cart by the side of the track. The donkey began to nibble at the grass.

'Here,' whispered Carrie, 'I guess there'll be people around here.'

'No, there won't,' I said.

I didn't care if there were. I knew it did not matter, anyway. I went on kissing her. She took the reins out of my hand. There wasn't a sound of the others. They were miles away by now.

'Say, what sort of a party is this?' said Carrie suddenly.

I took hold of her hands – I knew she did not mind. I looked round at the close trees.

'Here – let's get out of the cart,' I said.

The steamer sounded her siren just before midnight. We had to take the donkey carriage back to the hotel and join the rest of the passenger crowd on the landing-stage.

I don't know what had happened to our party. Perhaps they had gone on board by an earlier boat. We crossed in the launch with a bunch of Germans. They were all a little drunk and very sentimental, their arms round each other's shoulders, singing folk songs. I was dead sober. I thought how contemptible we must all seem sitting huddled together in the chugging launch, passing rapidly over the still water to the steamer with her glaring lights. The siren kept shrieking into the air, and the sound of it drummed so hard into my ears that I covered them with my hands knowing as I did so that it would help me not at all, and that this hideous sound was one which would be remembered. It was like the hooter of a merry-go-round at a fair. There ought to be swing-boats, and booths, and litter of paper everywhere and empty beer-bottles, and hot bodies pressing against each other tired from the day, and drunken breath on one's face. All these would have been part of the screaming siren and the throaty voices of the Germans.

Instead of which there was the calm unruffled water, and the grave mountains bathing in a white light, and a glimpse of virgin snow in the hollow of those mountains.

We were all wrong, we ought not to have been there at all.

The German women were ugly, their dresses bursting across their large breasts, and grease at the corner of their noses. I felt they had been good-looking earlier in the evening, but now nothing remained to them but the lost trace of powder smudged on their faces which they would not even bother to wipe away. The German men leant against them and peered down their necks and fondled their hands, and it was incredible to think they were being attractive to one another.

They looked at us, and we looked at them, and I knew we were alike and our smiles were the same, and we had all gone ashore to do the same thing.

Carrie had put the jumper on over her dress. She had put it on in a hurry, and it hung wrong, bunching out at the back. She had powdered her face without a glass and it was like a white mask of powder against her red hair, blowing anyhow over her eyes, and the lipstick was too thick on her lower lip.

She looked like a clown at a circus. She kept trying to join in singing with the Germans, and bursting into little high shrieks of laughter that jarred for no reason that I could tell, and then seeing I was silent she pressed close against me and whispered 'Baby', and fumbled about with her hands.

I wanted to be alone. I did not care to speak to anyone or listen to anyone. I wanted to be somewhere where there would not be a sound or a whisper of people, where there would be nothing but the peace of the mountains and the tremor of a white stream, and lying on my back looking up at the sky, and the ashes of a dead wood fire at my feet, and the still forms of the two horses standing under the trees.

The launch drew alongside the steamer, and we went up the gangway to the lower deck. The whole crowd of us wandered along to the smoking-room, Carrie still laughing excitedly, and clinging on to my arm. We found the rest of her party on stools round the bar. They waved and shouted when they saw us. Bill had Mary's hat on his head, and he was pulling faces and speaking in a high squeaky voice, pretending to be a woman, while Mary's brother had balanced his spectacles on his nose and sat with his hands folded, giving an imitation of a curate. Everyone thought everyone else was being terribly funny. Matty stood with his arm round Mary's waist and his face against hers. I saw Mary smile at Carrie as though to ask a question, and Carrie smiled and nodded back. I could imagine she would go along to Mary's cabin later, and they would giggle together and tell each other everything.

Carrie climbed on to a bar stool, and sat with her arm round my neck, while she tried to blow paper straws at Bill on the stool opposite. He ducked away, still speaking in the high falsetto voice, and then he dragged his stool next to her and whispered something in her ear which I could not catch, and she shrugged her shoulders and laughed again, and when he winked at me and began to run his hand along her leg she did not put it away. She looked up at me with excited eyes, hoping I would mind, wondering what I should do. I did not care what any of them did. I moved from her stool and stood next to the bar and asked for a drink. When I had finished they were all singing the chorus of some song.

Carrie was trying to make Bill dance, but he could not stand up straight.

I went out of the smoking-room without bothering to say good night to any of them. I went straight down to my cabin. I sat on a locker beside the scuttle and looked out on to the water and the blue mountains beyond.

The last of the boats had been swung up into the davits, and I could hear the rattling sound of the rising anchor, and the throb of the engines, and a clanging of a bell. The ship did not take long to get under way, soon we were turning, and heading for the outlet of the fjord with Balholm left astern of us like a painted village in a picture-book. None of it seemed real. It was a sham place in a sham setting. The colour of the mountains and the water and the sky were false and exaggerated as a child would paint them.

Balholm was a frosted cardboard village at the foot of a blue cardboard mountain, and the sky was a daub of olive green, and the water was a chart of crinkled silver paper. That was my last impression of Balholm, until we turned into a narrow channel, and another ridge of mountains and another stretch of water hid it from my sight. I knew then that my hatred of it was only the reflection of my own mood, and that it existed definitely as a thing of beauty like a jewel set in the bosom of a white lake, sheltered by the folding arms of the dumb mountains, shrouded by the rustling forest trees, fanned by the cool air from the skies, part of the snow and the singing falls.

Balholm was true and so were the mountains and the fjords, but I was the sham one with no measure of reality and no quality of truth.

I was like a little dancing marionette, jigged on an unseen cord, smiling, grimacing, bowing my head to the ground, my hands pointing this way, my legs that way, pulled at in all directions by a number of cords.

I sat on the bench locker with my head in my hands.

I would not look at the mountains any more. I was tired. I wondered if sleep would come to me tonight, and whether it would carry away the heaviness of my heart, letting me wake in the morning without this feeling that possessed me now that nothing would ever be the same again.

Maybe if I laid quite still with my hands pressed hard against my eyes I would remember the mountain path where we had ridden three nights back, and the horses outlined against the sky. I would remember the silence and the stillness of the air, the smouldering embers of the forest fire, the smell of my cigarette.

Perhaps, if I slept soundly, with no dreams, I would forget the screaming call of a siren breaking suddenly upon the air, echoing shrilly over the water into a black cluster of trees, I would forget the ugliness of passion, the silly excited laughter of a girl, I would forget my own beating heart, my own trembling body, my own sense of inexpiable degradation.

I got up and started to throw off my things. Then the door opened and Jake came into the cabin. I did not want to look at him at first. I turned my back and fumbled with the tap of the basin. He did not say anything either. I whistled a tune under my breath. I wished he had been drunk, or laughing, or cursing, or in some way dragging himself down to my level.

'You all right?' he said.

I looked at him then, and saw he was standing before the open scuttle with a smile on his lips, and his eyes calm and happy as though he had come straight down from the silence of the mountains, with the beauty of the things he had seen still clinging to him, and the pale light still shining upon his face.

'Yes,' I said. 'What happened to you?'

He began taking off his coat, stretching himself, smiling inwardly as one who is happily weary, happily tired, with a long sleep before him and a dream. He looked down at me from a great distance, unchanged, the same as he had always been, and I standing against the basin biting my nails.

'I just went for a tramp,' he said.

I lay in my berth, and he in the one above me, and it seemed as though we were back in the fo'c'sle of the barque *Hedwig* again, with his deep breathing to assure me of his presence, and however lightly I might speak his name he would stir, and answer me at once.

So that night I woke, after sleeping for an hour or two, and I felt I should not sleep again, for it was the broad light of day, although it was hardly half-past three.

I put my arms over my eyes, cursing this light that scarcely changed, and I yearned for the comfort of darkness that had not covered me for so long.

'Jake,' I said.

'Hullo, Dick.'

'What time do we get to Vadheim?'

'Any time soon, I should think.'

'How long do they stay there?'

'I heard something about an all-day excursion. The ship won't get under way again till sundown.'

'Jake – I don't want to go on after Vadheim.'

'Right.'

'Can't we get away first thing in the morning before the excursion party start?'

'If you want to.'

'We'll slip off when everyone's at breakfast, and you can settle with the purser, and then we needn't worry over anything, Jake.'

'I'll fix that,' he said.

'Where can we get to?'

'Anywhere you like, Dick.'

92

I'd like to clear out of these fjords altogether. I guess I've had about enough.'

I heard the unfolding of paper, and I knew he was looking at his map.

'There's a good road from Vadheim,' he said. 'We'll be able to get a car there, I've found that out already. This road takes us to right away up to Sandene on another fjord. We'll wait there, or we'll go on to Olden, and then perhaps we can pick up a boat that'll take us south once more.'

'That sounds the sort of thing, Jake. It will be good to get into the open sea again. I'm sick of this still water, and the close air, and the light never changing – I don't know. D'you understand?'

'Yes,' he said.

We were silent for a few minutes. Then I spoke again.

'Jake – who paid the bill at the hotel?'

'I settled up with the fellow in glasses,' he said.

'Was it all right?'

'Yes.'

'I don't want to have to see them tomorrow, Jake.'

'No – I understand.'

'I don't want ever to have to see them again.'

'No.'

'You know what happened?'

'Yes – I know.'

'I don't want to have to think about it.'

'No. Are you sure it's all right?'

'How d'you mean?'

'About the girl?'

'What, Jake?'

'You don't have to worry over her.'

'No.'

'Certain, Dick?'

'Yes.'

'It didn't matter?'

'No.'

'Did she tell you?'

'I knew she'd come away with that fellow Bill, anyway.'

'I see.'

93

'I think they're both like that – the other girl, too.'

'Yes.'

'It was all rather bloody stupid, wasn't it?'

'Never mind,' he said.

'You didn't say much yesterday, Jake?'

'It wouldn't have been any use.'

'Why?' I asked.

'I knew it would happen,' he said.

'When could you tell?'

'Back in the mountains.'

'What d'you mean? Everything was different there.'

'Yes – that's why.'

'God – Jake. I loathe myself so terribly.'

'You'll get over that,' he said.

'I feel like hell about everything.'

'It won't last.'

'D'you know how I feel?'

'Yes.'

'It's pretty damn filthy, isn't it?'

'Not really. It doesn't have to be.'

'I suppose everyone goes through this the first time.'

'I don't know. Some don't give a curse. It doesn't mean much to them.'

'It never did to me when I used to think about it. I thought a whole lot, too.'

'Yes, I know.'

'What happens if one cares about anyone, Jake?'

'It's all right then; at least, it should be.'

'How is it any different?' I asked.

'You don't think about yourself then.'

'I don't understand, Jake.'

'No, you wouldn't at the moment.'

'I guess I'll make a hell of a mess out of life.'

'I don't want you to.'

'D'you remember our last night up in the mountains, before Laardel? God! you must have had a hell of a laugh over me.'

'Don't be a fool, Dick.'

'I talked that night, didn't I?'

'What does all that matter? I understand. You'll learn to see straight in time, and not lose yourself about nothing,' he said.

'That's another way of telling me I'm young, isn't it, Jake?'

'Perhaps.'

'Where's this place we're going to?'

'Sandene, or Olden. It doesn't matter which. We'll find a boat, or we'll get on another road and strike inland to the railway.'

'Yes – that's good,' I said.

We did not talk any more after this. I dozed a while, not thinking much, and presently I heard the engines cease throbbing, and then the rattle of the chain as we anchored.

We had come to Vadheim.

We got away early before anyone was about. Jake settled with the purser, and then arranged with one of the fellows to take us ashore in a launch. I did not have to worry over a thing, he did it all. None of the passengers seemed to be up. They were all below in the cabins. There was nobody about except the chaps scrubbing down the decks and going through the usual early morning routine.

I could see the place where I had sat with Carrie in the afternoon, where we had put the rugs and the gramophone. I seemed to have lived through a hell of a lot of time there, and it had only been a few hours at the outside. It was funny that I did not have any feelings about it at all. None of it might have happened for all I cared.

I thought of Carrie and her red hair, and smoking a cigarette, and laughing, and stretching out her hand to the gramophone. It just did not mean a thing. As I stood now, waiting by the gangway for Jake, I could not even remember how I had felt. It was as though my imagination had stopped working, and would not hold pictures any more. I felt like I used to back at home when I went up to the deserted schoolroom and sat down before a blank sheet of paper without an idea in my head. I would sit nibbling the end of my pen, wondering how it were possible to exist as I did without the slightest substance of a thought. That was how it was now, standing by the gangway, waiting for Jake. I could not even recapture the memory of my mood when Carrie and I had come aboard after midnight. It was only a few hours back. There had been disgust, I know, and hatred of myself, and wanting to be quite alone, not even with Jake – most especially not with Jake.

That was gone now. It was like having been drunk and then seeing the fine morning and realizing that one did not have to take life so seriously after all, because all that sort of thing had nothing to do with the business of the day.

As for Carrie and the rest of them, they were not real any more. Not in the way they had been. Carrie was any girl I had met in a crowd and forgotten.

I could not understand why I should feel so impersonal towards her. I could not understand why yesterday I had thought of nothing but her, and today I was leaving the boat, glad to be done, and she a girl with a laugh, and I in a car soon with Jake not even bothering to remember the laugh.

I could not understand why I was not still excited, and why I did not want her any more.

It was queer that yesterday my body had mattered so much and now it did not matter at all.

When I had come aboard at midnight I had not known whom I hated most, she or myself, but now if she were to come and speak to me I should not be aware of any antagonism, she would only be a stranger, somebody out of a crowd. I could not see why desire should turn into degradation, and from degradation into nothing. One ought to go on either with the desire or the degradation. One ought always to mind terribly about things.

And here I was, whistling by the gangway, waiting for Jake, looking forward to driving in a car along a road. It was all wrong, somehow. I was glad that I did not mind any more, but it did not seem right that it should be so. It was almost callous towards myself – the self who had stood here last night with his hands burning and his body trembling. He had gone for ever, that self, like the boy who had seen ecstasy in the mountains, and the boy who had sung on a ship, and the boy who had wished to cast himself from a bridge. They were all gone, these other selves, and they would never come back again. They had vanished, like little thoughts and little dreams, poor has-beens that had lived in me and I in them, now thrown away into the dust, not even lingering as shadows to keep me company.

So, standing there on the deck of the cruising steamer it was as though I left behind me something that had been part of myself, and I wondered how it was that I left it without a regret. For here was I, calm, easy, thinking of the days ahead, and there was he whom I should not see again, troubled, tortured, exquisitely sad, the boy who had loved a woman for the first time. I had left him behind, but I was not any wiser than before.

Jake came out then, and we went down the gangway, and into the waiting launch, and so across the stretch of fjord to Vadheim.

I glanced back at the anchored steamer, and it was not even a place where I had lived, but only an incident, already half forgotten.

We found there were cars at Vadheim, and Jake was able to arrange for one of these to take us on to Olden. It was not long before we were both seated at the back of the car, and winding away from Vadheim and the fjord into deep wooded country that seemed fine to me because it was different from what we had just left. I glanced at Jake beside me, and it was good to see his dark hair falling over his eyes, and the long scar on his cheek, and the inevitable cigarette between his lips.

It was good to think that the steamer and Balholm had not really changed anything between us after all.

With each kilometre we went I knew that the distance was becoming greater between us and Vadheim, and my spirits rose because of this, so that I was aware of a sense of freedom in getting away from it as though there was something in its nearness that might have bound me to it in spite of myself. It was not the steamer, nor the fjord alone, nor even the girl, but all these things combined into an atmosphere that might have closed in upon me had I lingered there even a few hours longer. For all that was a web of my own weaving, and I, a sorry spider, to have been caught in my own mesh. Now I was clear, having made my escape, and I wondered if it would cling to me through life, this quality of desertion, of running from the thing I had created, of escaping in a sense from my own self.

I had stood in the library before my father, he with my wretched verses in his hands and his eyes turned upon me in interrogation, and I had gone from him not in rebellion at the life he had forced me to lead, but in horror at the self who had brought such a scene to pass between father and son. When I would have thrown myself into the river it was because I hated the coward who lingered on the bridge. This was I, then, twisting and turning in my tangled web, seeking an outlet when I had carefully arranged that there should be none.

It seemed to me, though, that there was madness in too great a depth of introspection, and however much I delved into my own instincts I could not change what I should find there, so it were better to shrug my shoulders and shake my head, to whistle and to laugh, and keep up a pretence that I did not care what came to me until the very believing of this pretence made it at length reality.

Still, there was no need to go into this now, for here was the car taking us along a winding road, and the mountains stood up around us and the forested hills, and the white streams ran, too, to keep us company.

Soon there would be high ground, and another fjord more beautiful than the one we had left, and Jake to turn to at a change of mood, and, anyway, I was alive and young, so why should I worry – these being the only things that really mattered.

Then I heard Jake laugh, and I saw him looking at me with an expression in his eyes that meant he knew what I had been going over in my mind.

'So that's that, and everything all cut and dried, eh?' he said.

'Yes,' I said, 'I guess I know where I am now.'

'You're thinking that after all it's a grand day, and this country's pretty good, and it's been an experience, and, anyway, you're not such a bad fellow – and perhaps next time. . . .'

'Yes,' I said.

8

We went from Sandene to Olden, and at Olden Jake had to pay off the car because it was getting too expensive. I had got used to his paying for everything now; I did not have any shame about it. It was not as though he were merely someone I had met; he was definitely part of myself and part of my life.

Sometimes I wondered what I should be without him, for never before had there been anyone in my existence that had counted, and the years at home seemed just a stretch of time without any meaning at all.

It seemed incredible to me now that I had ever lived as I had done, a pitiful figure crouching in my father's shadow, and the personality that had held so great a power for me had drifted away into nothing, compared to the living breathing creature that was Jake.

I thought about him sometimes, this father of mine, and how strange it was that the supreme influence of twenty-one years should have fallen away thus without my conscious knowledge of its parting. I knew that if I returned home the big park gates would close upon me and I should no longer be aware of this suggestion of captivity, but would travel along the chestnut drive feeling that the trees were smaller than before, an avenue now and not the sentinels of a shadowed cloister, and the very sweep of the gravel finally bringing to my view the grey stone of the house would hold no shudder of oppression, for these things were of the past, belonging to a dead childhood, and I would look upon the most familiar scenes of spent misery and discontent with new eyes. They could not hold me now, neither the house, nor the garden, nor the shadow of my father seated at his desk by the open window of the library; they could not hold me any more than a dream holds a child who wakes in the morning, seeing the kind brave light of day, and knows the little horrors of his dark night were of his own imagining, not lasting nor true.

All I had done to rid me of my ghosts was to fall in with Jake as my strength and my conscience, my leader and my companion, and he had washed away every memory of my bitterness and repression with a look, and a smile, and a word here and there; so that my home was a sleeping house in a still garden, my father a dreaming poet with no shadow of scorn in his eyes. I did not hate them any more; they were just a pattern in a finished screen, now folded and put away for ever.

I had sailed in a ship and felt the wind in my face, I had wandered in strange cities, I had ridden over the mountains, I had slept under a white sky, I had loved a girl with my body: all these little moments had been lived through and forgotten, nothing in themselves, making other patterns on that screen.

Only Jake remained, and I asked no more than this, his continual presence at my side, and long days and nights ahead of us, and laughter and talk, and an open road, and the sun.

We stayed a couple of nights at Olden, because Jake wanted to see the Briksdal Glacier and I to explore the fjord in a boat, and then we pored over the map and saw a road that would take us on to Marak at the head of another fjord, or if we turned east at Griotli we should strike inland for over a hundred kilometres perhaps until we came to Otta on the railway from Trondhjem to Oslo.

It was some fifty kilometres from Olden to Griotli, and we were lucky in this, getting seats in an open tourist car bound for Marak, thus taking us a good way on our journey.

I was tired of the fjords now; I wanted to get away to something different.

We struck east then at Griotli, where we found neither cars nor horses, so there was nothing for it but to start walking, and we reckoned that if we did twenty miles a day we should make Otta and the railway in five days or thereabouts.

We made packs of whatever kit we had, and slung it over our backs, and set off from Griotli knowing that time did not matter to us at all, and we could sleep in the hills or in the shelter of a peasant's hut, and food could be found at odd places.

We could rest when we chose, and walk when we chose, and the weather was grand, and we were together and we did not care.

Once more it was like being in the mountains from Fagerness to Laardel, and the fjords, and the steamer, and the girl might not have happened for the little I thought of them. I don't believe I thought of anything much during that six days' tramp from Griotli to Otta. Nothing mattered but the sun shining and the wind from the hills blowing upon my face, the feel of the hard road beneath my feet – ever and again striking off from this road on to the rough tracks and the hill paths – then throwing off my pack and lying beneath the forest trees with my head in my hands, and the sound of a rushing stream in my ears.

Back in the mountains there had been something of peace and exultation, an understanding of beauty beyond my grasp and a dumb longing to stand a little higher than myself, but here there was the glory of tangible things, the touch of earth, the feeling of water running over my hands, the smell of trees clustered together – the very knowledge of being alive with this world to live in.

Back in the mountains Jake had been the leader, I sitting carelessly astride my horse letting him follow slowly in the footprints of the other, with my spirit shaken by what I saw and timid of the thoughts that came to me, wrapped in a silent ecstasy; while here I climbed a grass track calling to Jake over my shoulder, he ploughing away steadily behind me, or I found myself alone on the road ahead of him, obeying some instinct within me that made me run like a boy and swing by the branch of a tree, throw a stone in a stream, shouting a song into the air. Then I would stand on a ledge of high ground, and wave my hand to him, a dark figure in the road below; and while I waited I kicked my heels on the ground, watching a blue shadow pass across the distant hills; smoking a cigarette with my face lifted to the sun, and I whistled a tune without words and smiled for no reason.

Presently Jake would join me, and we would sit there together plucking at a stem of grass, sifting the sand with our hands, chucking stones down into the valley.

I did not want anything to be changed; it could have gone on like this for ever for all I cared.

'This is all right, isn't it, Jake?' I would say.

'Good enough for me,' he would answer.

'God! I'm happy. I don't see how anything could be better than this.'

Jake laughed, and I knew why he was laughing.

'You don't believe a word I say, ever, do you, Jake?'

'Always, Dick. You're an enthusiast though, that's why I smiled. I wondered what would happen if it came on to rain and the wind changed.'

'I shouldn't care. I like a stinging wind and the rain in my face. Those aren't the sort of things that change me.'

'What price London now, Dick?'

'Any price you like. I feel fit. I feel grand – I'm ready for anything. Think of standing in Piccadilly and looking up at the electric signs – just before dark when the light is grey and the theatres are opening – and the traffic all jammed up anyhow in a block, and the smell of dust and food from a restaurant, and a news-boy shouting in your ear. . . . It isn't so bad, Jake, what d'you think?'

'You've never lived there, you make everything as a picture in your mind. You go through life doing that, don't you?' he said.

'I can't help it. I've always done it, even when I've hated things. No, this suits me, Jake, out here on this road with the hills behind us, and a stream at our feet. I feel like living every minute and holding on to it. That's what I want to do – to hold on to it.'

'You can't do that. When you live too fiercely it slips away from you, and you find you've missed the whole thing.'

'Yes – I've felt that.'

'Keep calm if you can – don't get blown about the place. You'll enjoy everything so much more, especially afterwards.'

'How d'you mean, afterwards?' I asked.

'When all this, and all you do later, is behind you.'

'Don't be a ghoul, Jake. I don't have to think of that. Now is the time that matters. I don't want to sit back and call up dead dreams. Memories – what hell.'

'No, it's the best time,' he said.

'How do you know?'

'I know, that's all,' he answered.

'What, being old, with a bald head and a pain in my back?'

'No – that's got nothing to do with it.'

'I don't get you at all. You have a whole lot of theories that don't fit in with mine.'

'I'm sorry about that,' he smiled.

'Now you're laughing again. You're a terrible fellow, Jake.'

'I can't stop myself when I look at you, with your eyes glaring, and your hair standing up on end – just letting yourself burn to a cinder with your terrific ideas.'

102

'How d'you expect me to live?' I scowled.

'I'm only ragging, Dick. I don't ask you to be different.'

'You'd like me to have comfortable, steady principles, and never feel hot over anything, and just take life as it comes instead of rushing to meet it half-way.'

'No, Dick.'

'Sure, you would. You won't be easy till I'm laid up in a bath-chair, with a morning paper for an excitement. Well, you'll be disappointed, Jake, I shan't live for that to happen to me.'

'What makes you think so?'

'I have a sort of hunch that I'll have a terrific time and then die –'

'Oh! we all think that,' he said.

'No, that's me all right.'

'You're a boy, Dick, and all your thoughts are boy's thoughts. Believe me, you'll wake up one day and find yourself a successful stockbroker with a big belly, unable to go without your early cup of tea.'

'And not minding?'

'And most especially not minding,' he laughed.

'There can't be any mortal thing worse than that, can there, Jake?'

'Of course there can. You'd be happy enough with your cup of tea. Try starving, being without clothes in winter, lying on your back ill, never getting better.'

'But those are big things, Jake, when you can curse and suffer. It's mediocrity I hate. Little days and little nights. Moving around in a small circle, knowing you don't matter.'

'Rot, Dick. Think of the million mediocre people who go to make up a world. They eat and sleep and marry and have children, and do their job and die.'

'I don't want to be like that,' I said. 'I don't care a damn about the rest of the world.'

'You belong to it. You'll have to care.'

'Not yet, Jake, anyway. Let me go on drifting.'

'What have I got to do with it?'

'Everything. You know damn well you can make what you like out of me.'

'That isn't true,' he said slowly.

'It is true. If you said "Dick, you've got to write", I'd say "Yes", and I'd get a piece of paper and a pencil, and I wouldn't leave them until I'd written something worth writing, something you told me was good.'

'Then what would you do?'

'I'd send it to my father and say, "Well, what about it?" and if he didn't like it I'd laugh, for yours would be the only opinion worth a cent to me.'

'You're becoming a responsibility, Dick.'

'You shouldn't have stopped me from going over that bridge,' I said.

'I see. So whatever happens, I'm to take all the blame, am I?'

'Sure.'

'Even if you become a stockbroker?'

'More than ever if I become a stockbroker.'

Jake laughed and threw away his cigarette. 'Come on, Dick. We've got to push if we want to reach Otta in two days.'

'Why do we bother?'

'Must get somewhere.' He stood up and looked down at me with a smile.

'I like hanging around here doing nothing,' I said.

'I know you do. You're born lazy right through. If you stay much longer in this country you won't become anything, not even a bank clerk!'

'The South Sea Islands would suit me, Jake.'

'I guess they would. You'd sleep all day and drink all night, and write dud poetry, and make love to native girls under a palm tree.'

'Sounds good,' I murmured, chewing a stem of grass.

'That's because I've made a picture of it. In reality you'd loathe the flies, and you'd loathe the rain, and you'd sit bored stiff with a glass of bad whisky listening to the small-town gossip of a local trader,' he said.

'I'd be disappointed?'

'Of course you'd be disappointed. You always expect too much.'

'You're hard on me, Jake.'

'I'm not hard on you.'

'Oh! hell. So we've got to push on to Otta, have we?'

'Yes.'

'You think its bad to drift like this? So we've got to find a train to take us to a city and I have to set to and do a job of work. Is that it?'

'I think it's time you took a pull on yourself, Dick.'

'Do you want me to?'

'You can leave me out of it,' he frowned. 'I'm thinking of what's going to be good for you.'

'I want to know what you feel.'

'Go on wanting.'

'No, tell me, Jake.'

'Tell you what?'

'If you were alone, what would you do? Where would you go?'

'Oh – if I were alone . . .' He broke off abruptly.

'Yes.'

'God knows.'

'I believe you'd strike up to the North Cape and lose yourself looking for icebergs,' I said.

'Possibly.'

'Instead of which, I've made you responsible for me, and you have to stick around.'

'That's right.'

'I don't see what you get out of all this.'

'Don't you?'

'No, I'm damned if I do. Listen, Jake, have we really got to cope with the world?'

'I think you ought to.'

'Maybe you know best. Jake, would you get sick of it all if we stayed out here?'

'No.'

'Never?'

'No.'

'Why do you go back then?' I asked.

'Because of you.'

'I don't understand you.'

'Never mind.'

'We're just going through some bloody idea of yours that it's slack to stay here and enjoy ourselves?' I asked.

'Yes.'

'You don't believe in being happy when you can?'

'Oh! quit talking, Dick. You'd argue till the skies fell.'

'Anyway, you haven't answered my question yet.'

'What question?'

'Whether you want me to take a pull on myself, as you say.'

'For your own sake, yes.'

'And you?'

'I don't matter.'

'Why don't you tell me?'

'I have told you.'

It was hopeless to have any sort of argument with Jake. He put one off all the time. I called him every name under the sun, and he only laughed. I tried to hit him, and he laughed again. We got up and pulled on our packs once more. I walked at his side, kicking a stone in front of me.

'You're bored with me,' I said.

'It looks like it.'

'You're fed up, that's it.'

'Yes.'

'I'm no sort of a companion. I'm a dud, and a fool. You wish you were back in prison.'

'That's right.'

'Jake – can't you be serious for one minute?'

'No.'

It was useless to speak to him at all.

'When we get to Otta,' said Jake, 'we've got to decide something.'

'What's that?'

'Whether we go north or south.'

'Let's take a squint at the map,' I said. He stretched it out, and we saw the dark line of the railway crossing Otta and bearing north to Trondhjem on the coast, or south to Oslo and Stockholm, and Copenhagen.

'Let's toss for it now,' I said.

He found a coin in his pocket. 'This is very serious, you know,' smiled Jake, 'a whole lot depends on this.'

'Come on,' I said, 'call.'

'No, you call.'

'I'll say "Heads".'

'Right.'

He flicked the coin into the air and brought it down on his palm, covering the face of it with his hands.

'What is it?' I said.

We looked. It was heads.

'You've won,' said Jake.

I looked back again at the map. I saw Trondhjem on a big fjord to the north, some two hundred and forty kilometres perhaps, and then south there was Oslo, and Copenhagen where we had been. But there was another line south-east crossing the frontier into unknown territory, marked white on our Norwegian map. And because I thought it would be different, and because I guessed Jake would have chosen Trondhjem, and because I really did not care at all, I laid my finger on this line.

'We'll go to Stockholm,' I said.

So the whole of our future depended on this flick of the coin and the choice I had made.

'Another city?' said Jake.

'Well, that's what you wanted, isn't it?' I said.

'For you.' He put the map back in his pocket.

'What would you have chosen?' I asked.

'Trondhjem, I expect.'

'It's too late now. Stockholm is where I take a pull on myself.' We were silent a while.

'I should have chosen the North Cape,' he said suddenly.

'Why?'

'It's farther away, Dick.'

'You wanted to get somewhere, I thought?'

'Not really.'

'How do you mean?'

'Not when I think selfishly.'

'How do you think, then?'

'I think of keeping away from cities and people, Dick, and staying out in the hills by ourselves.'

'Why?'

'I don't want you to grow up,' he said. He laughed at me, but I did not understand. We went on walking along the road.

9

We came to Stockholm just as the sun was setting, with the dark spires standing out against the rose-coloured sky. The lights of this spilled itself into the blue water, spanned by many bridges, and the square buildings like palaces gave back the reflection from their windows, casting a beam of light on to the wide streets, into the fluttering leaves of an avenue of trees, and on to the grey outline of the ships at anchor.

There could never be a more beautiful city than this. It was cold, austere, belonging only to the water.

Perhaps there were shops and traffic, and people passing one another in the streets, but I did not notice them. All I did was to lean over one of the bridges and watch the shadowed lights dancing in the water, this river itself framed by the group of buildings carved against the sky. Jake leant over the bridge beside me, and we said that this was like the Venice of our dreams; but here there was no picture postcard loveliness, no sweeping gondolas and pink palazzos bathing in a soft indolent air.

Stockholm was a northern city, her beauty stark and frozen even in midsummer, the blue water like the pure caverns of a glacier; and across the bridge I could see a wide cobbled square, and a white palace, and a crimson tower like a splash of blood standing in definite clarity, with no mist of a spent day to wrap them in a vague obscurity.

When the sun was gone they would be clearer than before, the bridges silver arches spanning a glittering lake, the buildings frosted carvings, motionless under a white sky.

I thought there should be snow upon the ground, and the jingle of bells, and a fur-clad coachman whipping his horse, blowing upon his hands, but there was none of this, because the air was warm, and the stone of the bridge hot where the sun had been, and a flaxen-haired girl passed me, hatless, in a thin dress. Warmth should not have belonged to this white city and this white sky, yet it was part of it, part of the still atmosphere and the still water.

There would be no darkness here, no diminution of light, and all through the night a cool whisper of a wind in the shivering trees, with the sky breathless and expectant, as though waiting for the dawn. I should never be weary here, I should never be at peace, for this was a place where restlessness would not be controlled, where some secret called to me, elusive round a hidden corner, where I must walk, and search, and wonder at something with no name.

It seemed to me we crossed a hundred bridges, and we walked a hundred streets, we had food by a garden and an open window, we slept and we woke again. We left the carved buildings and went and lay under an avenue of trees, we travelled down the river and came upon a thousand islands all alike, jagged rocks set in a deep pool with the trees bowing their branches at the water's edge. We bathed from one of these islands, slipping into ice-cold water under a hot sun, we watched the pale light flicker in the leaves, we saw the white sails of little yachts dance and shake their shadows on the stretch of water.

We came back to Stockholm, cold and carved against the frosted sky; we went into a theatre where a girl sang, her eyes as blue as the water under the bridges; we came out again and stood in the cobbled square with a dance band playing from an hotel nearby, and there should have been darkness and stars, and the feeling of midnight, but there was nothing but the still river bathing in a white light. And I had not found my secret, nor did I know what it was that called to me.

Once more we wandered by the waterside where the ships were anchored, ugly coal-fouled tramps, incongruous in their jewelled setting, their sides rusted, their grey decks blackened by smoke, and so to a street café, with the tables huddled close together, the smell of tobacco and the ring of glasses, the voices and the breath of sailors. We sat down in a corner and watched their faces, the broad square faces of Scandinavians. They seemed all alike, their pale eyes, their dull close-cropped heads, and suddenly there would rise from a group a great blond fellow with a golden beard, or a boy – a Dane, I think – with blue eyes and a pink skin like a girl.

They were mostly Swedes here though, and Finns, bullet-headed and flat-faced, and it seemed wrong that the forests and the mountains, the snow and the rushing streams, should belong to them, who lived like animals cooped in the hot fo'c'sle of a dirty tramp steamer. We sat here, Jake and I watching the crowd, scarce talking to one another, and listened to their monotonous guttural voices, that neither rose nor fell, and the sudden chink of money, or a laugh, or the scraping back of a chair upon the floor.

Outside the air was still and pure, and the sky was white and the water the same colour as the sky, but here there was a smell of drink and tobacco, heat and sweat over dirt, and it was good, this atmosphere of not thinking nor caring, and of men without women.

Next to us there was a man who sat by himself, who turned his eyes upon us from time to time, but mostly he kept them fixed upon the door, as though he were waiting for someone.

Sometimes he looked at the clock on the far wall above the bar, and he tapped his fingers on the table before him, then lit one cigarette, and then another, and still he glanced at us and back from us to the door.

'What's wrong with that chap?' I said to Jake; 'have you noticed his hands and his eyes?'

'Yes,' said Jake, 'I've been keeping a watch on him for a quarter of an hour. He's scared stiff. Don't say anything, but keep your eye on that door.'

I did not answer, but I shifted in my chair so that I could now see the man and the room, and the swing doors of the café without turning my head. My eyes dropped again on to the table, I began to lose myself in a train of thought, picturing the island where we had bathed that afternoon, and the white sails of the little boats dancing against the sun, and how it was that Stockholm should hold this café and that island, the two merging, making an impossible pattern, when Jake spoke again, his low voice, just in my ear.

'Did you see that?' he said.

'What?'

'Did you see how one by one they disappeared, with a glance at the clock, and now there remains no one but this fellow at the next table, the barman and ourselves.' I looked up and saw that in five minutes, whilst I had been dreaming, the café had emptied, the room was silent and the smoke hung heavy in the air.

'They've only cleared,' I said, 'it's five to one. Maybe this place shuts at one.'

'No,' said Jake, 'these places don't shut.'

'Well – what is it then?'

'Wait – there's something wrong.'

I glanced at him and his head was thrown back, and he was smiling.

'While you've been dreaming I've been looking at things,' he said; 'the barman went round to all the tables and cleared the glasses away. On each table he left a slip of white paper. When the crowd saw that, they laughed, or shrugged their shoulders, or didn't say a word. But they all glanced at the clock, and they went – every one of 'em. Look here.'

I saw that on our table too there was a slip of blank paper, which the man must have left when he cleared our glasses.

'What does it mean?' I asked.

Jake laughed softly. 'It's the notice to quit,' he said.

I looked towards the bar, and I saw the man gazing at us curiously, his arms folded, and then next us the scared fellow watching us too, his fingers tapping upon the table.

'Do you want to go?' said Jake.

I listened to the silence, and the sound of my heart beating, and I knew I was excited, excited enough to be afraid.

'No,' I said, shaking my head, 'no, let's stay and see this through.'

There was no sound, nobody spoke, and we went on sitting at the table.

'Jake,' I said softly, 'try English on this fellow – ask him what's going to happen.'

Jake moved ever so slightly in his chair, his shoulder turned towards the man, yet keeping his eye on the door all the while.

'You seem in trouble about something,' he said; 'can we do anything to help?'

The man made no movement to show that he had heard. He did not turn at the sound of Jake's voice. We knew then that he could not understand, that he had not even realized we were speaking to him, he thought we were talking amongst ourselves.

The few words of Norwegian and Danish were no good to us, and Swedish was an unknown language. This fellow was a Swede.

Jake got up, and taking the slip of white paper between his fingers he went to the next table and held it before the man's eyes, pointing to the clock and to the door.

The man shook his head and shrugged his shoulders, and then he began to speak very rapidly in a low hurried voice, spreading out his hands on the table, passing his tongue over his lips, and it seemed to me that he was in mortal terror of something, and he was trying to explain.

He spoke in Swedish, and we did not understand.

'What is it, Jake?' I said.

He made no answer, but he crossed the café to the bar and held the slip of paper before the fellow who waited there. This man did not speak, he only stared at Jake, and then quietly, as though Jake was not there, he went on polishing the dirty glasses. Jake came back to the table once more and sat down beside me.

'Dick,' he said, 'I've an idea this place is a hang-out for settling a quarrel. See how close we are to the water? It would be easy enough after you've laid out a fellow – to drop him in there. It would look like a drunk – having tripped over his feet on the cobbled stones – and finding the river instead. The crowd who were here tonight knew the meaning of the slip of paper. They got it at a quarter to one – it's now two minutes to. Whatever's going to happen, Dick, is going to happen at one.'

According to his theory, then, we had only two minutes longer. And still the barman polished his glasses, and still the other fellow tapped his fingers on the table.

It was sinister, queer.

'Why did the crowd clear?' I asked.

'It wasn't their affair,' said Jake; 'they don't want a mix-up.

They'll all be dumb, they won't say anything. Besides, there's the police to reckon with.'

'Police?'

'Yes. This sort of thing's against the law, Dick. The bartender knows it, that's why he didn't take any notice of us. He's not sure who we are. He's not going to give the show away.'

'What do we do, Jake?'

'We sit here – and wait.'

I did not see how anything could happen at a water-side café in Stockholm. There was no darkness here, no little mean streets and squalor; this was a cold white city, infinitely remote, there could not be hatred and murder under this light. Scarcely two hours ago we had been in a theatre, listening to a girl singing Swedish words to an American song, and we had come out and stood upon a bridge, and had heard a dance band playing from an hotel.

I looked up and saw the hands of the clock pointed to one. Then the door of the café swung open, and four men came into the room, and walked, without looking to right or left of them, straight to the table next us, where the pale scared Swede was waiting.

I felt my heart beating, loudly it seemed, like the ticking of a clock, and the palms of my hands were wet. I fumbled for a packet of cigarettes. The four men sat down at the table, and in the midst of them our first fellow looked like a fly in a web, a poor frightened thing overshadowed by his companions. He sat huddled in his seat, limp and unprotesting; he would make no effort to stand for himself, but would be blown swiftly – suddenly, as a flickering flame of a candle.

The four men pressed closer to him, their faces near to his, and one of them began to speak in a quiet, monotonous voice, and it seemed as though his tones were persuasive, as though he were suggesting that our fellow must see reason, and he smiled ever and again, showing a row of gold teeth, and a slow, false smile.

The scared fellow shook his head, he uttered one or two words, broken they sounded, and unfinished, and then he gazed up at these men who surrounded him to watch for the expressions in their eyes, and his face was grey like one who expects sentence of death. For perhaps two minutes there was silence and no movement, and then with one accord they all turned in their seats and looked at us.

I felt the question in their eyes, the wonder and the doubt, the mute wave of antagonism borne towards us. We went on smoking our cigarettes and the man with the gold teeth and the false smile spoke to us, but it was in Swedish, and we did not understand. He called out to the bar-tender, hovering behind his glasses, and the fellow shook his head and shrugged his shoulders. Once more the man with the gold teeth spoke, an order this time, for it was sharp and decisive, and the bar-tender crossed the café and shot the bolt into the door, and then turned without a word and climbed the rickety staircase to the landing overhead. We heard him open the door of some room, and then he must have gone inside, for he closed it, and there was no sound from him again. We were alone now, with the four men and the little scared fellow huddled in his chair, he glancing towards us like an animal in pain, showing the whites of his eyes.

The man with gold teeth spoke to Jake, no longer smiling, pointing to the bolted door, and Jake shook his head.

They all rose slowly from the table, forming themselves in a group, one of them laying his hand on the shoulder of the frightened Swede.

I looked at Jake, and he looked at me, and I saw him smile and straighten himself in his chair. And it seemed to me that the walls of the café dropped away and the grey light was changed, and we were standing in a circus tent with the hot sun streaming through a slit in the tent. There was a ring, and a crowd of men pushing their way up to the ropes, shouting and laughing, and Jake stood stripped with his arms folded, and this same smile upon his lips.

The air was hot, and there was a smell of sawdust, and trampled grass, worn leather gloves, and the warm hungry flesh of animals in a close cage.

A bell rang, and Jake moved across the ring towards me . . .

But in that flash we were back in the café again, and Jake was at my side, and the four men stood around their table staring at us.

Then I knew that there was going to be a fight, and I was glad, and I was not afraid.

The four men spread a little distance from one another, and came closer, and hemmed us in.

Suddenly the one with gold teeth pressed forward, but Jake was waiting for him, and I heard the crack of his naked fist on the man's jaw, and his head swing back. Then there was a shout, and a cry of pain and a table fell over, and I saw one of the men coming towards me, and I hit him, but he caught me somewhere above my eye and I went crashing down on to the floor, dragging a leg of a chair with my hands. I felt the blood run down into my mouth, and the pain of the blow throbbed like the crack of a whip and I remember thinking to myself: 'I must not give in – I must not give in,' so I rose unsteadily from the ground, where I had fallen, the hatred strong in my soul for the man who had hit me, and I saw him reaching for a chair to swing above his head, but I ducked and threw myself against him, my head in his stomach, and we went down again – this time he was beneath me, his fingers fumbling for my throat. I hit him again and again, smashing into his face, and I heard him whimper, and he struggled under me.

I lifted my head and saw two fellows trying to get Jake, but he shook himself clear of them, and knocked one backwards across a table, and he called out to me: 'You all right, Dick?' and he was still smiling, and his hair was falling over his face.

The chap with the gold teeth was crouching with his back to me, and swiftly his hand went to his pocket, and there was a flash of steel and 'Look out, Jake,' I cried, and Jake leapt aside, his arm over his face, while the knife whistled through the air and quivered against the wall behind him, two inches above his head.

I rose to my feet and swung into this man who had thrown the knife and missed, and he was taken unawares, and dropped like a stone, both of my fists smashing into his two eyes. And it was good to know that he was hurt, it was good to feel his mouth soft and bleeding under my hands, and I heard myself laughing, with the breath shaken from me in sobs, while a pain hammered under my ribs, and this is all right, I thought, this is all right.

Someone came up at me, and I did not care, I hit him and he went down, and then he came again, and this time I fell, but not before Jake had seen, and in a stroke he had sent my fellow crashing against the window, and there was a splintering crack of breaking glass. Now the lamps had shuddered in their brackets, and two were smashed by a chair thrown into the air, so that we moved about in the dim white light as shadowy figures, scarcely discernible, and I, struggling against the bar with some fellow, his hot breath on my face, saw someone run like a little beetle to the door, and struggle with the heavy bolt. I heard Jake's warning shout, for once more there was a whistle in the air, and the little beetle was none other than the frightened Swede, whose life we would have saved, but he threw out his hands as though to grapple with an unseen danger, and I heard his last scream of terror, his choke and his cry, and he went down on to the floor with a knife in his back.

I broke away from my man; I must have winded him somehow, for he fell loosely with a grunt of pain, and I ran to the door and stood above the wounded Swede, and tried to pull the knife out from between his shoulder-blades, but it would not come, and the blood splashed over me, and anyway he was dead. Near me men were fighting, I heard the scuffle of their feet and I saw Jake's face, white against a beam of light from the window, and his smile as he struck the jaw of a fellow who rose up towards him, and then I opened the heavy door and the white light streamed into the café, breaking the shadows into clarity. One of my eyes now was closed, the blood from it dry on my cheek, and my body might have been beaten all over; but none of this mattered and I was happy in a silly drunken fashion, not even sick at the poor dead Swede at my feet.

It was my voice that shouted in a high unnatural key: 'Come on, Jake, come on,' and they were my hands that fastened themselves round the throat of a man, and my feet that kicked something lying on the ground. For this was flesh against my flesh, and teeth that broke with my fist and the warm blood of a man I hated, and his cry of pain – crying because of me.

116

'Hullo, Jake,' I shouted, 'hullo,' and then I laughed for no reason, except that my pain was as great as the pain I had caused, and this was glory, I thought, and this was hell, and here was a man's fingers at my throat, and here was a great limp body under me, and 'Fight, you unholy bastard, fight,' I said.

Then from away down the street there was the shrill summons of a whistle, answered by another, and the call of voices, and the patter of footsteps running swiftly, and I heard Jake's voice near me, and the touch of his hand on my arm.

'Come, Dick,' he said, 'we'll have to run for it,' and I shook a man's grasp from my collar and followed Jake out in the street, where the white light shone as clear as dawn, and the water glittered.

A whistle sounded close now, round the corner of the café, and the rush of feet was near.

'Run, Dick,' said Jake, 'run for your life.' I tore after him along the wide cobbled street, my heart bursting in my breast, my limbs aching, and I could hear the sound of the chase behind us, and a shout, and another blast of a whistle.

My breath came harshly, and the stones were sharp under my feet, and Jake was like a fleet shadow ahead of me, glancing back at me over his shoulder as he ran.

'Come on, Dick,' he said, and I felt the laughter shake me in my exhaustion, a great wave of laughter that could not be controlled, yet I must go on running, running because of the hurrying footsteps behind me, and the distant shout.

There was a bridge which we must cross, and a narrow street, and the corner of a dark building, and so on into a square, and another street and once more by the side of the water where ships were anchored. Here I paused, for I could go no longer, and Jake waited for me, and we listened, breathless, for the thin echo of those following footsteps, but there was no sound of them now, nor of the shouting, nor the whistle.

There were ships all round us, quiet against the quays, ghostly in this pale light of morning, and we flung ourselves down in a black corner where there were barrels huddled together, and here we lay, panting, laughing, with the tears falling from my closed eye, mixing in the dried blood of my cheek.

Jake's upper lip was cut right open, and there was a swelling on his forehead as large as an egg, and as I looked at him I realized my own pain, my throbbing eye, my sore weary body, and I began to laugh, and I could not stop laughing, the sound tearing at my chest, while images floated into my mind, turning me sick and giddy, yet my laughter was uncontrolled.

'Did you see?' I said. 'Did you see that fellow with the knife in his back?' And I rolled over on my side, shaken and sobbing with this laughter that came from me, the tears of blood rolling into my mouth.

'Stop it, Dick, stop it,' said Jake, but he was laughing too, and I wondered who was mad, he or I, and whether we had really seen what we had seen, and done what we had done. Then, like a cold shudder and the sudden plunge of a warm body into water, we stopped laughing and we sat up and looked at one another, calm, sober, two solemn owls under a still sky, and I only conscious now of my pain and my weariness, and a dumb longing to sleep.

'We'll have to get away,' said Jake; 'we can't stay around here with those fellows on our track.'

'I don't care,' I said; 'we've finished them, they haven't any fight left.'

'I'm not thinking of them,' he said, 'I'm thinking of the police. It was their whistles that we heard, and their footsteps.'

'Maybe we could explain,' I said.

'No, Dick, there's the dead Swede with the knife in his back; we'd be as much in it as that bunch of chaps who did it. Who'd listen to us, anyway? We've got to quit.'

'All right,' I said.

We got up and began to wander once more along the quay. We came to the end of a jetty where a vessel was moored, a small tramp steamer of about two thousand tons, and there was no silence here, for she was coaling, and the lights of the jetty shone upon her, and we could hear the groan of the crane and the thunder of coal as it poured down the shaft into the hold.

In a glance we could tell she was a rough ship, no paint on her, her sides rusted, her decks unscrubbed, and a man on the bridge

118

lounged over the rail, keeping no order, cursing at the men, chaffing, familiar, their faces black with the coal.

We watched them for a while, and then Jake looked at me, and I looked at him, and I shrugged my shoulders, and 'This is our ship,' he said.

He left me and walked across a plank to the deck, and I leant against a post on the quay, not bothering to look after him, biting my nails, looking down into the grey water. The crane creaked and groaned, and the coal rumbled down the shaft, while the men moved about the deck, and out of the corner of my one eye I could see Jake calling up to the fellow on the bridge, who leant over, grinning, his hand to his ear.

I felt myself slipping away into a dream, a dream of a far mountain and a rushing stream, a vision of slender trees, and a snow surface, and a white fall crashing into a narrow fjord, but then these would not stay with me when the coal thundered into the hold, and a crane rattled, and Jake himself touched my arm, saying in my ear: 'Come on, her name is *Romanie*, she's French, bound for Nantes.' So I stumbled after him along the plank, not caring where I went, and he said to me: 'They've finished loading now, and she'll be away in an hour's time.'

I blinked up at the lights, and knocked against a rope with my feet, and somebody laughed, and somebody called out to me in French.

And soon we were working with the others on the deck, finding our way about, hungry and tired, and I knew that this man who moved his limbs and cursed was not myself, for I lay asleep somewhere, curled in a dark corner. Now I had a crust of bread in my hands, and was peering into a black fo'c'sle, and now there was a movement of a ship under way, and the thrashing of her propeller in the water.

And now I was looking up into Jake's face, he black and filthy with the coal, the swelling distorted on his forehead, and the black of my face was caked with the blood from my eye. It seemed to me I had lived a hundred years in a night, and somehow a strength had come to me I had not yet possessed, so I laughed up at Jake with his cut lip and his swollen temple, and I knew this was what I had wanted, this thrill of danger, this taste of blood, so that it was good to be young, and good to be alive.

Jake laughed too, and he asked me how I was, and 'Hell,' I said, 'you know I'm all right,' and we stood there together and watched Stockholm disappear, clear-cut like a jewel, aloof, mysterious, bathing in a white light.

10

The *Romanie* was a black ship run by a crew of devils, and Jake and I were devils too, living in a hell, filthy and unwashed, hungry and tired, blaspheming to a heedless sky.

She was one of those miserable leaking little packets, too narrow for her length and shallow for'ard, who toss about the North Sea and the Baltic looking for freights, always dirty, always wet, rolling in a ground swell as though she were on her beam ends, and when she was loaded lying deep in the water like a sodden bucket, never lifting to the sea, sullen and slow.

She belonged to some obscure company with a French name, and by the look and feel of her she ought to have been condemned, plunging and groaning as she did in the slightest sea, the inches of water in her hold pumped out once, and sometimes twice a day, while her skipper was a Belgian who did not know his job.

This was my impression from the start, and so I think was Jake's, for the fellow seemed to have no idea of time or discipline, treating the men as equals, lounging over the rail on his bridge, and going down the river from Stockholm he remained on this bridge, with a pair of glasses glued to his eyes, searching the thousand islands for bathing girls, while the black smoke from our stinking funnel swept into the pure air, and we must have looked like a clanking tin kettle hissing our way through the still blue water.

Once away from the river, though, and out in the Baltic, we met a high-running sea, and a strong wind blowing from the sou'-west, rain striking down from the low swift-scurrying clouds, and we were scarcely clear of the land when we realized what sort of a vessel we were in and what we might expect her behaviour to be.

The skipper, as I have said, was easy-going, good-natured and unreliable, and as if to make up for this he had for a mate a fellow who never kept still for a single moment, a concentrated bundle of nerves and fuss, who screamed and worried at the men, grumbling at our work, finding everything wrong and driving us all to the verge of mutiny.

They were a tough little crowd in the fo'c'sle of the *Romanie*. Besides Jake and I there were five Belgians, counting the cook, and a couple of firemen, both Dutch. We had no business to be there, of course, they were full without us, but the skipper accepted our services in return for our passage, and here we were, for better, for worse, tossed about on the Baltic in a dirty little tramp steamer, all because of the flick of a coin on the road to Otta. We were covering now much of the same distance as we had already done, on that first voyage from Helsingfors to Copenhagen in the barque *Hedwig*, but then the wind had been fair and the ship a thing of beauty for all her discomfort, and the Scandinavian boys were grand fellows, but there was not much romance in the dirty leaking *Romanie*, in this atmosphere of rust, and rain and coal, nor did I care about eating and sleeping beside these garlic-stinking bastards, who used any part of the fo'c'sle for any purpose. I hated them and I hated the ship, the only comfort was that Jake was there, and we could curse and blaspheme together. I don't think Jake lost his temper much; he seemed impervious to the coal, the dirt and the stink in the fo'c'sle.

We talked of going south after we reached Nantes. We imagined the sun in Africa, the hot sky, and the dust in the streets. There would be little restaurants with orange blinds reaching down from the long windows, and tables huddled together, and a fat smiling waiter with black hair and a greasy face, flicking at the flies with a cloth. There would be white houses with the shutters closed, and purple flowers creeping against the walls, and lying in the cool shadow of a eucalyptus tree somebody would sleep, dusty and brown, his head in his hands. The sea would sparkle there, like a sweltering sheet of paper, and the grass and the trees be burnt yellow from the sun. I could see the streets, the patches of vivid colour, a woman in a blue apron shaking a bright rug from a high balcony, then leaning over this, lazy, yawning, listening to a banjo played in a restaurant below. The smell of coffee, white dust, tobacco and burnt bread, flowers with a fragrance of wine, and the crimson fruit, soft and over-ripe. A girl looking over her bare shoulder, with a flash of a smile, gold ear-rings showing from thick black hair brushed away from her face, long brown arms, a cigarette between her lips. Night like a great dark blanket, voices murmuring at a street corner, the air warm with tired flowers, and a hum from the sea.

When Jake told me about Africa we were standing outside the galley of the *Romanie*, pitching and tossing in the trough of a great sea, the water running along the deck and from the galley the smell of oil and grease, and brown garlic soup, and soot coming from the cheap coal.

Somebody had drawn pornographic figures on the bulkhead above the galley; they stood out strongly in white chalk, the pathetic creations of a stupid mind, very crude and obvious, as a child might have drawn. The men added bits from time to time, changing the attitudes, scratching words beside the figures, and then roaring with laughter, like little schoolboys, finding a strange stimulation, flushed, and proud of themselves.

I wondered if I had seemed thus to my father when I laid my verses on his desk before him, and if he could have thought less of me than I did of myself. It was all incredible to me that these things had once happened.

Meanwhile we sweated and toiled on the ship, we rose and fell in the grey sea. There was every kind of hell on board the *Romanie*.

'When we get out of this,' I said to Jake, 'we'll live in luxury, deck-chairs under palm trees, and a waiter in a white coat bringing drinks when we raise a finger. We'll sleep all day, and reach out a tired hand for a great ripe passion fruit, while a dark girl stands behind the chair waving us with a paper fan.'

Jake did not say anything; he looked up at the sky and the wall of grey mist ahead of us, he watched the stern of the *Romanie* lift sluggishly to the high sea. 'Dick,' he said later, 'do you notice how she wallows in it like something tired of the struggle? She hasn't got any kick left; she wants to lay down her head and die.'

I wondered if Jake was joking at first, but when I saw his face I knew he was serious. He would not be an alarmist without reason; I trusted him about these things. When he said this I felt a little cold premonition of fear, and it was as though a voice whispered within me: 'I shall remember this.'

In any other danger there would be a thrill for me, but not in the *Romanie*, not out here suddenly in that wall of fog, drifting helplessly . . .

'Oh!' I said, 'we're all right now and making down the Channel. We can't get lost with the traffic around.'

'We've got a lonely stretch ahead of us, Dick,' said Jake, 'and we've got a couple of fools on the bridge looking after things. You don't know the coast of Brittany, do you?'

I did not want to have to listen carefully to his words. I said to myself it did not matter; I had seen a fellow killed in Stockholm, anyway – this was nothing to me.

'D'you think we'll be for it, later?' I asked.

I spoke carelessly, shutting from my mind a vision of sudden panic.

'I don't know,' said Jake, and he looked at me strangely, as though he, too, held vistas of unspeakable things, but having greater courage than I he looked into them closely, not putting them away from him. It was easy to laugh, though, all the same, standing as we did by the galley in security.

'Africa, Jake,' I said, 'we're going to live there better than we've ever lived, the first night we get ashore.'

'Yes,' he said.

I was sure everything would be all right. There was a kind of conceit in me that gave me a firm belief in safety. In spite of this, I hated the *Romanie*. We went on down the Channel, the mist never lifting, the seas running high, and the wind blowing continuously from the south-west.

Even though it would have meant beating against it, I would rather have been in the barque *Hedwig*. Had the wind and the seas increased we could have hove to, lying as snug as a house.

Not the *Romanie*, though, groaning and shuddering in each successive sea, settling in the trough of it as Jake had said, like a soul who is weary of living. In the fo'c'sle the sides of the ship

123

smelt of damp rust and iron-mould. The water ran in the bilges with a hollow sound. Outside the galley the cook had once hung a cloth, and he had forgotten to take it down. It fluttered now in the rain, sodden and grey, a torn rag. The bunting round the bridge was black with the soot and the rain.

The mate paced up and down, a small figure like a beetle in an oilskin several sizes too large for him.

The Dutch fireman came up for a breather; he put his head out of the round scuttle and sniffed at the rain. In the fo'c'sle one of the Belgians was playing on a mouth-organ; he drew in his breath with short, spasmodic jerks, and the tune came dolefully, a harsh, strained sound. Somehow the hearing of it brought back to me a memory of long ago, when I had been taken as a child by my mother to a bay some twenty miles from home. We had a picnic on the beach, and a mist had blown in upon us from the sea, even as this mist that wrapped the *Romanie* now, and listening I had heard the mournful tolling of a bell coming from a far distance across the bay. My mother told me it was a buoy, set in the sea to mark a dangerous ledge of rock, and when sailors heard the toll of it through the mist it served them as a warning, and they altered their course accordingly. The mouth-organ was like a poor thin echo of that tolling bell; it shivered its way through the air from the fo'c'sle to the galley door, borne on the wind and the rain. Someone began to sing against the tune in a different key, and then there was a great burst of laughter, and a silly, high French voice. It jarred horribly, and I shuddered for no reason. I hated the *Romanie*.

It was about half-past seven in the evening. We had passed the Ile d'Ouessant early in the afternoon; it had been fine enough to distinguish it away on the quarter, and then the wall of fog had come up again, and we ran away into this with the land left far astern. I had been up on the bridge, taking my stand at the wheel. The skipper had been beside me for a while, but when we came into the fog once more he shrugged his shoulders as though this was some trick the fates had played him, and after peering about him he altered the course he had just given me, then called to the mate for some sort of conference – mainly, I think, to impress me with their joint efficiency, and finally disappeared and leaving me with no confidence at all. The mate remained on the bridge, nervous, restless, and his very manner unsettled me, especially the way he kept turning his head and listening – straining his eyes into the bank of fog. It was as though he expected to hear something.

There was no protection from the weather on the bridge. The rain drove into my eyes, and I could not see ahead of us more than two cables' length or so. The ship groaned and plunged in an ugly cross sea. Deep inside me I had a feeling that neither the skipper nor the mate, nor any of us upon the ship, knew for certain where we were going.

Later I was relieved by one of the Belgians, and I went down from the bridge, and then for'ard to the fo'c'sle.

This mist had made everything dark. Somebody had lit the lamp, it swung in gimbals against the bulkhead, casting a yellow reflection on the faces of the men. One of them lay stretched in his berth, his hands over his eyes. There was a smell of wet oilskin, stale tobacco, and cheese. A torn magazine without a cover lay upon the floor. I lit a cigarette and went and sat beside Jake.

'What's happened?' he said.

'Nothing,' I told him; 'you can't see a yard ahead, and the glass is falling. I don't think the bloody little fool has any idea where we are.'

'He's keeping too close in,' said Jake; 'I don't know what his game is.'

'He's afraid of the high seas farther out,' I suggested; 'maybe he thinks she'll settle down to it and wallow. He must have realized by now she won't stand it. Do you think he'll try for Brest?'

'We're miles from Brest,' said Jake; 'this coast is hell – he ought to know that!'

'He doesn't seem to make any effort,' I said; 'you'd think if he wasn't afraid for his own skin he'd give some thought to the owners of the blasted ship. He'd lose his job even if he saved himself.'

'Not necessarily, Dick.'

'How d'you mean?'

'It might be a put-up job,' he said.

'Good God!'

'Yes, I know. But that sort of thing happens at sea. When a

125

ship is losing money over freights and she's not worth reconditioning, what's to prevent an owner making a bit on the insurance? Broken ships don't tell any tales.'

'Listen, Jake, no skipper's going to risk his life for the sake of his owner's pocket.'

'What about the skipper's pocket?' said Jake. 'He'd make on the deal, too, you may depend on that. A fellow like this Belgian of ours would split himself if he stood to gain anything by it. I know the type. Lazy, ignorant, good-natured, but crooked as hell.'

'I don't believe he'd have the guts to carry through with the job,' I said.

'Perhaps not. It needs an odd sort of courage. It wouldn't be so difficult, Dick, to run a vessel ashore on a quiet stretch of coast. There wouldn't be much danger, I mean. A skipper would blame the fog – and then invent a highly-coloured story of the fight he'd had. While all the time he'd waded ashore, and watched his ship break up on the rocks where he'd put her himself.'

'What about the mate – and the men?'

'Bribes, Dick, can quieten a whole lot of nonsense.'

It sounded convincing, this theory of Jake's, but even if it were true, I did not see how the knowledge of it would help us at all.

'Oh, well!' I said, 'he can send her to the bottom for all I care. I'm game for a swim or anything else.'

'Yes,' said Jake, 'so would I be if we were heading for a sand-bank off the coast of Holland, but if this fellow thinks he's being clever, running ashore round the Pointe du Raz, he's making the biggest mistake of his life, and the last one.'

I looked at Jake through the haze of smoke.

'You can't scare me,' I laughed; 'come on deck.'

He followed me without a word. The seas were running higher now than when I had been upon the bridge, and the mist had not lifted. The seas were grey, foam-crested, rearing into the air like strange giants with sloping shoulders, turning and rushing upon us out of the mist. A thin rain blew in our faces. Every now and then the deck was swept with a sheet of water, and the ship rolled heavily, wearily, as if she had no wish to shake free.

It would be dark soon. I could see the figures of the mate and the skipper on the bridge, standing beside the man at the wheel. The mate was gesticulating with his hands, and I could imagine the torrent of words pouring from his mouth. It seemed as though the skipper turned a helpless face and shrugged his shoulders. The chap at the wheel gazed stolidly before him, solemn as a mule. They were like dumb shadows in a moving-picture show. I knew how they would be in a crisis, pitiful, impotent, and swept aside. We watched them in silence, and we watched the curling seas sweep astern of the *Romanie*, and we listened to the rain. The mist closed in upon us, grey now and stifling, and night came like a dark cloud to cover us.

'I don't think,' said Jake, 'we can do any good by staying here.' This time it was I who made no answer, and he led the way back into the fo'c'sle, where the flickering lamp shone as a glow of queer comfort, and the Belgian boy blowing his mouth-organ seemed symbolical and a defiance of fear.

I can see them now without closing my eyes, dark figures on a dim background, sprawling in the cramped fo'c'sle under a guttering light. The boy with the mouth-organ sat on the edge of his cot with his legs swinging over, dangling to the berth below. He leant sideways, his cheeks puffed out, and his eyes closed, and ever and again he took the instrument from his mouth and wiped it on his trouser knee. One of the firemen lay on his back asleep, even the wail of the mouth-organ would not wake him. His face was upturned, and he had one arm stretched above his head, and one leg drawn up, a weird, strained position. He snored loudly, quivering on a scale with a tremulous shudder, followed by a deep, satisfying intake of breath. The sound of his snores was distinct and apart; it did not mingle with the tuneless jerky whimper played by the boy. Another fellow sat cross-legged, a jacket across his knees, biting at a piece of coarse black thread, and turning his eyes up to the boy with the mouth-organ, chaffing him, keeping up a barrage of words. He spoke a mixture of Flemish and bad French; I could not distinguish half of what he said. I think this was the fellow who had drawn the pornographic figures in the galley. He grinned at Jake and me, showing a great empty mouth and two yellow fangs drooping from black gums.

'*Tu l'as vu, le petit, avec son foutu machin,*' he said, '*quand on ne le regarde pas il s'en sert comme d'une petite amie, quoi! Assez, mon vieux, assez – tu me fais chier avec ton bruit. C'est pas une femme ça –* '

I hated his voice, and his high thin cackle of laughter. The boy up in the cot puffed out his cheeks and a high-pitched wail came from his mouth-organ, while the sleeping man spluttered and tremored beneath him.

I could feel the rush of the sea against the bows of the vessel, the thud and plunge of her head in the trough, and the walls of the ship groaned and screamed for relief, shuddering like a live thing in pain. There was a hiss of air above me, coming from some crack, a hollow echo of the wind on deck, and the water sucked and gurgled in the bilges beneath the planks.

'Oh! hell,' I said to Jake, 'I can't turn in and sleep and I can't sit here and wait. If there's going to be a row in this hole, let's make it loud and strong.' He smiled, he did not say anything.

'Here, you,' I called to the boy, 'stop that damned howling – *jouez quelque chose*. And you – *finie votre* bloody mucking with a needle – *chantez – chantez, tout le monde.*'

I climbed on a berth, waving my hands in the air.

'*Moi, je suis* conductor,' I shouted, '*suivez*, everybody.' I kicked the Dutch fireman in the pants. 'Wake up, you lousy bum, and sing.' He turned over, cursing, shaking his great fat head at me. The Belgians laughed, the boy climbed up beside me, screaming his mouth-organ in my ear. He played something, and we all joined in the chorus, whistling, yelling and stamping our feet. Somebody started improvising words to another tune, the boy followed it up, and I bent forward gravely, swaying from the waist.

'*Messieurs, mesdames, permettez-moi de vous présenter ma petite camarade . . .*'

The boy and I clung to each other lovingly, the Belgians hooted and jeered, singing at the top of their voices.

The ship rolled heavily from side to side, and we crashed down from the bunk, struggling, cursing, and we tried to dance on the floor, the boy sobbing for breath on his mouth-organ, the others clapping and stamping their feet.

There was a song about '*une blonde*', whose something-or-other was '*profonde*'. We sang, with actions of course, I following the words and grimaces of the boy, scarcely knowing what I said, shaking with laughter, forcing myself. '*Il y avait une blonde,*' answering a back-chat of questions.

'*C'était comme ça?*'

'*Deux fois ça, mon vieux.*'

'*Quoi! Plus grande encore? Pas possible.*'

'*Cherche-la – alors, ta blonde. Tout le monde va passer dedans.*'

There was another burst of laughter as the ship lurched again, and we lost our balance, sliding helplessly into a corner.

I saw Jake push the door, and a gust of wind came tearing through, sending the lamp a-quiver, while he kept his head and shoulder in the entrance, watching the weather.

I could tell that the seas had increased, and at that moment a sheet of water ran along the deck, sweeping its way for'ard, and part of it washing through the open door of the fo'c'sle.

'Keep it shut, you damn fool,' I said to Jake; 'd'you want to drown us?' – and one glimpse had shown us that the mist had now become part of the dark night, shrouded, horrible, and we could not even see the bridge because of it. We were sober in an instant, the laughter dying away, and the mouth-organ breaking off suddenly in the middle of a note. The bell rang then from the direction of the bridge, and we heard the voice of the mate shouting, while one of the watch staggered along the deck towards us from amidships, a swaying ineffectual figure in his streaming oilskin, his head bent, the wind tugging at him. We came out on deck as we were, I close to Jake, somebody following behind me dragging at a boot, muttering under his breath, and I saw one man look at another with white scared eyes.

The *Romanie* rolled now like a turtle in the water. The bell rang again, and she plunged from side to side, as though she had no power within her, but must drift wherever the seas should sweep her.

We were making no progress now, our speed was dead slow,

and we stood about peering at each other in the gloom, waiting for orders, waiting for some signal. The men called to one another excitedly, each one suggesting what should have been done, no one listening to anyone but himself. The hoarse cries of the mate seemed to come from very far away. I looked up at Jake standing beside me; he was very still, as though drawn within himself, and quieter than I had ever seen him. Then he turned to me with the smile I knew, bringing relief and a denial of trouble.

'If there's a panic,' he said, 'you'll be all right, won't you?' He spoke calmly, without a suggestion of fear, and I knew that wherever he was there would be safety.

'Yes,' I said, 'I'll be all right.'

We stood by, ready, expectant, straining our eyes through the mist and the darkness, turning our heads first one way and then another, listening – always listening.

It seemed to me that many hours must have passed, and there was no change, no new thing to force itself upon us, making a diversion however terrible, and we went on waiting there with the ship rising and falling in the high seas, and the soft rain blowing on our faces.

I wondered why the jerky, horrible rhythm of the tune of the mouth-organ should turn and twist itself in my mind, its little patter and jingle hurting me, keeping me from the full realization of what might come. I thought of the *Romanie* lying beside the wharf at Stockholm, the tall crane above her, the lights, and the thunder of the coal pouring down the shaft into the hold.

I saw Jake and myself running away from the café, a man stretched hideously with a knife in his back, and mingled now with the pattern of this was the Belgian boy, his hand to his mouth, wailing a tune.

'Jake,' I said, 'why don't they do something? What in the name of God is the use of all this hanging about – this waiting about? Why doesn't somebody do something?'

I listened to the pitch of my own voice; it was higher than usual, strained somehow. I caught hold of Jake's arm.

'You don't have to worry,' he said. I knew that, and I knew it would not do any good, whatever I did, whether I cursed or whether I stayed silent. I could not stand waiting, though; I wanted to be able to move about, to haul at things, to work in some way. I saw that there was relief in the excited chatter of the other fellows, in the string of curses.

'How long are we going to carry on like this?' I asked.

I went on talking without expecting an answer.

'They oughtn't to have left Stockholm,' I said; 'that's where the mistake was made, in ever leaving Stockholm . . .'

How I clung to them, my silly patter of words. 'To put some idiot in command of a vessel, who can't find his way in a fog – especially on this coast. A lot of bastards – that's what they are – a lot of bastards . . .' I said. Maybe if the mist cleared we would be able to get away, perhaps Jake was wrong in his calculations and Brest was not far, not really far. Yes, no doubt Brest would be quite close. When the mist cleared we could look around, and the skipper would realize he could not make a fool of us any longer. Brest would be all right. I was glad I had thought of this. I saw myself walking in the streets there, having a drink somewhere, leaning against a bridge. It was impossible that these things should not be.

'Jake,' I said, 'why in hell doesn't he go back to Brest?' My words were not convincing, though, not angry enough – they trembled in spite of myself, pleading a question. Jake looked down on me. His hair and his lashes were wet with the fog.

'We're not near there,' he said, 'we're not near anywhere.'

'Yes, but look here,' I started, and then I trailed off, unable to finish my sentence, unaware of the very words I should choose – 'Yes, but look here. . . .' I did not speak any more, I felt dazed and bewildered, as though some sort of stupor had taken hold of me and would not let me go. The silly jingle of the mouthorgan no longer haunted me. I made up a dream of standing in the garden at home, pointing the library window to Jake and saying carelessly: 'If we go in we should disturb my father.' It was funny how clearly the picture came to me. And I saw Jake walk through the open window, and touch my father on the shoulder, and they smiled as though they had known each other for a long while, and their faces seemed suddenly incredibly alike – merging finally into one.

'You know,' said Jake, the Jake in my picture, 'you know that Dick writes too,' and my father nodded, while I stood a little aloof, almost superior, rocking backwards and forwards on my heels.

'*Il y avait une blonde . . .*'

but then that had not anything to do with it at all. There was no need to bring that in. 'Jake,' I said, 'Jake . . .' and the picture went, and I was here on the deck of the *Romanie* beside him, peering through the curtain of mist. The bell rang from the bridge again. Somebody called out hoarsely from the fo'c'sle head. It was the Belgian boy, who had been stationed there as a look-out. He stumbled down the ladder towards us waving his arms. There was an answering shout from the bridge.

'Listen,' said Jake, 'listen . . .'

I caught at my breath, shuddering from head to foot, cold, alive. Suddenly there came to our ears the sound for which we had waited – the sound I had so often conjured in my imagination at safe moments, and now unmistakable and sinister, demanding to be heard. The roar of it drummed in my ears, horrible, unseen, so near yet intangible, drawing closer – triumphant and mocking at us who swept so steadily towards it, driven on and on, helpless in the cloud of mist.

Sullen and insistent it would not let us go, this sound of the sea shattered against rock, this crash of breakers on a hidden shore.

They ran blindly here and there upon the deck, sobbing, shouting, little figures of men, their faces grey with fear. I ran with them. I was one of them. We tore at the lashings of a boat. The mate passed me, lifting his hands, screaming something in my ear. I hit out at him, I struck him down, and my feet passed over his fallen body. Someone tore at my throat with his fingers, clinging to me, babbling like a little idiot child. I shook him from me, I pushed and thrust my way against the shoulders of the others, who fought wildly and helplessly with one another, caged animals bereft of all humanity.

And while we ripped the covers from the boat we turned our faces hither and thither in the darkness, aware of the roar of the

132

breakers coming to us out of the mist, and we cursed helplessly – bent backwards against each other in confusion, pitiless, unutterably lost.

Now the boat was swung out on the davits, and we clung to it, listening to no order, hearing no order, trampling upon one another in our fear and our distress. There were too many of us; we fought for our places with hatred in our souls, striking out desperately in a wild despair.

It was only then that I remembered Jake. I clung with one hand to the davit, I searched for his face amongst the pale idiot faces of the men pressed against me.

And 'Jake,' I called, and 'Jake' I called again.

He did not answer me, he was not there. I struggled to loose myself from the tossing arms that dragged me down; I did not want to be in the boat any more, I wanted to find Jake – he was not there, I had to find him.

'Jake,' I called, 'Jake . . . Jake . . .' and now I could not get away, and now the boat was swinging down from the davits into the sea, and I was fighting, cursing, tearing at the eyes of the men who clung to me – possessed by horror, stricken and insane.

'Jake . . . Jake . . .' I saw him for a moment, I saw his head flung back and his smile. I heard his voice call to me, a message of beauty never lost and never forgotten – 'You'll be all right, Dick,' and one swift vision of his splendour, unbroken and immortal.

Then we were gone from him, and there was no more after that but the sudden churn of water under us, the shock of the sea in my lungs, and my heart, and I tossed like a dead thing in the shattering roar of the white breakers, sinking down, down into the blackness of eternity, swept beyond him to some shore where he would never follow me, outcast and alone. And I was clinging with numb fingers to a ledge of rock, rising out of the water, and then I was swept past this, my hands above my head, in the suction of a breaking sea, and cast like a stone, into the face of stones, bleeding, broken, the surge of sand beneath my body. And stretching out my hands and he was not there. And calling to him, and he was not there.

And 'Jake . . . Jake . . . Jake . . .' like a soul lost in the wilderness, with nothing but the mist and the rain, and the sound of the breakers on the shore. And later, when the mist had lifted, I saw there were high cliffs about me, encompassing a wide bay.

The tide was gone out to meet the wreckage we had brought for her, while stark and naked on the black rocks the *Romanie* held her broken face to the sky.

I sat there alone, and I saw the waves shatter themselves upon her, and I watched the rain fall into the sea, and I watched the grey dawn breaking.

Part Two: HESTA

1

At first it was like living in a dream, an existence made up of shadows, where places and persons held no substance. Nor did it matter much where I went nor how I lived. Night followed the day, and there was the sun in the sky, or it would rain, or it would blow; there were barren stretches of land where no tree stood, there were stone villages, and little churches beaten by the wind.

There was a peasant woman washing her linen in a pool, there was a dog stretched lazily on the doorstep of a cottage flicking his tail at the flies. These things went on inevitable and undisturbed, but I did not see how I should have part in them again. It was as though the hum and the emotion of life continued around me, close, breathing and touching me not, so that I stood aloof in my own channel of existence, holding no communication with the great stream that would have passed me by. I did not matter, I was of no importance. Once I had stood upon a bridge with the certainty of death before me, and at that moment the call of living and the glamour of adventure had seemed stronger to me than they had ever been. I had looked down from a gateway and seen that the earth was good. Something within me had struggled for release, and cried for fulfilment. The air blowing upon my face, the stray dust beneath my feet, the murmur in passing of men and women, so dear, so familiar, the very sweat of their bodies and the smell of their clothes, these had drawn out to me in one last definite appeal. The tumult of living, the glory and the pain. The precious intimacy of little things. I wanted so much and so much. But that had all happened a long while ago, those old longings and those desires. I had lived them and they had not lasted. I looked about me now to see some trace of their departure, but they had vanished.

I did not care for them any more, not the sun, not the sea,

nor the sky, nor the touch of earth, nor the warmth of humanity, nor anything at all.

I had my life before me and I did not want it.

I was a dumb stupid thing, a mass of senseless clay having no meaning, weary and lost. I was someone with no limbs and no flesh, not possessing the consolation of a mind nor the fortitude of a sorrowful heart. I was without courage. Hope was a word belonging to another language which I did not try to understand. There was nothing but two eyes that framed a picture, haunting, mournful, a picture where every detail was clear and minute, drawn with a thin dark brush, escaping no shadow, no reflection of light. My picture was one of a grey morning after the mist had gone, and a wild, desolate stretch of beach frowned upon by cliffs of granite.

The tide was gone out and the sea broke upon the *Romanie*, she lying on a ledge of rock, weird and ghastly, lifted from the water. Her sides were smashed, her davits fallen, twisted and caught in a mesh of stay and cable. Pools were beginning to form on the sloping deck, and the sea ran in and out of the hold with an odd sucking gurgle. A bar had slipped from somewhere down to the main hatch, torn open and disclosed, and this bar kept banging against the iron sides of the ship, sounding with a strange hollow clamour. A ladder hung over the bows, broken and aslant; it must have been cast there in the panic and then left. Outside the galley the white cloth of the cook still hung upon its nail, fluttering in the morning breeze, oddly alive. Inside the galley the saucepans and the mugs would be undisturbed. The figures of the women in white chalk, they would still be there, grotesque and absurd, mocking the silence. On the surface of the water the wreckage floated placidly, drifting with the tide, torn timbers and iron plates, part of the propeller, a loose arm of a davit.

There were barrels, too, and broken bottles, cases of tinned meat, a cracked basin, a sack of peanuts – they rolled sluggishly backwards and forwards on the crest of a wave.

The smashed boat lay like a gaping shell tossed high and dry upon the higher beach.

Between two rocks there was a little pool of water, warm in the morning sun. A broken dish lay here and a cake of soap, while farther away was the brightly coloured magazine that once had lain upon the fo'c'sle floor.

Now that the wind had gone and the mist, the sea sounded hushed and still. Away to the left the high jagged cliffs ran sudden and sheer, grey boulders of rock, massive and impregnable. They stretched to a sharp definable point, like the edge of a razor, and before this the sea twisted and broke, as though crashing upon unseen things. A lighthouse stood upon a rock, and another lighthouse beyond. The sea at this point would never be still, would never be silenced, but would break for ever in a turmoil of hate and exultation, leaping, shouting, wave meeting wave in a sterile embrace, horrible and cold.

To the right swept a wide clear bay, and here the water was no longer bewildered, but ran in white breakers upon a stretch of yellow sand. It seemed as though this bay should be a refuge from the wild seas that crashed beyond the point, and there should be peace here and rest. The *Romanie* leant towards it on her ledge of rock as though she cried for the touch of sand. But there was no peace and no rest, for the bay was a wilderness and a desolation, where nothing lived and nothing cried.

And the sea left other relics strewn on the wet sand with the wreckage. Gently the tide relinquished them, regretfully, with a whisper and a sigh and the water streamed from them as tears stream at the sorrow of parting. They lay on the beach separated from one another, dark and motionless, with the sun warm on their pale faces and their soft glistening hair. They lay like sleepers weary from the day's toil, and now were happy and consoled, their heads pillowed in their hands.

This was my picture, and I wanted to become part of it too, to sleep there with the others on the shore, but they would not let me. I had to go away and live my life. I had no business to remain there lost in a dream. I had to break my mind away from it, I had to cover it, sadly, reverently, hide it in the shadowed untouched places of my memory.

I would never forget. I would never permit my picture to become dusty and worn. After all that had been and all that was to come, I should still see it, the rugged cliffs, the little lighthouse standing beyond the razor edge of the Pointe du Raz, the broken *Romanie* desolate, alone, and lastly, beautiful and forlorn, the sleeping figures in the Baie des Trépassés.

There were so many things to do. They kept me from thinking, after that first dumb stupor. To begin with, each fresh incident was a moment of horror and torture; there were people who clothed me and gave me food, there were questions to answer, and excited shouting faces coming upon me, one after the other, people touching me, stroking me, and I with my bad French not understanding what they said to me, being dragged away, sitting in some corner of a room – and a car rattling along a dusty road, a village, and more people and more questions. I suppose now that they meant to be kind. I suppose now that they were sorry for me. But I did not want pity, I only asked to be left alone, and this they would not do.

First they took me to a village called Plogoff. There was a pastor here. He could do nothing for me. I was not ill, I did not want to be helped. There was a peasant, too; he was kind, gentle, an old man, and he let me sleep in his cottage. He tried to keep the officials and the questioners away from me; he ordered the curious, straying people to go, who pointed at me and stared.

I was still dazed and uncomprehending; I heard the snatches of their conversation, their expressions of pity and dismay.

'*Ils sont tous mort,*' was one line that hammered itself into my head – '*Ils sont tous mort,*' and they brought back to me in a flash, vivid and strong, the picture of my sleeping figures in the Baie des Trépassés. That was the name, they told me, the Baie des Trépassés, and the lighthouse and the headland was the Pointe du Raz. So Jake had been right after all. Jake . . . I had not got to think about that, though; I had not got to give way to the knowledge that he was gone. He had said to me: 'You'll be all right.' And I would not disturb him with my sorrow wherever he should be, his arms outstretched above his head on the wet sand, his eyes closed, no smile on his face.

I would only think of Jake as he had been – long ago on the mountains above Laardel, astride his horse, standing against the background of the setting sun. I would think of him walking

138

by my side, laughing, whistling, kicking a stone as he went.

I would think of him with a tree behind him, and the wood fire casting a reflection on his face, and his grave eyes turned upon me, a cigarette between his lips.

All of that belonged to me; the sea could not take it from me.

Now there was the continuation of my own life. There were dull, necessary formalities to be gone through, these endless questions which must be answered for the satisfaction of people I did not know. I stayed two nights in Plogoff with the Breton fisherman, and then I had to go to Nantes and give an account of the wreck and how it had happened. All this fell upon me because I was the sole survivor. It did not bear thinking about too closely. I do not know why I alone should have been chosen out of ten men to carry on this business of living. It was supreme irony on the part of someone. I, swept to safety, broken, bleeding, but alive, carried by the sea to the bay after the boat had swamped, and the others – they came later, one by one, their arms above their heads . . . There was no need to go into all that.

So I went to Nantes, where there were questions to answer, and after this there was no more I could do to help them; but, to my surprise, I was given some money and some clothes as a small compensation. This was kind of them, I thought; I do not think that they were obliged to do it. I was free now of the entanglement of the whole concern, the *Romanie* would have no further claim on me.

I went to see the British Vice-Consul in Nantes. Here there were further questions to answer, further documents to sign. The worry of these little matters kept me from thinking. They gave me something to do. I was confused and inefficient in a strange country without Jake. He had managed things in Scandinavia; when we had landed there it had been as sailors before the mast. There had not been the necessity of passports and officialism. Now I had to go into this. I was an alien, I had not any means of support. The Consul advised me to return to England. From my point of view, this was out of the question. What would I do in England? I could not go home. I could not settle down anywhere. I should always be a wanderer, I knew that. Only now it would have to be alone.

On the road to Otta Jake had told me to take a pull on myself. I had never quite known what he meant. Anyway, there had been the flick of a coin, and my choice, and Stockholm, and then the *Romanie*. This was all because of me. And he was dead. Much he cared what happened to me now. I should never see him or talk to him again. There was no other thing to do but to go on with life somehow, taking what came and accepting it, not minding very much.

I had to get away from Brittany. The sea was no good to me, nor the wild rocks, nor the fields and the dusty roads. The huddled cottages, the grave burnt peasant faces, the chapels with their worn stones, their quiet simplicity, the villages sleepy in the midday sun: they were too silent and too pure for me.

At first I had wanted it, this peace and quietude, so as to be able to shut myself up with a blind stupor of grief, but now I felt that thinking was a bad thing. I thought perhaps that if there was noise around me and the movement of many people it would be better. I should not be so much alone if I were doing things all the time. I had to keep myself in some way, too. That was part of the stupidity of living. I had to eat and drink and have a roof over my head. It hurt me that I should have to do these things, that after eating or sleeping I should feel changed and easier in mind and body. I despised myself for being able to eat, for being able to lose consciousness in sleep. It was wrong to look up at the sky in the morning and be pleased to see the sun. It was wrong to buy a packet of cigarettes, to sit on a wall yawning after food, to smile in spite of myself because the sun was warm.

It looked as though I were not caring about Jake.

I was really very lucky. Things might have been so much more desperate. I ought to be grateful for small mercies. Both the British Consul and the agent from the *Romanie*'s company had been helpful and provided me with everything I needed; I had sufficient money therefore to last me for a little while if I was careful in the spending of it.

That was good enough for me. I would live from day to day. I had one idea in my mind, and that was to get to Paris. I said good-bye at the Consulate, thanking them for all their kindness;

people whose faces I did not know came up and shook me warmly by the hand, a little reporter from a local newspaper even took a snap of me – me, 'the ship-wrecked mariner', and I was put on the centre page alongside a picture of the *Romanie*, with half a column devoted to my personal sufferings. Yes, they were all very kind to me. Then I went to the station and bought a third-class ticket to Paris, and so away from Nantes and the taint of the *Romanie*, and what was gone from me, and into the start of a new life and new interests, forgetting the hell that had been.

The train was packed with sailors going home on leave, and we were all crammed together in the hard wooden carriage like animals herded in a truck. They were nearly all of them young, and in tremendous spirits, laughing and singing, hanging out of the window when we came to stations, calling out to girls, whistling, chaffing one another.

It was good to see them. I did not join in with them though; I had a paper which I pretended to read. I watched the country flash past, scattered villages and woods, hills and fields, till my eyes grew fixed on the pane of glass and it all seemed alike and I was not taking anything in, and then I grew tired of it and propped my head against my fist at the side of the carriage, trying to sleep, and the chatter and laughter of the sailors coming and going in a wave of sound.

We arrived in Paris about eight o'clock in the evening.

The name of the station was the Gare Montparnasse. I got out of the train and was swept down to the entrance with the rest of the crowd; there seemed to be a riot of noise and confusion, and everyone in a hurry, and a strange excitement and clatter, and I stood outside on the wide boulevard where there were trams and taxis rattling over the cobbled stones, and there were cafés everywhere, and people, and lights just beginning, and a good food smell, warm air, and dust, a gay screech of taxi hooters, somebody laughing, a flash of scent, and men and women being happy with one another, and it was Paris.

I found a room in the Rue Vaugirard. There was a street leading off the Boulevard Montparnasse. The room was stuffy and not very clean. It was cheap, though. It looked down on to the street below, and opposite was a wall with hoardings and posters. If I craned out of the window I could see the end of the street, and the red and white striped blind of the *tabac* at the corner where it led on to the boulevard. I looked round the room, at the cracked jug and basin, the red lamp-shade, the fat bed with a dent in the middle, and I tried to feel as though it were mine and I knew about it.

Then I went out and had something to eat at a small restaurant in the Boulevard Montparnasse, where there was a large menu written in mauve pencil that I could not be bothered to read, and remains of other people's bread on the table-cloth, but the food was good for all that – I had a tournedos, red and juicy, and some Gruyère cheese – and then some brandy, so as not to mind about things, and I leant back smoking Camel cigarettes, thankful for a tired body and a mind drugged by drinking too much, and I watched a fat Jew fumble about with a girl's breasts at the next table, she with silly goggle eyes and a greasy skin hot under make-up. I remember being glad that I did not have to go to bed with her, and then I got up and walked rather unsteadily out of the restaurant, blinking at the lights and the passing people as though they belonged to another world, and so back to my stuffy room, dead weary and a little sick, neither thinking nor caring very much.

I was glad I had come to Paris. I wondered about it at first, but after three days I was certain. There was no other place in the world that would have done for me just at this time. It was impossible to be really lonely in Paris. That was the importance of it – that was the whole thing – not to be lonely. There was no conceivable comparison between Paris and London. I leant over a bridge looking down upon the Seine, and I thought of that other time back in London on that other bridge. It could not happen here. There was something in the warm, dusty air that was against it. It was easy to forget myself because of a little tattered book in a collection of books on the side of the quay, because of an ancient man with a long white beard and a wide-brimmed black hat, because of Notre-Dame soft and grey above a network of bridges, with one white cloud in a pink sky; and then gathering these things to me and walking away from the quays in any direction, up the hill again to Montparnasse, rubbing shoulders with people who smiled, coming to a café where the sun-blinds stretched to the pavement, and there would not be an inch of room; somebody waving *L'Intransigeant* in my face, a smell of burnt bread and Camel cigarettes, and the sombre eyes of a bearded man and the red lips of a girl in a yellow scarf.

It seemed to me that there was no finality to these pictures; they were little flashes of life that broke in upon a line of vision and were gone because another came and then another. I went on sitting at my rounded table blocked by a hum of voices and a hundred eager waving hands, and I said to myself that if I was old I would consider these people as an explosion of gas, a waste of air, and energy to no purpose, coming to a crisis over nothing, but being young I wanted to be as passionate as they, and as warm. I wanted to share their enthusiasms and lose myself, too, in some belief, no matter what it should be, only for the zest and fire of the believing. It was not the faith itself that mattered, but the possessing of it. To be stimulated in any way; the rest was a side issue. I wanted to go deeply into things, not ever to stand apart with a half interest. Thus after these three days in Paris I pretended to be blindly interested in the glimpses of life that came my way, in the pictures that people gave of themselves, mirrored in my mind. The old things did not matter to me. I did not stand transfigured before the windows in the Sainte-Chapelle; I did not watch the shadowed arches in Notre-Dame, nor did I lose myself in narrow streets and in dim churches; I was aware only of the life that went on around me, the strange intimacy of a café, the familiarity of faces I did not know, and wondering how they lived – that man and that woman.

This, then, was the Paris of my first few days, an impressionistic study, patches of colour and flashes of gloom, a suggestion of fullness throughout, so that in some strange way I was dragged into the picture, caught up in it and carried along, and there was no time for reflexion, no time for being entirely alone in a room and thinking.

And this was good, for I did not want to be alone in a room and thinking. The sound of Paris took me away from the silence of the Baie des Trépassés, the laughter and clatter of the cafés covered the hollow whisper of the spent tide retreating from the hold of the *Romanie*. There was the fellowship of people who were strangers to me, becoming infinitely precious and dear, the broad back of a man with a straw hat on his knees, the flushed warm face of a woman tired with many parcels dragging at the hand of a child, and I clung to them and the supreme power they possessed of rousing a story in my imagination of what he was thinking, of where she was going, so that this might continue in a chain of stories, and never for one moment would I hesitate, and pause, and turn unconsciously to him who had gone from me and then be shaken in a wave of remembrance, and so be lost once more and alone.

I knew now that this sound and this movement of a breathing, living city were necessary to me, and the contact of people, never to be away from people. In some way I must mingle in their lives, be bound up with them, be recognized as one of them. Not be myself, solitary and absurd, creeping to a quiet corner. I had got to go on living, therefore I must live well, and quickly if possible, seeing much, drinking it all in, making some sort of a business of living, placing a value on everything I did, saying to myself: 'This is a good moment . . . and this . . . and this. . . .' Definitely I would stop in Paris, I would not go away from Paris. I was not quite sure how I was going to live. It gave me a thrill of excitement, this, the uncertainty of it – never being sure from day to day. And while I was sitting here in Montparnasse, on the terrace of the Dôme, lounging back with empty pockets, smoking American cigarettes, more than a little drunk, there would come to me the image of my father in England, the long windows opened on to the shadowed lawn, and he sitting there, assured, famous, the memory of me, his son, coming not to trouble the smooth continuity of his life that mattered so much. I could write to him for money, of course. It amused me to play with the thought. The inevitable eight-page letter, whining for assistance, admitting failure – the beaten puppy with his tail between his legs. Or sending a wire, a plain statement of facts, carrying it off with a high hand.

I would not do either of these things, not I. I would not be humble and accept his kindness – gratitude and the rest of it. I did not want those sorts of sensations in my life. I could hear the voices of his friends: 'He was so good to him, you know, so good to him.' Because he would send me the money if I asked for it. I knew that all right. He would send it willingly, without any reproaches, having expected such a summons for a long while. He would not even take it seriously; he would open the letter at breakfast with a little smile and a shrug of his shoulders, looking across at my mother. 'Something from Richard at last. In trouble, of course. We had better send him a cheque, and his fare home. Will you see to it, my dear? You had better read his letter.'

And then he would open *The Times*, folding it carefully, turning to the centre page, while my mother rather anxious and flushed fingered my close-written screed, worried that his breakfast might have been spoilt by my interruption, and ashamed that she had had a hand in the making of me, his son, who should have turned out so differently, who had been such a quiet little boy – no trouble – and now all this suddenly, all this. Such a worry, such a breaking up of the placidity of things. My father wandering off to the library, his indifference to me sincere, not even a cover of pretence, and then looking out of the window absently, his eyes fixed, an old man with no understanding, and back to his desk, giving the lie to this, steadying his pen with steady fingers, calmly, clearly, writing his way into the pages of immortality. . . .

No, I would not whine to him. I could stand by myself. I would not trade on his name or his relationship. It gave me a keen satisfaction, this feeling of intense individualism. The famous father, the outcast son. Being free of him, being a rebel, smashing at authority. I would show them all what I was made of – one day. Here was I, just nobody, drunk in a café, but I was more alive than he. Drinking took away my inferiority. I painted a picture of myself to myself, rather a devil, getting what he could out of life and not caring, then startling the world with some magnificent gesture. Living intensely, supremely. . . . Oh! yes, that was me all right. If I had been sober I should only have been a boy sitting at a little table on a pavement outside a restaurant, going back later to a solitary room, with no occupation, slightly foolish, very inexperienced and lonely – admittedly lonely, but

I was drunk and full of deep-worn theories, and this was Paris, and I was a grand fellow. I called stoutly about me, I cursed a waiter for the slow service, I bought a French paper which I did not read, I gazed slowly and critically at the legs of a passing girl.

Why should anyone doubt me? – I knew about these things.

There was a party at the next table. There was a man with a beard and full, protruding eyes, he kept smashing his fist on his knee and talking all the time. He wore a purple shirt, open at the neck. By his side sat another man, small and putty-faced, who hung upon his words, and there was a tall fair boy bending over their table now, a portfolio of drawings under his arm which I felt he would never sell nor have the courage to show, and there were two girls without hats, bad figures and good hair. They tried to look Hungarian, but were English all the time, and this did not matter to me, being drunk, they were not ridiculous at all. I was certain that they painted brilliantly and wrote brilliantly, but nobody understood them, and they were in advance of their age – one day they would be understood – but in the meantime they would work furiously, and burn with ideas, and be miserable for no reason, and talk too much, and all sleep with each other on different nights.

'I'm not drunk,' I said to myself, 'I'm not drunk at all.'

I listened to them gravely, catching snatches of their conversation, and every word they spoke seemed to me to be sincere and true. There was not an atom of absurdity in the man with the long brown beard. He was the apostle of a new faith. 'In art,' he said, 'sex is everything. You can't get away from it.'

I nodded my head as though I were sitting at his table, and I wondered if this was a very new idea or if perhaps I had heard it somewhere before.

'Every curve in drawing,' he continued, 'expresses a sex-urge. Unconsciously, of course, to people who deliberately blind themselves to their own impulses, but to us – to us who know, it is the very essence of creation. When I fling a straight line on to a stretch of canvas, I always remind myself that it isn't a line – it's a symbol, a sex-symbol. If I wasn't aware of this I shouldn't be able to draw at all.'

146

He paused, and we all stared at him in admiration.

'We've got to cultivate it,' he said: 'we've got to break away from this state of appalling passivity. We must acknowledge sex on canvas, but not as a product of civilization – it must come from within ourselves as a last definite protest. . . .'

I was lost in wonder at his flow of words. Then one of the girls spoke. 'Kroenstein says that there is no such thing as sex,' she announced; 'he says that it only exists in our imagination.'

Ha! Here was a poser. This would not be so easy for the fellow in the beard. If Kroenstein said a thing like that . . . I had never heard of him, it was true, but anyone with the name of Kroenstein surely. . . . Was I very drunk? My bearded man would not give way, though; he was determined to carry off the situation. He laughed, and leant back in his chair with a shrug of his shoulders.

'You're a little behind the times, aren't you?' he said; 'nobody has believed in Kroenstein for at least three months. He's gone right out.'

That of course was another matter. I felt sorry for the girl. Still, it was her own fault for trying to brag about her knowledge of Kroenstein. I smiled stupidly to myself and nodded my head. I watched the same figures pass up and down the pavement in front of the Dôme, stroll down as far as the Coupole, and then return again, crossing over the street to the Rotonde. The same figures, over and over again.

This was great, this brilliance, this noise, this clatter of traffic, and my head swimming and my eyes staring. I wasn't lonely – not I. . . .

I could hear the fellow in the beard holding the conversation again.

'You, Josef, paint in terms of rhythm,' he was saying; 'I can tell by your work that you're striving for some inner purity that you haven't yet learnt to control. You're sex-conscious, too, but it doesn't break the harmony.' The fair boy leant forward eagerly.

'You say it,' he exclaimed, 'you say it very truly. Rhythm has more importance to me than the sex.'

But here the putty-faced man shook his head, he laid his hand on the shoulder of the fair boy.

'Rhythm,' he said, 'will lead you so far – and then, pouf!' (he snapped his fingers). 'You come against a blank wall. Symmetry of design is the great thing to achieve, but you'll have to surrender to sex before you purify yourself. You'll have to surrender.'

The fair boy looked about him a little helplessly. I wondered if he would surrender to sex immediately or if he would wait until he got home. Then the other girl spoke, the fattest and plainest of the two. She wore horn-rimmed spectacles and she was spotty under the skin.

'If only,' she said, 'if only we really knew just what it was that our bodies wanted.'

They looked at her with respect; they were silent, they admitted that she had thrown across to them a thought of very deep intensity. I began to imagine a little conversation between the girl and myself.

'When I look at you,' I was saying, 'I know perfectly well what my body doesn't want.' And then she would crumple up like a child from a convent, and burst into tears. 'It can't be much fun for a girl,' I thought, 'unless she is pretty.'

I sat very still and watched the flickering lights of the Rotonde, while their voices went on and on, droning in my ear, and I was very far away, really. . . .'

After a while I shook myself out of a dream, and I looked at them, and I saw there was another man sitting at their table, and he was thin and very round-shouldered, and his face was olive green. He was the only one of them who wore a hat, one of those wide black ones that suggest no sense of humour – or possibly too much. He called for another round of drinks. He fluttered notes in his hands, hundred-franc notes.

'I wish,' thought I, 'that all that belonged to me,' and I fumbled in my pocket and drew forth a crumpled five-franc note. And this was all that remained, and I was drunk and I did not care. I looked across at them all sitting at the next table. The olive-green man was important; even beard and putty-face sat back and let him do all the talking.

'I want you to do the cover this month, Carlo,' he was saying, 'and I want you for once to give your mind entirely to me, not to let yourself be swayed by an impulse coming from your own indifference. I want you to express my thought in curves, and I suggest that the thought be called "Flight" – you can, of course, lend it something of your own treatment.'

'By "flight",' said Carlo with the beard, 'you mean to convey one distinct impression of the slipping away of the mind after the consummation of the body?'

'Naturally.'

'Then there must be no striving after tone effect?'

'None.'

Carlo seemed disappointed. I thought it was a damned shame he shouldn't have his tone effect – a damned shame.

'Of course,' said olive green, 'it must be formless, utterly formless. You can't connect any purity of line with impotence. Your curve must suggest relaxation – a negation of sex after the act.'

'Yes – yes – I understand.'

It was more than I did. I did not understand one bloody word of what they were saying. I had half a mind to tell them so, too. It would serve them right. None of this was real, anyway, so what the hell did it matter what I said to them? I got up from my table and dragged my chair after me. I pushed against one of the girls, and sat down, and struck my fist on the table.

'Nonsense,' I said loudly, and that was all. They gazed at me in astonishment. I could see the blank surprise in their faces. The fat girl was the first to recover herself.

'You get out of here,' she said.

I smiled at her politely, and then I remembered, and I shook my finger at her in reproach.

'You,' I said, 'are the girl who wants to know what to do with her body. That's right, isn't it?' She flushed under her skin and looked away from me in disgust.

'He's drunk,' she said.

I stood up again, and bowed to them very gravely.

'I think you are all so charming,' I said, 'so very charming.'

'Who are you?' asked Carlo.

'I'm a poet,' I said.

Olive green raised his eyebrows. 'We are not interested in you,' he said.

I looked at him a little sadly. 'That's where you make such a big mistake,' I told him; 'you ought to be interested. You need a wider, broader vision than the science of curves can ever give you. I don't believe in curves – I never did.'

'Are you a sodomite?' asked the other girl.

I considered this thoughtfully for a few moments.

'No,' I said. 'No, I haven't sufficient rhythm.'

'Supposing you go back to your table and leave us in peace?' suggested olive green.

'I would rather recite one of my poems to you,' I said.

This was very amusing. I was enjoying myself. Or wasn't I? I sat down at their table once more. 'My poem is a study in repression,' I said; 'I wrote it some time back, but I don't think it is really dated. In fact, between you and me, I think it's pretty good.'

I began to say the lines of the poem that once, long, long ago, I had laid on the desk in the library before my father, and he had taken the paper in his hands, and then let it flutter softly on to the floor.

And a boy had run away down the chestnut drive, flying from the shadows that pursued him. But I was not that boy any more, I was somebody else, escaping down another drive, escaping from another shadow.

'Perhaps you would like to hear some more,' I said when I had finished; 'if I can remember rightly there is one poem that deals with a different sort of sensation entirely.'

They looked at me stupidly, and their faces were flat, like ghosts, without any expression.

'Well?' I said later, 'and if the first was too thin for you, what do you think of that one?' I leant back, my hands on my knees, unconscious of ridicule, proud of my little triumph.

'Do you want another?' I said.

And when I had come to the end of my little repertoire I saw that they were smiling at me, and the olive-green man was rubbing his hands together, and the ugly girl's eyes were large behind her glasses. She breathed heavily, she leant against me, excited.

'It's marvellous,' she said, 'marvellous.' And the bearded man looked at me and laughed, and suddenly they were all aware of each other, as though this was the first time they were together. I hated them then, I hated them. It was all right before when I could fool them with their curves, and their rhythm, and their symmetry of design. Not now, though. They were different. It was not a game to any of us any longer. They were men and women with narrow, horrible minds, running round and round the same subject like moles in a trap, little moles, fusty and evil-smelling. And I was not so drunk as I thought I was.

'I'll be going now,' I said.

The olive-green man touched my sleeve with his hand. I shook him off; I did not want his hand.

'Those poems of yours are very good,' he said softly, 'very good indeed.'

I did not say anything; I knew how bad they must be if he should praise them.

'You would probably like to see them in print,' he said; 'every writer likes to see his work in print. I bring out a paper every month; it is circulated privately – among my friends in the quartier. I should like you to contribute something.' Little fusty mole in his trap. . . .

'No,' I said, 'no, I don't want to do that.'

'Oh! come,' he went on, 'you know perfectly well you do.'

'Yes,' said the putty-face fellow, 'yes, you really must.'

They smiled at me, nodding encouragement, and then at one another, and I hated the loathsome intimacy of their smiles. I did not know them. I did not see why they should get anything out of me, especially not that part of me.

'Perhaps it's a question of money,' began the other girl.

'Is that it?' they asked. 'Is that it?' and they hemmed in round me like spiders ready to suck. I shook my head, I wanted to go away.

'Look now,' said olive green, drawing out his note-case, 'if I give you a hundred francs, will you write down for me those three poems with a paper and pencil?' He snapped the bundle of notes before my eyes. I looked at the one on the top, crisp and yellow. 'I tell you what I'll do,' he said, 'I'll give you a hundred and fifty francs if you'll write down those poems and let me have the entire rights. I'll publish them in my paper under my own initials. You'll be free of them then of course, but isn't it worth it to you – a hundred and fifty francs?'

'No,' I said, 'leave me alone.'

The bearded Carlo got up, pushing away the table. 'It's no use,' he said; 'he's drunk, don't let's bother with him. We're wasting our time.' They all got up, they turned away from me, irritable, shrugging their shoulders.

I wanted the hundred and fifty francs, though. I wanted them badly. I could not let them go from me. Dirty little moles.

'Wait,' I said, 'wait – give me that pencil, I'll write down the poems for you.' They were friendly at once, helpful over-smiling. The pencil quivered between my shaking fingers, the words ran crookedly, anyhow, across the page. The bearded fellow patted me on the shoulder. 'That's right,' he said, 'you're a good fellow, we know that.' I did not care for his sympathy.

'Give me the money,' I said.

They gave the two notes into my hands, and then they gathered up the sheet of paper, and they all crowded together, their eyes searching it, their lips moving, pressing hard, eager to see the words once more, fearful lest I should have missed anything.

'It is all there?'

'Yes – it's all there.'

They moved away, and across the street to the Rotonde, not bothering about me any more, and I lost their backs in the crowd, and I did not bother about them either. I folded the two notes carefully, and put them with the five-franc note that had hitherto stood between me and starvation. I went back to my own table in the corner. A hundred and fifty francs. That was not so bad. A hundred and fifty francs for three poems. Dirty, fusty little moles. My mind was clearer now, and I did not want it to be clear. I called the *garçon* to bring me another cognac.

Still the figures passed up and down in front of the Dôme, and the lights flickered opposite at the Rotonde. The taxis rattled and screeched over the cobbled stones of the Boulevard Montparnasse.

I looked at my watch, the hands pointed to half-past one. I

had done well, very well indeed. I had sold three pornographic poems for a hundred and fifty francs, and I had not thought about Jake for three-quarters of an hour.

Paris was a grand place, and I was a grand fellow.

I went on drinking and sitting at the café.

2

Seventy-five francs I spent on drink. At that time it did not seem to me that there was any point in saving money. I had left the Rue Vaugirard, of course. It was not humble enough for me now. I found an attic at the top of a gaunt bare-faced building in the Boulevard Edgar-Quinet. There was a laundry beneath me, and a dirty *épicerie* where they put stale slabs of chocolate in the window, bottles of congealed sweets, and sticks of thin spaghetti. Flies used to fasten on to these, and drowse sleepily in the sun against the hot dusty pane.

My room was at the back of the building; it looked down upon a square court where all the dogs of the neighbourhood, poor, restless, flea-bitten mongrels, used to come regularly to make love. It was almost impossible to sleep, the heat was terrific, and no air seemed to find its way into the tiny room from the high window. I would wake up in the middle of the afternoon – I used to try to sleep during the day and spend the nights outside at a café – and there would float up to me from the court the boiled hot smell of dirty linen in soft soapy water; this was the work of the *blanchisseuse*, and the irritating scream of her voice 'Marcelle! Marcelle!' and then another smell of rubbish left in the corner of the yard, not cleared away, and used as a lavatory by people who did not mind, and the monotonous murmur of voices arguing in the room beneath me, a baby fretful and the smell of wet blankets and milk in a bottle, and then, sharp and sudden, the squeal of a bitch in pain, and a panting yelping dog, and somebody laughing, and somebody leaning out of his window with a fat belly and a white shirt, yawning horribly, and the rasping sound of a throaty, high-pitched gramophone playing the same tune over and over again.

And away down the boulevard the groan of a tram, the tinkle of its bell, and the heavy wheels of a cart lumbering over cobbled stones, the silly rise and fall of a taxi's hooter, and again 'Marcelle! Marcelle!' screamed the *blanchisseuse*.

I could not sleep, so I lay on my back and read the torn page of an old newspaper printed on green paper. I read the account of an assault in a wood near Rennes, and a thief battering a woman's head in Tours, and then the day's racing at Maisons-Laffitte, a cycling course at St Denis, and so on to the advertisements of '*masseuses*' at Montmartre, and pills for *impuissance*, and how to cure '*l'action brève*' by a special treatment guaranteed '*dans trois jours*'. Then getting up from bed, not bothering to wash or to shave, and yawning a little, and lighting a cigarette, and so down the grimy flight of stairs to the dusty street, and crossing the boulevard, and walking about to stretch my legs, and then sitting down at a café and watching the people, and drinking too much.

So, as I have said, I drank away seventy-five francs, and got myself a head like a closed-in barrel and a tongue like a lump of suet, and then I had enough, so I went to bed for two days, and slept as though I had never slept before, and I did not eat a thing and all I drank was the water out of a jug that stood in the corner of my room, tepid water with refuse at the bottom like brown sand.

So now I was sober, and conscious only that I was hungry and unwashed, and that there remained to me seventy francs or so, and something had got to be done with it, and I was without question the weakest damned fool that had ever gone under because he was alone.

Thank God I was alive, anyhow, and could feel as good as this, in spite of starving, in spite of having filled myself with drink, and thank God the blasted heat had broken at last, for there was a grey sky and a cool wind blowing, and a sting in the air like autumn.

I went out to a place and had a bath and a shave, and a haircut and my clothes brushed, and ate a grand meal, and I knew now that I was free again, although I should always remember, I knew I could come and go as I wanted, and my thoughts were my own, and I did not have to be haunted, but would keep it beside me as a thing of beauty set in a place apart; I could start with a clear mind and an untroubled spirit, and never again would I be tortured by the memory of Jake, nor the silent beach and the staring cliffs of the Baie des Trépassés. I crossed over from the Rive Gauche to the Paris that I did not know, the shops and the theatres, the jewellers' windows, the American voices, the Cook's tours. . . . And that gave me an idea for a job, for what could be more right and obvious than I standing, megaphone in hand, beside the driver of an open char-à-banc, with a sea of tired faces gazing up at me, horn-rimmed faces and Panama hats, white-haired old ladies, schoolgirls sucking sweets, and pointing to the right and to the left, waving my free arm: 'We are now coming to the Place de l'Opéra; on the right you see the famous Rue de la Paix leading to the Place Vendôme and' (the wretched attempt at jocularity) 'I dare say you ladies would like to take a peep into some of the shops if it wasn't for the impatience of the gentlemen.'

Ha! ha! the titter, the pathetic rustle of amusement, and a stout, red-faced old Englishman leaning forward in his seat, nudging his friend, straining to catch the eye of a scarlet-lipped, full-breasted little prostitute who crosses in the stream of traffic, slowly hesitating, hobbling in her high-heeled stumpy shoes.

'We're seeing Paris all right,' they say: 'Casino de Paris, Folies-Bergère, Montmartre after dark, and the things fellows tell you about that go on in the Bois.'

I watched them from the pavement, and it seemed to me ridiculous and a little wearisome that everyone must be incessantly occupied with the same subject, those Englishmen in the char-à-banc, that girl who glances away self-consciously, those two mouth against mouth in a closed taxi, that man pretending to read a paper at a kiosk, that fat priest into whose hand a passing advertiser thrusts a warning against syphilis – they were every one of them obsessed and aware of themselves, they were fusty and mole-like as my olive-green-faced man who had bought the pornographic poems to sign them with his own initials.

155

And I was one of them, I thought about it too, and we were all alike, whispering, nodding, smiling behind our fingers.

This is filthy, I thought, this is bloody filthy, and then I looked at a girl with long legs and a mouth, and it did not seem so bad after all, so that I laughed at myself, wondering why I should bother, anyway, and I sniffed at the air that was light and full of a good Paris smell, and the day had turned out fine, and I felt well, and things were fun, so I went to Cook's to find out about a job.

There was nothing doing there, of course; I was sent off to another office in another branch, and at the next place I had to sit in a waiting-room for an hour and a half while a little clerk with inky fingers and bad breath wrote my name in a book, was called to the telephone, asked me a question, and then telephoned again, finally disappearing for ever and then coming back and saying he was sorry, but he had not anything for me, and perhaps would I call in during the week. I felt like a drink, but that was no good because I had a new thing about not drinking, so I went soft in a café and had a struggle with something called a *café Liégeois*, and then out again in a search for work, wondering whether some sinister hotel would take me on as a night-porter, or if I should haunt the newspaper offices, poems in hand, and tell them in lofty tones that I was my father's son.

That was too easy, though, that was giving way, so I put the little idea away back in my mind, and I tramped around poking my nose into bureaux and offices, with a smile on my face that did not mean a thing, and I ended up the day in a totally unexpected position, selling shirts behind the counter of a sports shop in the Rue Auber.

It is not fair to myself to say I did not try. I did try, for three solid blasted months. I sold shirts during three weeks and then I got the sack because I had a drink I did not want on a Sunday night, and when I woke up it was eight o'clock on the Monday evening. So I crawled along to the Rue Auber like a whipped puppy on the Tuesday morning, but they did not think much of me, judging by the reception they gave me, so I went out with a wave of my hand, saying to myself that it had been worth it, anyway, on Sunday night, and the next thing I knew was that I was on a stool behind another counter; this time it was a Travel Bureau in the Avenue George Cinq, and I had to talk intimately about the comforts of a wagon-lit between Paris and Biarritz to spoilt young women who did not care to go. I became amazingly familiar with train services; I warmly praised the fittings of the third-class carriages that were attached to the non-stop running from Calais to Trieste; I suggested that it was simpler to reach the Oberland by the Engadine Express and not the Simplon–Orient, thus avoiding a change at Lausanne; I ran my fingers over maps with an air of intelligence; I extolled the advantages of a tour in the Massif Central from Carcassonne to the Gorges Basses du Tarn, a tour in six stages with one day's rest at Millau and everything included except wine.

Then, when my fluency had reached an astounding pitch, when I had quoted without a tremor the interesting fact that 'Sables-d'Or has all the amenities of a modern seaside resort, the absence of currents and the high temperature of the water allowing aquatic sports at any hour of the day, and little wonder that it has been named, and justly so, the Plage Fleurie', when I was called up to the manager in his private office, and was told that I wasted the time and patience of every client who spoke to me; anyhow, this Bureau was run for the purpose of reserving seats in trains, and not as an advertising firm for the hotels of the Côtes du Nord.

So once more I lost my job; that was after a fortnight, and now five weeks had gone by, and during the next five I became in turn assistant to a dealer in old furniture, period Louis Quinze, little gold chairs with cane seats, and stiff cabinets with straight legs; then I pressed clothes at a dry-cleaner's, straining away perspiration with camphor-balls, and then a lift-man at a *boîte-de-nuit* in the Rue Fontaine, where I left rather hurriedly in the middle of one night because I was expected to go to bed without any warning, some elderly lady rather long in the tooth having expressed '*une envie*', which I felt I could not satisfy even if I had followed the advice of every advertisement in the green paper; then I interviewed faith-healers who wanted their names put in the back page of the *Christian Science Monitor*.

Finally I opened the door of a dingy apartment off the Boulevard Clichy and showed nervous young men into one room, furnished with a table and a pot of ferns, where they waited restlessly until the adjoining-room – furnished with a sofa and a looking-glass – was left free for them by other young men, cured of their restlessness, for the payment of forty francs and the enjoyment of a quarter of an hour's interview, and sometimes less, with 'Madame', a charming, generous woman who sucked *menthe*, and told them to be sure and come and see her again, presenting them with her card. After this I felt that it was impossible to sink any lower; there was no greater degradation now that life could bring to me. I had reached the limit, and yet there was some solace in the fact that I was able to laugh at myself. That was the only thing that remained, the ability to laugh. The rest had gone – pride, ambition, self-respect, dreams, and thinking about Jake. The last little experience *chez* 'Madame', the pot of ferns, and the *menthe*, had broken these right up; it seemed to me that there could not be any mortal thing left by the sort of life she stood for, the sameness, the inevitability, the sheer appalling boredom of it. I knew that if I stayed much longer in her atmosphere of *menthe* I should lose even the quality of laughter. It had started as a joke, and now it was not a joke any longer; it had passed from a stage of disgust and loathing to a dangerous placidity and indifference. If I stayed there I should never be free, I should get warped and distorted like an insect in a spider's web. I had to get out of it, and get out of it quickly. I remember leaving the place suddenly one afternoon about four o'clock in a kind of horror that had never come to me before, a surge of revolt rising up in me like a wave of nausea, and I walked dazed and blindly along the Boulevard Clichy; then up the narrow streets – up – up – and climbed the back-breaking steps, and then out on to the space below the Sacré-Cœur, and sat with my chin in my hands beside a group of tourists and a lot of screaming little boys. I did not hear them, but I just sat there looking over Paris, shivering in the cold air, watching the dark sun set away in the distance beyond the hills of Meudon, and a chill mist rise from the Seine and settle upon the towers and the spires, and it was grey, it was winter.

So then I knew I could not go on living as I did; I was not built that way. I had not any strength and resistance, and I was not Jake, so I had to acknowledge to myself that this time, anyway, I was beaten. There was a little weak spirit in me that kept whispering and hammering at me, saying: 'It's not my fault, it's not my fault,' and I listened with a half-smile and a shrug of my shoulders. It went on to tell me that this life was not my life, that it was useless to fight, ridiculous to bluff out a pretence of existence. I was not built that way – no, not that way. The voice told me that it was my father who was to blame. He was responsible for this moment, this business of me dejected, helpless, sitting on the steps of the Sacré-Cœur. It was heredity, environment, upbringing, misunderstanding, all these clashing against each other making me what I was. It was his fault; it had nothing to do with my will or my desires.

So the voice went on and on, and I listened wearily, nodding my head, and I snatched at the crumb of comfort that it gave to me, saying that now it was enough. I had fought and I must give in; it was not surrender, it was giving in to understanding and strength. The arguments of that voice were soft and easy to hear, it had caught from me the trick of making pictures, and it drew a figure of me sitting at a desk curiously like my father's, with a pen between my fingers, writing, writing, covering the white sheets of paper with little black dots of words, and then another picture of me standing in a group of men, my father there too, his hand on my shoulder, and I was not only his son bearing his name, I was myself. . . .

So it came to me quite suddenly, lifting me from the despondency into which I had fallen, coming clearly out of a mist as though it had always been, that I must write – that writing was my thing.

Now that I was not stifled in that atmosphere of home, nor smothered by his presence, his will over mine, his silence compelling me all the time – it was my duty, now that my father was distinct from me and I no longer his rebellious shadow, now that I had learnt, however humbly, however foolishly, something of life other than myself – I would shake clear of lethargy, and make supreme above everything, untouched, pure, coming from within – this business of writing.

I would not write because I was expected to; I would write because I must. Because it was the strongest thing, and I wanted to be swept away by it to the exclusion of everything else.

Then I went down from the Sacré-Cœur, and the grey had faded now and darkness come, and the cafés and restaurants were open and ablaze with light in the Place Pigalle, men and women crowding the pavements, the men with their faces nipped from the cold, the women drawing their coats close, standing in the cafés by the glowing braziers, and a smell of steaming chestnuts filling the air.

I went away down to my funny small room above a coiffeur in the Faubourg Montmartre, where I had lived since the autumn, and I lit the gas and drew my chair up to the bed that stood for a table, and I kept my coat on because of the cold.

Then I dipped my pen in the bottle of mauve ink I had borrowed from the coiffeur, and spread out two sheets of paper before me that I had also borrowed – and I thought hungrily of the supper that awaited me, bread and sausage, Gruyère cheese and a Camel cigarette, and so, with my old hate gone and a new hope risen, I sat there and wrote a letter to my father.

It was difficult because I had never approached him with any intimacy before. I had been a member of his household, subservient to him; he had accepted me as a customary part of his daily life, aside from his writing, as a piece of furniture, belonging to the place, just a child and then a boy, but holding no inner life of my own, being only of importance because I was his son. Never had there been any words of meaning between us, no moments alone, no consciousness of our relationship, until that last day when I had flung my poems on to the desk before him, and even then no betrayal of what he felt towards me, only the question in his eyes, his face upturned to me. So I had to begin as one stranger to another, ignored, blundering, at a loss for words, unable to touch him by a call for sympathy, feeling with each stab of the pen that it was impossible ever to explain away the storing up of those years of anguish and discontent, culminating in that fevered declaration in the library. Nor could I

160

bring myself back to the reality of that time. I was different, I did not feel it any more. There had been ships since then, and riding over the mountains, and Jake. As I wrote I could not make them come true, the sensations of the old days. It read like a cold plain statement of facts; there was no depth behind it. I could not explain Jake either, my father would not understand. I could not say: 'I met a fellow called Jake and he made me see things differently. He's dead now. . . .' What had my father got to do with Jake? It was useless telling him about that.

Nor would I prostrate myself, be humble, be ashamed; it was not forgiveness I asked for; this new state of mine was not a state of being sorry; it was a definite appeal for understanding, an attempt for him to grasp my point of view, and above all for him to share with me my sudden cherished comprehension of writing.

I said to him: 'I don't know whether you ever expected anything much from me. I don't know whether I was important enough to you to become a disappointment. When I left home you may not even have been aware that I was gone. But in spite of the fact that we never knew one another I have something within me that belongs to you, that you have given to me without your conscious knowledge, and I long – beyond anything in the world – for you to tell me that you understand. However indifferent or antagonistic we may feel, we can't help being part of one another, you and I. Maybe creating me was a little thing, unimportant, something of a mistake, but I'm alive as much as any of your poems are alive; I came from you, and my body is yours, and my blood, and even though you never realized it, you let me grow from a child into a boy blighted in some hopeless inexplicable manner because of your own glamour. I had your greatness and your brilliance thrust upon me, and I was left untended and alone, lost in my personal inferiority, made wretched by the sense of it, loathing mediocrity because I was your son. Often I wished you dead, often I wished you to be a separate distinct personality that I could cherish stories of, somebody in a photograph of whom I could build up little fancies, little dreams, and smile, hugging my knees, when I listened to the things you had done, told me by my Mother, a different

161

Mother – more gentle, more tender – who would see in my face the memory that was you.

'And I would say to myself: "He was like me, he would have understood." But instead of this you were alive, you came and went about the house, and I was only a boy too shy to speak, so that from the beginning until the end our lives were not bound together as in the depths of me I longed and prayed for, and you were not my father and I was not your son.

'I missed all the joy that goes to make up the lives of other boys; I missed you not carrying me on your shoulders as a child, nor taking my hand when I was afraid, not laughing up at me from the ground as I climbed a tree or found a bird's nest, not throwing a ball to me across a field, not leaning with your hand on my shoulder. I missed not being able to run and tell you things, not racing over the lawn and dragging at you, pulling your arm excitedly, wanting to show you something; above all, I missed you as I grew older, missed not having you as a companion, not sitting alone with you, listening as you talked, and then you smiling at me, suggesting what I should do with my life, connecting me with you, giving me the warmth of your personality and the blessed security that we were part of one another, and you understood.

'It hurt me to be so terribly proud of you, and for you never to know and never to care; it hurt me that I could not ever say with any truth or meaning: "My father and I – my father and I . . ." '

As I read over these words it seemed to me that they sounded like little senseless protestations, coming too late, unable to change all that had happened, and I felt he would skip over them restlessly, rather bored, thinking to himself: "What is all this about? I suppose he wants some money." So I broke off and went on to tell him about my writing.

'Up till now I've existed more by good luck than anything else, I've knocked about, I've mixed with people and I've learnt things, and I know now that all that isn't any good to me any more, that I've got to write. I believe that if I stay here in Paris it will come to me and I'll give every ounce of energy to it I possess. I won't tire, I won't slacken. A fellow I knew – he's

162

dead now – said that if I ever wanted a thing enough, if I gave myself up to it entirely, I'd get it and I'd be all right. I think he knew me better than I did. It's not going to be hard starting if I feel you know about it and you understand.

'When you get this, and if you have not put me right away from your mind, would you send me a letter and tell me so? It would mean so much to me, so much. . . . I can live ridiculously cheaply in Montparnasse, but if you would write me a letter, that is what I ask for, beyond anything, so that I shall know at last that we are not apart from one another, you and I.'

After this the blank space, the hopeless search for words, and then giving it up, and writing down the childish conventional ending, so formal it sounded, so cold – 'Please give my love to Mother. I hope you are both fit, and everything is all right. – RICHARD.'

I posted the letter that evening; it was nine-thirty by the time I had finished, and I went out with it at once to catch the last post. Then I came back and ate my supper. It was a Tuesday, and I calculated that my father would not receive the letter until the Thursday morning, down in the country. He would probably take a day to think it over. Then, supposing he wrote on Friday, catching the afternoon post, which would leave Lessington at five-thirty – that would mean the letter would travel Saturday – no, I did not think it was possible to expect an answer before Sunday. Sunday at the very earliest, probably Monday. I would have to hang around for five days with nothing to do. In my mind I would travel with the letter, cross the Channel with it, lie beside it in the van from Paddington, watch it sorted in the Post Office at Lessington, rest in the postman's bag as he bicycled along the hard main road and turned in at the drive by the Lodge gates.

I wished now that I had not sent it; I wished that I was somebody else and that it had not anything to do with me.

I remembered a line I might have crossed out, I remembered a sentence I could have phrased better. And, anyway, I had not said what I had wanted to say.

Wednesday, Thursday, and Friday passed, hopeless days when I pretended to myself I did not mind; I had made too much of a thing, and on Friday afternoon I walked very hard in the Bois, to Boulogne and back; it was cold, and I could not keep warm any other way. And when I got home to my room in the Faubourg Montmartre, Friday evening, I went upstairs and opened the door, and there was a type-written envelope pushed under the door, lying just inside.

I took it in my hands and went over to the window, and stood for a few moments, not doing anything. Then I lit the gas and sat down on the bed and tore open the envelope.

I pulled out one slip of folded paper. It was a cheque for five hundred pounds. There was not any letter. I laid the cheque aside, and looked once more into the envelope to see if I had been mistaken. No, there was not any letter. I went on sitting there with the empty envelope in my hands.

3

I found a room in the Rue du Cherche-Midi. It was a fair size, and heated, not badly fitted up, at the top of the building, too, and I could put a chair and table by the window and look out over Paris.

There was a jeweller on one side of the house and a dealer in antiques on the other.

The Rue du Cherche-Midi is one of the longest streets in Paris; my end of it opened out into the Boulevard Montparnasse, so that I was back in the quarter I liked and close to my cafés.

I gave myself time to settle down and to look around and to buy one or two things. I had been going about looking like a tramp all the autumn, and now I tried to force myself to regular working hours, breaking off for meals and intervals of rest, but not at stated times, going out and eating only when I felt hungry, throwing myself on my bed and sleeping only when my brain seemed to close up like a shutter, and it was impossible to let anything through. This happened often, of course. I found it incredibly hard to concentrate, and I would sit at my table beside the window with a sheet of paper before me, something hammering at the back of my mind, struggling for release, and then my will refusing to give way, my thoughts straying, wandering in the air, following some trend of their own which I could not control. At other times words seemed to flow from me, effortless, tripping over themselves, and my pen tore across the paper as though it were guided by mechanical means, and I would cover sheets with this scribbling; then, flushed and excited, I would read over what I had written, to find it empty of meaning, spiritless, uninspired, not even the sentences hanging together, the very phrases clumsy and ill-framed, the dialogue stilted and unnatural, and most of what was written appearing to me in my cooler moments as unnecessary and superfluous to the main theme. It was cold too, sitting still, the *chauffage central* being poor at most times. I never sat without a coat with the window tightly closed, and my limbs would go numb and my fingers stiffen, so that I made the cold an excuse for leaving the room, and, going out into the street, crossing to the Boulevard Montparnasse, and dropping inside a café for something to eat or to drink.

I would tell myself that this business of sitting in a café saved me from becoming used and stale, that the change of atmosphere and the view of people coming and going opened and cleaned some recess of my mind, so that afterwards I could go back refreshed, stimulated, eager to work for several hours at a stretch; but somehow deep down I knew this to be false. I knew I would return to my room with my brain much the same as it had been before, only a little more distracted, a little more capable than ever of making pictures of what I had seen; pictures of a man sitting alone with an empty glass in front of him; a girl in a red hat looking over her shoulder, two Hungarians speaking with their hands, and these things were not any good to me and my writing; they were only solitary pictures, interesting to me alone. They were not of the slightest value; they carried me away to no purpose. I said that winter was a bad time, that it was hopeless to expect my mind to concentrate when my body was cold. Paris was merciless in winter, the air was stiff and harsh as though a frozen breath had blown from heaven upon the city, leaving it quite still, wrapped in a hard glaze, the very solidity of the cold penetrating the quivering frame of my body. I would come out of a café and stand at the edge of the pavement waiting for the traffic to pass, with my shoulders hunched and my chest caved in, the expression of my face set in deep lines, immobile and seared, and then walk swiftly, my head bent, the cold forcing its way within me, creating a vivid sense of pain. There was something cheerless and forbidding about my room in the Rue du Cherche-Midi; it seemed warm at first only because of the comparison with the temperature outside, and then after a little while the first temporary warmth would dissolve into a chill airlessness, and I would sit there with my coat on, my mind numbed, my body too, and my spirits at zero. The cafés were kind, though, the glow sent forth by the hot braziers, the relief given by a strip of matting after the frozen sting of a pavement. The comfort of other people's body-heat, all of us crowded together, and voices, and the smell of food; being hungry and tearing at the crisp burnt bread, spreading a spot of hard butter, the genial satisfaction of meat, covered in a strong sauce, yellow and steaming, and then the potency of Gruyère cheese, the gulping of bitter coffee, and breathing into my lungs the nearness of the people, the bustle, the clatter, the haze of cigarettes. There was not anything like this, the satisfying of hunger. It seemed to be the only thing that kept the soul alive. I had to walk, too, to bring some life into my body. I would fight against the timidity of the first encounter with the icy breath of the still streets, and force myself to stand straight, not bent and cowed with cracked lips and watery eyes; then I would get a tram from St-Séverin which took me to Boulogne, and walk like a madman along the deserted *allées* in the Bois, passed sometimes by horsemen, blue with the cold, their horses stamping on the stiff sand, the breath coming from their nostrils like a wreath of thin smoke.

In February the Seine was frozen, great cakes of ice floated on the surface of the water, blocked together, swirling majestically in the current of a stream, and it looked like the breaking up of an Arctic river, white and relentless, the ice lumps cracking and tossing against each other in strange confusion.

There was a certain exhilaration in this, that Paris should be in the grip of such a thing, the slow procession of crushed ice on the surface of the Seine. It was as if the idea of it had been thrown on to a vast canvas, a splash of grey and white, and the picture of it remained with me in the cramped space of my room, making me forget about the cold, remembering only the magnificence and strength of winter that burst unhindered, scornful of humanity, caring not at all. When the thaw came the streets ran with water, the rain falling from the leaden sky like a sheet aslant, spattering on to the cobbled stones, twisting round corners in a gust of wind, and a thousand-odd lights were reflected in the shining puddles, the striped blinds of a café, the black skirt of a priest, the rain dripping from a spout on to his broad hat, the purple coat of a woman bent under an umbrella. One day a watery sun showed itself for a few hours, and there was a break in the sky as large as a man's head, a little patch of pale blue, and next day I was awakened by a bird singing, and a streak of sun making a pattern on the floor, and when I went out there was a woman at the corner of the street in a green shawl selling oranges, a girl without a hat running in a check dress with a basket on her arm; the doors of the cafés were open, letting in the fresh clean air, and the tight black buds on a tree had loosened during the night, softened and were round, little shoots of green coming into view, curling like feathers.

People did not hurry any more; they were no longer nipped and strained, they wandered along the boulevards looking into the windows, they sat down outside the cafés and read a paper, somebody laughed, somebody whistled, and trams flashed past bright in the sun, a child bowled a hoop followed by a little barking dog, and a girl strolled on the arm of a young man, a new blue hat on her head.

Then I knew that the old winter was gone, and this was a breath of something new, sparkling and dancing in the air. I wanted to capture it somehow and hold it close, this trembling joyous thing infinitely precious, and I went on walking with no purpose, listening to the clash of bells from a church as they struck *midi*, a troop of boys running from school, their satchels slung over their shoulders, girls chattering, linking arms.

White clouds were spun in the sky, and the fresh wet streets echoed the blue and the golden spots from the sun. An old man stood by a kiosk with a straw hat and a cane, and a little red flower in his buttonhole. Surely a most ridiculous old man. There was a sparrow at his feet, hopping about, nosing for crumbs, absurdly expectant, and from a window above a café a woman leant shaking a rug, pausing an instant looking along the street, her dark hair caught in a sudden frame of light. Then she turned away, back into the room, and the old man sauntered across the street, swinging his cane, his hat on the back of his head, and the sparrow lifted his wings suddenly and rose into the air, fluttering, dipping, losing himself above the roofs and was gone.

I strolled along with my hands in my pockets, smiling for no reason, singing a song.

I knew now that I should be able to write, that the words I had already written would count for nothing, would pass by as though they had never been, and that when I went into my room I should throw open the window and let this fresh sweet air lighten the dull walls, and I would sit down with a new strength, that had not as yet been part of me, rising from within, powerful, beautiful and true. I would work as I had never worked before, purified, possessed, a light coming to me, breaking through the dark and dusty channels of my mind.

This was great, this was how I wanted to feel, this was the grandest thing that had ever happened. I went into the Coupole to get something to eat, and then to shut myself afterwards in my room, confident, supremely alone.

The restaurant was very full, I had to share a table with a girl. I looked down at her, excusing myself, and she glanced up with a flash of a smile, not answering or taking any notice. She wore an orange béret and she was eating macaroni, spilling it, twisting it round on her fork.

So I saw Hesta for the first time.

I remember I ate macaroni, too. I had never liked it before, but I glanced sideways at her plate, and somehow she made it look good, so that I felt that there was nothing in the world I wanted more than macaroni. She spread herself at the table, taking up more room than she needed. I sat on the edge of the seat. I felt I had no right to be there. It was too late to make some excuse and move away. The table was narrow, very cramped for two people who did not know each other.

It seemed silly not to be talking. Yet it was obvious that if I started some form of conversation it would only be because I was a man and she was a girl, and I had looked at her and seen that she was pretty. She did not seem to be aware of me at all, so I left it and went on eating macaroni. We handed butter and bread to each other without speaking. People passed up and down in front of our table. A boy with long hair wandered about with a portfolio under his arm. He seemed to be looking for a free meal. I felt that his pictures would be bad. The girl stretched out her hand and reached for her half-bottle of Evian. Her fair hair had slipped a little from under her orange béret. I thought suddenly that it was fun to be living alone in Paris and writing a book. She finished her macaroni and began peeling a tangerine. I had a tangerine, too. She spat a pip on to my plate by mistake, and then she spoke for the first time.

'I'm so sorry,' she said.

'It's quite all right,' I said.

We went on eating our tangerines. She was making a mess of hers, not breaking it into filters, but sucking it noisily, getting the juice all over her fingers.

'They're awkward things to eat,' I said.

'I don't think so,' she said. There did not seem much reason to go on with the conversation.

I pretended to be interested in something that was happening at the other end of the restaurant. I wrinkled up my eyes and stared thoughtfully, and then broke into a smile, acting very hard. I don't believe she noticed anything of this. When I glanced at her to see she was looking in the opposite direction. I gave it up as a bad job and offered her a cigarette. To my surprise she took one. I spoilt it, though, by bringing out a lighter that did not work. There was not even a flicker of a spark. She reached for a match as though she had expected this, while I went on jabbing at the wretched flint, blackening my thumb.

'It doesn't matter,' she said kindly, 'I always use a match myself.'

That did not help me, though, what she did; that was not the point. I had not made the beginning I had wished. I ought to have leant towards her carelessly, with a suggestion of confi-

169

dence, my left hand flaring the lighter to her cigarette, then shutting it with a snap, and calling to the waiter for my bill. Instead of this I sat meekly, accepting a light from her match, wondering what I should say.

She was friendly now, there seemed to be a bond between us because she was smoking one of my cigarettes.

'You are an artist, I suppose?' she asked.

'No,' I said. 'No; as a matter of fact, I'm trying to write a book.'

She looked at me gravely.

'That must be very difficult,' she said.

'Yes,' I said.

I was sorry I did not appear as though writing were easy to me. Perhaps she did not think I took it seriously.

'I've been working on it all the winter,' I went on hurriedly; 'I guess I'm too critical to let things slide along anyhow. I tear up a whole lot before I am satisfied.'

'Of course,' she said.

I did not see why she accepted that as natural. After all, plenty of writers just fired straight ahead. I felt as though I wanted to go on talking to her about my book; I would have liked her to sit there and ask me questions. Still, I had to get her things over first.

'What do you do?' I asked.

'I study music.'

'Oh! that's great.'

'Yes – I like it,' she said.

'Music and writing have much in common,' I said, trying to get back to myself again, 'and I should think Paris is about the best place to do both. What do you say?'

'Paris is quite nice,' she said. 'Nice' seemed to be the wrong word.

'No, you mean it's vital, terrific,' I said; 'you mean there's something about Paris that gives you a mental slap all the time, and you can't just sit still and do nothing. You've got to work, to keep up with the pace, the sting in the atmosphere.'

Suddenly I felt like talking a great deal. 'And it's not only over here in Montparnasse you feel it,' I went on, 'it's the other side too, the electricity in the air. There's nothing dead or used about it, everything is glowing, everything is alive. You stand in the Place de la Concorde, like any common tourist, and you look up the Champs-Élysées to the Étoile – that long slope, the line of traffic – why, it gets you, it does something inside you, you want to throw back your head and shout.'

She smiled vaguely, as though I were a fool.

'I prefer the country,' she said.

'Oh! sure,' I said, 'the country's all right; I love a day out in the country, but not to live, not for any length of time. Why, it's the same, it doesn't change, but here in Paris it's different every day, there's a throb of excitement all the time, a suggestion that any moment a tremendous thing is going to happen. If I lived out in the country I'd have to dash up every second in case I was missing something.'

She turned away, shrugging her shoulders.

'You're mad,' she said briefly, dismissing me. It seemed as though my words had gone for nothing.

'Where do you live?' I said.

'I'm staying at a *pension de famille* in the Boulevard Raspail,' she answered; 'it's fairly comfortable, but they are rather strict about hours. They don't like you getting back late. Not that I mind much, as I don't go out a lot, not in the evening. It's too cold, anyway.'

'Just the feeling that they minded would be enough for me,' I said; 'I wouldn't let myself be tied at all. I've got a room in the Rue du Cherche-Midi. Not much of a place, but I can do as I like.'

'Yes,' she said.

'It's marvellous,' I went on, 'not being stuck at some job that can't be left. You see, with writing I can choose my own time. I can work or be slack, just as it pleases me. I get away any time I like and come and have a drink.'

'I should find that rather distracting,' she said.

'Oh! Lord, no, not a bit of it,' I answered, laughing; 'once you get the hang of it you can empty your mind at any moment. Then when you go back you just pick up the thread where you left off.'

I could not make out whether she was impressed or not. She was looking at me, but her eyes seemed to drift a little way beyond.

I thought if I went on talking she would go on looking at me like that. It was the grandest thing. I tried to make my voice as monotonous as possible, so as not to wake her up out of her dream.

'It's no good waiting until ideas come,' I said softly, 'otherwise I'd just sit around and wait all day. I have to force myself, as much as a bricklayer forces himself to lay bricks. And I daresay it's the same with your music, you have to work your fingers at scales and arpeggios, you don't wait until some melody comes floating out of the air. You hammer away . . .'

She did not seem to notice what nonsense I was talking. She just gazed in the distance, through me as it were, and I knew that in a moment I would not be able to go on talking, but I would have to prop my elbow on the table and lean against my fist and stare at her, losing myself. It was not fair to look as she did. It was not fair to think we had sat through the whole of our lunch without speaking. Nobody in the world could talk more nonsense than I at that moment.

'You loving the country,' I said, 'I expect you're absolutely right about that; you don't have the look of belonging to this sort of rush and scramble, you ought to have things made easy, you ought to – I don't know what you ought to do. Listen, aren't you glad the winter's over?'

She laughed then, she seemed to wake up and take notice once again.

'What's that got to do with all you've been saying?' said she.

'A whole lot,' I said, 'but I can't explain; maybe you wouldn't understand, anyway. Gosh! I feel grand today. I felt grand when I woke up this morning. I leant out of my window and it wasn't raining, and there was a patch of sunlight on the pavement opposite, and a girl without a hat running along with a dog. The air smelt good, fresh and sweet, somehow, and the striped blinds of a café were fluttering in the wind. The puddles in the street were blue, same as the sky.'

'Those are nice feelings,' she said. I saw then that "nice" was a word of hers. 'In the Boulevard Raspail it's difficult to breathe in that way,' she went on. 'I share a room with another girl, she's Austrian, she sleeps with her mouth open and dark hair spread all over the pillow. She likes the window shut very tight while she

172

dresses, in case anyone should look in, passing by in a tram. That's silly, isn't it?'

'Very silly,' I said.

'So I miss the fun of getting up in the mornings like you,' she said.

I could see the Austrian girl lying spread-eagled in an untidy bed, her hands tossed awkwardly, her face putty-coloured and flabby, and this girl waking and sitting up very straight, her eyes solemn like a child, gazing at a square patch of sky through the window which she could not reach.

'Yes,' I said, 'but you get away from the pension, out in the street, and you walk along with the wind catching at your hair, and people passing you, laughing and talking, and an old woman selling flowers, and then surely you smile because you can't help it, and you feel fine.'

'I like the way you describe things,' she said; 'it's funny, but it's nice. I know what you mean about smiling and an old woman selling flowers. It's being happy for no reason. Do you put all that in your book?'

'Oh no,' I said, 'my book is very serious, there wouldn't be any point. I guess it would look silly written on paper.'

'I suppose it would,' she said.

'D'you know, I can't remember when I last talked like this,' I said, 'but it seems a long while ago.'

'I expect you get out of the way of it; always writing your book, you don't have time for people.'

'No, it's not only that. The fact is, I don't know anyone.'

'That isn't very nice for you,' she said.

'I haven't exactly thought whether it was nice or not,' I told her, 'it just happened that way. Maybe it's all wrong, maybe I ought to go about a bit, see places and do things.'

'You don't have to if you don't want to,' she said.

'It's all right for you,' I said, 'you aren't lonely ever, you can always talk and go around with girls.'

'Oh! girls . . .' she said, and shrugged her shoulders, 'I haven't much use for them, I'd rather be by myself.'

'I wish it was real spring, and not just the beginning,' I said; 'it's still cool to be out of doors a long time. If it was real spring,

173

and you hadn't anything else to do, we could get a train out to Versailles; we could walk a bit in the gardens.'

'I like Versailles,' she told me, not committing herself.

'There's a whole crowd of places to see,' I went on, 'round and about Paris. Even if you've seen them once, you can always see them again. Gosh! I think Paris is wonderful. I wish I were rich though, I wish I had a car.'

'Perhaps you'll get a lot of money for your book,' she suggested.

I did not want to talk about my book so much as I had before.

'Oh! I don't know about that,' I said, 'but if I had a car I could drive you right out in the country if you liked; you'd be able to stroll around. Why, Fontainebleau Forest will be looking splendid soon, the trees and everything.'

'What about your work?' she said.

'It's not so important I can't leave it now and again,' I told her. 'Why, it's bad to get stale, to get in a rut. That's a fatal thing to do. Do you study your music every day?'

'Yes,' she said.

'You should take a holiday now and again and go to it fresh,' I said.

'Well, I don't stick at it solidly for hours on end, I have my lessons at stated times, and then I go back and practise. I come out to lunch, like I'm doing now; then sometimes I have shopping to do, one or two things to get, or I wander about or I go into a cinema.'

'I've not been inside a cinema all the time I've been in Paris. I guess I never thought about it before. We might go this afternoon?'

'No – I've got my music.'

'Listen, you can chuck it for once.'

'No, I have a lesson.'

'That's too bad. You're mighty conscientious, aren't you?'

'I don't know.'

She called the *garçon* for her bill.

'I wish you'd let me pay this,' I said. She looked at me in surprise. 'Don't be absurd,' she said.

'No, honestly I mean it,' I went on.

'Certainly not; thank you very much all the same,' she said.

174

'Perhaps you're annoyed with me for suggesting it,' I said; 'maybe you think we haven't known each other very long.'

'Oh! it's not that. I don't want to be churlish. But I like to be independent.'

She was gathering up her things, her bag and her music-case. She was more aloof now than ever. I did not seem to know her at all.

'I'm sorry about the music lesson,' I said, 'but I do hope I shall see you here lunching again. Do you ever go up to the Dôme or the Rotonde for a drink?'

'I go there sometimes,' she said.

'I've never seen you there.'

'Well, it's big.'

'I'd have noticed, though.'

She was good when she stood up. She was small, and thin. She wore a sort of brown suit. She pulled her orange béret over one side, showing her left ear.

'Would you be at the Dôme tomorrow?' I asked.

'I don't know.'

'I'd give you some tea, or coffee or something.'

'That's nice of you.'

'If you're not there tomorrow perhaps you'd be there the day after, or some time during the week?'

'Yes.'

'That's fine. Why, if it goes on keeping warm like this, we could go out to Versailles one day.'

She smiled vaguely, looking over my head.

'I shall be late for my lesson,' she said, and then she held out her hand and shook mine gravely, politely, as though we were two people in a drawing-room.

'Good-bye,' she said, 'and good luck with the book.'

Then she turned and walked away down the long *allée* between the tables and turned the corner, and so out through the swing doors of the Coupole, her back very straight and slim.

I sat there thinking I might have walked with her as far as her music place. Perhaps it was quite a long way. I called the *garçon* and paid my bill and hurried out into the street, but I did not see any sign of her, and I did not know which way she would have gone. The sky had clouded over a little since the morning, but it was not cold. There were a good many people sitting outside the Dôme. I saw a fellow in a straw hat. Well, anyway, I had got to go back to my room and work. This was the day when I had promised myself to start really seriously. The winter was gone; it was March; there was not any excuse, and I felt fine, too. I ought to sit down and work until about eight o'clock in the evening. This gentleness, this little breeze, this kick in the air, had given me the grandest feeling. I had awakened in the morning knowing I would be able to work at last, and I had not changed at all since then. The air was marvellous. I was not hungry. I was not cold. It was fun talking to that girl. I'd go to the Dôme to-morrow about four o'clock. It would be fun if she made a point of going there often, at a certain fixed time, so if I got away from work I should know where to find her. It would be great if she went there every day, if we always had a certain table by the brazier. The *garçon* would know, he would keep it for us. I'd tell her about my book. She could talk about her music too. Maybe she would be able to get away into the country after all, one Sunday, surely. She'd like the forest at Fontainebleau. Especially if she was fond of the country. She really ought to see it.

Still, here I was back in the Rue du Cherche-Midi. It was a good thing I was so close to the Boulevard Montparnasse. I should not care much to live anywhere else.

I went upstairs to my room, and I leant out of my window. There was still a clean sweet smell, the clouds had not made any difference. A chair-mender came along the street, halting every now and then, blowing his thin bugle, gazing up towards the windows. A chained dog in a yard somewhere started to bark. He hated the noise. I could hear the grinding of a tram away on the boulevard. Then I shut the window and sat down at the table, searching for my pen, fumbling amongst my papers. There was a whole lot of stuff that ought to be written. I lit a cigarette, and began to concentrate, stabbing at the blotting paper with my nib, drawing little figures. It was queer, though; somehow I did not feel so much like working after all.

4

I went to the Dôme next day at four o'clock, but the girl was not there. I hung around for a good while, too. Perhaps she had been kept at her music lesson. Still, we had not made any definite plans. She did not have to be there, of course. I went the next day, too, and the next. I kept crossing over from the Dôme to the Rotonde in case she should be sitting at one end and I at the other, and I should miss her. She was not at either, though. I suppose she could not manage it. I walked one evening down the Boulevard Raspail to try and see if I could find her pension. I did not really go there because of that; it just occurred to me as I went along. I thought I might as well walk down the Boulevard Raspail as anywhere else. I could not see the place, though. One evening at the end of the week I went to the Dôme about six o'clock. It had been raining all the afternoon. I had stayed in my room and worked, in my fashion. I went out about six because the rain had stopped and I wanted a breath of air. I passed the Dôme more from habit than anything else; I did not have any real hope that she would be there. I stood on the pavement and bought a paper from the bawling fellow who sold them here every evening. I did not really want to read it. Then something made me look up, and I saw the top of an orange béret behind a crowd of tables in the Dôme. She was sitting right in the corner. I crumpled up my paper and pushed my way through to her. She was reading a book, and crumbling a *brioche* in her fingers. I had to touch her on the shoulder before she looked up.

'Why,' I said excitedly, 'whatever did you stick yourself back here for? It was just a piece of luck I saw you. I happened to raise my head, and spotted your orange béret. Well, how are you?'

She stared at me, marking the place in her book with one finger.

'What?' she said.

I stood on one leg, grinning stupidly, feeling a fool. I had somehow thought meeting her again would be different from this.

'I'm sorry,' I said, 'I expect I startled you. Only I've been here every evening hoping to see you, and been disappointed, and now

I have seen you it got me kind of excited for a moment – I didn't think.'

'It's all right,' she said; 'sit down,' and she smiled.

That was better. I drew a chair up next to her, and I smiled too.

'What's your book?' I said, not caring, and looking at her.

'It's nice,' she said; 'it's one of Kessel's. I always like his things. Do you know it?'

'No.' I fluttered the pages vaguely. 'No, I'm not much good at reading French.'

'I suppose you read a lot in English?' she said.

'No, not really, I don't get much time,' I said.

I did not want to talk about reading. 'What have you been doing since I saw you the other day?' I said.

'The same as usual, music lessons, practising – Oh! I went to a cinema, and I had dinner up in Montmartre the evening before last.'

'Did you? Why didn't you come here?'

'I never thought.'

'Didn't you once think of coming here?'

'No, I don't think so.'

'Why did you come today, then?'

'I was up this way.'

It was rotten to think she could have come if she had wanted, and she just had not bothered, and I had been hanging round every evening.

'Did you go in a party?' I said.

'Oh! No – just two girls from the pension.'

I was glad about that. It had probably been quite dull.

'How's the writing going?' she asked.

'The writing? About the same. I've worked most days, on and off. Listen, you're going to have a drink with me, aren't you? You'll have another cup then – here, where's that fellow gone to – or would you rather have something else?'

'I'm not thirsty.'

'Sure. What? Oh! yes, rather. *Un autre chocolat.* Listen, what were we talking about? I say, I'm terribly glad to see you. I might have missed you but for your orange béret. Always wear

178

it when you come here. I love this place, don't you? Look at that chap with the ginger hair – he's crazy. Gosh, this is fun – that *chocolat* looks rotten, have something else. Are you sure you aren't cold?'

She shook her head, biting her lip.

'I'm all right,' she said.

'You're laughing. Why are you laughing? I guess I'm a fool.'

'No – it's nothing. I wasn't laughing. Go on talking.'

There did not seem anything to say, though. I felt I had been stupid. I sat in silence, watching her drink her *chocolat*. After a while I forgot about being stupid, and I went on talking.

'Tell me what you did in Montmartre. Was it a good party?'

'I told you it wasn't a party,' she said.

'Oh no, nor it was. Did you like it, where did you dine, was it full of Americans? That's the worst of Montmartre, you can't avoid them. It's bad enough here. Wasn't yesterday a marvellous day? I thought you might have been here yesterday. I wondered what you were doing.'

'I went after my lesson to have tea near the Trocadéro,' she said.

'Did you? Where did you go? I know the Rue de la Tour; the tram stops round there on the way to Boulogne. Did you take the tram 16? I wish I'd known.'

'Were you there yesterday too?'

'No, but I'd have imagined you going along in the tram. Do you ever walk in the Bois? I wish it was summer, March is a dud month. There's a whole lot of things people can do in the summer.'

'What things?' she asked.

'Oh! I don't know. Sort of mucking about. I'd like to get one of those funny steamer boats and go up the Seine to St Cloud. Did you see it when it was all frozen in February? It was great. The Seine, I mean. Like an Arctic picture. Have a cigarette – you don't have to go yet, do you?'

'No,' she glanced at her watch.

'That's fine. We'll go inside if you get cold. I say – you couldn't have dinner with me, could you?'

'Not this evening; thank you, though.'

'Will you another evening?'

'I might perhaps – I'll have to see.'

'What sort of a place is this pension of yours? It sounds rotten. Do they let you out on time or what?'

'No, it's not so bad, really.'

'I'm hanged if I'd live in a pension. Do they treat you like a kid? How old are you – or mustn't I ask that?'

'I'm nineteen,' she said.

'Are you? In some ways you look younger than that, in other ways older. I don't know . . . Here, I'm being rude, aren't I?'

'No, I don't mind.'

'I haven't said anything awful, have I?'

'No.'

'It's wonderful of you to let me sit here and talk to you. Gosh! I get fed up by myself sometimes. I don't mean I like talking to you because I'm bored being alone, I mean – I wouldn't get any kick out of talking to just anyone – I'm rotten at explaining things. D'you see?'

'Yes – of course. It's nice of you. I'm like that, too, about not talking to anyone,' she said.

'Are you? That's marvellous, isn't it?'

I couldn't stop myself from smiling. It was fine to be able to agree with her over things. It made me feel in with her, as if I knew her very well. Somehow I could not be such a fool if I thought the way she did. That's how it struck me at any rate. It did something to me to be able to talk to her. I wanted to agree with anything she said. I also felt mad, too, as though I were a little drunk, as though life were terrific all of a sudden, as though I wanted to shout. Or else never to say a word, to be struck dumb, to go on sitting there at the Dôme and looking at her. All these feelings mixed up in an incredible fashion. Mostly I was humble, though. I would abase myself, I would grovel with my face in the dust.

We sat for a while without talking much, watching the different people in the café. She was amused at them, she had a funny little smile all the time. I watched her, I did not mind about the people. I wished I knew how to draw. Artists must get a lot of fun out of drawing. I would draw her nose and the curve of her chin. I drew her profile on the table with the end of a match. It looked like nothing on earth. I rubbed it out with my elbow. She was quite unconscious of me. After a while she turned and looked at me, smiling.

'It's nice here, isn't it?' she said. I had not quite realized about her full-face before. It struck me, all of a sudden, that she was beautiful. I could not answer a thing. I just had to go on staring.

'What's the matter?' she said.

I felt myself going very red, it crept up above my collar, spreading to my forehead, my eyes.

'Sorry,' I said; 'I wasn't thinking for the moment. Yes, this is a great place. I always love it.'

She glanced down at her wretched watch. 'We have dinner at the pension at seven-fifteen,' she said, 'and they like one to change. I must be going. I shall be late in any case.'

I jumped up, too eager, too keen, overwhelmed by my new thing of wanting to please.

'Could I walk down the Boulevard Raspail with you?' I asked.

'It will take you out of your way,' she said.

'No – no – I'm in no hurry, I'd just love to, I'd like a walk.'

I paid the bill, and we crossed over the street. We came too soon to the pension. It did not look much of a place. There was a frowsy woman looking out of a top window. She did not see us, though. There were crowds of things I felt sure I should have said, but I could not think of one of them. I was afraid she might be bored if I asked her to come to dinner one evening. What would be the fun of going with me from her point of view? I could not imagine anything much worse. So that all I could say to her outside the pension was: 'I do hope I shall see you again,' and she said: 'Yes, I hope so, too,' and I said: 'Tomorrow, perhaps?' and she said: 'Yes, perhaps,' and I had to let it go at that.

She went inside the pension then, and I waited a minute, and then I turned and walked up the Boulevard Raspail once more.

I wondered if I should go back to my room and work, and then I thought that, after all, I had worked most of the day and there was not much point. It was not good to overdo things. So

181

I went and had some dinner, and then I dropped into a cinema and saw a bad picture. Somehow I had never thought of doing this before. It made a change. It would give me a fresh outlook on the book. I wished the girl had been with me all the same.

We were sitting at the Rotonde one afternoon. She had just finished her music lesson. I had got the table early, and had sat there waiting for her. I managed to see her nearly every day now at about five o'clock. It was a good time. She would be thirsty after her lesson, and a little tired. She had come one day, and then two days later, and then the next, and then the next, so that it had become a habit. She just arrived, either at the Dôme or the Rotonde, and I was always there. I used to work most of the day and then look forward to five o'clock. It gave some purpose to the day. It was wonderful to look at my watch about four and think there was only one more hour. I never did much work after that. I would knock off about half-past and then make a business of going over and booking a table and settling myself, and waiting for her. I wondered how I had existed before, when every day had been alike. Now I did not know how I could have gone on if it had not been for five o'clock. Something jumped inside me when I saw her walking along towards the café swinging her music-case. She always wore the orange béret. I called her Hesta and she called me Dick. I nearly split myself with talking, and she nodded, agreeing with what I said, or sitting very still, looking away, going off into some dream. I was not quite so humble as I had been. I discovered I had theories about things, I rather laid down the law. There were a good many matters it was fun to discuss. I had a queer feeling that deep down she was much more intelligent than I was, but she was ignorant of this, and it made her seem young. I liked this, I liked her being young. I felt I knew a whole lot. I was very old, I was very wise. I talked about life. When she looked at me, though, solemnly, with eyes that might have been sad, that were very deep, that I did not understand, then I was humble again, then I stammered and was lost, then I was young.

It was at these moments I was not content with just seeing her for an hour or so, at the Dôme or the Rotonde. I wanted her to

182

have dinner with me, to go to a cinema afterwards perhaps, and then a drink and a sandwich, and then to take her back to the pension. An evening with her, from five, say until eleven. There could not be anything better than that. Yet I ought to be content with my hour in the afternoon. I ought to be satisfied; it was hell how one always wanted a little more.

We sat then at the Rotonde and she was drinking an orangeade through a straw.

'Of course, people make the most absurd fuss about sex,' I was saying; 'they go on as if it was the only thing in the world that mattered. And it's nothing really, it's just a little phase in life that scarcely counts. Men and women ought to make love like they play a game of tennis; they ought to consider it a healthy, physical necessity, and no more.'

'I don't know,' she said thoughtfully, 'it leads to all sorts of complications.'

'It shouldn't do,' I insisted; 'that's where the mistake is made, in taking it so damned seriously.'

It was fun having this sort of conversation. It meant we knew each other well, we were modern, and we hadn't any old-fashioned ideas. I could talk about anything to Hesta.

'The thing is,' I said, 'that children are brought up all wrong. They aren't taught to have any sense of proportion. The truth is kept from them like a shameful secret. So they get a wrong idea. I think education ought to be entirely changed.'

'How would you change it?'

I thought for a moment, I was not quite sure. It was easy enough to talk, but difficult to keep up.

'Why, I'd have kids learn not to expect so much,' I said; 'I'd have them know everything before they were grown up, so that they would not be disillusioned afterwards. They ought to be told that it means nothing, just nothing.'

'Yes – but then everybody would go doing things all over the place,' said Hesta, 'and women would have babies all the time.'

I laughed, she was very young.

'Oh no,' I said, 'that would be kept well under control. Besides, people only do things, as you call it, because they've been told it's wrong. If they thought no more of it than shaking hands nobody would bother.'

'You said it was a physical necessity?'

I frowned, I was getting rather mixed.

'Yes – I mean that, too. At least – it depends on the individual. It's no use laying down rules. I mean – here, will you have another drink?'

'No, thank you.'

'I wish you didn't have to go back to that beastly pension so soon. You will have dinner one evening, won't you?'

'Yes.'

'What about Friday?'

'I might on Friday.'

'We could have dinner and then go to a film. We could go to the Studio des Ursulines.'

'That would be nice.'

'It doesn't matter, then, you being late occasionally?'

'No, not occasionally.'

I did not know how I was going to wait until Friday. Even then it might not come off. She might be ill or something.

'You will come, won't you?' I said.

'Oh yes, I'll come,' she said.

I could not believe it was true. I wanted to get up and order people about. I sang out for the waiter, tilting my chair. I told him to bring me a drink.

'There's half an hour before you need get back,' I said.

Then I went on to lay down the law about marriage.

'I just don't believe in it,' I said. 'The very idea of tying two wretched people down for life – it's barbaric. It's insulting to even the average intelligence. Of course, in fifty years' time nobody will be married at all.'

'What about children?' she asked.

'Oh! that will be arranged by the State,' I said vaguely; 'there'll probably be kind of institutions run for the purpose. I dare say polygamy will come in, for men and women; I mean, both sexes will do as they choose. There won't be hard-and-fast laws. Of course, nobody will think any the worse of a girl if she has a hundred lovers or only one. But the idea of marriage – gosh! –

it makes me sick. Two damn fools sitting down at a breakfast-table day after day, just because some parson has mumbled a few words over them. A settled home, probably very drab, and the man getting home tired and irritable, and the woman always having babies and losing her figure, and going on pretending they like it . . .'

'You don't make it sound very attractive,' she said.

'The whole thing is rot,' I said firmly. 'Who invented it, any-way? Some old idiot in the Bible. It makes me sick. The sen-timentality, the pathos, the incredible muck talked about – I say, are you getting cold?'

'Just a little.'

'Oh! Hesta – Lord, what a damn fool I am, keeping you here in this draught; why didn't you tell me? – here, come inside.'

'I ought to go.'

'No, no, you needn't go yet. You've loads of time, you don't have to go. Listen, I've got so much to say. Sit down again, please sit down. Look, here's a table just by the door. Have another orangeade. Yes, do, one more orangeade. The time goes by so fast, you only seem to arrive and then you go again. We don't have a moment. Ever played this game with the paper off the straw, Hesta? Everyone does it at the Dôme. Look, I tear the paper in sections, making the figure of a man. Here's his arms, here's his legs, there's his bit of a head. See? Then I blow drops on it from the orangeade in the straw. Look, watch him wave his arms, watch his body writhe. It's good, isn't it, it's good?'

She laughed, leaning her arms on the table, close to me, her hair just touching my cheek. I did not want her ever to move. I felt excited, queer.

'It's good, isn't it, it's good?' I said.

We had dinner on Friday evening, and afterwards we went along to the Studio des Ursulines and saw a Russian picture. We sat in the very back row up against the wall, and there were students next to us, and boys who had come just for the fun of making a noise, so I made a noise too and stamped my feet on the floor when the lights went up, and whistled and howled when a bad film was put on the screen.

185

Hesta did not do anything; she laughed quietly, and watched us making fools of ourselves. I was a little above myself altogether. I could not get over the excitement of being there with her. Before dinner we had sat at the Dôme as usual, and when it was a quarter to seven, the time she generally had to go back to the pension, and she did not move, I could not believe it for a moment, and I had to turn away to hide my smile. She would have thought me a fool if she had seen me. I could not even talk much at first, I wanted to be still and undistracted, I wanted to be able to appreciate the fullness of it.

'You're very silent,' she said, and I had to give up looking at her and suggest somewhere for dinner. I wondered why she bothered to go out with me at all. She was probably bored the whole time.

We only seemed to have been at the Dôme a few minutes when I looked at my watch and it was a quarter to eight, and then we went along to the Viking for dinner, and that was gone in a flash too, so that all I had of it was a picture of her laughing in front of me, twisting something on to the end of her fork, and I bending towards her saying: 'This is fun, isn't it, Hesta?' and her nodding, and then a waiter passing, someone talking Hungarian behind us, and it was finished, she straightening her béret, I calling for the *addition*.

It was hopeless the way time did not stand still, not for a fraction of a second, that there was never an occasion when I could grasp the whole intensity of pleasure, examining it, breathing it, holding it softly with my hands and saying: 'Now I am living, now . . . now . . .' It was nothing but a series of flashes quivering before my eyes, dancing themselves away, and being in the restaurant, and sitting beside Hesta in the Studio des Ursulines, and strolling along the streets afterwards looking for a stray taxi: these were all reflexions that I had not gathered, but mocked me when they had gone and the minute had passed, so that afterwards, alone again, and she at the pension and I undressing in my room in the Cherche-Midi, I would have to make a thing to myself out of all these flashes, and imagine they had been greater than they were. The memory of her shoulder touching mine, and her hand on my knee, her face upturned, laughing at the film, seemed to me now to give a deeper thrill than I had experienced at the time; thinking of it produced a delight and a pain I had not felt when it was happening. So I wondered how much of all this was reality and how much was imagination, but at least the thought of her had become an obsession that would not leave me, and I gave way weakly, making no effort to withstand it. I was conscious now that scarcely for a moment did I think of anything else.

After the evening at the film I was restless and dissatisfied with going back to the old routine of seeing her at five o'clock. The next evening, when she rose to go at a quarter to seven, I had to remember that the night before she had stayed, and now it was all over, and perhaps another whole week would go by before she would come out with me again. The five-o'clock meetings had lost their value.

I pretended that knowing her, anyway, was a marvellous thing in itself, and that I must beat down my restlessness and my irritability at being dissatisfied with what I had, so when she was gone I would go to my room and throw myself into a frenzy of work that meant nothing, for there was her face staring at me across the table, sometimes solemn, sometimes gay, her eyes larger than any eyes had ever been, the fair hair slipping down from under her orange béret.

So that working was not any good to me, eating and sleeping were not any good to me, nothing was any good to me but seeing her, and that not occasionally, but all the time.

On Easter Sunday she came with me to Versailles, and after that we made a fixed thing of every Sunday going into the Bois and walking if it was fine, or staying in Paris and seeing a film if it was raining. She liked going to concerts, too, because of her music, and I would go with her, not understanding much about music, her sort of music, but just for being next to her and watching her face, enrapt, immobile, following the meaning of it. At Versailles she fell into a mood of sadness that it was no longer a palace, when people had walked in the galleries, proud and supreme, kings and princesses, the sweep of dresses rustling on the floor, the hum of voices; and now there was a guide with a flow of meaningless words, and us not bothering to listen, and a man

187

yawning behind his hand, and a group of schoolgirls giggling at a young soldier who had followed them.

'Oh! Dick ...' said Hesta, 'Oh! Dick! ...' and she did not go on with her sentence, and I said: 'What is it?' and she sighed and looked out of the window in the mirrored hall, down the long avenue and the last two trees at the end, between which the sun set in a ball of fire, and she said: 'All this – it's gone, never any more,' and I did not know whether she meant the beauty of what had been, the colour and the pageantry, the something that was France and was now nothing but Americans in straw hats, saying: 'Jesus!' caring not at all, or whether she meant our little day, and our being together, that would never happen in the same way again.

I took hold of her hand and smiled and said: 'It's all right,' and she said 'Yes,' and she smiled too, and we went out of the palace and into the gardens, and I went on swinging her hand, but we did not say very much.

It was warm at the end of April, like a heat-wave, premature and sudden; the trees were a riot in the Bois, and the chestnuts bloomed in the Champs-Élysées; the cafés hung out their sun-blinds, and their sun umbrellas, and people sat out, limp and dusty, tired after one day, the women in thin dresses and no sleeves, the men with hats tilted at the back of their heads, wiping their brows with handkerchiefs.

In the Place de Concorde the fountains played, and children ran bare-legged in the Tuileries, the sun beating down on the gravel paths, colour everywhere, blossom, a smell of early summer, open taxis massed together in a block below the Pont d'Iéna, a gendarme whistling, waving his arm, and then the traffic sweeping over the bridge, the water of the Seine grey and sluggish beneath. Hesta could not bear staying indoors at the pension in this weather. She would come out in the evening with me two or three times a week now. We would sit at a café and have a drink, watching the people, or we would go over to the other bank, into the Paris we did not know so well, where there was greater heat, and more glitter and noise, more people, a certain excitement and suggestion of gaiety different from our Montparnasse. Here we were younger, and yet older in a thousand ways; here we were not so light-hearted, not so gay, but wrought and bewildered in a new way, I restless and swept by a strange excitement, impressed by all these people who were wanting the same thing as myself, and Hesta, lovely beside me, flushed, not so remote, and we were aware of each other, laughing, looking away, catching our breath.

One evening we had been inside a restaurant where there was music, my sort of music, a saxophone throbbing beneath the melody, a moan and a sigh, and something that went on beating, getting quicker and quicker. Then they played a tune, low and humming, a little wailing note coming from nowhere, and the time was perfect. There were people dancing. I said: 'Dance?' to Hesta, and she nodded, and we got up on the floor, too. I knew I was no good at this; it would not be any fun for her, but for me it meant holding her, and, being very close, her hair touching my cheek. She seemed small, smaller than I had realized, and she moved as though she had no will of her own and was part of me. I did not know what was happening at all. I just went on holding her, and she held me, too, and it was unlike anything that had ever been before.

When the music finished we went, she had a coat over her arm and a béret in her hand, and we passed through the doors and into the street, the lights flickering, people's faces passing us, meaning nothing, and I shouted for a taxi – a yellow Citroën came grinding up, stuffy and closed, but it did not matter, and we got in, not speaking, not knowing what was going on anywhere or where he should take us. I took hold of her, burying my face in her hair, and I felt her heart beating and her body trembling. I had never dreamt it possible that I could go on kissing anyone for so long. Still I did not speak, but clung to her, not letting her go, and she lay quite still, and then turned away, with her head against my shoulder.

'Hesta,' I said, 'Hesta, darling, you don't mind, do you?'

'No – I don't mind.'

'It's so marvellous, being with you; I couldn't go on any longer, Hesta, not doing anything.'

'No.'

'Put your arms round me.'

189

'Why?'

'I want you to. Put your arms round me.'

'Where's the taxi taking us, Dick?'

'I don't know – it doesn't matter. I love you so terribly.'

'Dick – they'll make a fuss at the pension if I'm late again.'

'No, they won't. It doesn't matter. You can't go back yet;
you can't. I'm not going to let you go. Hesta, you must keep
your arms round me; you must. I've got to kiss you again. I
can't help it. Oh! darling – Oh! darling . . .'

There had never been anything like this.

'You're not angry; say you're not angry?' I said.

She took my face in her hands, and I saw her eyes were troubled,
sad.

'I don't want you to kiss me any more,' she said; 'I want you
to take me home,' and her voice was a little shadow of a voice,
coming from far away, bewildered and lost.

'You don't hate me, do you?' I said. 'Hesta, if you only knew
what this means to me, loving you. Darling – don't go away,
please don't go away.'

'You know I don't hate you,' she said, and her voice was still
muffled and strange, as though it were frightened of itself. 'That's
why I want you to take me home. Tell him where to go, Dick.'

'If I say drive straight to the Boulevard Raspail, will you
put your arms round me again, will you kiss me, too, like you did
before?'

'Yes.'

When the taxi drew up in front of the pension she pushed me
away, and she sat very still in her corner, looking out of the
window, her hands on her lap.

'Hesta,' I said, 'tell me what you're thinking; you're unhappy,
darling, you're sad.'

'No,' she said.

'What is it?' I said.

She looked back at me then, and she was solemn, and she came
close to me once more and put her arms round me, her face
against mine.

'It's queer,' she said.

'What's queer, beloved?'

'All this . . .'

'Why, my darling, why?'

'I don't know. It's queer to me. I've never loved anyone before.' she said.

'Oh! darling . . .'

'I never wanted to love anyone. I wanted to be free. And now it's come, and I don't know what to do about it. Dick, what am I to do about loving you?'

'Hesta, sweetheart, it's marvellous, so marvellous . . .'

'I've never felt like this, Dick.'

'Felt like what?'

'Queer – I can't explain. Let me go now.'

'No, darling, no.'

'Please, Dick.'

'You're not angry with me?'

'No – no.'

'We'll go on being like this?'

'Yes.'

'I love you, Hesta, more than anything in the world.'

'Dick . . .'

'Let me kiss you once more – just like that – that's all. Darling, it's so wonderful, don't be sad. We won't ever be serious, will we, never, never?'

'Not if you don't want to.'

'I'll see you tomorrow?'

'Yes.'

'At five o'clock.'

'Yes.'

'We'll have dinner?'

'I don't know – I don't think we can, not again.'

'I'll see you, though.'

'Yes.'

'Good night, darling.'

'Good night.'

She was indoors, and I paid off the taxi and walked home up the Boulevard Raspail to the Rue du Cherche-Midi, not seeing where I went, nor what was in front of me, nor anything at all.

Knowing her now made the knowing of her before a small and pitiful thing. Then she had been an incident, something to look forward to at the end of the day, a relaxation, a method of casting oneself away after work, but now she was the whole purpose of the day, the reason why I went on living, and I stayed in my room and wrote only because it was a means of filling the time until I should see her. Generally she managed to meet me for lunch, and this at least was an hour, hurried perhaps and difficult, but better than nothing at all, and then she would have to go off to her music, getting away again at five to meet me at the Dôme or the Rotonde. If she could not manage dinner with me she would slip out of the pension for an hour or two afterwards, and these meetings, which once would have been miraculous and exquisite, were wretched snatches of time to me, gone in a flash, so that it seemed I was always outside the pension saying good night, and never sitting at the café waiting for her to come. The first part of the time would be spoilt by my restlessness and my hurry of looking forward to the last, and the last part was spoilt by her fretting she would be late at the pension.

We would take a taxi and tell the fellow to drive anywhere – the Bois, of course, was too far if Hesta had to be back – and so he would rattle along the streets and the boulevards, bumping over the tram-lines and the cobble-stones, and I going mad with Hesta in my arms, thrown from side to side by the filthy, jolting taxi, not being able to do anything, feeling like hell, not even kissing her properly. And then in a moment we were in the Boulevard Raspail, the drab front of the pension looming up ahead of us, and she was combing her hair, distant and remote, and I was staring moodily in front of me, my hands in my pockets.

'This is hopeless,' I said; 'we can't go on like this,' and she would stare at me bewildered, and put her hand on my knee, and say: 'What's the matter, Dick? What's the matter?' and I did not know how to explain, pushing her away almost roughly, and then holding her close again to say good night, and she would kiss me, not knowing what she did to me, and then was gone, and another evening spent.

It was not always like this, though, because on Sundays there was the day-time, and we went to places and saw things, and there was not the fever of being absolutely alone, thinking of nothing but ourselves. Now that there was this business of intimacy between us I was no longer shy of her, no longer speechless when she looked at me, no longer humble. It made a whole lot of difference. The very fact of kissing her and holding her, it meant that I knew her well and I never had to be awkward in front of her, that there was no strangeness left for us. There was the fun of being together, of laughing at the same things, of swinging hands across a street. There was the fun of going over what we had thought when we first saw each other, I looking down above the table in the Coupole at a girl with fair hair under an orange béret, and she glancing up and not taking much notice, seeing any sort of man without a hat.

It seemed to us that there wasn't a past and there wasn't a future, but this was our time, this bright day, this warm evening, and these little momentary plans meaning so much and so much.

She did not talk about her music, nor I about my book; they were tiresome bothering things not worth the trouble of mentioning, part of the day's routine, like cleaning our teeth; and we did not talk about war or death, or other men or other women; but we sat at a table and looked and laughed, and lost ourselves in looking, and did not talk at all.

There was the fun of nonsense, of pointing up at the sky above her head and saying: 'See that patch of blue, the square bit, between the two clouds, you can have that . . .' and she sucking her lemonade through a straw. 'What, that bit, only that?' and I, considering the matter for a moment, screwing up my eyes: 'Maybe you can have the clouds, too.'

And knowing we were fools, and other people could not hear, and reaching for her hand, and kicking at her ankle, and, anyway, that man who went out of the café leaning on a stick was old, old . . .

So we jumped up from the table, and swung along the streets, and we laughed at a fat priest climbing on a bus, and we laughed at a thin boy with long hair like a girl, and it seemed there had never been such laughter and such fun, until we were in the taxi and then I wasn't gay any more, but tortured and distressed, with her face against my shoulder, and her hands around my neck.

And 'Hesta, darling, what's going to happen about us?' I said. 'What's going to happen?' and 'Aren't you happy?' she would say, and she would not understand.

One Sunday it was a funny grey day, heavy and spitting rain, but it was hot, too, so that we did not want to be inside at a cinema or anywhere much, and we had coffee after lunch by the Luxembourg, and then went into the gardens to stroll about, to amuse ourselves with the people. There was an old woman selling balloons, and Hesta had to buy one, swinging it by its cord in the air like a child, and I bought one of those lemon *sucettes* on a thin stick, and we walked along with sober little bourgeois families, dressed in their blacks, gloved and furred, staring at us as though we were crazy.

There were two priests, large and greasy, glancing about them from side to side under their broad black hats. 'I don't like priests,' said Hesta, and I asked her why, and she said she hated to think of their bodies under the robes, and she was sure they had queer habits.

Then we saw a young Saint-Cyrien out with his sisters; we were certain they were his sisters, for he was red in the face and bored, and they were hanging on to his arm; and we saw a fat woman on a seat fanning herself, screaming in the ear of her neighbour.

And we saw a tall Englishman, very correct, white-haired, cane in hand, walk solemnly along a gravel path, and a girl flounced past him, rouged, mincing, lifting an eye, and he stared at her stiffly without a quiver of his face, but when she had passed him he turned round slowly, his eyes beady, enquiring, and followed, solemn as ever, along the path where she went.

There were children running with hoops, a little boy throwing a ball into the air, and a tiny girl who fell flat on her face, baring her round behind naked to the world. And we laughed, and I said: 'It's fun, isn't it?' and Hesta said: 'Yes, it's nice,' and we went on being happy, and looking at people and things. Suddenly the sky seemed to burst over our heads, and the rain came down. Everyone ran for shelter. We were near to the entrance, and there was a rank of taxis just outside, so we got into the first one that was there.

'Where shall we go?' I said.

'I don't know,' said Hesta.

'You don't have to be back for ages?'

'No – not till this evening.'

'Do you know of any film?'

'I can't think – suddenly.'

'It's hopeless, isn't it?'

'You're getting wet, Dick; come in out of the rain.'

'Well, what shall I tell him?'

'I don't know – anywhere, it doesn't matter. You're getting soaked.'

'Shall we go to my room?'

'Yes – why not?'

'Shall I tell him, Hesta?'

'We might as well.'

I gave the man my number in the Rue du Cherche-Midi.

'I can't think why we've never thought of that before,' I said.

'There's always been something to do,' said Hesta.

'Well, it's a great idea, anyway,' I said.

The man was a fool about finding the number. He kept peering about him, and he went a few yards too far. I tapped on the glass and he pulled up the wrong side.

'Oh, it doesn't matter,' said Hesta; 'which door is it? We can run across.'

It was still raining hard. She bent her head and ran, laughing, and crouched in the doorway, and when we were inside she took off her cap and shook the rain out of it.

'Are you wet?' I said.

'No, not very,' she said.

I led the way upstairs to my room. I was afraid she would think it was awful. I mumbled something about it being untidy. She came in, swinging her béret in one hand, and her balloon in the other, and she looked round, and peered out of the window, and saw vaguely what it was like.

'It's nice,' she said.

'Oh! it's not bad,' I said, and I went and covered up my writing things with a piece of blotting-paper and then I thought perhaps that was conceited, as if I had thought she would go over and look at them.

She sat down on the bed, her back against the wall, and the balloon floated up to the ceiling, staying motionless in one corner.

I gave Hesta a cigarette, but I did not sit down; I moved about the room. It seemed odd having her there. She made it different. I knew it would not be the same when she had gone. I was shy and awkward, as if we weren't ourselves, and suddenly I did not know what to talk about.

'I wonder how long it will go on raining,' I said.

'I don't know,' she said.

We might have been two strangers in a dentist's waiting-room. I felt she ought to be turning over a magazine. I sat down on the bed, too, swinging my legs on the floor, forcing a whistle. Our cigarettes gave us something to do.

We did not speak for a long while. Then: 'I saw Briand the Minister this morning,' I said.

'Did you?' said Hesta.

I turned and looked at her and I could not go on being stiff any more, so I put my arms round her, and she smiled, and we weren't shy and strange then, but ourselves again.

'Oh! darling, I love you so much,' I said, and she held me very close, and I kissed her eyes and her mouth, and she clung to me, and we lay down together on the bed.

I said: 'Hesta, darling, Hesta,' and she said: 'Yes?' and I said: 'Can't I love you?'

She said: 'You are loving me.'

'No,' I said, 'really, I mean.'

'Oh! Dick – why?'

'Because I want to so terribly; I can't go on any longer, sweetheart, it's impossible – I must.'

'No – Dick.'

'Yes – darling – yes. Let me, say you'll let me.'

'I don't want to.'

'Oh! darling, it's because you don't know. Please, darling, let me.'

'No . . . No . . .'

'You don't care about me?'

'Dick, it's not that, you know it's not that.'

'What is it?'

'It's – I can't explain. Suddenly like this, it's not – I don't know.'

'Darling, you're making too much of it. It's nothing, my love, it's nothing. It doesn't mean a thing.'

'Oh! Dick, it does.'

'No, darling, not a thing. I love you so, you needn't be afraid.'

'I'm not afraid.'

'You won't have a baby, I promise you.'

'It isn't that . . .'

'Oh! darling, let me, I can't not – darling, please.'

'I don't want it to be like this. When I've imagined it – oh! Dick, it's been different, it's been lovely – we've been away somewhere, not suddenly in your room like this – not the daylight . . .'

'Hesta, what does it matter where it is? I want you more than anything, whether it's a room or a wood or it's night or it's eleven in the morning, none of that counts, darling. You don't have to be afraid of anything, darling, I promise you. Not a thing . . .'

'You don't understand.'

'Oh! don't go on thinking and worrying, Hesta; forget everything you've ever thought about. I love you so much, so much.'

'No, Dick, please.'

'Yes, darling. Yes. You've got to let me. Yes, I don't care . . .'

It was still raining. I stood looking out of the window, smoking a cigarette. People were passing in the street below bent under umbrellas. A little cat crept from the doorway of the shop opposite, and ran across the road, sleek and wet, his tail outstretched.

I could hear the bell of a tram as it stopped in the Boulevard Montparnasse. The sky did not seem to have cleared at all; it would be a wet evening. Outside on the parapet was the stump of the cigarette I had smoked the day before.

I watched a blind blowing backwards and forwards on the second floor of the house in front.

Hesta was still lying on the bed. She was staring up at the balloon that hung from the ceiling in the corner of the room. It did not seem to move at all. I chucked her a cigarette, but she did not take it. I wished she would not look so young. She had never looked so young as this. I went on gazing out of the window and smoking my cigarette. I kept my eyes fixed on the tiles of the roof, and it seemed to me that, suddenly, out of nowhere, born from a thought, I saw Jake's face looking at me, and we were in a circus tent, with the hot air about us, and the crowd swarming against the ropes. Jake – looking down at me.

It was something of horror, something of fear, and then it was gone.

Hesta was sitting up now, pulling at her dress. Why did she have to look so young? I did not know what to do, I did not know what to say. She glanced up at me, and smiled, and she seemed a child, with a child's smile. I wondered whether she expected me to sit beside her, and take her in my arms, and kiss her. If only she would not look like that. If only she were different. The orange béret lay at her feet.

The rain kept on all the time. Hesta looked up at me, waiting for me to be the first to speak, waiting for me to do something, to say something, as though in some strange way she asked for comfort. I did not know what to do.

I threw away my cigarette. 'Oh! hell!' I said, 'let's go out and get bloody drunk . . .'

5

After that day we did not meet so often at the Dôme or the Rotonde, but Hesta would come along to the Rue du Cherche-Midi instead. She did not want to at first; she always made some sort of excuse, and would pretend she was thirsty and longing for a drink at a café, or she would say there was a film she wanted to see.

198

It was not any good, though, she had to give in. We would be sitting at the Dôme perhaps, not speaking, I very moody, irritable, scarcely answering when she did say something, and she would lay her hand on mine and look across at me.

'Dick, you're funny today; tell me what's the matter?'

And I would shrug my shoulders. 'Nothing, what could be the matter?'

She would sigh helplessly, and insist. 'Please tell me, Dick; I know there's something, I can't bear it.'

Then I would laugh as if I did not care, and say: 'You know perfectly well, let's forget about it.'

She would hesitate, and look about her as though she were afraid people were staring at her, and then say: 'You mean, you want us to go along to your room?' And I said: 'Yes, but it doesn't matter.'

'If you want to so much, I'll come, Dick.'

'No, why should you?'

'Yes, Dick – it's hopeless sitting here, let's go.'

We would get up, I still sulky, not looking at her, and she quiet, oddly remote, and we walked along not talking much, but once back in my room I would hold her very close to me and say: 'Darling, darling, I was beastly at the Dôme just now, but it was only because I want you so terribly that it sends me crazy. Say you don't hate me, say you're happy to come here . . .'

'Yes, Dick, if it makes you happy.'

'But not only me, darling, you, too – it must be for you, too.'

'Yes – it is, I promise.'

And then afterwards everything seemed to be all right again, and I did not feel irritable and moody, and nothing mattered, and then I thought we might as well go out and have a drink, or stroll around, because there really was not much point in staying indoors any longer. I felt fine, gay and irresponsible; I felt like laughing at all the other people, and what fools they were, and I would walk with Hesta back to her pension, and if she could not get out again that evening it did not matter so very much, because, anyway, we had just seen each other.

So soon Hesta got into the habit of coming straight to the room, and we did not meet first at the café. The meeting part seemed forced now, a waste of time; it meant hanging about to no purpose, when we might have been in the room. The summer was definitely starting now, and on Sundays, and sometimes other days, we were able to go into the country. We went to Barbizon several times, and after lunch walked right into the thick of the forest, striking away from the tracks and the paths, and we used to lie down under the trees.

We found a special place, a sort of sand-pit with rocks behind us and ferns, very high above the trees, so that we could look down and there would be nothing but the forest around us as far as we could see, like a carpet made up of trees, and every describable colour of green. I had not ever seen trees like that except in Norway. I tried to remember always that it was Fontainebleau, and France. I did not want to think about Norway.

We lay down in our pit, with a beam of light coming down upon us through the trees. We never saw or heard anyone at all. Hesta went on getting lovelier; I could not seem to stop wanting her, she was so lovely. She gave up wearing her béret. She wore a yellow dress and she did not have any hat. Her hair was cut very short. I slept sometimes with my head in her lap, and she would sit still, cramping herself stiff rather than wake me.

'You ought to have told me,' I said.

'I liked you being there,' she said.

Hesta was funny, she asked questions, she wanted to know things about me. It was a bore having to talk over what had happened before. I was not interested in myself of the old days any more, of my home, and my father and all that. I was only interested in our lives, and living in Paris, and what we did.

'Tell me, Dick, I want to know everything you used to do,' she said; 'I want to know what your home was like, and what you thought, and – I don't know – just about you as a little boy.'

'Oh! it was deadly,' I said, 'there isn't much to tell. I can't think of anything that would amuse you.'

'It isn't for being amused,' she said, 'it's because – I can't explain – I want to love you in that way, too, as if you were a boy still, belonging to me.'

'Darling,' I said, feeling for her hand – but I wasn't really listening.

'Why did you run away, were you so terribly unhappy?' she went on.

'I expect I was a damn fool,' I said yawning; 'I was bloody ignorant, and I didn't know a thing. Sweetheart, how marvellous your skin is, just there, where your arm finishes – Gosh! I'll go crazy . . .'

'But tell me,' she said, 'didn't anyone ever understand you. I can't bear it – if only I'd known you.'

'That would have been good,' I said lazily, 'if we'd known each other as children – I guess we'd have been a filthy couple. They'd have sent us to a reformatory for immoral behaviour.'

'Dick – I do understand you, don't I, better than anyone?'

'Sure, sweetheart.'

'Better than your friend, that man you went away with, who got drowned?'

I did not want to talk about Jake.

'Oh! that's different,' I said; 'never mind about that. Darling, you're so lovely, so lovely, come close to me, near; can I do anything to you I like, can I sort of tear you in pieces?'

She was still thinking, though; she was still staring up at the trees.

'Oh! Hesta, beloved,' I said 'don't let's be serious. You said you wouldn't ever be serious. Life's too short, darling . . .'

And I put my arms round her and kissed her, and held her, and now it was she who smiled, and she who clung to me, saying: 'I love you, I love you.'

It was not very satisfactory, this business of Hesta living at the pension and me in my room in the Rue du Cherche-Midi. She was always having to get back just when I most wanted her to stay. Her music lessons, too, interfering with everything. Then even though she did come round to my room most days, it had to be at a definite time, and that spoilt things. Perhaps I would not be in a good mood until just before she was leaving, and then there was no time. Or she would be in a bad mood, nervy or tired. We would have little scenes over nothing at all. I used to say it was her fault and she would not answer, but I felt she thought it was mine. We went on like this through the summer.

Some days it was marvellous, a Sunday perhaps, and we would

have gone to St Cloud by a steamer up the Seine, amusing ourselves with the people, and come back in the evening to dine at the
Coupole, and so home to my room, where she would stay until it
was time to go. That was perfect; we loved each other and it was
finished, and anyway there was tomorrow.

Other days were bad. She would arrive when I was trying to
get some work done on the book, hopelessly difficult at all times,
and perhaps at that moment a flash of something like the truth
and meaning of writing would come upon me, so that I could not
bear to let it go, and she would sit on the edge of the bed smoking
a cigarette, while I tried to convey my flash into words of meaning.
It wouldn't be any good, though. It was impossible to concentrate; however still and unobtrusive she would be I knew that she
was there. She worried me, she sent away the flash, she crept into
my mind.

'It's no good,' I said, pushing away my paper and pen, 'I
can't write.'

'I'll go,' said Hesta, 'I'm in the way.'

'No,' I said, going over to her, 'I want you more then I want
the book.'

But somehow even that was not true. I was not any good for
either, writing or loving. They would not work side by side. The
memory of that flash spoilt the loving. I could not surrender myself entirely to Hesta, nor she to me. We were aware of that hidden flash between us all the time. We were not either of us happy.
We were not together. There was not satisfaction in anything
that happened. Afterwards it would be late, she would have to go,
and it all went for nothing. It was a waste. She would smile at me,
but I felt all the time she was wondering why she had bothered to
come. She was only being kind, and her kindness had not helped
me. The thought of the good days would no doubt force itself into both our minds, and we would wonder why it was not always
the same. We would not reproach each other, but we would put a
black mark against the day for having been a failure.

It left us uneasy, bewildered, not knowing what to do about
it.

Then she went, and there was not even a moment to talk, to be
ordinarily affectionate, to be glad about being with each other;

there was only time for the mechanical, 'I love you, darling,' and 'See you tomorrow.'

One day I said to Hesta: 'It's hopeless, you know, this life of yours at the pension. It spoils everything.'

She looked at me thoughtfully.

'I wish,' she said, 'I wish that we could be married.'

'Oh! darling.' I stared at her in amazement. 'You can't mean that. Why, marriage is terrible. You know how often we used to talk about it.'

'Yes,' she said, 'but somehow it doesn't seem so bad now.'

'We can't,' I went on, 'we wouldn't love each other half so much. Being with you wouldn't be a thrill any more. You'd just be my wife. We should take each other for granted.'

'I don't see that it would matter,' she said.

'Darling, you don't really want to be married. You haven't thought what it would be like. Seriously now, have you?'

'Yes,' she said.

'No, Hesta, you can't have. Why, at once life is stale, ordinary, going on the same day after day. Surely you haven't suddenly got moral scruples, have you?'

'Oh! Dick – that's horrid of you . . .'

'Sweetheart, I'm not being horrid. But marriage – you'd feel tied and so would I. The very respectability of it would finish things for me. It's perfect as we are, never being quite sure.'

'Sure of what?'

'Sure of life, love, you – I don't know. Listen, do you really want to get married?'

'Not if you don't want to.'

'Don't you see it would be awful?'

'Perhaps . . .'

'You do see?'

'I expect you're right, Dick.'

'Besides, there's no need. We don't have to worry over other people. You're independent and so am I. That guardian doesn't mean a thing, does he?'

'No.'

'It's not as if you were poor.'

'No.'

'What made you think of it?'

'Just an idea. We won't say anything about it again, Dick.'

'Darling, it's wonderful in a way, just to think you thought of it – I mean, as if you cared about me a bit – but it would be awful, wouldn't it?'

'Yes.'

'The thing is, you must leave the pension and come and live with me here.'

'There wouldn't be room.'

'Sure – I'll get the room next door. It's empty. I asked about it the other day. It'll be all right. It doesn't matter what you do here, anyway. Tell you what. We'll sleep in one room and use this as a sitting-room.'

'What about my piano?' she said.

'Oh! Lord. Listen, have you got to go on with your music after this term?'

'I can't give it up, Dick.'

'Couldn't you give it up for a bit?'

'I don't want to . . . P'raps I could go and practise somewhere; there must be places.'

'We might buy a piano if it comes to that,' I said.

'No, it would disturb your writing.'

'Well, I don't know.'

'What can we do?'

'It's up to you, darling. I want you to come and live with me more than anything in the world, but if there's going to be a scene about your music . . .' I shrugged my shoulders.

'I might give it up for a little while.'

'Honestly, darling, I don't see that it would do you any harm,' I said.

'It will be so hot, too, later on, won't it?'

'Terribly hot.'

'And, anyway, term ends in a few weeks. Perhaps if I don't practise through the summer the rest might help my fingers.'

'I'm sure it would, sweetheart.'

'I'd like to have worked up for the concert next term, though. The Professor is giving a concert, Dick; it's very important, famous people go, and he only picks out his best pupils to play. It sounds conceited, but – he said something about me.'

'Well, you can always see, can't you, later?' I said, rather bored.

'Yes – I suppose so. . . .'

'And you'll leave the blasted pension and come here, won't you?'

'Yes, Dick.'

'We'll have the most perfectly marvellous time, darling. It won't seem true at first, when you don't go back at nights.'

'It will be nice. . . .'

'You can do whatever you like all the time; we might go away a bit in August, we might go to Fontainebleau and stay.'

'Could we go to the sea?' she said.

'Oh no – not the sea. I hate the sea.'

'The mountains?'

'Mountains are bloody. . . . No darling, we'll go somewhere, never mind now.'

'I'm going to look after you, Dick.'

'Sweetheart – I don't need looking after.'

'Yes, you do.'

'Darling. . . .'

'You need looking after more than anyone, and I've wanted to for so long, Dick. I'm going to do so much for you.'

'Are you?' I said.

'Yes, as if I were years older than you, and you were dependent on me. I shall love it. All day – getting sausages for you, anything.'

'Sweetheart. . . .'

'Running out and buying you Gruyère cheese. Mending things – I can't mend at all. You don't mind, do you?'

'No.'

'When I think about it I have a pain here, in my heart, as though I can't breathe, because it's too much – too much.'

'Oh! Hesta, beloved.'

'Dick – I do wish I could have a baby.'

'A baby? Good Lord! whatever for?'

'I don't know. Sometimes I think I'll die unless I have a baby.'

'Hesta, darling, you're crazy! I can't imagine anything more of a cope. Think of it screaming about the place.'

'Yes.'

'Gosh! you make me laugh more than anyone. You – and a baby. What a mad idea. It's the funniest thing I've ever heard. It's a joke, isn't it?'

'Yes . . . it's a joke.' She turned away.

'I guessed you couldn't be serious. Listen, when are you going to leave the pension. Soon, very soon?'

'I'll try.'

'This week?'

'No.'

'Next week?'

'Perhaps.'

'I can't wait to have you here, Hesta.'

'It won't be long.'

'You'll get fed up with me sweet.'

'Why?'

'I shan't ever leave you alone.'

'I don't mind.'

'You're not going yet, are you?'

'What's the time?'

'We've nearly an hour, beloved.'

'Shall we go to the Dôme?'

'No, Hesta.'

'We can't go on staying here. . . .'

'Yes, darling. Darling, come here. You're going to stay. I want you to stay.'

She came and lay down beside me, and put her arms round me, and we were together.

And I said later: 'This is our thing, isn't it?'

'Yes,' she said.

'Nobody else, ever?'

'No, never.'

'We'll always go on being happy?'

'Yes, always.'

Hesta's term finished at the end of June, and she came to live with me in the Rue du Cherche-Midi. She told the people at the pension that relations had come over from England and taken a flat in Paris, and they wanted her to be with them. To her vague guardian she wrote that she was sharing a room with a girl who had left the pension and was studying music, too. She said that it was quieter in the new place, and it would improve her French. Nobody made any attempt to find out the truth. It did not seem to matter at all what she did. There were no worries of that kind. I was afraid that Hesta would be lost without her piano at first, but she said it was all right, and I forgot to ask if she missed it after a while. She said there was fun in buying things to make the two rooms attractive. She loved the Rue du Cherche-Midi; she used to wander up and down in it in the mornings, while I sat in my room trying to write, and she would come back very excited with an old chair under her arms, or a little cupboard, or a quaint picture dragged from the depths of one of the dusty little shops.

'It's nice, isn't it?' she said, and I smiled. 'Yes, that's fun,' and went on with my writing. I had left the book for a while and had started a play. I had written the first act. I was very pleased with it; it seemed such an achievement to have written the first act of a play. I was uncertain about the length, though; I was not sure how long an act should last. It did not take any time to read through. Perhaps that was only because I knew it so well, and the words flipped by, scarcely read, known from memory. I finished the act one evening, flushed and proud, and we went out to celebrate.

We had dinner, and then drove in a taxi round the Bois. We had drinks at the Grande Cascade. It was good, leaning back in a chair, looking at Hesta, lovely in a blue frock, and knowing we loved each other and lived together in a couple of rooms in Montparnasse, and we were both young, but we knew a lot, and I had just written the first act of a play.

I read it to her the next day, and she said it was wonderful. I was not sure if I could go by her, though.

'You mustn't say that just because you love me,' I said; 'you must tell me what you really think, without any prejudice. I shan't mind.'

'Honestly I like it,' she said; 'I shouldn't tell you if I didn't. Of course, one thing strikes me – it's lovely to listen to, but you know what people are about action in a play – nothing seems to happen very much, does it?'

'I don't know what you mean,' I said; 'there's action the whole time. It keeps going from one thing to another, it all comes in the dialogue.'

'Yes,' said Hesta, 'but people like to see things too, they don't just want to be told what's going on. And that man – I think his speeches are just a little too long. Nobody in real life could go on like that without getting out of breath. A good deal of what he says doesn't seem to have much to do with the story.'

'Hang it, darling, all those lines are pretty nearly epigrams, though I say so myself. They're supposed to give polish; haven't you ever read Wilde?'

'Yes.'

'Well, then?'

'But, Dick, Wilde's lines were very short and to the point; this man goes on and on.'

'He's a great thinker; that's his character.'

'I see.'

'And, anyway, you have to have talk in a play. Dialogue is the main thing. I couldn't write the sort of stuff that's full of pistol-shots, and murders, and rot.'

'No.'

'There'll be more action in the second act, of course; the first is more like a prologue.'

'I see.'

'You don't like it?'

'Yes, I do, really I do. I think you're terribly clever.'

'No, you don't, you think it's rotten.'

'Oh! Dick, how can you say that?'

'I know.'

'Honestly, it's wonderful; I promise you it is. I don't know how you do it at all.'

'Oh! well. . . .'

'Promise me, Dick, you don't think I don't like it?'

'Well, you didn't sound very keen.'

'I love it, I love it. You do believe me, don't you?'

'I suppose so.'

'Come over here and let me kiss you. You look all grumpy with your hair ruffled, like a little boy.'

'You're laughing at me.'

'I'm not. It's only when you look like that I have to smile, I love you so.'

'I expect I'm a dud, anyway.'

'No, my angel, you're the most marvellous writer that's ever been.'

'That's a bloody lie.'

'Don't be cross, sweetheart. Really, it's a lovely, lovely play.'

'Is it?'

'Yes.'

I went and knelt with my head in her lap. Being with her was better than any blasted writing. She bent down and touched the back of my neck with her lips.

'Go on,' I said.

'You must go and work, Dick.'

'I don't want to work any more.'

In July the heat began to be terrific. The rooms were as stifling and as unbearable now as they had been icy in winter. There did not seem to be any air at all. We dragged the mattress before the window and tried to sleep on the floor. Hesta damped a sheet in water and hung it in front of the window. We tried fanning each other in turns, but this was so ridiculous that we burst out laughing in the middle, and then got hotter than ever because Hesta would be looking lovely and I could not leave her alone. The days were terrible. I tried to write with a bandage of cold water tied round my head, and the pen slipped from my fingers, slippery with sweat; ideas were stubborn, my mind was clogged and greasy. Workmen were doing something to the building opposite; they had erected scaffolding, and they started knocking and hammering about six in the morning and went on all day. They had long iron planks they kept smashing down on each other, and bolts that had to be driven in, and then one of the fellows had a barrow full of stones he emptied every few minutes, the sound of all this mingled with the scrape of a spade. It was inferno.

Hesta kept the shutter close, to keep out the noise and the

heat, and then it was dark. She went about with nothing on but a thin dressing-gown. The workmen whistled and called out to her when they caught a glimpse of her. The heat seemed to tire her even more than it did me, although she had nothing to do. She looked very white, and she was thinner, too. She used to lie down most of the time on the bed and read. I supposed that all this wasn't doing her much good. The heat did not help my second act either. Hesta would look up from her book. 'How is it?' she said, 'getting tired?' And I would answer irritably because it was not going well, and I had scarcely written five lines, and I wondered why she had to ask me at all. I began to kick at sitting there day after day with nothing to show for it, my mind hazy and woollen like a blanket, my body weary for no reason, flabby for want of exercise and air, and the thought would come to me that last year I had been riding a horse in the mountains of Norway with Jake.

And a queer, almost irresistible longing would steal upon me to chuck everything, to chuck writing and Paris and Hesta and to get away alone again on a ship with the wind in my face. The feel of a deck, and the smell of the sea, and the voices of men only in my ears, and then coming to some other port I did not know, with new faces and new words, a shadow by a street corner, and leading from a city there would be trees waving on a hill-side, and a path across the mountains.

'What is it, Dick?' said Hesta, and 'Nothing, darling,' I answered, but I went on staring out of the window biting the end of my pen, with a dream drifting farther away from me, disappearing like a little white cloud in the sky.

'You look dreary, sweetheart, and sad,' said Hesta.

'Oh! I'm all right, it's the heat,' I said.

Somewhere, though, there was a ship leaving a harbour, a grey barque towed by a tug, and when she was clear of the land the sails were shaken out upon the yards, filling slowly with the wind, and a man looked down from a tremendous height upon the deck below, the breeze in his hair, his hands blistered by the ropes, and he saw the coast slip away from him like a thin wisp of land, smudged and dim, while beneath him the green sea curled away from the bows of the ship, and he was alone and free.

Somewhere the tall trees shivered below   mountains, and the sun set behind a purple ridge, casting a pink fingerprint upon the unbroken snow; the falls crashed down into the valleys, and there wasn't any sun, there wasn't any heat, only the still pure air and the white light.

'Perhaps,' said Hesta, 'it would do you good if we went to Barbizon. We could stay in one of those little hotels.' Her voice brought me back again, and I saw the village of Barbizon, the one street with the artists' houses on either side, the rail-line for the train, the lumbering char-à-bancs arriving every lunch-time with their crowd of tourists.

'Yes,' I said, 'we might as well go to Barbizon as anywhere.'

'You seemed to like it so much two months ago.'

'Yes,' I said.

So we went to Barbizon in the first week in August.

During the next few weeks I seemed to let loose all the energy that had been stored within me for so long. I used to walk for miles. I should think I explored practically every inch of the forest. Hesta got tired easily, she came with me at first, but she found it difficult to keep up with my pace. I was always a long way ahead, and then I would have to pause and wait for her, she a little figure in the distance scrambling through the bracken and over the stones, tearing her dress and scratching her bare legs.

'Could I sit for a bit, do you think?' she would say, panting, brushing her hair behind her ears. 'I would love a tiny rest just for a moment, but you go on, you don't bother about me,' she said.

I would feel a swine dragging her after me on these expeditions, but she would keep protesting she was not really tired; it was only that she was not used to the pace.

Then, after the first few times, she said that she knew she was spoiling the day for me, and would I go off alone, because she would be perfectly happy in the garden of the hotel at Barbizon; it was restful and quiet, she had plenty of books, and, anyway, she had a piano in a queer room that nobody ever used.

I said I hated that arrangement, but I soon found it was all right, and I could now go terrific distances without having the thought of her lagging behind to worry me, and it was nice to imagine her sitting quietly in the garden at Barbizon or mooning over her piano, and it was fun getting back to her in the evenings. Not seeing so much of her during the day seemed to make me appreciate her all the more when we were together. I had a new thing suddenly about being alone. It was as if I had made a discovery. It was strange, it had never appealed to me before. Last year, back in the mountains, I could not have borne a moment of it alone, I would have been lost and helpless without Jake. There used to be a tremendous excitement in the idea of a crowd of people, even people I did not know. Voices, laughter, the suggestion of life going on at a terrific pace, things happening continuously, sound, movement, and men and women. Now I felt as if I had not gathered the intensity of those days in the mountains with Jake, as though all the time I had observed the outward beauty of what I saw, and had not seen the inner peace and loveliness that were there. I had always been in a state of excitement to get on to the next place. If I was there now I would not be excited any more, I would linger a long while in the same shadow of a tree, I would not bother about a little path winding away over a hill. And there would be a pleasure in this very sensation of complete solitude.

It was strange, feeling all this. I supposed it was the reaction after the heat and the turmoil of Paris; it was the result of brain-fag, of worrying over the play. I was glad now that we had come to Barbizon.

The shelter of the clustering trees seemed a protection, the movement of the leaves in the forest sounded like a whisper, a message of sympathy and understanding. So I would walk, and walk, and then throw myself down upon the grass under the trees, and lie there, quite still, losing myself in a sleep that had no dreams. After that, after the weird and inexplicable exulta-tion of being alone, it was good to get back to Hesta. It was good to feel her arms round me, and her cheek against my cheek. This was the best part of having her, the physical tangibility of her, feeling her, holding her, sinking into some great depth of silence that seemed the embodiment of peace and security. I wanted her to let me stay like that, not to be roused, not to go

212

through the fever and unrest, the antagonism and the crisis of love, but for all my mental protestation, my first mute disinclination, the very holding of her would prove this impossible, the touch of her hands against my back made resistance a sorry thing, and the old slumbering longings stirred within me, so that I had to give way, I had to deny passivity and be her lover. And I would be glad to give way, I would not want the peace and the security any more. Even this she spoilt, though, by not accepting the understanding born of physical contact; she would search beyond this, she would try to wander into my mind, to share that with me, to be part of this as well.

'What are you thinking, darling? Tell me what you're thinking?' she said, and she would not see that this had no connexion with the business of our being together.

'Nothing, sweetheart,' I said, and I wished she would be quiet; I wished she did not have to speak, but would let me be there next to her, feeling her with my hands.

'When you're alone in the forest all day, what do you have in your mind, Dick? Do you plan about your books, do you make stories, do you think of me ever?'

'No, beloved, I just walk around,' I said, 'I guess I don't think of anything much.'

'Not of me, ever?'

'When I do think I suppose it's about you, Hesta.'

'Tell me,' she said, holding me close, 'tell me what you think. Say things to me.'

'I don't know what to say, darling.'

'Say nice things, whisper them to me.'

And it wasn't any good. The only possible words that would come to me were 'I love you', and they had been said so often I could not believe she asked for them again.

I did not see why she wanted this thing of words; that was not the way I felt.

'Let's just be us,' I said, 'and not bother about all that.'

So she had to surrender then and take herself from my mind, and I knew at once when she was gone because there was an understanding between us at once, a single purpose that did not interfere with my thoughts locked away that I did not remember, and we loved each other simply without contradiction, and we were happy in our own way.

We had three weeks at Barbizon, and then I thought we might finish up with a fortnight at a gay place before going back to Paris, because after all it would be amusing to see people again, and to have the fun of spending money we could not afford. I did not know about places, nor did Hesta, and because we saw they had cheap holiday tickets we went to Dieppe. We stayed in a little hotel in the town.

The market-place was grand, and we used to potter around the stalls buying things we did not want. We bathed twice a day, and Hesta tanned a gorgeous brown, getting rid of her old pallor. None of the women I saw were anything like her. They could not touch her. Seeing her there amongst them gave me a marvellous feeling, because she looked so good, and as we were nearly always in a crowd, either at the Casino or on the beach, I found myself being terribly in love with her, and when we were finally alone back in the hotel I could not leave her alone. It seemed to me I had wasted a lot of time at Barbizon going off walking by myself all day when she was there. I tried to make up for it at Dieppe. We were both crazy. We did not mind. I thought I would just let myself go entirely and be mad before settling down again in the Rue du Cherche-Midi, and writing steadily through the autumn. I would have to be serious then, I would have to work; besides, the money would not last for ever. I should have to work on the book and get it published, and finish the play, too. That would all be when I got back. Meanwhile, forget everything but having nothing to do and being with Hesta. I wanted to make myself sick with loving her, so that afterwards a sort of weariness and satiety could come upon me, and I could go on with my work quite calmly and not be aware that she was there. I thought if I loved her a lot now I would not want to love her so much in the autumn, and then it would be all right for my book.

So beyond the market-place and the beach we did not bother a great deal about Dieppe. We went into the Casino sometimes, and Hesta heard a concert or two, but I remember nothing of all that, only our room at the hotel looking over a square, and there was a theatre opposite, and every morning an old man used to wander beneath our window with a sack over his shoulder, calling for old rags and bottles.

Hesta wore no stockings and no hat. She looked a child. Sometimes I felt rotten about it, I felt she ought not to be so young.

I have a picture of her in my mind sitting cross-legged on the bed without anything on. It was a terribly hot evening, and she had thrown her things off, and was combing her hair. I lay in a chair, looking at her, smoking a cigarette.

'I wish,' I said, 'that you were a prostitute.'

She laughed. 'Whatever for?' she said.

'Because then it wouldn't matter so much. It wouldn't matter a damn what one did,' I said.

'It doesn't matter now,' she said.

'I don't know,' I said; 'it's wrong, you're only nineteen.'

'Age doesn't count. I feel older than that, much older; I feel I've lived a long time.'

'If you were a prostitute I could treat you anyhow, and just walk out, not caring.'

'Do you want to?' she said.

'No – that's why it's difficult sometimes, being us.'

'You know,' she said, 'you were awfully right about not marrying. It's more fun like this, isn't it? I mean we don't feel settled at all. We can either of us go away if we like.'

I was surprised when she said this. Somehow it was all right for me to talk down marriage, but it looked wrong coming from her.

'You've changed your views,' I said.

'Oh well! one gets a different outlook after a while,' she said.

'You're not getting fed up?'

'Dick, darling, don't be absurd. I love you more than ever.'

It was funny, all the same.

'It would be nice if you didn't have to write and we could travel about all the time,' she said.

'What about your music?'

'It doesn't mean so much to me now. I don't know why. Being with you is the only thing that matters. I wish, Dick, we just went from place to place, and it was always as mad as it is now, in Dieppe.'

'We'd end up insane, sweetheart, a couple of mad things in an asylum.'

'I'd like being mad that way,' she said.

'Only three days more. We'll be back in Paris this time next week, Hesta. You won't mind, will you? We'll have had a good time.'

'Yes – a lovely time.'

'Shall we go over to the Casino, darling, and see what's going on?'

'No – let's stay here.'

'Don't be lazy, babe; put on your things.'

'No.'

'Why, darling?'

'I don't want to go out.'

'Don't you?'

'No – Dick, come over here.'

6

I did not mind getting back to Paris after Dieppe. It was as if I had exhausted my capacity for pleasure, I no longer wished to be slack with myself, and indulgent. I had had all that, I had got what I wanted out of those five weeks. I had emptied my brain and only bothered about the rest of me. It had been good, too, giving way, not thinking; it was a physical satisfaction that had brought strength in itself, a new freshness and an inward purification.

Now I knew I could go right ahead. The old dreams of Jake and Norway came to me no more, they did not hover close, ready to absorb my thoughts, as they had done during the heat of the summer. It was as though I had said farewell to them for ever. And Hesta was not an obsession. This was most important of all. No longer an obsession. She would not stand between me and my writing; she had her own place, and her own value. I did not fully understand why these things were. I did not understand why in June I had sat at the table in my room, with a blank page of paper in front of me; and the knowledge of her lying

216

on the bed in the next room with a book had made the action of writing a mental and physical impossibility, while now in September I was able to write easily at almost any hour of the day, and whether or not she lingered in the house was something with which I had no concern, nor could it affect me in any way. She did not possess me, the image of her was not continuously before me as it had been, and the tearing need of her physical presence had loosened its grasp in some dim mysterious fashion. In June I had to keep getting up from my chair and going into the next room to see if she were there, and the very sight of her, the feeling that she was close, was a tremendous disturbance to me, so that I could not control my will, and the time of writing was as nothing compared to the precious intensity of the time of loving.

Now I could sit in my room unmolested and calm, and the knowledge that she was next door was such a thing of certainty that it ceased to be a means of distraction. Even if she went out I knew she would come back; I knew she would be always there for me when I did want her. So I could put her aside, confident and undisturbed. I was curiously free, I could think now as I liked.

In June she had been so much in my blood that I had lost all liberty of thought and action; I belonged to her, I was possessed soul and body. To free myself of this I had been forced to break down her barriers of individuality and restraint, I had gone away for these five weeks with the idea of ridding myself of her by the very excess of love, by making her enter into submission and so with her own complete surrender she would fasten the chain on herself and give me my liberty. I had succeeded. I loved her more than ever, but I was free. She was no longer dominant, she was subject to me. She was part of the house, part of my life, part of the general order of things. I did not ask her what she thought about it; I accepted her as such. The summer was gone and now I could go on with my writing.

Adventure and love seemed childish immaterial things beside this business of ambition. It was a queer abstract quality; it seized hold of me, and lifted me towards some weird unattainable height, lost and happy, and I did not know what I wanted, but I knew that it was there, waiting for me, like a hidden secret, beautiful and strange. I had to reach out and find it.

I did not know whether I asked for glory and success, whether to achieve something meant words on a printed page, and my own name beneath, the material obvious satisfaction of people speaking to one another about me, of any man in any train reading what I had written, knowing me and I not knowing him, or whether it meant the glow of an inward exultation having no connexion with outward form, a happy privacy that none could share, the baring naked of myself to myself. I did not want to be a forced self-conscious writer, ready with a title and a dedication, but no story to tell, no mood to interpret; I wanted to reach the truth and the meaning of sincerity.

Somewhere dwelt the shadow of my father, the father who had reached his own fulfilment, but would not believe in that of his son. The desire to prove him false was interlinked with my ambition, and I could not sever them. He was not personal to me, he was not a man of flesh and blood who had denied a message of hope and sympathy to the son he had begotten; he was a poet who would not stand for ever on his little peak unrivalled, but one day I would meet him face to face. He would lower himself then, he would bare his head and be ashamed. I should not be deterred if there were many stumbling-blocks in my path: I had a new strength now to break them down. No one would stop me from reaching my mountain. I would be to myself like a leader among men.

I did not speak of these things to Hesta. They were mine alone, they were not for her. She was a woman, and we travelled different ways. I think she understood this much at last, for she had given up trying to enter into my mind. She no longer questioned me. She accepted me as I was, and she kept what I had given her. She was there, part of my background, there when I needed her. I had my writing, and I had her. These were sufficient unto me. So I sat all day in my room in the Rue du Cherche-Midi, and gave myself up to this power of writing, more dangerous than adventure, more satisfying than love.

We had an Indian summer in October; for ten days the sun shone like June. It was like the whisper of a temptation to break from work, and to take Hesta away into the country while it lasted. I had a vision of the forest at Fontainebleau with the leaves turned golden, falling softly upon the ground, and the short green bracken that had surrounded us in early summer grown high and yellow, with curling, feathery fingers.

Just one evening I considered in my mind whether or not I should suggest to her our going. We were coming home after dinner at the Rotonde. She was holding my arm and swinging her cap in her hand. I wondered whether I should say to her: 'Darling, would you like us to run away for three days, and forget everything during those three days but this last glimpse of summer, and the fun of it, and you and I alone?' or whether I should say nothing that night, not give way and speak on an impulse, but wait for my feelings in the morning.

I hesitated for a moment, and then I decided to wait until the morning. When I woke up the sky was overcast, and there was a patter of rain against the window. Hesta lay asleep, her head on her arm. If it was raining I did not see there was much point in our going. Perhaps the weather had now broken, anyway. Perhaps, when I came to consider it now, coldly and calmly, in the grey morning, and no longer sitting at the café with the last light casting a finger on the yellow of Hesta's hair, perhaps it would be a stupid thing to do. Hesta was asleep, I could not discuss it with her. Yes, I supposed it was stupid. I would not think any more about it, and, anyway, I had writing to do.

After that day the weather was fine in intervals, but it never seemed to me to be fine enough to make the excuse for leaving Paris. So we did not go away, and in a week the old warmth was gone, the leaves scattered themselves about the ground, leaving the trees naked and shorn, and a little harsh breath of a wind blew sharply at the corners of the streets.

I forgot about the Indian summer. I had finished all three acts of my play, but the third did not satisfy me entirely, and I was re-writing the opening scenes. With a little care it should be all right. After that I planned to revise my novel and alter the end, also to tighten up the structure of it. I did not think it was quite long enough either. There seemed to be no ending to the output of work I should do. It was exciting, interesting; I could not help but feel myself someone of importance. When I had sufficient material my ambition was to go over to London and find a publisher. I did not think it would be a difficult matter. However, that was all for later.

It occurred to me one day that term must surely have started for Hesta's professor of music, but she had not said anything to me about it. I remembered this one afternoon when we had finished lunch.

'By the way,' I said, 'what's happened about your music?'

'I know,' she said; 'it's rather awful, isn't it, how lazy I've been.'

'Well,' I said, 'I suppose now your old term will have started and you'll be wanting to go on with it again.'

'It seems such ages since I've touched a piano,' she confessed, 'I believe the Professor will be horrified. To tell you the truth, I'm a little scared.'

'You can do just as you like about it, can't you?' I said.

'Yes,' she said.

The next morning she went off to see the professor and to arrange about another course of lessons.

I had quite forgotten she had been until the evening came, when I had finished work for the day. We had been silent during dinner, I rather full of my thoughts and my play, and she even quieter than usual, passing me things without a word.

I watched her crumbling a piece of bread in her fingers, and suddenly I wished she would be gay and laugh, because I could do with some gaiety now that the day was over. I did not want her to look dull like that; she ought to have been ready to fall in with my mood.

'Don't look so bored,' I said.

She looked up at me and smiled: 'I'm not bored.'

'Well, do something to your face, darling.'

'I'm sorry, I did not know I was being dull. Besides, I thought you were worried over your play.'

'Oh! no, it's coming along all right; I'm quite satisfied.'

'I'm so glad, Dick.'

'Oh! darling, you don't know what a kick it gives me, being able to write. I can't tell you.'

'I can guess.'

'No, you can't. You've no idea. It's grand. I mean there's something about writing . . . By the way, how did your old lesson go off, I forgot all about it till this minute?'

'Oh! that.'

'Yes. Was it fun?'

'No, not exactly.'

'Boring, I suppose.'

'It was funny seeing the Professor again.'

'What did he say?'

'He didn't say much.'

'Made a scene, I suppose, because you hadn't practised. Old fool.'

'Oh! well . . . .'

'I bet your fingers were a bit stiff at first, but they'll soon loosen up.'

'Yes.'

'When is the concert?'

'The end of November, I think, or the early part of December.'

'You'll have to work.'

'I'm not going to play in the concert.'

'Why on earth not?'

'I'm not good enough.'

'Who says so? Why, you told me yourself he wanted you to play.'

'Yes, but that was four months ago. It's different now.'

'I don't see, darling.'

'I haven't practised at all, Dick, all the time. The other students worked right through the summer. They're ahead of me now. It's quite fair.'

'Seems a damn shame to me.'

'No – I understand. It's my own fault. The Professor told me that with music you've got to work and work, never stopping, never letting anything else interfere. That's the only way to get on. I haven't bothered, so now I'm just one of his ordinary pupils who don't matter.'

'Aren't you disappointed?'

'I was at first. I don't know, I don't think I mind very much. I don't seem to be keen any more. I've lost it.'

'Poor old sweet.'

'It's all right.'

'Will you go on having lessons?'

'I might as well, twice a week, anyway. I can practise there. Besides – it will give me something to do.'

'Well, it's rotten luck. I think the chap's a fool, doesn't know his job. Good thing for him you didn't kick up a fuss.' I fumbled in my pocket for my cigarette-case. Then I had to ask the *garçon* for a match.

'What were we talking about?' I said afterwards. 'Oh! yes, your music. What a bore for you. Do you know, darling, I think I shall be able to get to work tightening up the book next week; it will be rather fun going back to it again. I've thought of a new ending which is really good. You remember the old one was too sudden? I'll explain you the new idea.' I leant forward excitedly, and went on to tell her about my book. It was quite late by the time we got home. Going over the new idea with her seemed to have stimulated me somehow; I could not rest, and I went over to the table in my room and sat down with the thought of noting down one or two little things. Once started, I did not seem to be able to leave it. I forgot the time. I heard Hesta calling to me from the other room.

'Aren't you coming to bed?' she said.

'I shan't be long,' I shouted; 'go to sleep if you're tired. I won't wake you, anyway.'

She was silent a little while, and then she called me again.

'Dick, it isn't good for you to go on working so late. Do stop.'

I pretended not to hear. I did not answer. It was very important to me what I was doing.

Presently I heard her footstep, and she came into the room, in her pyjamas, and knelt beside me.

'It's nearly two o'clock,' she said; 'you must get some sleep; honestly, you can't sit here all night.'

Why did she have to come in, she might see that it irritated me, just as I was on the flash of a thought.

'Oh! darling, do leave me alone,' I said, 'you know how I hate being fussed. I'll come to bed when I'm finished. Why should you worry? Do I stop you from sleeping?'

'It's not that,' she said, 'but you're always late now. It goes on and on.'

'Well, damn it, darling, I can't help it if I write better in the evening.'

'Oh! God,' she said, looking white and queer, different from herself, 'always this old writing. There's never anything else, all the time, day and night, you and your writing.'

I stared at her, scarcely believing what she said.

'Sweetheart, you're crazy. What on earth is the matter?'

She slipped away from me, she sat back on the floor, small and thin, clutching her knees, shivering in her thin pyjamas.

'It's never like it used to be,' she said, and her voice was strained and funny, as though she might cry.

'All day you sit here and do your writing, and in the evening too, very often. We never go out like we did in the spring and the summer.'

'Go out?' I said. 'How do you mean, darling, go out where?'

'In Paris, to have fun, to laugh, to look at people. It's different now, it's been different ever since we came back.'

'Hesta, love,' I said, speaking rather gently as if she were a child, 'you know I have to work, you know it's the most important thing to me. You can't expect me to fly around with you all the time, in Paris, and all over the place.'

'You did in the summer,' she said.

'Well, it's no good comparing the summer with now,' I said; 'we can't always go on doing the same things.'

'It's because you don't want to,' she said.

'Darling, that's ridiculous.' It would be easy for me to lose my temper.

'We had a marvellous holiday, we had a grand time, and now you're kicking that we have to settle down,' I said. She stared up at me, white and wretched, biting the back of her hand.

'It's not going about that I miss,' she said, 'it's being with you, it's the fun of us together. It's all gone, we don't laugh like we used to do. I can't explain. I get so lonely. . . .'

'Lonely?' I could not understand. 'How can you be lonely? Why, I'm here all the time,' I said.

'Oh yes, you're here – stuck at your desk. You and your writing. But you don't care whether I'm here or not.'

'Listen,' I said, 'we've got to get this straight. You know I love you, and you're just making this scene because you're bored. Are you bored?'

'It's not boredom. . . .'

'Well, get something to do, darling. Go on with your music lessons.'

'What help is music to me now? I can't even play.'

'That's bloody rot. Of course you could play if you wanted to.'

'Supposing I don't want to?'

'Well, damn it, sweetheart, that's your look-out, isn't it?'

'Music meant everything to me, Dick, until you made me forget it.'

'Oh! I made you forget it, did I?'

'You know you did.'

I picked her up from the floor where she was crouching, and held her next to me.

'Sweetheart, we mustn't row like this. We mustn't. It's not a bit of good. I guess you're disappointed over that concert, and it's rotten, babe, just rotten. It's not us, to quarrel, you know that.'

She put her arms round my neck.

'I don't want to quarrel,' she said, 'I don't want anything but you.'

'You've got me,' I said.

'No,' she said. 'We're never happy now like we used to be. It's never the same as Barbizon or Dieppe.'

'I love you every bit as much. You don't understand, Hesta, you're part of me, you're here. Don't you see?' I argued.

'What's the good of that to me?' she said.

'How do you mean?'

'What's the good of it, that settled thing, that quiet love? I want you so much in that other way – like Dieppe.'

I held her very close. I did not say anything. It gave me a profound and staggering shock, this coming from her.

'Since we've been back,' she said, 'we've scarcely ever been like that. You've always had your writing, or else you've been tired, you haven't thought about it. You don't know how I've felt. Sometimes I thought I'd go mad.'

'Darling,' I said, 'darling.'

I did not know what to do. I did not know what to say. How was I to know what she felt? How was I to know? It was terrible for her to say this thing.

'You mustn't,' I said, 'Hesta, sweet, you mustn't be like that. It's ghastly – it's – I can't explain. A woman should never tell a man she feels like that. Never. It's terrible – it's all wrong.'

'Why?' she said. 'Why – I don't see . . .'

'Sweetheart, it's beastly – it's making a thing of it; it's – it's unattractive. It's all right for me to want you, but not for you – at least, never to say. It's terrible, darling.'

'I can't help it,' she said. 'I can't alter myself. I did not know before I started how it would be. I never cared to, and you used to beg me and beg me, and be wretched until I did. Now that I want you, now that you've made me want you, you say it's beastly – you say it's wrong.'

This was appalling. I did not know what had happened.

'I'm sorry,' she said, 'I didn't know you would think it so awful. I didn't think it mattered, telling you.'

'It doesn't matter,' I said.

'If it's so unattractive,' she went on, 'perhaps you'd better send me away. You'll be put off me.'

'Listen,' I said, 'you're not going to worry any more. You're going to forget about all this. And tomorrow we'll see if the hotel at Barbizon will take us for a week. A few days away, out of Paris, will be wonderful. We ought to have gone before.'

'Oh! Dick,' she said, 'you can't just because of me. You can't – I won't take you from your writing.'

'Sweetheart, there's no argument about it. We're going. See? I want to get away – I want to get away just as much as you. . . .'

I did not work any more that night. It was raining the next day. It scarcely looked hopeful for Barbizon. We decided we would wait a day or two until the weather cleared.

I took Hesta to dinner and to a theatre instead, and the following afternoon we had tickets for a concert. She said she enjoyed it, she said she was happy and everything was all right. I was

225

worried, though; what she had told me had interfered with my sense of security. It was as if I had failed to understand her, it shocked me to realize I did not know anything about women. There had been a smooth regularity in my life since the summer which she had now disturbed. What had been perfect for me she had spoilt with this admission of her own loneliness. She had made herself into a responsibility, and I did not want that.

In my mind there had been my writing and her, and she had fitted into it to suit me, but now I saw these things were apart and could not be brought together. I wished she had not told me, I wished she could have gone on in some way without letting me know.

A responsibility – I had not bargained for that. And then she had lost interest in her music, she had lost the enjoyment of her own talent and the pleasure of being alone. I thought of her as I first knew her, cool, indifferent and remote, wearing her orange béret, not listening to what I said.

I wondered why she had to change. Perhaps I seemed different to her, too. These were problems, deep, intricate and hurtful, that we could not discuss with one another. We were lovers, but these things must remain unspoken.

I thought, however much two people may surrender themselves and become part of each other, they must realize, with a little sensation of helplessness, that they are always alone, in some great depth of solitude. I wished there was someone who could tell me what to do. Someone older than myself, experienced and wise, who would have understood.

After Hesta had told me how she felt, I could not think of anything else for three days; in spite of taking her about, in spite of the forced distraction, the thought lingered there, in the back of my mind.

During the interval at the concert I sat without speaking, my eyes fixed on the empty platform, and she reached out for my hand and held it between hers, and I looked at her and she was smiling.

'What's wrong?' she said. 'Aren't you liking it, are you miserable?'

'No,' I said, 'it's a splendid concert. I'm all right.'

226

'What are you thinking about?' she said.

'Nothing, darling.'

'You always say that, you always make this pretence of never thinking. Tell me, Dick, you look dreary and grey.'

'I don't know – I was thinking about you.'

'Me?'

'Yes.'

'Tell me.'

'I was just thinking over what you said the other night – you worried me a little; I feel I've not treated you right. I guess I've been a bore at times, Hesta.'

'No, darling – never, never. Don't think about what I said, I didn't mean it. I was silly and tired, and besides, you needn't worry, I'm happy – terribly happy.'

'Are you, sweetheart?' I said – 'are you sure?'

'Yes, Dick. These last few days have been so wonderful, I feel a beast for saying what I did the other night. You won't remember, will you? Promise me you won't. I'm happy, darling – happy.'

'Really?'

'Look at me.'

The second part of the concert began again after that, and I went on holding her hand as though we were a boy and a girl out for the first time, shy of love, having to touch each other. Somehow I felt easier after that. I glanced at her, sitting beside me, and it seemed as though the white drawn look had gone, also the thin lines at the corners of her mouth, and there was no longer a haunted shadow in her eyes. She had said she was happy. She looked happy. Perhaps I had been making too much of a thing of all this. Perhaps there was no need to be so serious. She had been disappointed about her music, and then tired, and I in my turn had been irritated and excited with the book. We had caught each other that night in difficult moods. In a week or so I would laugh at myself, I would know I had been a fool. A scene over nothing at all. Losing my sense of humour.

Hesta looked lovely. She was all right. I whispered across to her in the darkness: 'I love you.'

The next day I felt that I could go on with my book. I asked Hesta first if she minded, and she said of course not. So that was a good thing, and I worked all day, but I left off quite early in the evening. The next day I worked a little longer, but made up for it by taking Hesta to a theatre in the evening. The weather was cold and grey.

'What about Barbizon?' I said.

'I leave it to you, darling,' she said.

'It wouldn't be too good this weather, would it?'

'I suppose not.'

'I mean, if we got there and it was like this, it would be pretty ghastly, eh?'

'Yes, Dick.'

'We'd only get fed up.'

'Yes.'

'What about putting it off till later?'

'Next week, perhaps, or the week after?' she said.

'Something of that sort. The fact is, the book is going so strong, at the moment it seems almost a shame to leave it. But you've got to tell me first you don't mind, you've got to promise you're happy.'

'I promise I'm happy. I promise I don't mind,' she said.

'We'll go some time, of course.'

'Yes.'

'Meanwhile, I should go on with your lessons, darling, I really should. I'm sure they're good for you, and music is marvellous, isn't it, and, anyway – Oh, I should.'

'Yes, Dick.'

'That's right. Then I don't have to worry you're bored?'

'Of course not.'

'Darling. Then we're happy, aren't we?'

'Yes, we're happy.'

Somehow we did not go to Barbizon after all, Hesta not reminding me about it made me forget. She seemed content with her music lessons, and so I was able to concentrate once more on my writing.

7

In a flash I can see the progress of that autumn and the coming of winter. The grey afternoons, dark at half-past four, getting up from my chair and closing the shutters outside the window, feeling the radiators with my hands and wondering why they gave out so little heat, and then back to the table looking about for my pen, rustling the pages of my writing-block. Hesta, singing up the stairs, going into the next room so as not to disturb me, and then flinging her music-case on to the bed, and moving a chair or opening a drawer.

I would go on writing and yet be aware of the life that continued around me, the comfort and the familiarity of little things. There would be Hesta's book lying open on the floor, and her sweater hanging over the back of a chair. On my table were some flowers she had placed there in the morning. My cigarettes stood on the mantelpiece beside a silly stuffed cat I had bought one day for fun, and here also was a snapshot of Hesta taken in Dieppe. Her things and my things, part of each other, part of our life, and the room next door with the one divan in the corner, and my old coat hung on a hook on top of her mackintosh, my shoes lying untidily under the dressing-table, hers beneath a chair, and our tooth-brushes in a jar, and a sponge we shared. All these making up the atmosphere of Hesta and me, she coming to the sitting-room later and I looking up and saying: 'Chuck me a cigarette, darling,' and she saying: 'What about dinner?' patting the side of her hair, walking over to the mantelpiece. Scraps of conversation, she standing with a frown, putting her finger down her throat: 'I believe I'm getting a cold,' and I not listening wholly: 'Haven't we any aspirin?'

Undressing together at night, Hesta with a sensitive skin always scratching at herself when she took off her things. 'I forgot to tell you, the wretched *blanchisseuse* is down with 'flu, what are we going to do about the laundry this week?' and I, leaning over the wash-basin, my mouth full of rinsing water for my teeth, shrugging my shoulders, then spitting out the water, rattling the brush round the glass: 'I should ask the daughter to find somebody.'

Lying in bed, the accustomed warmth of her body, the scent of the eau-de-Cologne she used on her skin, then yawning, settling myself in comfort by her side, caressing her mechanically with one hand. 'Remind me to get that book in the morning,' and she: 'Oh! so funny. I saw one of the girls from the pension this afternoon; she didn't see me, though.'

Falling asleep later, she on her side, me on my face, neither of us moving much, used to each other's positions.

Sitting down to a meal at the Coupole, and glancing at an English paper, crumbling up her bread when I had finished my own. 'You know, darling, I think this place is going off, the service is shocking,' then she leaving half-way through to be in time for her lesson. 'Will you remember, Dick, to buy some *chocolat*: we've finished it all,' and I saying 'All right,' and going on with my food, following her vaguely with my eyes as she swung through the doors, then looking down at the paper again.

In the evening, cutting work for a while, lounging in a chair, trying to read a French novel and missing half the meaning, with Hesta opposite me, squinting as she threaded a needle, bad at darning a hole in her stocking, sewing it up in a knot.

'Some of the people are quite amusing this term; another girl and I are going to play duets, and she has a brother who composes.'

'Really?'

'It's much more fun if one knows just two or three of them. I never bothered before, I don't know why.'

What was the meaning of *crépuscule*? I never could remember. I couldn't bother with a dictionary.

'There's rather an intriguing person who is quite new. The Professor says he is brilliant, he's a violinist, but I haven't heard him play. I bumped into him in the corridor yesterday. He gave me a sinister look.'

'What does *crépuscule* mean, darling?'

'Twilight, I think. There's a dictionary somewhere. This queer man is Spanish, I believe, but he spoke English all right – he said "I'm very sorry" without an accent.'

'Fancy,' I yawned.

'Oh! Wanda, the duet girl, asked me to go back with her to-

230

morrow evening and stay for some supper, and practise together. Is that all right?'

'Sure, sweetheart.'

'I won't be late, anyway. I believe, though, they're giving some party at the end of the week, she and her brother; they've asked me to it. It might be fun.'

'Yes.'

'It's not as if we go out much,' she said.

I turned over two or three pages of the book. There was a lot of description that did not matter.

'Oh! rather, you'll enjoy it,' I said, reaching for a cigarette, not listening much.

She bit off a piece of cotton with her teeth and I went on reading the book.

The novel was finished, I read it and re-read it, and copied out pages that were scratched and dirty, and then laid all the pages on top of one another, and slipped a large india-rubber band round the whole of it. It looked grand. I put it carefully away beside my play.

I remember standing up and stretching myself, and then going over and leaning against the mantelpiece. My heart was beating, and my hands were trembling for no reason. There had never been anything like the thrill of writing the last word, of drawing a line at the bottom, of blotting the page. The breaking up of tension, the culmination of excitement, the supreme effort of that final word.

'That's that,' I said aloud to myself, 'that's that.' I was excited. I was happy. I wanted to walk swiftly somewhere with the wind in my face.

'Anyway, I've done it,' I thought; 'whatever happens, I've done it.'

I felt as though I were tall, way up above everyone else. It would not matter what they said to me. I would go on alone in my own way. There was my father standing in a group of men, and one of them said to him: 'It is really your son who has written this?' and he, looking from one to the other, rousing himself from his lethargy, a little confused: 'Yes, I believe so – Yes, it is Richard.'

Then I would come walking into the room and stand before

231

him. Pictures leaping and thrusting themselves into my mind. I stood before the mantelpiece, lost in my dreams, and the door opened, and it was Hesta.

'Hullo,' she said, 'I'm back early, aren't I? What's wrong with you? Is the book being a nuisance?'

I tried to be casual, I tried to hide my smile. 'It's finished,' I said.

'Darling – how clever of you.' She came across to me and kissed me, and then wandered into the next room. I thought it would be different from this. I was aware of a little blank sensation. I followed her into the bedroom.

'What's the rush?' I said.

'Wanda and the rest are coming to pick me up,' she said; 'we're dining and going to a concert. Out of the way, sweet; I want to get at my other dress.'

I stood aside while she fumbled with her things.

'You didn't tell me you were going out?' I said.

'H'm, darling, I did. I told you this morning. You must have forgotten.'

I wandered about while she changed.

'You're very thick with these people,' I said.

'Well, they're amusing, I can't help liking them. Where's my belt? Oh! darling, have you seen my belt?'

'There it is, on the floor.'

'I never can find a thing in this room.'

'Will you be late?' I said.

'I don't know. It all depends. Don't wait up for me.'

'I shan't sleep till you get back.'

'Oh yes, of course you will. You'll be tired with your book.'

'How many of you are there?' I said.

'Wanda and her brother, and a divine couple of Hungarians and Julio.'

'Who?'

'Oh! you know, Dick, the violinist man; I've often told you about him.'

'I don't remember,' I said.

'Yes, darling, I have. You don't listen. Look out, you're treading on my other shoe.'

'Is he in love with you?'

'Don't be silly,' she said.

'Is he?'

'Of course not. Do I look all right? Do you like this hat?'

'Why do you never wear bérets now?' I said.

'I'm sick of them. I don't feel like them any more. Say you like the hat,' she said.

'I don't know. I suppose it's all right. It looks queer, right off your face.'

'It's the fashion,' she said.

'You never used to worry about fashion. Why do you have to put all that red on your lips? That's new for you.'

'You are personal, all of a sudden. I like red lips, they suit me,' she said.

'Who says so?'

'Oh! Wanda and people.'

'Do you have to go by them?' She shrugged her shoulders.

'Darling, how trying you are!'

'It's not like you, it's like any other girl one sees. Red lips, hat off your face. You had a thing of your own. Why spoil it?'

'You don't understand, Dick, you've got so used to me dressed anyhow. You don't appreciate me like this.'

'I don't know.' I kicked my heels on the floor. There was a taxi blowing a hooter repeatedly in the street below.

'There they are,' said Hesta, 'I must dash.'

'What a filthy row,' I said; 'where are you going in the taxi?'

'We're dining in Paris, some new place Wanda knows. Good-bye, darling, have some dinner, and look after yourself.'

I stood by the window and watched her get into the taxi. Some fool of a man was in the street, his hat in his hand, and he was smoking a cigarette through a long holder. He took hold of Hesta by her arm and laughed down in her face. Bloody cheek. They climbed in the taxi and it drove away. I wandered back into the other room, bored, irritable, kicking at the floor. I did not see why she had to go out with those fools. I wanted her to be with me, happy, and talking about things. It was damn selfish of her. She had spoilt all the excitement now of having finished my book.

It was a week now to Christmas. I thought I would wait until after the New Year and then go over to London and see about finding a publisher to read my book, and perhaps give his opinion on the play at the same time. I was not sure yet how I should go about this business. I might send the MS. to house after house, and it would be returned to me because it had not been properly read. Even if I had a personal interview with the head of the firm, I could not be certain he would go through the book himself. These publishers must be constantly bothered with unknown writers, making claims upon their time.

Yet I wanted to win through on my own merits; I hated the idea of trading on my father's name, of getting my things read just because I was his son. It was all very difficult; I resolved not to decide anything before I arrived in London.

I asked Hesta what we were going to do about Christmas. Now that I had finished the book and was no longer working we could surely celebrate in some way.

'What do you think, darling?' I said.

'I don't know, whatever you suggest,' she said. She was sitting on the floor in the sitting-room, putting some pink stuff on her nails.

'That looks queer for you,' I told her.

She shrugged her shoulders and laughed. 'Hands are very important,' she said.

'You oughtn't to have long nails when you play the piano,' I said.

'My piano-playing doesn't mean much these days,' she said.

'Aren't you really keen any more?'

'I don't know, I don't think about it much. What were you saying?'

'Oh! about Christmas. Where shall we go, darling?'

'Go?'

'Yes. Barbizon or the sea? It's all the same to me.'

'Do we have to go away, Dick?'

'How d'you mean?'

'Well – Paris is fun in itself. I can't see there's much point in shivering at the sea somewhere, or mooning about in Barbizon.'

'Oh!'

'What do you think?' she said.

'Darling, I thought you loved Barbizon.'

'So I do, in the summer. Not now. How long did you want to go for, anyway?'

'As long as we liked. Spend Christmas and the New Year.'

'I see.'

'You don't seem keen, darling,' I said.

'Well, darling, I don't know. Of course I had planned one or two amusing things. Wanda is giving a party on New Year's Eve, and we had thought of motoring somewhere Boxing Day. They suggested you should come too.'

'Very kind of them.'

'Don't be sniffy, sweet. They're terribly good fun, and they'd love you to come.'

'I don't care about it.'

'Yes, you would, you'd adore it once you got to know them properly. It would be such fun, all of us together. You'd like Wanda, she's very attractive.'

'I've seen her, I don't rave. All that hair curling down her neck.'

'Most people think she's beautiful.'

'They can have her, then.'

'Oh! darling, you've got on your screwed-up grumpy face. I have to kiss you when you look like that.'

I had to take my handkerchief and wipe my face after kissing her now. She would leave great marks of red from her lips.

'Hesta.'

'What is it?'

'Put your arms round me.'

'Suddenly like this?'

'Yes.'

'This doesn't happen very often,' she said.

'I want it to happen now.'

She laughed, digging her nails in me, biting the corner of my ear.

'No,' I said.

'Why?'

235

'Be like you used to be, still, just holding me. I hate this new stunt of yours.'

'I can't help it – I have to do things,' she said.

'You ought to let me do them.'

'Why not both of us?'

We laughed, and I lifted her up from the floor.

'You're a wicked woman, darling.'

'Don't you like it?' she said.

'No.'

'It's your fault, all the same.'

'It's not.'

'Yes, it is. You started me.'

'Oh! darling . . .'

She was very small and light to hold. I kissed her closed eyes.

'What am I going to do with you?' I said.

She opened one eye.

'Let's go in the other room and see,' she said.

I gave way about staying in Paris for Christmas. Perhaps she was right, and it would have been dreary at Barbizon.

We went over the other side and had a swell lunch on Christmas Day, and we ate and drank too much. So we had to come back and sleep all the afternoon.

On Boxing Day there was the expedition with these friends of hers to Chantilly. The fellow called Julio had a car, and drove it himself. I think he fancied himself at the wheel. I did not take to him much. Hesta sat in front with him, and I at the back with Wanda and another Hungarian girl. The girl's husband and Wanda's brother crouched on the floor. It was absurdly over-crowded, I thought we would have an accident. It came to me suddenly that if this had been eighteen months back, I should have been sitting on the hood and shouting, thinking it the grandest fun, longing for a puncture just for the thrill of danger, and here I was now, sober as a judge, between the two women, watching Hesta's back ahead of me, bored, wondering about my book, thinking all these people were fools and making too much row.

We had lunch at Chantilly, but the château was not open. The fellow called Julio smoked through his amber cigarette-holder and talked a lot of muck about music. The women lapped it up, even Hesta, her chin on her hands, staring at him across the table. I felt hot for them all. I wandered away and had a chat with the old lady who ran the hotel. There was a kid, her grandchild, playing in the courtyard. He was very friendly, and pulled at my hand to show me something. I loved to hear a kid talk French, it sounded so clever. I chucked a ball to him, and he stumbled after it rather unsteadily on fat legs.

'*Vous voulez jouer avec moi?*' he said, in a deep bass voice.

'Sure,' I said, laughing, and he stared at me puzzled, a finger in his mouth. We went on chucking the ball backwards and forwards to each other. It was fun. Presently the others came out of the hotel.

'Hesta,' I called, 'come here, I'm having a grand time, there's the most marvellous child . . .'

'What have you been doing?' she said; 'it was rather rude going off like that.'

'Sorry, darling,' I said, 'but do look here, I've never laughed so much.'

'You are mad.' She glanced at the little boy. 'Come on, everyone's waiting and we're all driving to some place farther on.'

She seemed impatient to get back to the car. I gave my kid a two-franc piece.

'*Pour acheter des sucettes,*' I said. I shook his hand gravely, and then followed Hesta to the car.

She was peering into the looking-glass from her bag, smearing the red on to her lips with her finger.

'Shall we sit as we did before?' she said. She looked as though she were enjoying her day. We spent the rest of the week fairly quietly.

On New Year's Eve there was the party with Hesta's friends. I hated going, I wanted us to have gone somewhere by ourselves. Even if we had dined out in a crowd of people, we could have got back home by midnight and been together.

It was our first New Year. I felt we should have done a thing about it.

Hesta seemed keen on the party, though. It was a fancy-dress affair. We were going to have drinks at Wanda's room first, and then go on to the other place and dance. Hesta dressed herself up as an apache. She had black trousers and a crimson shirt. She made up her face all white, with no colour at all except on her lips, and she brushed her hair behind her ears.

She stood in front of me, her hand on her hip.

'Well?' she said.

She had a new manner with me now at times, flirting with me, as though we were strangers. It was silly, rather. All the same, she looked marvellous.

'If you were a boy I'd be sent to prison for an unnatural offence,' I said; 'you rouse my worst instincts. Come here.'

'No,' she said, 'you'll spoil me; I mustn't be touched.'

'Have we really got to go to this party, darling?'

'Of course, be quick with your things,' she said.

I had not coped at all. I had bought a cheap pair of velvet trousers and wore an old shirt of Hesta's with a handkerchief knotted round my throat. God knows what I was meant to be. I looked a bloody fool, anyway. We found a taxi and went along to Wanda's rooms. They were all there, and several other people besides. Hesta seemed to know them all. Her pal Julio was late, and when he did come he made a terrific entrance, acting like hell, fancying himself no end, all got up as a toreador.

'Doesn't he look wonderful!' screamed Wanda. They all crowded round him. He laughed and shrugged his shoulders, pretending to be careless about his effect.

I rather stood in a corner, talking to a plain girl who looked all wrong draped in Eastern robes with bangles jingling. She asked me if I had been to Persia, and I said 'No, I hadn't,' so that wasn't much fun, anyway, and we were both glad when somebody shouted: 'Come on.' I did not speak to the plain girl again the whole evening.

When we got to the dancing place there was some muddle about the table, and we could not have one long one, but two or three squashed together. The atmosphere was appalling, thick with scent and cigarette smoke and the silliness of fancy dress.

Hesta was miles away. She waved to me, smiling, and I waved back. Wanda was next to me. She was dressed as a Hungarian peasant. She looked all right. She was not such a fool, after all, and she asked me about my book. She seemed interested, wanting to know about it and what I should call it. She was not boring with her questions, and, anyway, she was good-looking.

The party was being quite fun, and there was plenty to drink, too. After a while we got up and danced. Wanda rather stuck herself into one, but it did not matter. She danced well, and she used a good scent.

'Why don't you come out with us more often?' she said.

'Oh! I don't know,' I said, 'I'm generally working.'

'You work too hard,' she said.

The band played a good tune that did something to me inside. Wanda hummed vaguely under her breath.

'I love this,' she said.

'So do I,' I said.

We held on to each other more.

'You're more human tonight,' said Wanda: 'I'm terrified of you, as a rule.' I laughed. 'Oh! rot,' I said. It was all rather fun.

Then Hesta passed with Julio. She smiled vaguely at me. It bored me seeing her with him. Why did she have to dance with him, anyway? I wondered if she was enjoying it. It must be a bore being a girl, having to say 'Yes' when a fellow asked you. Seeing Hesta dancing with Julio spoilt my fun of dancing with Wanda.

When the band finished the tune we moved back towards the table, and I hoped we should reach it before they struck up again, otherwise I should have to ask her whether she cared to go on.

I pushed her rather, to get to the table in time.

'Have a drink?' I said.

It was nearly midnight before I found a chance of dancing with Hesta. She always seemed to be surrounded. It was queer seeing her with people and knowing what she was like alone. She seemed to put on another manner here. Laughing, raising her eyebrows, saying things in a different way. She talked louder, too, I thought.

'Come and dance,' I said.

Once I held her I realized how little it had meant holding Wanda. The very knowledge of Hesta made it perfect. My hand resting on her body, accustomed, my chin brushing the top of her head.

'Darling,' I said, and sighed for no reason.

'You seemed to be getting on very well with Wanda,' she said.

'She's not bad.'

'Talking and laughing, anyway. I saw you. Then you pretend you don't like parties. What were you laughing at when I passed you dancing?'

'I can't remember,' I said.

'How much do you like her?'

'Don't be silly, sweetheart,' I said.

It was all right for me to mind Hesta dancing with Julio, but it seemed stupid for Hesta to mind me dancing with Wanda. It was boring talking about it, anyway.

'Darling,' I said, 'do you remember that first time we danced, last spring, and we didn't say anything, and afterwards we found a taxi; do you remember?'

'H'm,' she said.

'It was wonderful, wasn't it? I wish it was then, I wish we could go back.'

It gave me the same thrill just to think of it. I felt sentimental, foolish; I had probably drunk too much. I wanted us to be home in the Rue du Cherche-Midi.

'Let's go,' I said.

'No, we can't. Don't be absurd,' she said.

'It'll be midnight soon, darling. We'll stick together, won't we? You'll dance with me when it's twelve o'clock.'

'Yes, if they dance.'

She was clapping her hands mechanically, glancing over her shoulder. The band started another tune.

'You don't have to go back,' I said; 'let's go on dancing.' We had one more, but she went to the table afterwards, I hating letting her go. There was a scene now everywhere, with paper caps and streamers and nonsense. Then the lights went out and immediately there was confusion and laughter, and excited voices. 'What's happening?' said Wanda, beside me, pulling my arm.

'I suppose it's twelve o'clock,' I said. She was rather a fool after all. I looked around for Hesta, but I could not see her. Then the clock struck, and afterwards the lights went up again and there were cheers, and people shook hands and kissed each other, and the band began to play, and everyone shouted and

240

sang. It was all very forced. Hesta was laughing, and throwing a streamer at someone. She did not seem to see me. I had to get up and dance with a girl in green that I did not know.

We were having breakfast one morning. I sat up in bed, stirring my coffee, and Hesta was curled up on the end, half dressed, buttering a *croissant* for me.

'I think I'll go to London on Tuesday,' I said.

'Oh! will you really?' she said.

'I think so, darling, I want to get all this business settled, and I'm not sure how long it will take altogether. You see, if they undertake to publish the book, even then it probably won't be done for a few months. I'll have to ask for an advance.'

'How are the finances?'

'Not so good. I've nearly come to the end. That cheque lasted over a year, you know, just. You don't have to worry, though.'

'I've my own allowance, anyway.'

'Yes, but I'd rather you used mine.'

'Have another cup, Dick?'

'Yes, I think I will. Well now, if I go over on Tuesday I can start routing up my father's publisher on Wednesday morning.'

'You've decided to do that?'

'I think it's the only way. It's beastly, but it can't be helped. I'd never get a hearing otherwise.'

'Can't I come with you?'

'What – to London?'

'Yes.'

'Oh! darling – I don't think you'd better. I'd adore you to, of course, but I honestly think I must see this through alone.'

'What shall I do when you're away?'

'It won't be long, darling. You'll be all right, with Wanda and the rest.'

'Yes. . . .'

'You won't be lonely, will you?'

'I suppose not.'

'Why, you're always going out these days, anyway.'

'It will seem funny.'

'I'll be as quick over it as I can. And think how marvellous it will be coming back, saying I've sold the book.'

'H'm.'

'I shall miss you like hell, but I'm sure it would be a mistake for you to come to London, darling; you'd be bored, hanging around all the time.'

'Yes.'

'Cheer up, sweetheart, we'll have the time of our lives when this business is through.'

It was an excitement to me, to be going to London. I had to buy a bag and some things. I had lived anyhow for such a long time now.

Hesta packed for me. She was not much good at it, but better probably than I could have done myself.

'Put the MS. at the bottom,' I said, 'and see that it's not crushed. I can't give the publisher something looking like lavatory paper.'

'I'll fold your suit over it,' she said; 'the edges won't curl up if there's your suit to keep them flat. Of course you ought to have it typed.'

'I'll get that done in London,' I said.

'Do you think you'll want two pairs of pyjamas?' she said.

'What? I don't know – Shove 'em in, at any rate.'

It was a business packing; I was not sure what I should need in London.

'All these ties, Dick?' she said.

I was searching furiously through a drawer. There did not seem to be any links.

'Oh! damn and blast, I can't find a thing. What, darling?'

'These ties – you never wear this blue one.'

'Don't fuss me, sweet, I don't know what I'm doing; put all the ties in. I don't care. Can I borrow your comb?'

'Yes, I can get another.'

'Oh! Lord – look at this shoe. The heel is trodden right down. You might have seen and sent it somewhere.'

'You never wear that pair. How could I know? Dick, listen – you don't seem to have socks that go with that dark suit – and there's one here full of holes.'

'Look, beloved, is this hat too awful?'

'Pretty bad. Perhaps if you wear it on one side people will think you're an artist.'

'I wish we hadn't left everything to the last minute,' I said.

I scarcely slept at all the last night for thinking of going to London, and wondering about the publisher, and hating to leave Hesta. I got up early the next morning.

'I wish you didn't have to go,' she said, looking away from me, her face hard and queer.

'So do I,' I said, but I didn't mean it really, because I wanted to go deep down, and I kissed her feverishly, and then tore into the other room to see that I had my passport stamped by the British Consul in Nantes. It was strange, looking at it, holding it in my hands, for all that seemed very long ago, and then Hesta came and worried me with keys.

'How pathetic you look in that photo,' she said, 'like a little boy lost.'

I shut it up quickly, and bent down to fasten my suitcase.

'You'd better find a taxi in the Boulevard Montparnasse,' I said.

There wasn't time to do much thinking, because everything was so hurried. Hesta came with me to the Gare du Nord. I went by the ten o'clock train, travelling second-class. The porter stowed my case away on the rack, and I walked up and down the platform with Hesta.

'I promise I won't be long,' I said, 'and you mustn't be lonely; you go out and have a good time.'

'Where will you stay?' she asked.

'I'm not sure, I'll find a little cheap hotel.'

'You'll write, won't you?' she said.

'I can't promise, I may not have much time. You mustn't count on it.'

'*En voiture – messieurs, mesdames,*' someone shouted.

'I've got to go, darling,' I said.

I kissed her hurriedly, blindly; I didn't want to admit to myself I cared. I leant out of the window looking down on her on the platform. She seemed so little, like a child, and scared.

'You've never left me before,' she said.

'I'll be all right,' I told her; 'I'll come back soon. London won't alter me.'

'That's not the point,' she said.

'What is it, then?'

But at that moment the train began to move slowly. 'Dick,' she called, 'Dick.' I waved my hand, I smiled, I couldn't very well shout out before all the people on the platform that I loved her.

'Take care of yourself, babe,' I said. I went on looking out of the window, and watching her figure become smaller and smaller till it was swallowed up in a mass of moving figures, and then we turned a corner and I could not see the platform any more.

I settled myself down with a paper and began to read, and though I was excited about London and the book, I felt empty, somehow, dull. . . .

8

I arrived in London about a quarter-past five. I knew that there were many small hotels round Bloomsbury way. I got hold of a taxi and told the fellow to drive me in that direction, and I would tap on the glass when I found somewhere I liked.

It seemed warmer in London than it had been in Paris. It was so different though, dreary, with a hint of fog. A lonely place to arrive in. It was difficult to see much in the dim light. The streets were very full, people standing in queues on the pavements waiting for buses. The shops looked weary and used, there was a general atmosphere of Christmas being over, and the whole cold month of January to be faced.

The taxi lumbered around Russell Square. The fog was thicker here, every house seemed to be an hotel, and none particularly inviting. I finally tapped on the glass before one in Guilford Street. A page-boy came out to take my bag. 'Have you booked a room, sir?' he said. 'No,' I said.

I had to follow him along to an office and look through a shutter at a woman in spectacles. She was difficult at first, saying it was full.

'It will be for a week, probably longer,' I said.

'Oh! in that case . . .' she began. I had to sign a book while she did things with keys.

'Take the gentleman to No 58,' she said.

There wasn't a lift, we trudged upstairs to the third floor. The boy showed me into a small room with a sloping ceiling. It was cold, no central heating. Stripes on the wallpaper and a thing in the fireplace like a fan. A maid came along with hot water in a brass can. I opened the window and smelt the fog. I could hear a newspaper-boy shouting at the end of the street: 'Late night final.'

'What time will you be called in the morning, sir?' asked the maid.

'I don't know,' I said.

'Breakfast in the dining-room from eight o'clock on,' she said.

I wanted to be back in Paris, going over to the Dôme for a drink. London wasn't any good to me.

I went downstairs and there was a lounge with people sitting before a fire. There was an old lady with white hair, knitting, talking to a man in pince-nez. The rest were reading papers. I picked up a paper, but the news was not interesting to me, who had not been in England for so long. At seven o'clock a gong sounded for dinner, mournful and hollow. I sat myself at a little table in a corner. There was a vase of sad flowers. There were waitresses dressed in black, and no one raised their voice above a whisper.

I thought at first somebody was dead, but after a while I saw it was just England. The bread was cut in little squares from a tin loaf, and there was tepid tomato soup, followed by tepid cod, followed by tepid steak, fried potatoes and cabbage, followed by tepid castle pudding.

'Coffee in the lounge, sir?' asked the waitress.

'No, thanks,' I said.

I lit a cigarette and went and looked up the address of my father's publisher in the telephone-book. I found it easily enough. John Torrence, Ltd., 33, Lower Bedford Street. Torrence himself was dead, but I remembered his partner, Ernest Grey, a tall thin fellow. He used to come down and stay at home. He would remember me. I wondered what story my father and mother had told after I ran away; whether they had said the truth or whether they had made

245

up some tale of my having gone abroad. Grey used to come down about twice a year, and of course my father always saw him when he went up to London to attend some dinner or give a lecture. I would not make a long business of my letter. I would just ask for an interview, mentioning my book. I found a pen and some paper in the lounge.

Dear Mr Grey [I wrote], You will be surprised to get this letter from me. I have been abroad for nearly two years. I would be very grateful if you could give me an interview some time. The fact is, I have written a book, and a play too, and I should so much like to have your opinion and your advice. I shall be staying here all the week, and hope to have a reply from you soon.

I wondered if it seemed cool. I did not know how to write letters.

I posted it; he or one of his secretaries would open it in the morning. There did not appear to be anything to do now but wait. I went up to my room, bored, vaguely depressed.

I kept wondering what Hesta was doing.

I had never known London very well. Sometimes I had come up for a few days with mother from home. We used to stay at the Langham Hotel. She would take me with her when she did her shopping. I remembered going to Shoolbred's and Peter Robinson's and as a special treat I was given an ice at Gunter's.

There was the theatre, too, when I grew older, the front row of the dress circle at a matinée, and then long, dull dinner-parties in the evening, when I must change into stiff clothes, and escort my mother to friends of hers and my father's, where I never spoke a word, but sat glum in my chair, my ears tingling, my hands very nervous with the knives and forks.

There was a little sense of shame when, because of my youth, I left the dining-room with the ladies, and upstairs in the drawing-room my presence also seemed superfluous, so that I wandered awkwardly to a bookcase, pretending to examine the covers and bindings of the volumes, and I would overhear my mother saying in a low tone to our hostess: 'Yes, Richard is a great reader.'

They would leave me undisturbed – Richard who would also write one day, they supposed. How nice if he had inherited some of his father's genius, and they did not suspect that the row of books meant nothing to the solemn-faced boy who stood with his back turned to them, but that he was yearning to be free of their quiet atmosphere, free of the scraps of earnest conversation, and away somewhere, anywhere, in the streets of London, with other men and other women, doing strange things that they would never know.

So I had this memory of London, and another one too, a memory of hunger and distress, loneliness and poverty, black thoughts hammering at my mind, and coming to a bridge that spanned the river, leaning against this, staring down into the cold grey water, and the hand laid upon my shoulder and the voice in my ear.

This was a memory that lingered with me like a message of hope and a whisper of beauty, but it hurt because of the beauty. I did not want to think of it, nor of the shabby restaurant with the table in one corner, nor the twisting turning streets, the throb of traffic, the warm dusty air, the call of adventure round a hidden wall, nor the sudden swift vision of a ship at anchor amidst the lights and shadows of the Lower Pool. This was another London, belonging to another time; now I was a writer who would have business with a famous publisher, and I was living alone in an hotel with my MS. safe upstairs in a trunk and a woman waiting for me in Paris. Life was very earnest, life was very sane. I did not swing along the streets with my hands in my pockets, I sat over my lunch in the City, a copy of the *Spectator* propped against the glass in front of me, and I looked about me studying the faces of men. I went one evening to a Russian play, and 'This is marvellous,' I thought. 'This is marvellous,' but really I was not quite sure, really I wondered whether the dramatist had been laughing at me up his sleeve.

I clung to the illusion that I was very busy, I went over my MS. once more, I straightened the pages, and then I took it to a typing agency in the Strand, and left it with them, loath to be parted from it, but in two days it was with me once again, and this meant another reading through.

It looked different typed, braver, more mature. I read literary papers, I scanned the criticisms of recent books to see if there were any that resembled mine. I resented them all; it seemed to me too many people wrote in England, too many people had ideas.

On the Friday a letter arrived for me with the crest of John Torrence, Ltd, on the back of the envelope.

It said Mr Ernest Grey would be able to see me on Tuesday morning at eleven-thirty. This, and no more. The letter was typed by the secretary, signed with his signature. I supposed this was customary, I supposed I could hardly expect an answer from Grey himself.

Meanwhile, I must live till Tuesday. The dragging by of a week-end. It was winter, too. I went from cinema to cinema, bored by them all. I wondered how being alone in a city could ever have seemed an adventure to me, and a thrill. The atmosphere of an hotel, the mournful emptiness of having no one to speak to and nothing to do.

For the first time I began to envy people who had homes. A set-tled home, somewhere that belonged. Furniture one knew, things one had bought. Food that was not restaurant food. Clothes hung properly in wardrobes. I began to imagine a small house some-where with a garden, and coming back to it, weary and content. I imagined not existing from day to day, but continuously, a calm even day of living. Things done for one, and one not being aware. The efficiency of servants, the pleasant monotony of order. I imagined Hesta with her hair rumpled, gardening, and then going in to change, and a maid bringing out to me an evening paper; or the comfort of dark evenings in the winter, the curtains drawn, a blazing fire, dogs about the place, sighing and stretching them-selves, and Hesta lying on a sofa reading a book. I imagined the security of settled money, of a steady income, putting my car away in a garage, and coming into my own house, picking up my own letters in the hall. Looking about me, calling 'Hesta?' and then a child shouting from a room overhead, running on to a landing, peering through the banisters, and I glancing up, laughing, saying 'Hullo!'

I wondered why I had ever despised these things, why they had once seemed pitiful and absurd. I wondered why the placidity of a home seemed necessary to me now, and why I no longer yearned for the turmoil of a ship upon the sea.

Once there had been a path across the mountains, and restlessness, and an urge to fight, and a dream of many women, and now there was a home that was my home, and peace, and relaxation, and no dreams but the reality of one woman. I did not know if it was I who had changed, or the world that had changed about me, but so it was, and I could not call back the dreams that had gone from me.

I stood on the doorstep of No. 33, Lower Bedford Street. I was shown into a room, where there were pictures on the wall and books on the table.

I felt shabby and wretchedly immature with my MS. under my arm, wrapped up very hurriedly in brown paper. This was where my father would stand perhaps, leaning on his stick, glancing about him at the prints, but supreme in his self-confidence, and then walking slowly to the other room where Grey would seize him by his hands, saying: 'They surely did not make you wait?'

I waited, though, unimportant, rather foolish with my brown-paper parcel, and in ten minutes the door was opened and I followed a man along a passage to another room.

Grey was standing with his back to me, stooping a little, warming his hands at the fire. He turned round as I entered, he smiled, and I saw he had not changed.

'Well, Richard,' he said.

I went forward and shook his hand.

'It's very good of you to see me,' I said.

'No, no, I was glad to get your letter. A little astonished, perhaps, but glad. Sit down, won't you?'

I did so, and was silent. I was not sure whether I should speak or he.

'Where have you been all this time?' he said.

'I've lived in Paris now for over a year,' I said, 'but before then I travelled a bit, I saw round Scandinavia, I went on a ship.'

'Quite an experience, I suppose,' he said.

'Yes,' I said.

'I haven't been to Paris for many years,' he went on – 'I dare say it's all very changed now. Americanized and so on.'

'I like it,' I said.

I wondered why there was a need for this conversation. Wasn't he going to ask me about the book?

249

'Scandinavia I don't know at all,' he said; 'it must be very wonderful, of course. Yes. The fjords and the midnight sun. Did you go very far north?'

'Not as far as the Cape,' I said.

'Oh! you ought to have seen the Cape. So now you're back in England again. How long are you going to be here?'

'Well, it rather depends. . . .' I began.

'Have you been home at all?'

'No,' I said.

'They don't know you're here?'

'No.'

'I was down there a few months ago. Your father was looking a little tired, I thought. Been overworking himself. We're bringing out his new book this week.'

'Oh?'

'Yes. Finest thing he's ever done, in my opinion. It's an epic poem, you know, very long, quite different from his shorter pieces. There is a strength and a beauty in it that leaves you breathless. I had no idea he would produce something of this sort, at his age. His grasp of psychology is astounding and his understanding of human nature. He has called it *Conflict*.'

'Oh yes.'

'We've included three or four shorter pieces as well. There's a lovely little thing, a description of a summer evening after rain, which literally gave me the impression of stillness, of silence, and the drip of water from an avenue of trees. I wish I had a copy up here.'

'Yes,' I said.

'He's the biggest man in the world of letters today, Richard. He'll go down to posterity as the poet of the century; we all know that.'

'Yes,' I said.

He sat for a few minutes, staring before him, his thoughts busy with my father. I said nothing, I looked at the carpet, hugging my brown-paper parcel on my knees. Then he broke himself away, he smiled, he reached for a cigarette, and turned to smaller things.

'Well, Richard,' he said, 'and what's all this about your writing a book?'

It seemed to me I could see the vision of my father slipping away, remote, impregnable, on some far-distant plane, and here was I, humble and obscure, running hither and thither on the silly earth.

I stammered and hesitated, searching for words.

'I brought it with me. I wondered perhaps . . .'

He nodded encouragement, he watched me kindly, the kindness of somebody old to somebody young.

'Is it a novel?' he said, and he spoke gently, too gently.

'Yes,' I said, and the words fell from me now, tumbling over one another. 'I've worked on it, off and on, most of the year. I was terribly keen, I couldn't leave it at times, and then of course there were breaks, going away and the summer. But I've been over and over it, time and again; I don't think there's anything superfluous in it now. It's difficult for me to judge, but I have worked hard and hope it's good. I think it's different in a way from the ordinary novel; I've tried to see things from a new angle.'

I stopped, breathless, searching his face. He flicked the ash from his cigarette into a tray.

'And the play?' he said. 'Didn't you say something in your letter about a play, too?'

'Yes,' I went on, perhaps he would return to the book later. 'Yes, there is a play. Of course I realized that it needed an entirely different technique. I wrote the play first. I think the book is the better of the two; it's a little more human, it deals with people from an outsider's point of view – seeing into them, as it were – but the play is lighter, more cynical – I – it's rather difficult to explain.'

'I see,' he said.

I wondered whether he would ask me to read some of it to him then. I cleared my throat in case.

'Well, Richard,' he said, 'I'll tell you what I will do. In the ordinary course of events, your MS. would be handed to one of the readers, and he would make his report in a week or so. But I have a great regard for your father, Richard, and because you are his son I will ask you to leave your package here with me, and I'll take it back and glance at it this week-end. How does that suit you?'

'Thanks terribly,' I said.

He stood up, he held out his hand.

'I'm afraid I must send you away now,' he said; 'I've got a great deal of work on hand at the moment. I'll write to you after the week-end, and we'll see what can be done. Good-bye. I'm glad to have seen you again.'

Once more I was walking along the passage, and out of the door, and so into Lower Bedford Street, hoping that the man passing would see me standing carelessly on the steps of the great publishing house and would wonder who I was, and I strolled slowly down the steps, smothering a yawn, acting to myself, but deep in my heart questioning what I should do for a whole week until I heard from Grey again.

Whenever I picked up a paper I seemed to see a notice of my father's poems. There was a whole column devoted to him in *The Times*, his picture flared up at me from the *Telegraph*, and when I passed a book-shop there in the window stood the small slim volume in its pale grey wrapper, and ranged behind it the collected edition of his works.

I wondered if any younger and impetuous writer would seize his chance and launch forth some virulent attack, but there was no suggestion even of this; it was as if my father stood on his little pinnacle above the rest of mankind, secure and supreme. 'His mastery of the English language is unequalled among the writers of today,' I read in one paper. 'The exquisite symmetry of his phrasing, his intimate comprehension of the beauty of sound are rare qualities belonging only to genius. His depth of psychology. . . .'

I threw the paper aside and laughed. Psychology. There was a father who had a son, he had not written a poem about that. '*Conflict*,' I read, 'deals with the dual nature of a man, and the continuous struggle for supremacy in a living soul. The poet's insight into the unchanging spirit of humanity. . . .' 'Insight' was a good word. My father was great on insight. I had lived with him for twenty years and I ought to know. 'His intimate understanding of the deep unspoken desires that lie sleeping in the breast of every one of us. . . .' So the papers said. I thought of him turning his eyes upon me in the dining-room at home: 'Yes, Richard must bicycle into Lessington.' Intimate understanding, and I pedalling down the hard main road. What a lot of insight that turned out to be!

I left the papers in the lounge at my hotel, bought a copy of *Tit-Bits* and laughed at the jokes. I then saw a picture at a cinema in the Euston Road, where chorus-girls tickled old gentlemen below the waist, and there was a tart beside me who fumbled with my knee. I let her fumble – and it was all great fun – and I hoped my father would continue to write his bloody poems, for why should I worry?

But though I strolled along the street afterwards with my hat on the back of my head I was not happy. I went into a shop and bought the book, and so upstairs to read in the room of the hotel alone. And as I read I saw that all that the papers had said of him was true; it was no use standing out against him, for here was beauty bare, and the meaning of dreams, and anguish and ecstasy, and all that I had ever wanted and all that I had ever known. Here was the tremor of life itself, the wonder and the pain, the voice of a lonely soul lost in the wilderness, and he called out to me from his desert places not as a father and a man, but as a spirit kindred to me, ageless, one of my kind, and I knew him then as I could never know him in the flesh, reaching down to me from some impossible summit, bringing me to his side.

And he had written this alone in his dark library, and I had sailed in a ship, and lost, and loved, and we would not come together and speak of these things, but because of his poem we were near to one another and we understood.

Somehow the week passed, in seeing things, in walking, in thinking of Hesta, in reading. I came to lose my dislike of London, for there was something tender in it and strong. Behind the sullen grey barrier, unfriendly at first and hard, there was a purpose more forceful and deep than the clatter and jingle of Paris. I felt there was a continuity in this place that would never be disturbed; there would not be blood and thunder, laughter and tears, but a solid belief in the normality of men and women; there was tradition here, and age, and beneath the exterior of cold indifference a certain restfulness and peace. I thought I would have to talk to Hesta about London. . . .

During the Sunday I pictured Grey at his home with my MS. in his hands, I saw him turn the leaves, I saw his lips move as they registered the phrases. First he would scan the book, and then the play. Would he understand why I had written this and that, would he see what I had seen?

Perhaps he would not be in the mood most necessary. He would have friends to lunch, and bridge afterwards, then yawning, fling himself into a chair saying: 'I suppose I must glance through this fellow's stuff.'

I wanted him to be grave, to be silent, to read slowly, deeply, to sit late over a sinking fire careless of time and then to call to his wife: 'I think I have made a discovery.' I would not build too many fancies in my mind.

On Wednesday there came a letter from him – his own hand-writing. My heart beat very fast and my hands trembled. He said:

My dear Richard, Would you be able to lunch with me tomorrow, Thursday, at 1 o'clock at the Savoy? Ring through to my secretary if this is all right.

Yours sincerely,
Ernest Grey.

I wondered whether I should wire to Hesta. It was better to wait, better not to make a fool of myself. I arrived at the Savoy on Thursday at five minutes to one. He came in alone; he had not brought anyone to meet me.

'Glad you were able to come,' he said. I did not tell him that there was no other possible engagement I could have had, that all the week I had lived only for this moment.

We sat down at a table by the window.

'What are you going to eat?' he said. I studied the menu, I did not care. He took some little time in the ordering of his food, and I chose what he had chosen. I smiled at him as a show of confidence, but the palms of my hands were wet.

'I can't stand this cold, can you?' he said, glancing out of the window. 'Now I should like to take a month off and live in the sun for a while down South. That's the life. No worries, no business. Do you know the Riviera at all?'

'No,' I said. 'No, but I should like to go.' I kept forcing little pieces of hard toast into my mouth.

'Oh! well, you're young, there's time for all things,' he said, 'and, anyway, you're quite a traveller as it is. Tell me now, is Stockholm a very remarkable place?'

I saw there was no help for it; I saw I must make an attempt at conversation. Too anxious to please, fearful of seeming dull, I plunged into an account of the places I had seen. I remembered details I hoped would interest him, the colour of buildings I had not really noticed, a description of scenery that in reality had passed me by.

'Most interesting,' he said, 'most interesting.' And all the while the time was passing by, and he chewed his food thoughtfully, bringing in anecdotes of his own, stories of past things, so that I must laugh and seem amused. And then a break in the conversation, and his glance at the waiter. 'Will you bring two coffees?'

I sat quite still, watching a little crumb on the cloth.

He lit a cigar, slowly, so slowly.

'Well, Richard,' he began, 'I looked over your things on Sunday, as I said I would. Tell me now, how long did you say you had been writing?'

'About a year, off and on,' I said.

'Yes, yes, I see.'

The waiter brought the coffee. I stirred it with my spoon, round and round, never taking my eyes off the cup.

'I will explain to you, if I can, Richard, just exactly what I felt when I had read your book. It seemed to me, from the very first page, that you were dominated by the thought of your father, that his image was so constantly before you he was cramping your own personality, you could not escape from the idea of his greatness. Do you follow my meaning?'

'Yes,' I said.

'You were writing as though you wished to be his echo, as though you were stalking in his shadow, and the result was not the result that he obtains, but a false contorted version of his

255

style, a grotesque resemblance, like a strange caricature. It was false, Richard, it was insincere.'

I went on stirring my coffee.

'In the middle,' he said, 'you appeared suddenly to change your mood. You were yourself, no longer a feverish imitation, but the self was not a writer, Richard, not someone who waits secure and alone guarding his talent for himself, but a young man, tossed here, tossed there, influenced by one mood, influenced by another, in love perhaps, uncertain, doubtful, a young man who forces himself to write, but was born without the gift.

'I am telling you this, Richard, because I believe in telling the truth; I believe that life must be faced, by all of us, and you are your father's son, you cannot run away.'

My heart was not beating any longer; I was steady, calm.

'You mean it's no good?' I said. 'You mean it's useless going on.'

'I don't want to hurt you,' he said, 'I don't want to seem indifferent to you, hard. Whether or not in later years, after some little suffering, some little experience, you are able to write I cannot at the moment say. I think in time you will discover that the urge that came upon you to write during the past year was no more than an expression of extreme youthfulness, a phase that was necessary to you before maturity. It was only because of your father that you chose to write. If you had been born the son of somebody else, it would have been painting perhaps, music, acting, any of these things. And whatever you had chosen you would not have succeeded, because it could never have come first with you before your own personal inclinations. Your father sits alone, Richard, a genius, secure and safe in himself, caring for nothing and no one, while you live and love, and hurt yourself, and are miserable, and are happy, and you aren't a genius, Richard; you are only an ordinary man; and though these words of mine are heartless to you now, one day you will be glad I've told you, one day you'll understand.'

I heard the band behind the palm trees play a loud gay tune, and a woman passed in front of our table, laughing over her shoulder.

'Yes,' I heard myself say. 'Yes, I understand.'

'I'll send your MS. back to your hotel. You will like to keep it, of course. I had a glance at the play too, Richard, but I am afraid we can do nothing with it. If I thought there was the slightest chance of the book making good I would suggest one of the smaller publishers, but I think even they would realize it falls short of what is required for even a moderate sale. Of course, it might be accepted because of your name.'

'I should not care for that,' I said.

'No – I did not think you would. Now, Richard, tell me, have you any plans for the future?'

How should I have any plans?

'I don't know,' I said; 'I suppose I shall go back to Paris.'

He asked for my address in the Rue du Cherche-Midi, and I gave it him.

'If you are ever in any trouble or perplexity I want you to let me know. Somehow I think you have had what you needed out of Paris. I think that London is the place for you,' he said.

'Perhaps,' I said.

He called for his bill. He rose from his chair.

'Where are you going now?' he said.

To save him embarrassment I murmured something about an appointment.

'I can drop you anywhere,' he said. 'I have a car outside.'

I said 'No', I thanked him very much.

'Don't let yourself be down-hearted at what I have told you,' he said. 'I don't want you to feel that you have failed. I want you to look upon what has been as a phase, as a casting aside of your boyhood. You were made for other things, Richard, for other things.' He smiled at me, and the commissioner opened the door of his car.

'I'd like to do what I can for you at any time,' he said, and then he shook my hand.

'Good-bye,' he said, 'and good luck.'

I watched the car drive away. Then I went out and sat in the gardens at the back of the Savoy Hotel.

There was no need to stay in London any longer. If we had finished lunch a little earlier I could have caught the afternoon train.
It was too late now, I would have to go first thing in the morning
instead. I would fill the rest of the day by seeing to tickets, by
packing my bag and settling my bill at the hotel. I knew that this
would take a small space out of time, but I pretended to myself
they were large matters, requiring much energy and foresight. I
had sat for nearly an hour in the gardens by the Embankment, and
the light was fading now, and it was cold. I got up and walked
away, my collar turned up, my hat low over my eyes. This time tomorrow evening I would be in Paris, anyway. And Hesta would
be there.

I tried to arrange in order the things that remained to me,
but my mind was a queer contradiction of itself, and my
thoughts wandered from Hesta to my father, and from my
father to Jake. Mostly I think they clung to Jake, his hand on
my shoulder, his smile, and his voice that came to me now as from
a great distance: 'You'll be all right,' he had said. 'You'll be all
right.'

I wondered what this belief in me had meant, and whether he
had known how things would be.

It seemed to me his words had gone for nothing, and here was I,
alive to no great purpose, and there was he, a poor fled shadow of
a man, drowned and forgotten in the Baie des Trépassés.

I went on walking along the Embankment, and then I turned
upwards again, and came to an Underground station. There I took
the Tube to Russell Square, and found myself once more before
the hotel and the page-boy standing on the steps.

In spite of shock of the breaking up of an idea, life had to go on,
even after this, in irritating ways.

I discussed the weather pleasantly with an old man in the
lounge, I announced my intention of leaving in the morning, I
smiled cheerfully to the woman in the office, and picked up an
evening paper.

I seemed to hear Grey telling me, slowly and calmly, what I had
always known, that I was an ordinary man. I was no genius, and I

had been born without the gift of writing. All that had been a phase, he had said, and the casting aside of boyhood. Even before I read my father's poem I knew this. I knew from the very beginning, when I had covered my doubting fear with a brave show of carelessness and a gesture of pretence. I knew that if I had been born to write it would have come from me effortless and unrestrained, compelled by some dim travail of its own, forceful, like a strange necessity.

It would have been unhindered by the turmoil of emotion and the touch of passing things, it would have rested immune from contact, precious and untended.

Instead of this I had blustered and sworn, too anxious and too eager, arrogant in my determination, seeing myself as a figure, watching my own antics. I was an ordinary man.

So I turned the pages of my paper and I saw that in Wood Street, Ponders End, this day a woman of the name of Marsden had been knocked down by a tram and killed, leaving two children of five and three; but what was that to me, I thought, what was that to me?

Grey would be leaving his office now, he would remember perhaps, just before he went, to tell his secretary to send a certain MS. to my address. And so out of the building, and into his car, sighing, a little weary from his day's work, thinking no more of me.

It seemed that Aston Villa had played Sheffield United this afternoon, and had won by two goals to nil. Which perhaps had caused excitement in many homes.

I sat in the lounge and waited for the gong to sound for dinner; then I had dinner and after that I sat again in the lounge, and so the evening wore away.

My MS. arrived by the last post in the evening, and when I packed my bag I placed it as carefully as Hesta had placed it before, at the bottom of the case, but this time my father's poems were on top. Then I covered them both with my pyjamas and Hesta's dressing-gown; so that was the finish of them and the passing of my phase.

When I left London the sun shone and there was a strange clarity and brilliance in the sky, the morning air brisk and keen, seeming the forerunner of a lovely day. The journey to Paris was long, interminable to me, who had bought no books and no papers, and must stare out of the window and watch the passing scenery.

I had not wired to Hesta, but she would be there.

As yet I had made no plans in my mind for either of us. Something would have to be done. I thought that we would not go on living in Paris. That belonged to the phase, and the phase was over. There would have to be some little adjustment of myself before my mind was properly attuned to the new condition of things. The old restlessness and hesitation, the weakness and the indecision, these would have to go. I would start again in a while with a fresh outlook. The sort of life we had been leading was no good to her. I must recognize that. It was no good to me either. I did not want to grasp at life any longer, to try first one thing and then another, to be under the control of a suggestion and a mood. I was weary of uncertainty. I wanted to be sure. I wanted to see my life ahead of me as settled and secure. The old nonsense of excitement and danger was no more than a fable, an invention for children, a continuation of a dream.

I thought of the stability of London, and the strength of it, and then the careless indiscrimination of Montparnasse, those friends of Hesta's, the wandering in and out of cafés at all times, the lacking of method, of any proper concentration. I would take Hesta away from all that. We would be married, we would have a home somewhere, some definite foundation. It was no good hanging about and playing at life. This was what we had been doing all the year, playing at life. We had not begun at all. Hesta and I would be married. I remembered once, long ago, she had said something about wanting a baby. I don't believe I listened much at the time. I wondered why. Perhaps I had been thinking of other things. Maybe that was what Hesta needed in life, maybe that was necessary to women – having children. I had not considered it before. She did not seem to care as much for her music as she had. Perhaps that was only a phase, too. Perhaps Hesta was an ordinary woman like I was an ordinary man.

One day, Grey had told me, I should be glad of this. At the moment it seemed ridiculous and a little sad – ordinary men and women, going on and living their lives. The picture of this clung to

260

me as the train swung through the dull flat country of northern France, and the man who sat opposite to me, his grey hair, a paper in his hands, and a quiet woman at his side, yawning, blinking her eyes as we passed by the station of Amiens; they were like us, I thought, only they had travelled a little farther.

The man yawned, too, and folded his paper. He put his spectacles away in a case. 'We have a good two hours yet,' he said; 'we might go along to the restaurant car later and have some tea. They do you well on these French trains.'

The woman, his wife, smiled, and nodded, fumbling with the magazine on her knee, pretending she had no wish to rest. The man settled himself more comfortably in his corner, he sighed, and closed his eyes, he composed his features for sleep. Perhaps he had written a book, too, when he was young, and had sailed in a ship, and had ridden across the mountains. Once, long ago, he had worshipped the body of that woman, and they had been lovers. I watched his jaw relax and his head sink from the high cushion to rest upon his hand, and she stretched out and placed her coat over his knees in case he should be cold.

And he went on sleeping, aware of her care for him, a shadow of a smile upon his face, safe in his corner. I looked out upon the rushing plains, the long white roads, the thin avenues of trees, and I wondered if it was really as pitiful as it seemed, this returning of mine as a writer who had failed, or whether it meant no more to the course of my little life than a shadow means, cast in early morning by a cloud on the surface of the sky.

I took a taxi from the Gare du Nord to the Rue du Cherche-Midi. The train was punctual, arriving at six-fifteen. I had not prepared anything to say to Hesta. I was tired now, weary from the journey and the reaction of the previous day. I did not want to have to make excuses for myself, speeches of defence, protests at fate and fortune; I only wanted her to put her arms round me and to understand. I would be a boy again, I would lay my head in her lap, saying nothing, feeling for her hands. When the taxi drew to a standstill against the pavement I glanced up at the window, but there was no light, and I had to face the disappointment of her not being there.

I paid off the taxi and let myself into the house. I went slowly upstairs, hoping perhaps that the absence of light would mean she was resting in the other room, but when I came there and felt for the switches on the wall, I saw that she was not there, and both the rooms were empty.

I threw my bag down on the floor and wandered between the two rooms, trying to make the familiarity of them come to me as a consolation. Somehow they did not give out the warmth I had expected; they were friendless, drear.

Her things were not spread about the bed, there was no ash upon the floor, no stray sheet of music on a chair, no general disorder that was part of her presence.

The rooms were too tidy, too cold; they looked as if they had been left a very long time to their own company, and had gone back to their original silence and formality, forgetful of the atmosphere we had created. The bed was not our bed, it was a piece of furniture, stiff and absurd. People had never loved one another there. I sat in a chair and lit a cigarette, helpless suddenly, aware I was alone. I felt as though I were waiting for something to happen, and I did not know what it would be. I went on sitting in the chair and it was dark outside, and soon the cafés would be filled with people for dinner, and the business of evening would be started, but I did not know what I should do. I thought that if I went on waiting Hesta would come.

Then I began to feel hungry, and this was an irritation to me, because if I went out to get some food I might possibly miss her returning, and our meeting would be spoilt, for I wanted her to come in like this, into the dreary room and find me lonely and hungry, unwelcomed, a wretched homecoming, and the realization of this would hurt her, I hoped, so that the sight of her suffering would cause me to forget my own pain.

I knew that I should have sent her a wire, but this was no excuse to me in my present state. I felt that instinctively she should have guessed of my return.

Then hunger proved too much for me, and I left the house, and so out into the street again, and across the Boulevard Montparnasse to the Coupole, where I had dinner.

I looked about for some sign of Hesta or her friends, but they were nowhere, and afterwards I walked up to the Dôme and to the Rotonde, but they were at neither of these places.

It was beginning to rain, and the discomfort of this added another chill to my depression, and I walked up and down, hoping that in some way I should make myself ill, and she would come back and find me thin and wretched, stretched on the bed, delirious, perhaps dying . . . I put my hand to my side and coughed. Already I was ill, already I was suffering. I went back to the Rue du Cherche-Midi, wondering if I should find her there waiting for me, reproaching herself, having seen my bag on the floor and now my things unpacked, the lights turned on.

There wasn't anybody, though, and the silence of the rooms mocked me, sneering at me for my pretence at make-believe. So I bent and undid my case, and threw my things anyhow on to a chair. I came to my MS. and my father's poems, and at the sight of these I sat staring for a while, lost in the dreams of a phase that had gone.

Then I opened the door of the wardrobe and I was surprised for a minute to see how empty it seemed because of the absence of my things, and as I looked I became aware that it was bare for another reason, and that it was not only my clothes that were gone, but hers too, dresses that she wore, a heavy coat, a suit that usually hung behind my own.

I opened the drawers beneath the dressing-table, and these were thin too, scanty of her things, brushes and creams, a box of powder, the litter that was hers, now absent, swept away.

I stood in the centre of the room, looking from the gaping wardrobe to the bare dressing-table, and I tried to make some sense to my mind from all this, but my brain was numbed and strange, and all I could do was to glance down foolishly at a little used lipstick in my hands, which I had taken from the empty drawer.

When I awoke the daylight was flooding the room from the window. I had forgotten to close the shutters before I fell asleep. I looked at my watch and I saw that the time was half-past nine. I had lain in the bed dressed as I was and had slept there, until the light had wakened me.

I remembered with a little shock of realization that here I was in my room in the Rue du Cherche-Midi, and Hesta was not beside me. I sat up on the bed and lit a cigarette and tried to think. Perhaps she had been lonely and had gone to stay with Wanda. Perhaps she had been frightened at living alone in the rooms by herself. I had sent her a letter the first day of my arrival in London, and nothing after that. She must have known that letters were not my thing, she surely had not expected to hear from me every day. She knew I would come back. That was all that mattered. I had not even bothered to give her the address of my hotel. I had not thought all this came into our lives. We knew one another. She would wait and I would come back. That was all. It was simple enough.

Yes, of course she had gone to stay with Wanda. They had made up a party somewhere. She thought I was still in London.

I got up, uncertain, anxious in my mind, and I opened the window wide and looked down into the street, as though I expected to see her there, staring up at me, waving her hand. And there was only the street and the sound of distant traffic, and a woman brushing the steps of a shop with a broom.

I began to shave, watching a strange face in the glass that was not mine, and the shudder of apprehension grew upon me, holding me fast with cold still hands.

I heard a taxi hoot some way up the street, and the hooting drew nearer, and then there was the screech of brakes as it drew to the pavement in front of the house.

I stood still where I was, the shaving-brush in my hands, and I did not move.

I heard a door slam below and the sound of footsteps coming up the stairs. Yet the taxi did not go away, it continued where it was in the street below. I wondered why she had not sent it away. The door of the other room opened, and I heard her walk across the floor. She did not come into the bedroom. I hesitated a moment, and then I went to the door, the soap melting on my face, the brush still in my hands.

Hesta was bending over the table. I could not see what she was doing. I waited, wondering whether I should speak. Then she turned suddenly, looking over her shoulder, and she stood up, and stared at me.

We went on looking at each other without speaking.

'You've come back,' she said, and her voice trailed off, odd, uncertain.

'Yes,' I said.

I smiled, and then moved towards her, wondering why we must be unnatural to one another and strained.

'I came back last night,' I said: 'I wondered where you had gone.'

I saw she had a piece of paper in her hands. She laid it aside, it was blank, and it fluttered to the floor.

'I was just going to write you a letter,' she said.

'I never gave you my address in London,' I said; 'it was stupid of me, you might have wanted it, in case anything had happened.'

Then I wondered why she should write me a letter if she did not know where to send it.

'You couldn't have posted it, anyway,' I said.

'I was going to leave it here for you,' she said.

I frowned, puzzled by her words.

'I don't see there was any need for that,' I said.

She got up and went and stood by the mantelpiece. She fingered a little ornament, putting it in its place. Her face was different, queer somehow, and strained. I knew then that I had to ask a question, that I could not go on pretending to myself that everything was all right.

'What's happened?' I said. Then her eyes swept my face, lost and strange.

'You shouldn't have gone away,' she said; 'I told you at the time and you didn't listen. You shouldn't have gone away . . .'

The soap was dry and harsh on my face now, but I did not bother to wipe it off.

I went over to take hold of her, but she shook her head and pushed me with her hands.

'No,' she said, 'no, it's no good.'

Her voice was hard, she stared past me, over my shoulder.

'Tell me,' I said, and I fingered her dress, not looking at her.

She waited a minute, as though searching for words, and when she spoke it was not her speaking, but somebody else.

'We're not going on any more,' she said; 'we've come to the end of this.'

'How do you mean?' I said.

She said: 'It isn't any good any more. It's all over. That's what I came to write and tell you. It's all over.'

'I don't understand,' I said, and I took hold of her hand and held on to it, as though this were some measure of safety.

'I don't understand.'

Her voice went on, dull and monotonous, repeating the same thing.

'I told you not to go away,' she said; 'I knew what would happen. It's no use saying I'm sorry. Sooner or later it was bound to be. You didn't see that, you just went away and you didn't seem to mind.'

'You mean you don't love me,' I said, 'it's finished, it's gone?'

'Love,' she said, and she shrugged her shoulders and laughed. A funny sort of laugh that wasn't hers.

'I don't know anything about love,' she said, 'but whatever was is spoilt and done with. We don't belong to each other like we did. I couldn't help it, it happened. Life's like that, it's queer. I'm sorry. I can't say anything more than that, can I?'

'What is it?' I said. 'Why are we changed?' I couldn't believe the truth of what she was saying. I thought she must be following some silly idea in her mind.

'You see, you don't mean what you did to me any more,' she said; 'once you were everything, and now I've lost it, the thing that was you. Since you've been away I've been with someone else.'

'No,' I said, 'no.'

'Yes. I had to, I wanted to. You know what I was like, you know. You shouldn't have gone.'

I did not listen to all that. I only had before me the vision of her with some man, doing our things.

'You didn't let someone, Hesta,' I said, 'you didn't, not with you?'

'Yes — ' she said.

I went on staring at her.

'No,' I said, 'no – it isn't true. You're not like that, cheap, stupid, giving yourself to anyone.'

'It is true,' she said.

I sat down on the arm of the chair with my head in my hands trying to think some way out of all this.

'No,' I said, 'it's not true, you're lying. It's too filthy, too bloody filthy.' I went on repeating this to her in an effort at persuasion.

'Too filthy, too bloody filthy.'

She did not seem to see.

'You told me once it didn't mean a thing,' she said. 'Those were your words: "It doesn't mean a thing." In here, in this room. The first time it happened with us.'

'That was different,' I said; 'you can't go by that, you don't know what you're saying.'

'You can't get out of it,' she said. 'You can't prevent what has been with me, with us, with other people. You made me in the beginning and now it's too late to alter things. I have to go on now – I can't go back to where I was.'

'Is it Julio?' I said, 'that fellow . . .'

'Yes,' she said. 'It didn't seem to matter once you had gone.'

She told me this gravely and calmly with her hands clasped in front of her. She was cool, unperturbed.

'Oh! darling . . .' I said. 'Oh! darling, darling . . . what have I done . . .?'

'You mustn't mind,' she said. 'I felt rather awful at first, too. And then it was so natural, so inevitable, and I wanted to, anyway.'

She did not realize, she was only a child.

'You can't,' I said; 'Hesta, my Hesta, you don't understand. It isn't a little thing, it's the beginning of degradation, the loss of everything that's lovely and perfect in you, it's the start of a life that leads to nothing but misery and humiliation . . .'

'Why?' she said. 'I don't see that. Besides, what does it matter?'

'It does, darling, it does matter.'

'I don't look upon it in that way,' she said. 'I want it, that's all, and it doesn't matter who.'

'No, no, Hesta . . .'

'It's too late, Dick, to go on in this way now. Too late. It's my own life, and I shall live in the way that's easiest for me. Once there was music, and then there was you, and now there's this. It can't be helped.'

'We've got to fight this together, Hesta, we've got to get out of it. We're going to be married, darling; do you understand? We're going to be married.'

'No.'

'Yes, darling.'

'No, Dick, you're being ridiculous, you don't seem to follow what I've been telling you. We've finished, you and I; it's over. I can't go on with our life. I want new things . . .'

'Hesta, sweetheart, what you've been telling me is something that hurts more than I believed it possible to be hurt, but we can get over it, we can, if we try together. I want to look after you, to take you from this. We've got to start again, we've got to. We're going to be married . . .'

'No, I don't want to be married. Once, yes, last year, but you didn't listen then, you said marriage was old-fashioned and absurd. I agree with you now, too. It is absurd. I wasn't made for that. I'm going away – I want to be gay, to have fun. I'm going with Julio.'

My horror for her future was blinded by my loathing at what she had done, and I could see nothing but pictures in my mind, evil and distorted.

'You're not going away with him,' I said. 'He can't have what I have had, not you, Hesta, he can't . . .'

'What's the use of all this?' she said. 'You should have thought of it before, months ago. You didn't bother, you've never thought of anything or anyone but yourself.'

'Hesta . . .'

'No – never, for one moment. It was you, you, all the time. Nothing mattered except what affected you. Loving, living, going away, it was you who came first. You did not think of me, and how I felt. I did not count. What's the good of trying to look after me now?'

As she spoke it seemed to me I was not there listening to her, but standing beneath a lamp-post in a dark London street, and the light of the lamp cast a shadow on the face of Jake beside me. And I leant forward, ashamed of my curiosity, saying: 'Anyway, what had he done?' and Jake turned his eyes upon me, gentle, strange. 'Just been selfish,' he said, 'and thinking about his body.' And then far away, the whisper of a voice, remote, and distant from me.

'I killed him because he'd spoilt the life of some woman I'd never even met.'

Then I was in a circus tent, stretched upon the ground, the life ebbing from me, the life that I loved – so painful now, so dim, and Jake looking down upon me, Jake's eyes that would not leave me . . .

'You didn't bother to think,' said Hesta, 'that was all, you just didn't bother. P'raps it's not your fault, p'raps it's just something to do with us both being young.'

Only I didn't die, it was Jake who had died. Jake had been drowned in the Baie des Trépassés, and I was here, alone, and listening to Hesta.

'What are we going to do?' I asked her, and I looked up at her as though she were strange to me now, some other woman, in some other life.

'I'm going away with Julio,' she said.

I was calm and indifferent, all feelings seemed to have gone from me.

'That won't last,' I said. 'You won't stay together for long. What will you do then?'

'I don't make plans ahead,' she said. 'I'll wait and see. I'll enjoy myself; somebody will turn up.'

'I want you to stay with me,' I told her, but my voice was toneless somehow, lacking conviction.

'No,' she said, 'that's over, you and I. You only ask me because you have to, because you feel responsible. You want to save your own conscience. We could never be the same together. You know that. Not after the other thing. You'd always be thinking of it. Even now, when I've only just told you, you feel different to me, quite different.'

'No,' I said, 'no.'

But I knew she was speaking the truth. Already I was another man and she was another woman.

'You don't need me either,' she said. 'Why, I've realized that for a long time. You have your writing, that's the only thing that counts with you.'

'My writing?' I said.

'Yes. You'd give up the world for that. You gave up me.'

I looked at her, not saying anything.

'You'll go on as you've been doing all the autumn,' she said. 'I can't stand that any longer. You'll soon forget all this, us, and what we've been. You'll be successful, with your book published and your play produced, and people talking about you. That's what you want, isn't it? That's what you set out for?'

'You don't understand,' I said.

'Yes, I do,' she said, 'I've known always, in the back of my mind, it would end like this. Last spring I wanted to be married, I wanted to have a baby, and a home, and to look after you, us being together always – like ordinary people. But you told me not to think like that, you told me it was worthless and absurd. And now you'll be free, on your own, famous soon with your books and happy; and I'm going to be happy too, in my way, in the way you taught me.'

She picked up her bag and her hat from the chair. She began to powder her nose.

'You used to say: "Don't let's ever be serious", didn't you? I always think of that now. I'm never serious. I laugh at people and things. It's the only way. So I shall say that to you, now – don't let's ever be serious, Dick – life's too short.'

She laughed, cramming on her hat. 'I don't think there's anything I want to take. I've moved everything I needed last week. Do you suppose you'll go on living here?'

I didn't think it could be true, somehow, the strange normality, her voice, natural and calm.

'I thought Julio and I might go down to the South,' she said; 'I long to be all day in the sun. He's got a little money, I believe. I don't know how. Probably sponges on vague relations. As a matter of fact, he's quite nice, Dick.'

Was she saying all this to me? We were like two people meeting over tea. I tried to bring myself down to reality.

'You're not happy,' I said.

She stared at me blankly. 'I?' she said. 'My dear, I'm terribly happy. It's such fun, feeling that nothing matters.' She looked at me, smiling, a new Hesta, confident, strangely self-possessed.

'Well, there's nothing more to say, is there?' she said. 'I'm glad I've told you, and you've been sensible. Not like men in books, murdering women. We had a good time in a way, didn't we? I've got a wretched taxi ticking away in the street.'

'You're not going?' I said.

Still I wasn't quite sure, still I would not believe the truth.

'Yes. There's no point in staying here. I only came to write the letter, you know. It was a shock, seeing you in the doorway. That's why I was stupid at first.'

She looked round her, smiling vaguely. 'Funny old room,' she said; 'there have been nice times here. Lately, I've hated it, though. It's been different for so long. You had better go and dress, Dick. You haven't finished shaving, have you?' She stood by the door, holding on to the handle.

'How funny if we meet in a few years, and you're terribly famous,' she said. 'I shall come up and speak to you, and you won't recognize me. You'll say: "Who on earth is this little creature?" and you'll peer down at me over the heads of publishers. I wonder whom I shall be with then. Be happy, Dick, with your writing and vague women who come along. You mustn't mind about me. I shall have fun, you know . . .'

She gave me a flash of a smile and was gone. I heard her footsteps down the stairs, and then out in the street, and the slam of the taxi door. It was the same as when she had come, only the sounds were reversed. The taxi started with a grinding of gears and went away up the street, hooting, the sound becoming faint as it merged into the traffic of the Boulevard Montparnasse.

I stood still, as I had before, and I picked up the shaving-brush that was lying on the table.

10

If this had been a year ago I should have gone out and got drunk. I should have gone on drinking until there were no thoughts left in my head, until I was stupefied and senseless, and then I would have returned to my room and lain face downwards on the bed to sleep for three days. Then when I woke up, hard and sober, I would have gone out and got drunk again. I did not do this now. I went back to the glass in the bedroom and finished shaving. I think I shaved with greater care. And I went on dressing. And I sat down and began to sort my things. And I was hungry, and I had lunch somewhere in Paris. I walked over to the other side. I crossed a bridge that spanned the Seine, but I did not pause to lean against the bridge and to look down upon the water. That belonged to another phase, even more distant, which I had almost forgotten. I came back in the evening and had a long conversation with the woman who lived on the ground floor, and from whom I had rented the rooms.

I told her we should not be living there any longer. I told her we were going away, very shortly, possibly within the week. She said she was very sorry. I said I was sorry, too. She said we had always been '*très gentils*' and that we had never caused her '*des soucis*'.

I told her it was very nice of her to say that. She said she would always remember us. I said we should always remember, too. She asked me what were our plans, and where were we going. I said the plans were not very definite yet. It was all a little difficult, a little sudden. She told me she quite understood. Life was like that, she said. '*On ne sait jamais*' . . . from day to day. It was the same for everybody. I said: 'Yes,' many times, and we sighed and we shrugged our shoulders.

I told her that Mademoiselle had left one or two things she did not want to take away. Would she care to have them, or her daughter perhaps? She clasped her hands and the tears came in her eyes, and she said we were too good to her, much too good. I said: 'No, no, not at all,' and she came upstairs with me, and I let her rummage about in the bedroom and find what she thought would be useful to her, amongst the remnants of the bare drawers and shelves. She made a little bundle. There was an old coat, I believe, and a blouse, and checked skirt, and an ugly red dress I had never liked. She said she would be able to do something with this, even if it was a little too small. She thanked me again and again with the tears in her eyes. I couldn't think of anything to say. I said: 'Ça va. Ça va . . .' but I felt that these were not the right words. As she left the room I saw that on the top of the bundle was an orange béret, very dusty and worn.

After that I went across to the Dôme and had a drink.

In the evening I brought the divan into the sitting-room and made up a bed for myself, quite comfortable, in the corner. I did not want to use the two rooms. I had all my things in my bag, leaving the lid open, so that I could pull out anything at any time. The other room was quite empty now. It looked as if nobody had been there. I had the door shut, like it had been when I first came, and had only rented one room.

It seemed quite all right like this. I was out most of the day too, coming back in the evenings to sleep. I spent most of my time looking in the windows of the various travel bureaux, gazing at the highly-coloured posters which served as advertisements for different places in France, in Europe, in the world in general.

I remembered my old job in one of these bureaux, and my familiarity with the express routes across the Continent. I was trying to decide where I should go. There seemed to be so many places. I could not believe in them, somehow, not the truth of those posters. They appeared to be false and unlike anything in life. I could not believe in the height of those mountains, nor the depth of those forests. The seas were a little foolish, too calm, too blue. The ships were painted ships. The islands were dream islands, and the sun in Africa was a great round ball of a sun that could not possibly exist, and the natives were only ordinary men and women, who had put feathers in their hair for fun. I was not deceived by them. I was not taken in by the glittering domes of a white city, nor the waving green branches of a tree, nor the gold of scattering sand, nor the deep blue of the sea.

Once I would have wanted to explore these places, but now I did not care to; now I knew they were not so beautiful as they seemed.

People were so wise who stayed at home and read – people in arm-chairs, with their feet in a fender. They ate, and they worked, and they slept, and they died. Those were their lives, I envied them.

Still, I was not sure where I would go. Whether East or West, whether China or Peru. Probably they both looked alike. The thought of the discomfort of the journey bored me this time. I had very little money left; it would mean roughing it again. I did not fancy a steerage passage, poverty and squalor. Sailing ships were cramped and dirty. I did not care to wear myself out, working before the mast. There was no excitement in rough seas, only danger, and danger was an uncomfortable thing. I might travel across country, huddled in a train, but this would mean hanging about frontiers, questions, the monotony of language which I should not understand. Going from one town to another, not minding whether I saw them or not. Adventure had lost its glamour for me.

I realized that I would have to decide upon some course, because I had told the woman I should be leaving the room in the Rue du Cherche-Midi in three days' time. I would have to turn out, anyway. And I had done with Paris. I went back then one evening after dinner with a map in my pocket, and I was determined to resolve upon some destination, even though it should be the South Pole. I would be a child again, and spread out the map upon the table, and close my eyes, and point blindly to an unknown spot, and, whatever it should be, that would be my place. It would be quite a little amusement in its way. I hurried my steps in the direction of Montparnasse. When I went into my room I saw that there was a wire lying on the table. I went over and took it in my hands. I could not open it at first. It seemed too much like a miracle, too much like waking from a dream. I wondered what Hesta's words would be, and whether she would say the time of coming back. I wondered if he had left her without money, and if she now asked me to go to her. I wondered if it had hurt her to send this wire, I wondered if she was sorry for what she had done. I tore open the envelope, and took out the slip of paper.

It was not from Hesta, though. The wire was from Grey, saying that my father was dead.

When I came to Lessington the sun was setting behind the church tower and a little cloud hovered high in the air above the spire, caught in a shaft of light. The station-master touched his hat when he saw who I was. I shook hands with him, and he was suitably grave and solemn.

'This is a great loss to the country, sir,' he said, 'and a great loss to us. People are deeply grieved in Lessington, sir.'

'Yes,' I said.

He looked at me uncertainly, as though he had not expected me to speak.

'You've been away a long time, sir, haven't you?' he said.

'Yes,' I said.

Outside the station the Daimler car was waiting. I sat inside, formal and alone. In the old days I used to ride in front beside the chauffeur. It all seemed very long ago. We went along the main road, where I had bicycled so often as a boy. We turned in at the lodge gates and down the long avenue of trees. When I had left the chestnut blossom had been out, the soft blown petals lying upon the gravel. The flies had danced and fluttered in the air, thick under the low branches. The rooks had called to one another from the woods beyond the meadows. Now it was winter; and the trees in the avenue were bare. There was a heap of litter and ashes at the turn, where a fire had been. I could smell the bitter tang of wood smoke and leaf mould.

The season and the scents had changed, but that was all. Everything else was still the same. The car came round the bend, and there was the great sweep of the house before me, the grey stone, the tubs before the door, the white porch, and the lantern overhead. My mother's spaniel, lazy and fat, rose upon his feet, wagging his tail as he saw the car. The curtain blew softly from the open window of the dining-room.

I went into the hall, and there was that same smell of an old ceiling, and the leather seats of chairs, weapons upon the walls, and logs burning in the great open fireplace.

I crossed the hall and stood for a moment at the other end, looking out upon the lawns that stretched down to the lily pond below. There was the same silence, the same hush upon the terrace, with the little grey statue of Mercury poised ready for flight, his hand to his lips. There were starlings searching for worms on the lawn.

Then I turned and went into the drawing-room and here were my mother and Ernest Grey, she very strange to me in her black dress, and smaller than before. I went over to her and kissed her. I wondered whether she would cry, whether she would begin to talk about my father. But she asked me if my journey had been comfortable and if I would like to have some tea.

I said 'No', I did not want anything, and then she looked at me and said: 'You've grown, Richard, a great deal. You've filled out, I think.'

I said: 'Yes, perhaps I have.'

'There's no doubt about it, is there?' she said, turning to Grey.

'No,' said Grey. 'No, I think you're right.'

'Your father always said you would be a big man,' she said; 'of course you were very lanky when you went away.'

We sat, the three of us, and we wondered what we should say.

'I'm glad my wire found you,' said Grey. 'I was afraid you might not be there, might have gone.'

'No,' I said. 'No, I hadn't gone.'

'I've put you in the little West room, Richard,' said my mother; 'your room had not been used since you went, and I was afraid it might be damp. It was always rather a cold room in the winter.'

'Yes,' I said, 'but it doesn't matter. I don't mind where I go.'

'You will be near Mr Grey in the West room,' she said.

The spaniel came up to me, sniffing at my legs, and I bent down and stroked his ears.

'Well, Micky,' I said, 'you surely remember me? Poor old Micky, good old Micky.'

'Micky has got very fat,' said my mother.

'Yes,' I said.

'Micky is fond of his food,' said Grey. There was another pause and I went on stroking the spaniel's ears.

'I shall have a little rest before changing for dinner,' said my mother; 'it's at half-past seven as usual. You must have a bath if you want to, Richard. The water should be hot.'

'Yes,' I said.

She rose from her chair, and went out of the room, the dog at her heels, panting across the polished floor. I stood up, too, and wandered to the window. It was getting dark now. 'Your mother has borne up wonderfully well,' said Grey. 'I am hoping she will not break down at the funeral tomorrow. Such an ordeal for her. I am glad you came at once, Richard.'

'How did he die?' I said.

'Heart, very suddenly, on Friday evening. Apparently he had complained of feeling tired at dinner. He went into his library afterwards, and your mother came in here. At ten o'clock she went in to see whether he was ready to go upstairs. She found him there, Richard, in his chair; a terrible shock for her. He was quite dead. He did not appear to have suffered at all, and he was leaning forward in his chair, his hand on his desk. I think he must have been stretching to reach his pen. It must have been very terrible for your mother, all alone.'

'Yes,' I said.

'I came down on Saturday morning. There have been reporters, messages, wires, the usual thing. It's a blessing you are not on the telephone, you escape the horror of that. You saw the papers, I suppose? The Prime Minister's tribute, I was glad of that. Your mother read all the papers. I think she was proud.'

'I wonder what will happen now,' I said. 'She won't want to go on living here, will she, now that he is dead?'

'She was talking to me about that this afternoon, Richard. She is so calm, she does not mind what she says, or how much she speaks of him. It's as though it helps her, speaking of him. She said she will never leave here, she wants to stay on, because of him. I believe she has in her mind some idea of keeping the place as it has always been, as though he were still alive.'

'I couldn't do that,' I said, 'not if I were her. I should have to go.'

277

'She's no longer young, you see, Richard, this is her home. Her roots are here, the whole meaning of her life. Even now that he is dead she will go on, with her memories, and it will be her consolation, living with them.'

'Consolation?' I said.

'Yes, Richard. Memories are very beautiful things, when you are old.' I moved away from the window.

'I want to look into the library,' I said. Together we left the drawing-room and crossed the stone hall to the library. I opened the door, and the room was in a half-darkness, for no one had been in to draw the curtains, and the grey evening light cast shadows on the floor.

'Your mother wishes it to be left like this, quite untouched,' said Grey. 'She will dust it herself. Look on the desk. She put those flowers there this morning.'

I turned on the little lamp by the desk. 'What was he working on, do you suppose, when he died?' I said.

'If he had been well enough in the spring,' said Grey, 'he was to have given an address at the University at Edinburgh. I believe he was already making notes for his speech. See this pencilled scrap of paper, and these words, "You young men who are before me now . . . " and then here below, underlined, "the courage to endure." This was obviously a sentence from his speech. I believe these to be the last words he ever wrote.' I held the piece of paper in my hands. 'I wonder why he wrote this?' I said.

'Your mother told me she had no idea what the speech was to be about. He had not even spoken of it to her.'

'I wonder if I could keep this?' I said.

'I think your mother meant his papers to be untouched, Richard.'

I laid the sheet back upon the desk.

'I had never realized,' said Grey, 'that this library was such a peaceful room. I can understand your father was able to work here. No sound, no disturbance, and then in summer the long windows open on to the lawn.'

'Yes,' I said.

Then we went out, and I shut the door behind me. We stood in the hall, warming our hands before the fire.

'What do you suppose you will do, Richard?' asked Grey.

'I've made no plans,' I said; 'I'm not going back to Paris.'

'There will be no need for you to worry about money, of course,' he said.

'That's being premature, isn't it?' I said.

'No, I don't think so. I think you will find your father has left you everything.'

'No,' I said. 'No.'

'He showed me his will once, Richard, about a year ago. I don't believe he altered it since.'

'A year ago?'

'Yes.'

A year ago I had written to him for help and he had sent me a cheque for five hundred pounds, but no letter. 'Did my father ever speak to you about me?' I said.

'No, Richard.'

'Never? Not after I went away, not last year, never, at any time?'

'No, Richard.'

I went on warming my hands at the fire. 'I don't want money,' I said; 'if what you say is true, Mother can have all that, to keep up the place. I think, after all, she is right to wish it so, as if he were still here.'

'You must get something definite to do,' said Grey, 'you must come and live in London. Have you given up all thought of writing?'

'Yes,' I said. 'Yes, that's over.'

'Have you ever thought of going into the City?' said Grey.

'I don't think so,' I said.

'I could give you a letter of introduction to Sir Malcolm Fordryd. You've heard of him, I suppose?'

'I don't know,' I said.

'He's a big banker. If you started with him, in his firm, it might be the beginning of something, Richard. Bit of a grind at first, perhaps. Office hours, you know, steady work. The regular routine of many men. I believe it would be the thing for you.'

'It's very kind of you,' I said. 'I shall have to think about it.'

'You could find a comfortable flat in town,' said Grey, 'you would go about, you would meet interesting people.'

'Yes,' I said.

'You're no longer a boy, you know; you'll have to make something of your life.'

'Yes,' I said.

'If you would like it, I would suggest you let me put you up for my club. You'll need a good club if you live in town,' he said.

'Thank you,' I said.

After a while the dressing gong was sounded.

'You had better go up and have your bath,' he said.

'Yes,' I said.

I paused on the corridor, hesitating a moment before I went to my room in the West wing. Then I walked slowly in the opposite direction, and I stood outside my father's room. Softly I turned the handle. The room was in darkness. I felt my way across, and switched on the light above the bed. He lay there, his face unchanged, the same as he had always been. Only now his eyes were closed. They did not stare up at me as I had feared.

I wondered whether he was really there, sleeping and untroubled, or whether he had gone away. I wondered why he should have given me his body, and kept from me his mind. I wished that he could have left some message for me, some word to show me he had understood. Something for me alone. Not his money. Instead I must be content with four words written on a scrap of paper to a group of young men he had never known, a strange farewell. I would leave him here, in his home, in his own atmosphere, created for himself; I would leave him with my mother, with the house and the hushed garden, quiet, in this sleep I could not understand. I would not disturb him, nor meddle with the papers on his desk. All that I would take with me would be the memory of a scribbled message – faint words – that he had not left for me. '. . . the courage to endure. . . .' So I turned away, and put his calm dead face from my mind, and I went along the dark passage to my room to dress.

11

I like living in London. There is a peace about it that I have never found in any other place. My flat looks down upon a little square, and there is a garden in the middle of this, a lawn and trees. The sound of the traffic does not come to me up here.

My flat is very comfortable, and I have a man to look after me. He sees to my things. He keeps me in order. We have long conversations about people and places. Ernest Grey found him for me.

Grey has been a great friend to me. He found me the flat too, and he gave me an introduction to Sir Malcolm Fordryd, the banker. I think I ought to do quite well in time. As Grey said, the work at first seemed a little tedious and long. I like it now, though. The regular hours suit me, and it is interesting, too. Apparently Fordryd told Grey he was very pleased with me, and I showed promise of doing things. I find this distinctly encouraging.

Grey put me up for his club. I dine there most evenings. Fellows there have been extraordinarily kind. I go out often, I know many people. Sometimes I remember what Jake said about me being successful one day. I suppose it will come true. It's all very different, of course, from what I dreamed. But then dreams are apart from the business of living; they are things we shed from us gently as we grow older.

Jake would smile if he saw me now. 'You'll be all right,' he said. He was never wrong. I think he always knew what would happen to me. Adventure and excitement, sorrow and love, they were all phases of my life that had to be.

Jake and the sea, Paris and Hesta, my writing, too: they were only phases – that, and no more.

I found my MS. the other day at the bottom of a drawer. I sat up one evening and looked through it. I laughed a great deal. I wondered how I could possibly have written it. It did not sound like me at all. There was an old snap-shot of Hesta, too, torn half across. One that was taken at Barbizon. I had forgotten she used to wear her hair so short. I put it back with the MS. at the bottom of the drawer. It's rather nice to look over these things.

The other day, after leaving the City, I drove to the bridge across the river where I had stood the first time with Jake. It was an evening, too, and the sun setting behind the spires, throwing great crimson patches on the water. I realized then something of the peace of London, the dim buildings shrouded in a haze, the beauty of the tired sky, the strength of the dome of St Paul's against a stray white cloud. The water ran beneath the bridge brown and swift, as it had run before. And once there was a boy who leant against this bridge, and dreamt of adventure, and the sea, the shouting of men, the call of strange countries, ships, and the loveliness of women.

I stood there for quite a little while, remembering my dreams. Looking back, I suppose I wasted my years. Maybe I spoilt the beauty of youth, let it slip through my fingers, shut my eyes to the swift passage. If it came again perhaps it would be different – I wonder. Whatever happens, though, I shall have had my time. It cannot be taken from me.

I am happier now than I have ever been. The restlessness has gone, the indecision and also the great heights of exultation, the strange depths of desolation. I am secure now, and certain of myself. There is peace and contentment.

From my window I look down upon the little square. The trees are green in the garden opposite. There is the clean, fresh smell of an evening after rain. Somewhere, on one of the branches of the trees, I can hear a bird singing. A note that sounds from a long way off, sweet and clear, like a whisper in the air. And there is something beautiful about it, and something sad. At first he is lost, and then he is happy again. Sometimes he is wistful, sometimes he is glad.

He seems to be saying; 'I'll never be young again – I'll never be young again.'

London, June–July, 1930.

More About Penguins

Penguinews, which appears every month,
contains details of all the new books issued by
Penguins as they are published. From time to time
it is supplemented by *Penguins in Print*, which is a
complete list of all books published by Penguins which
are in print. (There are well over three thousand of
these.)

A specimen copy of *Penguinews* will be
sent to you free on request, and you can become
a subscriber for the price of the postage. For a year's
issues (including the complete lists) please send 25p
if you live in the United Kingdom, or 50p if you
live elsewhere. Just write to Dept EP, Penguin Books
Ltd, Harmondsworth, Middlesex, enclosing a cheque
or postal order, and your name will be added to the
mailing list.

Some other books published by Penguins are
described on the following pages.

Note: *Penguinews* and *Penguins in Print*
are not available in the U.S.A. or Canada

Jerusalem the Golden

Margaret Drabble

'She wondered what her mother would have made of
Amelia, Magnus, Gabriel, Clelia and Annunciata,
let alone Sebastian and Candida.' Clara's mother
would have made very little of them, but the girl
from Northam was very much at home in their
'tender, blurred world'. After all, it was so much more
'real' than the world of the folks back home.

Clara could become the golden girl and have real
affairs with married men, just like in the novels.

With this, her fourth novel, Margaret Drabble won the
James Tait Black memorial prize for fiction.

Also available:
A Summer Bird-Cage
The Garrick Year
The Millstone

Not for sale in the U.S.A.

The Garrick Year
Margaret Drabble

Theatrical marriages – glamorous . . . scandalous
. . . bitchy . . . brief? Or are they in fact just
like anyone else's?

This novel takes the lid off one such marriage:
inside we find Emma, married to an egocentric
actor playing a year's season at a provincial theatre
festival, David, her husband – and Wyndham the
producer.

The mixture turns rapidly to acid.

Not for sale in the U.S.A.

Up, Into the Singing Mountain

Richard Llewellyn

Huw Morgan sails from the valleys to join the
struggling Welsh settlers in Patagonia and finds
that the tight-knit pioneer community is consumed
by the same violent passions and fierce prejudices
that drove him from his homeland. Richard
Llewellyn's prose surges with power and life,
and *Up, Into the Singing Mountain* is a worthy
sequel to *How Green Was My Valley*.

Not for sale in the U.S.A.

Also available

Down Where the Moon is Small

The Flight of the Falcon

Daphne du Maurier

It is over 500 years since Duke Claudio the Falcon
lived his brutal, twisted life in Ruffano. But this is the
twentieth century. The town has forgotten its violent
history. Its university has a shiny new commerce and
economics building: pointing to a golden future and
flouting the dusty humanities – and inhumanities –
of the past.

But have things really changed? Clearer and clearer the
parallels are drawn. Through murder, humiliation and
outrage – to the horrifying flight of the modern Falcon,
climax to a raucous travesty of a festival.

Also available

Gerald: A Portrait
The Birds and Other Stories
Frenchman's Creek
The Glass-Blowers
The House on the Strand
Hungry Hill
Jamaica Inn
The King's General
The Loving Spirit
Mary Anne
My Cousin Rachel
The Parasites
The Progress of Julius
Rebecca
The Scapegoat
The Blue Lenses